Traveler's Tale

First Book: Discoverings

One Man's Adventure
into the Mind of Christ First Book

ROGER FIOLA

authorHOUSE®

AuthorHouse™
1663 Liberty Drive
Bloomington, IN 47403
www.authorhouse.com
Phone: 1 (800) 839-8640

Published by Petersgate Press, LLC, in conjuction with AuthorHouse™
Carmel, CA

Published by AuthorHouse   08/20/2015

ISBN: 978-1-5049-2368-2 (sc)
ISBN: 978-1-5049-2369-9 (hc)
ISBN: 978-1-5049-2367-5 (e)

Library of Congress Control Number: 2015911391

Print information available on the last page.

To all my faithful companions on this life's pilgrimage,
and especially to my bride and fellow adventurer, Laney

Joseph: O Mary, what sweet thing is that on your knee?

Mary: It is my son, the truth to say that is so good.

Joseph: I'm glad I lived to see this day, to see this food. I marvel much at this, His light that shines so brightly in this place. In truth, it is a wondrous sight.

—*The Tile Thatcher's Play: The Nativity*, a mystery play of the York Pageant (ca. AD 1376)

Preface

The books in this series are works of fiction. They are about encountering and connecting with the interior experience of the divine within each of us.

This is what they are *not*. While they are based on historical facts and are respectful of the Hebrew and Grecian context of Jesus's life and the nascent church, the series is not another opus on the historical Jesus. There are libraries full of fine, scholarly books that deal with that subject.

Some exchanges, events, and sequences are the products of imagination, included in the hope that they will move the narrative toward an end that serves the lessons of Scripture. Mostly, this is the story of one man's encounter with God and the changes it made to his life. The man is Traveler. He is everyman and everywoman, perhaps even including *Yeshua*, the man we call Jesus. The historical references and research only serve to provide a backdrop, the realistic scenery for the mystery play of our own salvation.

If you remember this, then perhaps you will be able to move through Traveler's story with the right mind-set, not questioning whether this or that scene is possible or really took place but instead asking what lesson or understanding is trying to reach you through that scene.

If a passage is particularly unsettling, put the book down and reflect upon it. What does the disturbance feel like? How would your heart or mind change if this truly happened?

This is not a book on facts but one that uses some facts to bring you to a richer connection with the divine, a connection that I believe exists naturally in each of us.

It could also be expressed as the connection of love.

Okay. Let's begin with an imaginary bow between us. Like two monks who meet on a dusty Himalayan trail, we greet one another, hands folded prayerfully as we exchange a soundless greeting.

"*Namaste*!"

"The God in me reverences the God in you!"

Roger Fiola
Carmel-by-the-Sea, California
Easter 2015

Acknowledgments

This series is the result of a suggestion by my spiritual director, Sister Lorita Moffat, on February 4, 2011. It grew from a spiritual exercise into this book and the succeeding volumes, inspired by many spiritual teachers over the years: Saint Ignatius, especially from his <u>Spiritual Exercises</u>; Judge Francisco Firmat, for leading me through them; Richard Rohr; Thomas Keating; and Eckhart Tolle. One of my mentors, Caroline Myss, encouraged me and led me to the awesome talents of Ellen Gunter, who helped me fashion the narrative form of the books. Thanks also to James Finley for his sage advice and beautiful approach to the understanding and experience of the Christian contemplative and for his insights into the mystics.

I am ever grateful for the advice of Bruce Chilton. I sought his guidance, which led me to Charlotte Heltai, whose scholarly research helped make the settings and historical context of the book more realistic. I am appreciative of the efforts of AuthorHouse in assisting me in getting the words printed and doing so beautifully.

There are many others who contributed to my efforts or encouraged me: Maria Canavarro, Steve Squier, Damian Lynch, Teresa Andersen, Isabelle Ulfig, Judge Nancy Stock, Judy Patno, Bob Lanphar, Frances Rossi, Byron and Donna Beam, Dave and Gaye Brobeck, brothers Dale and Rich, and the Sperry family at whose home I wrote a substantial part of this and the following books in the series.

Finally, gratitude to Laney, my wife, and my children, Alexandra and Andrew, who gave me their suggestions but, more importantly, gave me the space alone in the early hours of the morning so that, in peace, I could witness the Spirit coming to me and gracing me to write these many words.

Franciscus, Episcopus Romae

FROM THE HOLY FATHER'S FILE "J.Castro"

Item No. 1

CALIFORNIA UNIVERSITY NEUROPSYCHIATRIC HOSPITAL

CONFIDENTIAL MEMORANDUM
DATE: … ██████████

To: His Holiness, Pope Francis
00120 Casa Santa Marta
Citta del Vaticano
From: Edward Ironsteen, MD, Medical Director,
        California University Neuropsychiatric Hospital

Your Holiness:

Firstly, it was both a great surprise and, of course, a high honor to speak with you personally by telephone yesterday morning. Although not a Catholic, I admire your efforts to resolve conflict and bring peace to the world.

Your particular interest in this unusual case is certainly understandable. The hospital's general counsel obtained the requisite legal authorizations from my patient, so it is my pleasure to enclose some of the diagnostic findings you requested.

In all candor, I might add that, as a clinician for thirty years—and as a published atheist—I do not attach any belief in the content of his statements. Religious themes are a common occurrence within several psychotic disorders and usually exacerbate present grandiose illusions. Obviously, I know of little external evidence to corroborate the elements of his narrative. Yet his delusions remain consistent, which is common in these disorders. However, what strikes me is the patient's appropriate affect, his seemingly concrete orientation toward his present situation and the clear, organized way in which he articulates his delusions. This makes for the most intriguing and seamlessly consistent set of narrative sequences I have ever encountered in my nearly four decades of professional practice.

The amount and level of detail is remarkable and, in my experience, unique to this case. If it were not outside of what we know as possible, one could easily believe he witnessed what he said he witnessed.

Additionally, there are the other physical manifestations, which may be self-inflicted but cannot as yet be determined.

These especially appear to have garnered the personal attention of Your Holiness. Our enclosed notes and studies may raise more questions than answers for you. Be assured that my staff and I are available to assist you or designated members of the Holy See at any time.

Furthermore, in return, I am hopeful that your findings or insights, if shared with the hospital, may shed light on the patient's therapeutic process and guide him and us toward his possible recovery, which, to date, has been elusive at best.

Until our next communication, I remain

Sincerely yours,
Dr. Edward Ironsteen

Franciscus, Episcopus Romae

FROM THE HOLY FATHER'S FILE "J.Castro"

Item No. 2

CALIFORNIA UNIVERSITY *NEUROPSYCHIATRIC HOSPITAL*

NOTES: INITIAL CONSULTATION
IRONSTEEN, E. MD.
DATE: ███████

    Patient self-admitted this afternoon, accompanied by his spouse. His physician and my former colleague, Dr. Michael Kohen of Monterey, referred him to California University and asked me to consult with him personally, because the patient has attracted a great deal of public attention. Dr. Kohen knows that Cal-U has had many high-profile patients, and handling the media will be a component of his stay at the hospital. The patient was a middle-aged, well-dressed, Caucasian man of medium height, although underweight. He presented courteous and cooperative, and appeared well oriented to his surroundings. Both his wrists were bandaged, I assumed from an attempted suicide, but I did not have any data to support that conclusion yet.

    He said he was a Stanford alumnus and efforted affability by joking about the upcoming Stanford/Cal-U game, but he was unable to mask his symptoms for more than a minute or two. His facial complexion was gray, and overall, he had an exhausted but agitated affect. His spouse, also middle-aged, appeared drawn and deeply concerned about her husband. He complained of sleeplessness and night terrors, sweats, as well as other symptoms of stress.

    I asked him *why* he had come into the hospital today. Composing himself, he replied definitively that he would not answer questions that begin with the word *why*. At that point, he dropped suddenly to his knees, putting his hands over his eyes. When asked about his wrists, he coughed, then told me he was afraid because "slaves of the demon" were chasing

Continued on Page Two of Notes -Santa Madre! +7.

PART I

IN THE RIVER

FIRST CENTURY PALESTINE

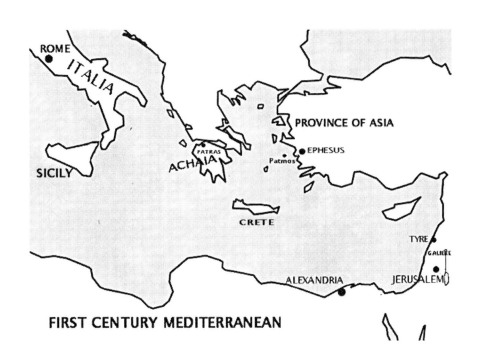

FIRST CENTURY MEDITERRANEAN

Chapter 1

AD 2003, and the second year of the presidency of George W. Bush, Monterey, California

"Jesus!"

A brilliant shaft of orange light, as brief as a camera flash, hits the windshield, making it opaque, like a blank, glowing movie screen. In split-second blindness, I hit the brakes. Squinting, I strain to focus. Painful brightness. Then suddenly, like a magician's reveal, the light's gone. Sight returns.

As the heavy Benz skids, a rabbit darts out of the pine and oak forest to my right.

"Shit!"

It stops dead in front of my car, takes a frightened look at me, and then bounds across the road. I wrestle the wheel to the right. In hot pursuit of the rabbit, a golden mountain lion veers so close that its tail whacks my left headlamp as the car slides on the pine needled asphalt. I avoid hitting the lion but almost slam my front end into the thick trunk of a live oak.

The rabbit's pause to look at me was enough to make the difference between life and death. The lion's jaws lock onto its neck, quickly executing the kill and then swinging the limp corpse twice, the rabbit's lifeless legs quivering as misfiring nerves play out their last gig. It's now become a lion's breakfast, and I'm shaking like a plucked guitar string.

"What the f—"

I left my house only a minute ago. I grew up in this area, but I've never seen a mountain lion before. Rangers post warning signs on all the hiking trails up and down the coastal range, but strangely, the first one I ever see nearly dances with my Mercedes in a gated golf community.

Without missing a beat, dead prey firmly locked in its jaws, the lion stands there, pinning me with a fierce focus. Without hurrying, it moves up the hillside, vanishing perfectly into the scrubby bushes beneath the oak trees. The quick life-and-death struggle is over before I can register my near wreck, but my heart pounds furiously. I feel the adrenaline pouring into my hands, and they tremble as I keep my death grip on the steering wheel.

Whoa! Am I blacking out? Was there some chemical or drug laced into my coffee?

Last night's dream was like that. My memory cancels out most dreams when I wake up, yet the residual feelings remain. Especially the disturbing ones I've been having lately. Yeah, I remember now. A leopard was chasing me through woods like these, and I went diving for safety in a black hole near a stream, like the adrenaline-junkie spelunkers who go freefalling into those yawning, massive caves in Mexico. Yet, chased or not, I wanted to dive in. Had to.

Mountain lions, rabbits, dreams—what kind of batshit-crazy, Alice-in-Wonderland crap is going on here?

Now I'm drenched in sweat, my breaths pumping in and out of me, mouth caked-clay dry like Death Valley in summer, and I take a gulp from the bottle of Fiji resting in the square cup holder I had made for the car. Still shaking, I decide to get back on the road and discover that I've absently turned the ignition off.

When did that happen? Snap out of it, Jack!

I start it up and edge onto the road, slowly making my way to the community entrance. When I reach the gate, I wave to the young guard and roll my window down.

"Morning, Mr. Castro," he says, way too cheerful for this time of day. He's studying to be a minister. "How 'bout those 'Niners last night?"

"Yeah, good game. Hey, just saw a mountain lion, Josh. Damn near had a wreck. Hit my front headlight."

Okay, my voice sounds normal. Jack is back.

Josh looks shocked and then eyes my car's front end. He moves closer, runs his hand over it, squats, and looks underneath.

"Car's fine. Not a scratch. But I'll report that. Never seen one around here!"

He asks me for specifics, but I cut him off.

"Later, Josh. Meeting in San Jose."

"Go!" He waves me off, and I make the requisite left onto the highway leading to Starbucks where I'm meeting my assistant, Tyler. We are heading up to San Jose for the conference I'm speaking at this morning. I'm in crop insurance. My firm handles most of the gigantic ag-business policies in the sprawling Salinas Valley and California's Central Valley beyond. A dry cough takes me out of my thoughts, and suddenly it feels like liquid lead pumping through my veins. Starbucks is not happening for me right now. I need a few minutes alone.

My eyes land on a familiar sign for the small wilderness park where my two teenage daughters and I often hike on weekends. Ordinarily, the words *teenage* and *hike* aren't two words that go together, but the girls do trek along with Dad on a regular basis. Other weekends, my non-hiker wife, Sharon, joins us as we sail Monterey Bay.

I try to distract my thoughts and think of my family as I struggle to chill out a bit. It's not working.

Impulsively, I veer sharply to the right across the lanes to the exit. The guy behind me slams on his brakes and lays on the horn as I rumble onto the narrow road leading into a small parking area. Even though there is no one else around, I move neatly between the white lines of the first space. I leave the car idling, and even though it's fifty degrees, I turn on the air conditioning. I try to lengthen my breaths, but short gasps are all I can manage. My clammy fingers still grip the steering wheel like it's a goddamn lifeline. I lift them off, and the joints respond with pain. Then I force them to unlock my noose of a tie. Allowing the lids of my eyes to close, I decide I just need a minute. I reflexively gulp some air and smell the forest.

Man up, Castro!

When I open my eyes, I am surprised to see that I am not alone after all. Close by, there's a homeless man rummaging through the trash containers for his daily bread, which consists of cans and plastic bottles.

Why am I here? My actions are unpredictable, and I like predictability—and logic and probability. Everyone admires that about me. In fact, they rely on it, which is why I'm invited frequently to be on boards. Even the Roman Catholic bishop recently asked me to help with the restoration of the old mission church in nearby Carmel-by-the-Sea, and I'm only nominally Catholic—barely nominally.

Come on, Jack. Get it together. I'm okay. I've got fifteen minutes to kill before meeting Tyler.

Mindlessly, I grab the slice of cold cheese pizza wrapped in wax paper that lays on the passenger-side floor. It flew off the seat during the dance with the mountain lion. My wife passed my favorite breakfast to me as I bolted out the door this morning. I brush off the paper, good as new. Maybe I'll take a bite or two in a minute. Pizza in hand, I get out of the car.

As I approach the homeless man, I see that he is barely more than a boy, maybe twenty-five—twenty-six, tops. Under a ragged woolen cap drawn partially over an unexpected pile of thick blond hair, I see his deep-blue eyes pinning me. This guy's carrying a load of Viking DNA, that's for sure. His skin's the color of rust, weathered beyond his years, and I can see that his brief life has been tough. He backs up a step, guarded, as if I'm there to take him in.

Seriously, kid? I mean, am I a ranger in a German luxury car?

I check my self-aggrandizing thoughts and muster up some humility. There's a tragedy standing here before me. I raise the palms of my hands, thumb across the wax-paper-wrapped pizza, showing that I mean him no harm.

"I am doing nothing wrong," he says.

"I'm not here for trouble," I reply as he gives me the practiced once-over, glances at my car, then back to me, thinking for a moment. "Do you have any spare money, for I am hungry?" he says, but I smell the wine on his breath.

"And thirsty too?" I ask sarcastically, immediately regretting it.

"No. Well, yes. I drank some leftover wine from these old bottles and some beer from these cans," he says, pointing down to the contents of his half-filled trash bag, "But it was all old. It tasted not good."

His speech sounds off, correct but not right. I shove a twenty at him, and he accepts it, glancing at it briefly. Funny, but it seems like he doesn't care about the paper money at all—though he has a definite interest in the pizza.

"Some bread would be good," he says. Calling pizza *bread* sounds weird, kind of foreign, even though the kid's accent is totally Californian. Dismissing it and being hungry myself—and therefore not so generous—I tear it in half and give the bigger part of the triangle to him.

"Thank you, sir," he says, eating a chunk of it instantly. "Very good! God bless you." It's the ritual blessing every homeless person seems to give. I often notice that only homeless people voice a blessing to me these days.

After a moment of watching him chew, I'm finding that this little exchange is calming me down. Strange. So, I decide to expand my peace and give him the other half as well.

Glancing at my watch, I decide I can do it: take that moment by myself. I feel better, but I still have to walk and get some air, be outside with the trees—just for a few minutes. A chill runs through me again, and then I'm flushed, my heart racing. I've heard of people having panic attacks, so maybe this is what it feels like. I start to half jog down the path into the forested area.

"Ah, sir, where are you going? I mean, you are not dressed for the trail." There's real concern in his voice.

"Only taking a walk, kid."

Nothing unusual here—just a guy heading off into the woods wearing an Armani blazer, a gold Patek Philippe, and a pair of handmade Italian loafers. Totally normal. If he rolls me, the kid won't have to go Dumpster-diving for quite some time.

Wincing as those arrogances pass through my mind, I hear the man coming up behind me, and I go into defensive mode, sensing I'm going to have a problem with him. I spin around and glare fiercely into his dirty face. *Ninja Insurance Guy*! Another camera-flash of orange light, here and then gone.

Off-balance and distracted, I blink and then straighten up to resume my tough-guy posture.

"What?" I say as menacingly as I can.

"Nothing, nothing, sir," he says, backing off. "But take great care. I mean, just be careful." Another odd turn of phrase. I haven't heard anyone except characters in classic British TV shows say something like "take great care."

The orange light flashing, this weird-talking homeless kid, the dead rabbit and the lion, the dream leopard—all of these bizarre, random events defy any summing up. My brain can't piece the puzzle together, though it desperately seeks a connecting reason. As I turn again, walking down toward the seasonal streambed, the park-bench Shakespeare shouts out one last thing, irritating me with a very formally phrased warning.

"And, sir, do not be afraid."

Chapter 2

Without light or guide, save that which burned in my heart.
This light guided me more surely than the light of noonday
To the place where he was awaiting me.

—St. John of the Cross, *Dark Night of the Soul,* stanzas 3, 4
(ca. AD 1579)

AD 2003, a forest near Monterey

Pounding into the woods, determined to reach the creek, compulsion rockets me forward with each step—another goal, another achievement. I'm stressed to the max, I know. I've been waking up drenched in sweat this last week, leaking saltwater from every pore. I get it. Mine is a jam-packed, moving target of a life. We take nice vacations, but even those serve an educational purpose for my girls, so we're nonstop tourists on every trip. And I guess it's obvious to everyone around me. Even Bronson, my old frat buddy, summed me up after one of our annual hikes in the Big Sur Mountains two weeks ago.

"Dude, you like your life to churn," he said. "Nothing's changed since Stanford—except your address." Of course, he's one to talk. He runs a Fortune 500 financial company on Wall Street, so he is on the move twenty-four seven himself.

But Bronson's right. I do like my life to churn. Boredom, too much quiet, scares the shit out of me. When things quiet down too much, I'll stir it all up again, both at the office and at home. But I also know that eventually my body will give me some pushback, and as I continue down the trail, I let myself guess that's what this is. Stress from the churn. Fatigue aided and abetted by the disturbing circle-of-life moment I just witnessed.

Not quite. There was that dream leopard too.

Something feels out of control.

Where am I going? The sensation returns, the tickle in the center of my chest. It's an ache more than pain. There's a feeling attached to it, always the heavy feeling, like lead. Not sadness but something akin to emptiness. Hollow. Makes no sense. I know my life's incredibly full. By every metric America has, I possess all a person could want, and what I don't have, I know how to get.

Walking deeper into the forest, I can't hear the highway traffic anymore. It's cooler in here. I check my watch and see that I have ten more minutes. But this is where I want to be, have wanted to be. For almost a month, maybe closer to six weeks now, I've felt this same gnawing hunger within me, a deep longing to discover something I can't put into words. It's eluded me, staying far enough away to be just out of reach, like that mirage I see when driving in the desert, that watery lake that ripples on the highway but keeps receding as I approach it.

Like the unreachable mirage lake, this longing has haunted me, disturbing me at the office and at home. Last week I made a conscious effort to stuff this damn feeling back into the mental hole out of which it came. As usual, I was successful—at first. For the balance of the day it was gone, and I thought I had it licked. That night, the first dream came, and the following morning at 4:41, I awoke, terrified, drenched in sweat. After the morning shower, I felt the longing claw at me again. Like today, I can stuff it down for an hour or two. When I think it's gone for good and I get back to being my upbeat self, enjoying my life, something like that bloody moment with the mountain lion slaps me like a backhand across the face, plunging me right back into it.

Wineskins.

Yeah, it did begin that night six weeks ago when the Mission's pastor, a tan Sicilian-American who as a teenager mowed my parent's lawn, spoke at our building restoration meeting about old wineskins and new wine, something from the Bible. Apparently, you can't transfer new wine into old wineskins because they'll burst. I know all about wine, because much of the Salinas Valley is now dedicated to growing grapes—except, of course, that they don't use clay jars for vinting or animal bladders for carrying wine these days. I have never seen a wineskin, so Father Joe's point was lost on me. We were there to discuss retrofitting the old church. Was he arguing to tear it down and build a new one?

"I'm not talking about structures or property improvements," he explained to a board member who asked that very question. "I'm talking about us stepping out of the old and familiar ways, our comfort zones—those old wineskins that are no longer elastic—to expand anew into what we are really here on earth to do."

I knew I was on earth primarily to sell insurance, so I found myself still missing his point. I chided myself for becoming involved in a quasi-religious thing like this committee. I knew better.

"What does this old wineskin, new wineskin mean?" some mature, carefully coifed woman asked.

I was thinking, *Jesus! How long is this sermon thing going to go on? I have notes to prepare for the office meeting tomorrow.*

"In the first century, vintners would take the grape juice and put it into a bag made from the skin of a goat and tie it off," Father Joe said. "As the juice fermented into wine, it expanded the skin, which was very elastic. After the vintner emptied the wine out, he or she could not use the old skin again because its elasticity was gone; it had become brittle. If filled again with new wine, it would burst under the pressure."

I was getting this point and found it spot on. Sometimes I feel like I'm about to burst, like today. All this made me more uncomfortable and antsy.

"Father Joe, excuse me, but what does this have to do with ensuring the church's roof doesn't cave in during an earthquake?" I asked him. He needed to tie this together because I was not there for Bible study.

"You are all embarking on the project to save one of the most beautiful historic buildings in California," he said, "but it is also a place that has been used by generations of people for sacred purposes. Regardless of your faith, or lack of it, you may encounter this sacred aspect during your work for the committee and find it challenging and confusing. For some of you, it is new wine and you may need to grow a new wineskin to receive it."

"Otherwise, we'll burst?" I asked with a chuckle. He smiled warmly.

"There are a lot of ways to burst, Jack!"

Light laughter rippled around the table.

There are a lot of ways to burst, Jack. That hit me hard.

On the drive home, the aching started eating a hole in my left side. That night, I wondered if all I was supposed to do with my life was to get richer from selling more insurance to more corporate farmers. That question seemed to drive the longing deeper into the new cavity inside me. I kicked myself again for becoming involved in something religious.

Even though the girls go to a top religious prep school, I stay away from it all. I was raised a Catholic by my *Californio*-Hispanic father and Missouri Irish mother, but by the time I was twelve, we became Christmas and Easter churchgoers. I found more meaning gorging on the donuts offered in the parish hall on Sundays than in the Mass itself. Still, I remember reverencing the moment of Communion, taking the consecrated wafer and sipping from the chalice of wine. Of all the prayers, standings up, and kneelings down, I seemed to value only that taking of the bread and wine. But even that was not enough to keep me attending church.

I have no taste for dogma. I hold my life together without religion, keeping right with myself by observing a personal philosophy that includes a sensible set of values: be loyal and responsible to my family and friends, have integrity in my business dealings, and help people in need when I can. I'm hardworking, consciously privileged, and scrupulously liberal. I brushed all this with the thinnest and vaguest belief in the divine. Being a scientific and pragmatic man, I understand the common person's God to be nothing more than a comforting and childlike device people conjure up to calm their psyches on the journey toward death as well as to infuse meaning into life's inevitable and unfortunate circumstances. Like most people today, my daily so-called creed results from what I can see and experience directly.

Until the wineskin talk, I was fine, and many times, I mentally kicked myself. My buddy was right; I do like to stir things up. But those *things* are ordinary and practical. I'm afraid that I have now stirred up something that is much larger and stranger than I can handle.

I've raised the bar on myself.

Hang in there. I'm huffing and puffing. Never breathed like this when hiking with the girls. Almost there. Walking a few more paces, the little creek comes into sight. Part of me thinks that I should turn around here, knowing that I'll be late now. I reach to lift my cuff and check my watch, but I pull it back down again.

I don't care anymore.

I'm not calm or comforted, and there're no explanations. There are only questions and the insane longing that pulls at me with greater and greater intensity.

I turn to glance behind me and see that the homeless kid didn't follow me. Back to his trash cans again, no doubt. Damn, I'm relentless! How consistently superior can I feel?

Boom!

I feel a new rush of adrenaline, but this time it carries a seismic wave of anxiety. A primal urge then rises in me. I run.

I'm scared shitless, pure and simple. Yet I find I'm not running back to the car but toward the streambed, deeper into the forest. What's going on?

My feet pound the rest of the way down to the creek, which is only a trickle, and I look up, huffing and puffing, through the twisted oak branches at a cloudless blue sky.

The time was seven thirty the last I checked. The sun is only two hours into its arc across the sky, and yet it peers at me like the giant eye of the universe. I place a hand on my chest and feel blood pushing through the neck and pounding through my temples. My body feels electrified, heavy.

"I'm talking about stepping out of your comfort zone to see what you're really here on earth to do …"

Dude, I'm way out of my goddamn comfort zone!

"Whoever you are out there, up there … stop torturing me," I implore. "I'm no good at guessing games. Just tell me what the hell you want from me! Show me! Now!"

Even the birds cease chirping as I stand there blinking into the soundless blue above me.

Nothing.

Then a light breeze brushes the bough of the oak nearest me. I don't feel it, but the tree's crisp leaves flutter like the soft whipping sound of a thousand playing cards clothespinned to the spokes of a thousand children's bicycles. The thought evaporates as everything around me begins to grow dim.

Then there's another golden flash of light. This time I'm surprisingly calm.

After that, like an iris on a gigantic camera lens, the light closes. I'm in a brown darkness, and I hear soft thrumming noises that seem to hold me like a Caribbean hammock. My mouth can't open, but I must be breathing. There's a sense of someone's arms holding me—not human arms though. It's something bigger than arms. They enfold me, and it feels amazing. That sensation changes from stillness to movement, lifting me so I fly straight up, and then plunging me downward into blackness with the loss of gravity. It's like a blind bungee jump, except that I've never bungee-jumped. This flying and plunging is exciting, but I notice that no air rushes against my skin. Muted lights appear and disappear. Then there's a change in air pressure, a humid warmth, unfamiliar smells, and a foreign lightness in the air.

I'm on solid ground. My skin prickles. I smell pines and the fetid scent of earth. There's the dimmest light leaking in to my left.

The moon. Uh, wait. The moon?

How did it get to be night?

My eyes open wide now. The animal side of me searches for bearings, danger.

As my vision adjusts to the dark, I look up and somehow know instantly that I'm standing under the brilliant stars on a mountain. It's weird, but I know somehow that I'm near the ancient city of Ephesus in Turkey.

Only it ain't now.

It's a long time ago.

My knees buckle with the shock.

Straightening up, I feel a scratchy sensation all over my body. Looking down, I am stunned to see that someone or something has stripped me of clothing and put me into the rough, tunic-like garb of the times. There is a jagged, neatly stitched seam down the front where it appears someone has sewn it back together after it was ripped apart. I also find that I am sporting sandals, except they're like no sandals I wear around the house on weekends. These lace up the legs. They are a little big but surprisingly comfortable.

Whose clothes are these? And how do I know where—and when—I am?

I did visit what was left of Ephesus once when my family and I took a vacation cruise, but only toppled marble fragments and ruins littered the site we toured with a guide. I get the understanding that it's definitely not in ruins now because I'm here in the month of *Germanicus*, or September, in the year 796 AUC, *Ab Urbe Condita*—from the founding of the city of Rome—a date that corresponds to the year AD 43. And the current Roman emperor is …

Claudius!

For three years now. There's no George W. Bush yet, and there won't be for a long time: one pleasing fact for this Democrat.

Humor is not working. Still edgy. Where's this intel coming from?

Yet these instant *knowings* are like downloads that keep coming in a steady stream with no apparent source. I breathe slowly, trying to muster up some calm. And it happens, suddenly and weirdly. An inner tranquility moves like liquid anesthesia coursing through the veins. Only I will not go to sleep. Far from it. I am cautious, hyperattentive, and focused—like the mountain lion I just saw—accepting what is front of my eyes and deciding to move with it.

I look up to a brilliant night sky as a shooting star streaks by in a flash, making an exquisite, perfect arc. It vanishes in an instant, dying in a glorious streak of light. I breathe in deeply and exhale my relief.

It is still the same earth and the same sky.

Chapter 3

To the roots of the mountains I sank down;
The earth beneath barred me in forever.
But you, LORD my God,
Brought my life up from the pit.
—*Jonah 3:6* (ca. 400–500 BC)

AD 43, and the third year of the reign of the emperor Claudius, Ephesus

"Shit!"

The smells of urine and crap climb up my nostrils like invading Mongol hordes storming the castle walls.

Covering my nose and mouth, I see that I'm next to the latrine! If I thought I was dreaming, I know now that I'm fully awake.

Needing to put geography between that smell and me, I begin to climb toward a stone house about fifty feet up the hill. It's so quiet here, no airplane noise. I make my way up the dark path through another forest. Cypress branches dip and sway to the lightest breath of wind. The evening is warm, and lamplights flicker in the windows of the house. I can hear a distant drum, the percussion of merrymakers in an unseen house nestled somewhere down in the trees. They must keep everyone awake around here.

Before the cruise to the Mediterranean five years ago, we spent time as a family studying all the ports of call. We learned that first-century Ephesus was a wealthy, sprawling city of the Roman province of Asia, the name given to an area that comprises western and central Turkey in our century. Its wide marble avenues, impressive temples, and extensive libraries made it an influential nexus of culture and thought in that era. I'm on a hill about three miles from the old city.

With relief, I now can smell a mixture of delicate scents: the fragrance of the pine trees and even the faintest aroma of baking bread. To my left, there's a large fountain I know people use for baptisms, or *immersions* as they call the rite in this time. This is a place where Christian people live. The expectancy of something immanent builds as a silver whirlwind whips up beside me. The pebbles around the fountain rattle and clack, and the water undulates when the miniature cyclone sweeps its surface. Spooky.

As I'm staring at the swirling, glinting dust, I can smell a different scent now.

Flowers.

Snapping my head to the right, I jump when I see a woman standing like a ghost only a few feet from me. I didn't hear her approach. Like the rabbit on the road, she appears suddenly, unexpectedly, silently. She seems to be my wife's age, perhaps two or three years younger than my forty-three years, with some strands of gray mixed with the red tresses of her youth. The light from the lamp she is carrying is surprisingly bright, but the flame flutters in the wake of the little whirlwind. Moving her elegant hand in a sweeping gesture, she motions me to follow her. It's as if she has been expecting me.

As she turns to take the lead, the lamplight shines on her, and I see her features for the first time. Her skin is an unusual, light-gold in color, and her face is like an ancient sculpture with high, prominent cheekbones and regally arched brows. She's dressed like one of those religious statues: a single tunic-like gown gathered with a belt at her waist and a woolen mantle over her shoulders. I can see her smoldering, dark eyes studying me, sizing me up.

"My name is …" I stop to clear my throat.

"I know who you are, Traveler. Much like the prophet Jonah," she says as I reflexively look around me.

Who the hell is Traveler?

I suddenly realize that she is speaking about me, and in the language of this time. But I can understand her as perfectly as if she is speaking American English.

Really? How can this be happening?

When she says something, I hear my native tongue, which won't develop for, like, another seventeen centuries! At the same time, she hears what I say in whatever language she's speaking. And it feels weirdly natural, seamless. My mind clicks, searching for rational explanations, but finding none, it gives up.

Okay. She wants to call me Traveler. Good with me.

"Please be kind enough to follow me, Traveler," she says. Her voice is soft and melodious but full of intelligence and authority. She smiles brilliantly but doesn't introduce herself, and I don't ask. We continue walking, and I take all this in stride, which is amazing. Even the earthy and feral odors here don't bother me any longer. As I follow her up a path inlaid with river stones, my sandal catches on the edge of one, and I stumble. She expertly grasps my arm and holds it firmly until I get my balance back. Her unexpected strength surprises me.

"You must work out," I say, and then immediately wince at how lame that must sound.

"Yes, I enjoy working," she replies. "I like to keep busy."

I'm grateful that the translating software doesn't hold all the American idioms of the twenty-first century. I can't really picture her jogging on a treadmill and wearing a headband. She holds the lamp closer to light the walkway and looks gravely at me.

"The stones are uneven and the pathway hard, so take each step with care; I will keep the light close," she says in a slow and deliberate way.

Her words are laden with subtext. I sense it but don't understand it—yet. Who is she? As I follow her, my analytical mind breaks out into a full-on inquisition. I seem to know where I am. From the stink, I know I'm not dreaming, and I doubt that I'm dead. So what's really going on here?

I consider the possibility of time travel.

Come on, Jack.

I'm not in one of those old 1950s sci-fi movies. My mind tells me this isn't rational, so it's not real.

Yet, *it is* happening! So what caused this?

Stuffing down the churning Castro mind, I let my sandaled foot take the next step. As we approach the house, I see in its somber lines something very familiar. I've been here before. It looks like that house called *Maryema*, where ancient tradition has Mother Mary living her last years. She was supposed to have died here. The family toured it on that same trip. On my desk at the office, there's a photo of my wife and girls in front of it. Yet it seems different, more unkempt, less manicured, and of course, unpaved, as it would be in its time.

If this is that house, could this be Mother Mary herself? No.

As confusing as all this is, I know that idea's too crazy to add to the parade already marching through my head. Yet here I am, walking up a path in another age with an unfamiliar woman dressed like a statue, who seems to understand why I'm here. As we arrive at the modest wooden door, she places her hand on the lintel, giving her peace, and I follow her lead. She turns to me, looking deep into my eyes, and I see her fully for the first time.

"We will go in now," she says. "You are tired from your journey." Her words are soft and reassuring. Listening to the sound of her voice and the melody of her speech makes an ordinary sentence take on the quality of music, beginning on a higher pitch and then descending with a wistful quality. I stop myself again, puzzled by this somewhat romantic mind stream. Shaking it off, I lower my head to enter the house.

Once inside, I see that there are only three small rooms. What passes for a kitchen merges with the sizable space I'm standing in. It contains a large stone hearth where a fire serves as the main source of light. On the floor in front of the hearth, a sleeping mat is rolled out and waiting. She clearly expects company.

Is it only me?

In the corner of the room, there are sitting cushions and a low table, or possibly a bench, made of weathered, gray wood. A brown blanket that looks like wool lies folded neatly on top. Next to this main room is her sleeping chamber. The aroma of fresh bread fills the house, and my stomach rumbles. I remember that I gave away my Sharon-wrapped pizza to the homeless man.

Thinking of her, I wonder how to measure the time since then? Hours ago? But it's roughly two thousand years before that forest morning. I wonder if time's rolling on there as well as here.

My mind spins and whirs, but I refocus on the woman moving gracefully into the kitchen area. From a small wooden box, she retrieves a goatskin bag. I remember Father Joe saying that the ancient wineskins were made of goat bladders. She unties one end of the bag and carefully pours wine into two simple clay cups. As she pours, she glances up at me with the most serene expression.

"This is wine from my homeland, from Galilee. When it arrived, it was new wine, but that was some time ago. It should be ready to drink by now."

"Was it put into a new wineskin?" I ask, topping my previous Greatest-Idiot-Award-winning question. Her eyebrows rise.

"Well, yes, of course," she says, patiently stating the obvious as she dilutes the wine with water from a clay pitcher, "It could not reach its fullness for so long in an old skin."

Taking out a large pan of the region's flatbread, she delicately breaks off two pieces. She invites me to sit on a cushion near the hearth, and she walks very carefully over to me, holding the two cups. She offers the watered wine and the bread, and I gratefully accept. Still warm, I chew the bread slowly, savoring its texture rather than swallowing it whole. It tastes much like pita bread, only coarser and chewier. I'm thirsty, but out of respect, I try not to drain the cup too quickly. The diluted wine is a deep red vintage, sweet with the hint of honey and other herbs I knew they added in this century.

"Is this a Cabernet?" I hear myself ask stupidly as I eye the cup in my hand, instantly regretting the words as they leave my lips. Apparently, my dumbshit questions are not going to stop.

"No, it is a cup," she replies, curious.

The Cabernet grape does not exist—at least by that name—in the first century. She moves on.

"This house belongs to Johanan. They call him Ioannis the Apostle here."

Another brain download feeds me, and I swallow hard.

She knows Saint John? Seriously? I mean, the real Saint John, the apostle of Jesus?

She speaks about him as if he's still alive. Wait a minute. Of course, he'd be alive. It's only AD 43. I shake my head like an impatient horse, and she pauses a moment to let the intel sink in.

"Johanan purchased it so that our friend could live out her days in peace. This is the place from which she left us." She sweeps the air with her arm, indicating the entire house, and glances thoughtfully into the fire as if remembering this friend.

The woman sits down next to the wall, leaning her back up against the stones, her head resting slightly on one of the gray-green river boulders that form the interior walls. As I look at the surface of the stone shining in the lamplight, I wonder how many human heads have rubbed it smooth over the centuries. That's when I notice a small shelf right above where she sits. On it rests a roughly fashioned clay fish with a coin sticking out of its back where the dorsal fin should be. It looks like a child's bank that failed to accept the coin completely. Its weirdness wrestles my attention away for a moment, and she notices.

"A friend made that for me when I was very young," she says and then takes a deep breath. "There is so much to tell." Offering no more, she returns to resting her head on the stone and reaches for the blanket on the bench. "Where to start?"

Start what? Clearly, she's settling in to tell me a story. But what story? And why? My older daughter always loves to tell me, "Ohmagoddad, just roll with it!"

I've shot back two thousand years in history and am now dressed like an extra in the movie *Gladiator*. Insane scared but fascinated at the same time, I guess I'll sit here and see what's next.

Okay, let's roll.

The woman gathers the blanket's reddish-brown folds comfortably across her lap as if more for protection than warmth. She draws in another deep breath, taking a moment before opening some personal box of memories. Then, sighing and bundling the blanket near her face so it brushes her cheek, she closes her eyes as if she feels the hand of a lover lost long ago.

"The time of Yeshua with his followers was short, but so much took place. So much." Her voice trails off sadly. After a silent moment, she regains her composure, straightens her head, and smiles warmly.

"Wait. Did you say *Yeshua*?" I ask her.

Suddenly, like a clap of thunder banging inside my head, I remember a movie where all the biblical characters' names were pronounced in Aramaic. I was surprised that Aramaic rather than Hebrew was the predominant language of the Holy Land in the first century. In that movie, "Yeshua" was the pronunciation of Jesus's name! When she says it, it sounds different from the movie pronunciation—almost like "EE-show' ah," with the "ah" being nearly silent—but I know she's saying

"Yeshua." With this news, my stomach seizes up, hard as a fist, and my head goes light.

She saw him? She actually saw … Jesus? Seriously, Jesus himself?

The woman gives me a minute and then looks at me as if she has just made a decision.

"But for you, we should start with the Immerser. Yes." She nods. "The Immerser." In the back of my mind, I register that she's speaking of John the Baptist, but I'm still reeling from her voicing the name of Yeshua.

Jesus frickin' Christ, what is going on here?

My heart is on fire with a hundred questions.

Who is she? Can this actually be happening? To me? Am I going crazy? Okay, okay, take a breath, Jack. Take another. Breathe. Okay.

"Uh, when you say, ahem, *Yeshua*, you mean, like, the man from Nazareth who was crucified under Pontius Pilate, died, and was buried"—I am reciting the Apostles' Creed to her—"and rose from the dead? On the third day?"

Her eyes suddenly fill with tears, and she sniffs. It's personal to her. The flippin' creed is personal to her?

Who am I with here?

Dabbing her eyes with the blanket, she doesn't say anything. She merely inclines her head slightly to answer yes.

"I am sorry to make you sad, lady, but why am I here? May I ask you that?"

Her expression doesn't change, nor does she seem challenged by the question. She leans toward me, moist eyes intently burrowing into mine.

"I will answer that question only once, Traveler. It is simple, really. You opened up." She says it casually, as if I should know what that means.

Opened up. What is this? Therapy?

"Sorry, I don't understand," I snap back quickly and maybe a little harshly.

"When you open up, what is inside and what is outside come together," she says to my blinking bewilderment. She sees she's not getting through to me, so she decides to heap more confusion on top of it. "You may not understand now, but you will. When the outside and inside become one, even for a moment, then you are ready to encounter all that you need."

What do I need?

I don't voice that one, because I understand none of this, really. She has that part right. However, I feel something else, something besides confusion. There's the breathless excitement of adventure in all of this, the allure of a voyage of … well, discovery. I feel as if I'm captaining a ship into uncharted waters never traveled by anyone before. This prospect thrills me, even if I must let go of my death grip on certainty and predictability. And right now, letting go is not only fine with me, it's compelling. I am surprised at how easily some part of me says *yes* to this. I can contain my excitement no longer. I have to know.

"What was Yeshua like?" I blurt out, and the enormity of that unanswered question hangs in the air like the blimp at the Super Bowl.

She closes her eyes and nods as if people have asked her that question a thousand times before, yet she understands, more than I do, why I need to hear.

"I will speak more of him later, but I will say this now: he is not very different from other men when you first encounter him, when you see him from a distance. He is of average height, not tall like you, but strong of arm and handsome of face. At thirty summers, he still had all his teeth. A man.

"But when he comes closer, you see his eyes, and you know here is no ordinary man, no simple son of a Nasrene tradesman. He can still your breathing and change you from the inside out. Indeed, after meeting Yeshua, even your breath is never the same again."

She speaks in the present tense as she gazes at the wall absently, her fingers gently kneading the blanket. Maybe that is a glitch in the translating software. Her eyes return to meet mine, more in wonderment than in sad remembrance.

"That is why he is amazing. To understand this with the human mind is a challenge. To understand it with the heart is a homecoming."

The way she talks is amazing, like an accomplished actress reading poetry.

"From the stories, you will see that Yeshua did not yet know what lay before him. He knew that he was someone singled out by Elohim, but when I met him, he was yet uncertain where Adonai would lead him."

I feel my forehead and cheeks burn red.

I have been to enough Jewish services to know that *Adonai* means the same as "Lord" in Christianity, but I have not heard of *Elohim* before. She pronounces it in a way that sounds a little like *Allah*, the name of God for Muslims.

"Elohim," I say, stumbling over the pronunciation, "means …"

"The same as the one Yeshua called Abba, or Father," she replies.

"In other words, God," I say. Her eyebrows knit together in a pretty frown.

"Gaw-ud?" She repeats the curious sound. I decide to set it aside for now, because apparently, some words don't translate. *God* must be one of them. So, *Elohim* is the name of God and *Adonai* is Lord.

Good to go.

"I am ready to listen to whatever you wish to tell me, my lady."

She smiles, and for an instant, I can see the young woman she must have been when she first set eyes upon Yeshua.

"You are very kind," she says, "but please call me Miramee."

"Thank you, Miramee." Even repeating her name is a pleasure.

"And, Traveler, we have already begun, but rather than me telling you about the Immerser, he can speak for himself," she says with a relaxed smile.

What does she mean? Is the Immerser going to appear now?

I take a deep breath as I realize that I'm the traveler, the Jonah in the belly of the whale. The man learning is the one who moves around, not the teacher.

"I am ready," I hear my voice saying.

"Go now to the Immerser with Elohim's peace," she says. Nothing happens.

Oka-ay, go where? How?

More nothing happens.

My mind kicks back into gear. Besides the incomprehensible opening-up stuff she spouted, I still don't know why I'm here. I don't know why this is happening to me. Even though I keep stuffing them down, questions continue popping into my mind like popcorn at a movie theater.

How can she send me to John the Baptist himself? And why me?

Pop. Pop. Pop.

I'm no holy man. I'm an insurance guy—a damn *good* insurance guy—but I'm no Nelson Mandela or Mother Teresa. As I try to settle my mind and cut off these thoughts, I remember what Dad told me when Gabriella was born, when I was unsure of the whole fatherhood thing.

"I didn't know what to do with you at first," Dad said. "You didn't come with instructions, Jacky." He's one of three people on earth who can call me Jacky. "Life gives you the answers as you go along. Just have the guts to do what you need to do next, and don't ever throw in the towel."

As I'm remembering that sports bar moment, something inside me breaks loose, like a glacier cracking and dropping a chunk of ice into the sea.

Whatever is coming, let's do this.

She sees that I am now ready and nods. "Close your eyes."

Eyes closing.

Chapter 4

AD 29, and the sixteenth year of the reign of the emperor Tiberius, Herod's stone fortress near the Dead Sea

It's dark in here.

I blink, opening my eyes wide, trying to adjust to the torch-lit space. I draw in a deep breath, and the stink of human waste and sweat makes me gag. It's so putrid, I can't control my body, and vomit into the straw on the cold and slimy stone floor. Wiping my mouth with my sleeve, I feel raw and disoriented.

Where the hell am I now?

"Machaerus. That is the name of this place." As if reading my thoughts, a man's deep voice sounds from the depths of the flickering shadows.

I turn in his direction, trying to wrestle control of the trembling vocal cords in my tightening throat.

"Where is Machaerus?" I ask. "I do not know where that is." I am unable to stifle the waver in my voice.

"It is the fortress of the tetrarch Herod Antipater," says the faceless voice. "He calls himself the king of Galilee. You are his prisoner, as am I."

Slowly, I can make out the form of a man sitting opposite me on the floor, his back up against the iron bars of the cell. I'm close to being insane scared. I'm no wimp, but I've never been in a prison cell before. And this isn't a cell; it's a stinking cage at the zoo.

As my eyes adjust to the light, I see other cells and water dripping down the stone walls that divide them from one another. Rats scurry in and out of the bars like mechanical toys that never run down. I hear groans and phlegmy coughing issue from the dark vaults around us, but then I notice something very incongruent to this scene: there are strains of music wafting from above, as well as the faint sounds of people laughing—like *at-a-party* laughing.

What kind of prison has a mixer going on upstairs?

"We are here so close to the tetrarch, because we are the ones he fears the most," the man says. "Herod Antipater follows the old adage, which is to keep your friends close but your enemies closer!"

He chuckles at his own wit and breaks into a fit of coughing and wheezing. He's sick, as anyone who lives in this shithole would have to be. My mind rattles around, trying to recall if I've heard anything about this place. When we toured Jordan three years ago, I know we went to the Dead Sea, and the guide said something about a castle built by Herod the Great on a hilltop a few miles south of our resort. It was so damn hot that day, no one cared much about another pile of ruins, so we passed.

Was Machaerus the name of that castle? I think it was. And these walls look pretty thick. I'm sure they would still be around in the twenty-first century.

"Why did you come here?" he asks.

"Miramee sent me to meet the Immerser."

There's an awkward silence as if that name doesn't register.

"What could the Immerser say to you?" he asks finally.

Feeling uneasy with this man's questioning, I scoot about a foot farther away from the vomit. I gingerly place my hands on the slick stone floor, not wanting to know what makes it so. I switch off any thoughts of the pestilence potential here and refocus on the man in the shadows.

Then it comes to me again: this man is John the Baptist, the one whom Miramee calls the Immerser!

"I came to ask about Yeshua. I believe that is how you say his name." I try to keep my composure in his awesome presence.

"It is," he replies as if trying to calm me down. "What shall I call you?"

"She called me—uh, I am called Traveler ... Sir, um, Your Holiness."

The Immerser ignores that and shifts his butt a little closer to me.

"Well, Traveler, I know Yeshua of Nasrath. He is my kinsman."

The invisible, deep tones of his voice start to really spook me, but then my eyes finally adjust to the gloom, and I see him clearly now. He is as grizzled as a black bear, his long hair and beard unkempt. He wears a crudely styled animal skin. He really is like a caveman but even wilder looking. I feel his eyes burn into mine, which is bizarre, considering the low light. He used the words "is my kinsman."

Is this a time when Jesus is living?

I get the download that it's AD 29, so yes, he must still be alive!

I take shallow breaths. My elbow slides off my thigh, and I nearly flop over with the realization. This is too much.

"You have come far and to this place to talk about Yeshua," he says. "I know Elohim wishes me to speak to you when I would rather be silent." He shifts his weight, and the chains on his ankles pull and rattle.

"Why?" I am puzzled.

If Jesus is his cousin, why doesn't he want to talk about him to anyone and everyone who asks?

"Do not chase reasons, Traveler," he replies. "It leads to convenient and comfortable mistruths. You can never find what you seek tonight by asking that question."

Out of respect, I bow my head and wait for him to begin. The music continues to play above as the celebration amps up. I can make out an instrument that sounds like a harp, only tinnier and less elegant— probably a lyre. There are also drums, cymbals, and other types of percussion that are harder to identify. Like an old, scratched phonograph record, the passage of music repeats over and over, its tempo rising to a crescendo and then falling back to the slower, more primary rhythm. The Immerser sits in silence with me, listening to the music.

"For many years, I heard no musical instruments play. Now that I am a prisoner and live in this wretched place, I hear beautiful music all the time," he says. "Elohim always gives us something to cherish, even in the darkest days of life."

In the context of this time period, I understand that any instrumental music is unusual enough for common people to consider beautiful. Too bad he was born before *really good jazz*.

He moves from his thoughts and looks at me directly, piercing me with his eyes again.

He's ready to begin.

Chapter 5

The Immerser:

A clear, hot morning. A mist of flies hovered around my head, and I turned sharply to the right.

Standing next to Andreas, my disciple, on the riverbank, I saw a man removing his outer garments and staring at me. A sensation shot through my chest like an arrow.

Yeshua.

I had not seen him for seven years. Clearly, he was more mature, a little more filled out, with our familial look about him. He wore only his loincloth, and he waited for my signal. I raised my arm, and he waded in. As he drew closer, I could see that he was strong and tightly muscled. His gaze carried a deep compassion. I felt as if I were looking into a bottomless cavern. My breathing changed—not shortening or lengthening but rhythmically—as if responding to a sudden difference in the air around us. I wondered if my disciples had exaggerated the reports of his healings and the many deliverances from demons. I was deeply concerned that a number of my disciples thought he was the Mashiach.

You look confused again, Traveler.

The Mashiach is the Holy One of Israel, whose birth the prophets foretold. Alas, many men posed as the Mashiach and came to me, seeking my blessing, which I did not give. I know my calling is to prepare for the coming of the Mashiach, but I had not yet received a revelation about his advent or even if he had already been born. Our people hunger for him, yearn for the freedom promised by the Holy

One of Elohim. Many think he will come to free the land from the Romans and reestablish a self-governing Israel, but I knew Elohim would have a greater design for his Anointed. I knew Yeshua was not another pretender, but I questioned whether my wiry cousin was the Mashiach of Israel.

I still do not know, but on that day, I could not ignore the fiery sensation he ignited inside me.

I heard a shout.

"I came for immersion!"

I did not see Yeshua's lips move. I looked behind me but saw only the witnesses standing on the riverside. No one there had said or even heard it.

"It is a sign for many. Do it!" It was another shout, a different voice coming from a different direction.

Startled, I scanned the opposite bank and saw Yeshua's mother. She is Miryam of Nasrath, my mother's dear cousin and beloved of so many others that she is known affectionately as *Eema*, the name a small child calls his or her own mother. His brother Yakov, nicknamed *Tzadik* or *the Just*, stood next to Eema along with Andreas.

The name stuck to Yakov because the people of Nasrath also called Yosef, his father, *the Just*. Even as a boy, Yakov was fair-minded, balanced, and serious, like a judge. Hence they called him Tzadik too.

With blank expressions, they all stared back at me. My large black dog, Aderes, was also there, wagging her tail. When Yeshua waded close enough, he stopped, and we said nothing to one another. Yet there began an unspoken dialogue without pause or lapse.

Suddenly, I felt the sensations again, pure energy, as if a part of the sun had come to earth and stood before me as a man. Imbuing a man with godlike attributes is not only preposterous but also blasphemous. As familiar as my cousin was to me, he was a stranger that day.

He should be immersing me, I thought.

Yeshua closed his eyes, bowed his head, and knelt in the clear, shallow water. The *Ruach Kudsha*, that which you call Holy Spirit, then revealed that I should fully immerse him and not simply pour water from my shell upon his head. Therefore, I helped him up, and we waded a few steps farther out, into the middle of the river. As I laid a hand on his shoulder, a wave of calm rolled up my arm and into my body.

I mouthed a silent prayer, put my hand on his face, and leaned him back. I immersed him in the cool, gently moving waters of Mother Jordan for the first time, with the witness of the sun and even the full moon, which hung dimly but visibly like a white circle of bread suspended in the late morning sky.

After I lifted him from the waters, I felt an immediate and profound sense of relief. Then, to reveal that I had stirred up other dark and malevolent forces, sharp pains stabbed through my hands as if knives were piercing them.

The excruciating pain almost caused me to drop him into the water. I set my jaw firmly. Nothing, *nothing* would prevent me from performing this sacred act!

I sensed the forces of good and evil swirling around us—perhaps all the forces of heaven and earth.

By this time, Andreas had entered the river to assist me as he had done many times. He is a tall, pensive man, a fisherman with huge hands and a larger heart. I shook my head at him as I raised Yeshua up and prepared to do the second immersion. This was between Yeshua, Elohim, and me. My kinsman opened his eyes and looked past me into the sky. I lowered him again. Severe cutting pain continued, stopping my breath. Tears flushed into my eyes as my hands faltered again, but I did not drop him.

No power of evil will prevail, I thought.

Like a small whirlwind, the forces circled Yeshua, and when I raised him again, I saw their gray and brown vapor-like fingers attempting to touch him. A brilliance emanated from him that kept the fingers at bay. They could get no closer to him than a hand's thickness. I looked into his eyes. There seemed to be light behind them.

Like shining gold.

He is the Light in silence, I thought as I detected a subtle and unspeakable power course throughout my body. Rather like warm oil being rubbed into my skin, except that I felt the sensation on the inside.

With the third immersion, as the water ran off his face and hair, Yeshua stood up in the river, still blinking at the sky—and then he gasped. I looked up and saw, about a man's height above his head, a dove or a radiant white sunbird. It hovered for a moment and then darted off into the wilderness east of the river.

"May this water purify you from your sins and strengthen you among the flock of Elohim, his people, Israel!"

Yeshua's light increased, and for an instant, I thought he would burst into flames. As I led him to shallower water, I motioned to Andreas, and he waded out to join me. The pain was gone, and I now felt lightheaded, yet I could see with a new sharpness and definition. Everything around me was suddenly so clear that I had to squint.

A wild wind from the west lashed the water's surface, and the river soon raged ferociously. The fearful onlookers began to shout and gasp as the current, which had been clear, now ran opaque with silt, flowing violently in different directions. The wind whipped the people with sand and dirt, needling them as they covered their faces, and some ran for the shelter of nearby tents. I kept my arm around Yeshua's shoulder as I walked him out of the water. He seemed to waver and be less sure of his footing, but I felt heat emanating from him, and I sensed something had come to completion. He had a different air about him. Andreas and Tzadik quickly dried him off and wrapped him in his robes, but he remained in this trancelike daze.

"He is as cold as winter water," said Andreas, and I noted that this was the opposite of what I sensed.

Yeshua gives a different impression to each person. As I thought that, the color instantly returned to Yeshua's cheeks and forehead. He was now clear-eyed and aware.

"I depart at once," he said suddenly, the first words I had heard him speak. Yeshua's voice has a richness that commands authority.

"Where are you going, Rabbuni?" Andreas asked.

"Into the desert wilderness," he replied.

"You should not go without a companion," said Tzadik.

"I am called alone."

The exchange was over, and Yeshua nodded a farewell. He looked into my eyes and put a hand upon my shoulder. I reflexively offered him my waterskin, but he refused by placing his hand upon the weathered one strapped to his belt. He would take nothing extra into the desert, not even another waterskin. I understood this and blessed him.

Then, without saying farewell to his brother and mother, Yeshua walked steadily away from us toward the east, almost pushed forward by the fury of the storm. He tripped once and almost fell. Andreas reflexively lurched forward to go assist, but Yeshua regained his footing and disappeared into the billows of rusty sand.

As we lost sight of him, the wind died down as suddenly as it had started, and the air became still once more. The waters flowed gently, returning to their crystalline clarity. Insects and birds reappeared and resumed their music in the warmth of the midday sun. Yet Yeshua was gone, and I felt the question come again, opening a nagging, empty hole in the center of my body.

Is he the One?

Chapter 6

AD 29, and the sixteenth year of the reign of the emperor Tiberius, Machaerus

The Immerser falls silent for a moment.

The smells have lost their intensity, and I marvel at how adaptable the human nose is. I'm in no hurry to leave right now. The Immerser is alone here and seems to be enjoying my companionship.

"I had a dream that morning before I woke up next to the dog, Aderes," he says. "She always slept right by me, an island of warmth against the cutting cold of the desert." He misses his pet. Very human.

"In the dream, I remember clearly a small house in Nasrath. I entered the house and saw that no one lived there anymore. It seemed to have been a carpenter's house, because some long-unused trade tools lay neatly in a corner, gathering dust. There was a rusting saw, along with a wooden clamp, plane, and mallet, among some others. Over the tools, a large spider sat in fearsome guard on his large, silver-spun web.

"I remember thinking that this was the family home of my cousin, of Yeshua, but there was no sign of his mother and their family. A child I did not know, a small boy with hair as silver as the spider's web, walked in from the sleeping chamber and stared silently at me.

"'Where is your father? Where is your mother?' I asked the child, but he did not speak.

"Like a mute angel, he motioned me to follow him into the darkened room. As I did, the spider shot up and down his web in a crazed and desperate motion as if trying to attack me, but he could not. The silver web was his carefully constructed trap, but it also trapped him. The boy

36

led me into the darkened room, and I became very fearful. Yet I was curious as well, hungering to know if Yeshua and his family were in here. The room was as dark as a starless night; I could not see my hand in front of my face. Its shadows were like the darkness of this prison, only deeper, as if the blackness could enter inside me. The boy was gone, the spider was gone, and the house was gone. Only the blackness surrounded me. Was this a tomb? I wondered.

"Suddenly, there appeared a shaft of blinding white light, a warm brilliance. 'This is my beloved son,' a man's voice announced lightly and calmly. It was not loud. Rather, it was more like a breeze rustling through a leafy tree bough.

"The white light faded back into the darkness. Then another powerful shaft of golden light with orange flecks illuminated a different part of the blackness. I could see the floor covered in straw, a floor much like this one, yet the straw in my dream was fresh. In one corner, I could see a pile soaked red with blood glinting in the beam of light. That was all I can remember. Strange. Stranger still that I felt drawn to tell you it."

He pauses for a moment, replacing the memory in the box and shelving it back into his mind.

"What else did Miryam say to you?" he asks me in a different, brighter tone of voice.

"Who?"

He gives me a long stare, taking in the full measure of my ignorance.

"The woman you call Miramee."

"Why did you call her Miryam?"

"On a rare visit, one of my disciples told me that Yeshua has a woman disciple he calls Miramee. I am told he is quite fond of her. She is from the desert, although everyone else calls her by her given name and the city of her birth." He leans back against the bars. "Her full name is Miryam of Magdala. They call her Magdalene. Only Yeshua—and now you—call her Miramee."

"Miryam of Magdal—" I stop midword. My heart jumps, and I feel my skin flash hot and cold as the realization hits me. My host, the woman who kept me from falling, handed me bread and wine, and sent me on my way is none other than the beloved disciple of Yeshua, Mary Magdalene. As incredible and difficult to believe as all of this is, the Immerser is telling me the truth, and I feel both exhausted and elated.

The beloved of Yeshua!

And I'm sleeping in her house!

Questions continue to roil about in my brain. The Immerser is amazing, and his presence calms me down again.

Keeping our silence, we hear only the whistle, strum, and beat of the musical instruments above us. It's an unspeakable honor simply to be here with him, listening to bad music and sharing these few moments of his life. The littleness of all this opens into its majesty, and it's enough just to sit here with him. In the dim light, I can see him pinning me with his stare. I can even make out the wild man's eyes crinkling as he smiles.

"You are learning, Traveler," he says.

I hear the distant strains of music soften as the Immerser closes his eyes, and my own vision fades again into darkness. I'm falling down the hole again. Rapidly and calmly falling … into black.

My senses are on full alert as streaks of light zoom past me in the darkness. The nose is first to notice the difference as the dank stink of the prison becomes the aroma of hot soup cooking. My skin pricking at me informs me that I am out of the foul clothes I was wearing and back in my freshly cleaned Ephesian garb. There is a whooshing sound like that of a heart beating through a stethoscope—not syncopated, though … steady. I feel tremendous energy up and down my body, and I know that if I can feel this, I must still be alive.

Chapter 7

AD 43, and the third year of the reign of the emperor Claudius, Ephesus

Holding the bowl of steaming soup, Miramee takes the small, careful steps she took earlier, as if she is terrified of spilling a drop. I'm still jittery from the meeting with the Immerser, yet I'm relieved to be back at the stone house, watching Miramee perform these ordinary tasks.

I'm watching her now with even more curiosity, for although I know she is the Magdalene, she possesses such dignified humility that, to me, she remains simply Miramee. I want to suspend this moment in time to savor it, locking it deep inside me.

"I am still very frightened when I carry something hot," she says as she carefully hands me the bowl. "When I was younger, I had the falling sickness."

"What is the falling sickness?" I ask, taking the bowl, my fingers lightly brushing hers.

"You know, when you suddenly fall and … writhe upon the ground?" she says.

"Epilepsy?" I ask, and her expression is blank. "Seizures, right?"

"Yes, although I do not have them anymore," she says.

As long as I've known him, my uncle's had to take medication to keep his seizures under control. I'd never heard of anyone recovering from epilepsy.

"People do not understand the illness, and they become frightened," she says.

"How long did you have the falling sickness?" I ask. More at ease with her now, I sip the delicious soup.

"There will be time for that question later. But now that you have met the Immerser, you need to move to the next—"

"Wait. Wait. Miramee, please," I say, cutting her off midsentence. She stops, dumbfounded. Obviously, she's unaccustomed to people interrupting her.

"You have another question, Traveler?"

"More than one. Miramee, I mean no disrespect, but I have no idea where I am or why I am here. You said that I opened up, but that is not enough for me."

"What can I help you with?" she asks.

"Thank you. Well, for instance, I am a guy who is in a business with many rules. The rules govern whether someone receives a payment or not. If the rules are not kept, the agreement is cancelled, no payment is made."

"Go on," Miramee says.

She seems to be having no trouble following me as I try to explain the cancellation of an insurance policy.

"I am from two thousand years into the future, and yet I am here, eating and talking with you and the Immerser. I am breaking the rules. Therefore, am I not changing the future forever just by being here? Am I not cancelling something else out? Am I terminating myself?"

Miramee sets her bowl down on the low table beside her and wipes her hands with a tan-colored cloth. She peers deeply into my eyes and remains silent for a full minute, which feels longer. Doubts seize my mind with questions.

Did I offend her?

What's she preparing to tell me?

Does she even understand?

Will she throw me back down the rabbit hole anyway?

My brain slowly unwinds like a child's toy. The spaces of silence become longer as I look back into her eyes in the flickering light of the fire.

"I will tell you what I know. You are here, but you are there as well—both places—and perhaps many other places as well. Most people who are aware of this are *rabbunim,* or masters, themselves. Seldom does someone who is not prepared, untaught, venture into the Kingdom."

"What kingdom?"

Is it some kind of parallel universe? Another dimension of some crazy kind?

Miramee looks at me tentatively. I guess she doesn't come across greenhorns like me very often.

"The sovereign presence of Elohim," she says to my blinking expression, which is as blank as a four-year-old having algebra explained to him.

"That is the Kingdom. The sovereign presence."

Okaaay. Totally lost.

She sees it.

"You talk about rules. Here are some you will learn while you are here. You will not change the shape or sequence of anything to come, because your true body is still where your home is. This body …" She touches my sleeve. "… is real, but it cannot affect anything around it permanently. You will learn that."

"So I can eat something and it will turn back up later, uneaten," I ask, incredulous.

"Once your attention is called to something else, what has happened will go back as it was before. This is for you, and it has been made possible for you alone."

"Why?"

"I don't answer that question. That question leads to distraction," she replies. Hmm, she sounds like the Immerser. Must be a type of group speak.

"All right, then. What are the other rules?"

"Your words can be heard and some of them remembered, but most will be forgotten once your presence is gone—except if you serve as a tool of the Father's revelation to someone else. All of us are used if we are open. Do not be disappointed if you try to warn someone and he or she does not understand you. You do not decide what Elohim reveals to anyone. Where you come from, you know many things that people here must not know, so if you say something that does not belong in their ears, it will become noise … the noise of your native tongue."

This bends my mind, yet it's intriguing.

"Also, any gesture or written word that does not belong in the eyes of anyone here cannot be seen. Your actions have no permanence."

"So, I'm a ghost?" I ask, smirking, and she laughs delightfully.

"No. You are as real as that bench, but only for a short time here."

"And if I break the rules?"

"These rules are like life itself, unbreakable," she says. "Therefore, you need have no concern about them. They take care of themselves."

"Can I be hurt? Can I die here?"

Miramee is silent again, and her smile vanishes.

"You must always take care, for it is a body and you are in foreign lands in another time. It bears all the risks to which any human body is subject. You remain a creature of Elohim—as we all are."

"If I die here, then I die there too?" I'm not liking the direction this is going.

"Elohim grants us the gift of life in a body, and in the fullness of time, the gift is returned to him. This does not change, even though you are here right now."

"You know, Miramee, maybe I should go home," I say.

I may have to flick the chicken-switch, considering the weight of this. I have two girls who need to make it through college, and this isn't like a video game where I get multiple lives. If I fall off a cliff or some guy with a horned helmet axes me in the first century, it's permanent, and I am leaving my family high and dry. Sharon would have a seven-figure monster mortgage to pay off.

"Traveler, the angel protects," she says. "You may return whenever you wish, but you are here because you need to be here and you desire to be here."

I feel the longing-like something gnawing at my gut. Is this the pain of the new wineskin growing around me?

If so, I see how a guy could burst with all this going on. I trust my judgment. Always have. There are risks here—real, insane, deadly risks, to be sure—but seriously, in the seven or eight odd decades we get to lope around on this wet asteroid, who gets a chance to do this, to witness something like this?

For now, I'll go with my gut and move through this weird reality, taking only measured, cautious steps. I'm good at keeping my head up and staying on purpose, so I'll know when to pull the plug if this goes too far. Besides, according to the rules of impermanence, if I die here, I'll vanish and turn up dead in Monterey—and there I have five life insurance policies on me. Sharon won't really be left high and dry. She'd be without me, sure, but she'd be taken care of—grieving but taken care of. Practical Jack Castro's mind is satisfied.

Okay, Traveler can continue.

"What's next?" I ask.

Miramee's smile returns. "You will meet other brothers and sisters at a point in their lives when they are ready to share what they have witnessed with you. People can only speak to you in precisely the right order and at the appointed time. It may confound you at first, but soon you will begin to understand the order."

"How will I know them?" I ask, bewildered at the enormity of this.

"You already understand that," she replies.

Yes. I have received downloads on the Immerser and her, about the places and the times. These downloads aren't instantaneous or complete. Instead, when I seem to be looking the other way, they fall into the mind subtly, in pieces, and become part of it. It's sort of like a heavenly mail carrier slipping letters, one by one, through a slot in the door of my mind.

All this elaborate briefing, all this trouble these important people are taking just to inform me!

Me?

While I've absolutely no self-confidence issues—in fact, it's just the opposite—I realize, with only a brush of self-assessment, that I'm no Nobel peace laureate, no modern day saint. I'm only Jack Castro from Monterey, another face in the crowd—unless you're one of my farmers with a failing crop. And in this time period, I know my professional expertise is about as valuable as *chicken crap on the pump handle*, as my Missouri grandpap used to say.

I'm going to take another crack at this.

"Why me? Miramee, why?"

"If I knew the answer, I would not say. That is the first lesson. If your thoughts stick together around the question *why*, your mind can become mired for a long time, sometimes forever. If what happens around you makes no sense to you now, then the time is not full. Elohim reveals all in the appointed hour, and you must continue in faith until then. Can you trust what I am saying, Traveler?"

I sit back, understanding her, though dissatisfied with her answer.

Should I trust her? Do I have this thing called faith?

Not up to now. I'm in a business where faith is not part of the equation. If a good thing happens, then it's good, and the policyholder sends in his or her premium. If the bad thing happens, then the company pays the policyholder. There isn't much faith involved. Really, it isn't a large part of life in America or Europe anymore.

So, I get back to the question: can I trust this sexy, radiant woman wrapped in a blanket across from me?

I look deep into her dark eyes, and I see myself reflected back, the image of a man who has seldom trusted in his life. My father was in insurance, like me, and my mother worked in security for the Department of Defense. Everything in our lives was about certainty, safety, covering all your bases—and covering your ass. The people surrounding me at home are there because they have earned my trust over years of experience. I play life when the odds are in my favor. In my book, taking chances against the odds is for losers and dreamers. People can only earn my trust the hard way—with time.

Miramee leans forward with a slight frown. "Traveler, can *you* trust *me?*"

Damn! This is a stretch. I trust few people, but this is Mary Magdalene. Yeshua himself loved her. If she merited that honor from Christ, who am I *not* to trust her? From my childhood religion classes, I remember that she was one of the few people who stood with his mother at the foot of the cross. She's got guts. And unlike St. Peter, she never denied Yeshua. If she wants me to do this, then Yeshua must want me to do this too.

I sip some soup and nod at her.

"I guess I am growing into that new wineskin," I say. She stares at me as if I just read the deepest secret of her heart.

"What did you say?" she asks as her breath quickens.

"The new wineskin, you know, the story from the Bible?"

"What is a Bible?" she asks with the slightest trace of a scowl.

"You know. From the gospels. Jesus's, Yeshua's story about growing new wineskins."

"You have heard the triumphant message? Who told you? The Immerser could not know. That was later, much later."

"It is in the book of Yeshua's teachings," I say.

Miramee's face tightens into a fearful expression.

"There is no *book*! There are some writings by a Greek, who was an enemy. That is all that has been written down, for none of what was said was ever meant to be read, only taught from the lips of another follower! That is the reason he picked the apostles, the messengers!"

She clearly does not know about the written Word that will come a few decades later, or about the resulting explosion of the church into hundreds of Christian sects.

I shut up. Something just slipped through; the rules here are not watertight.

Seeing how this rattles her to the core, I realize that this is dangerous stuff. I respect rules. But maybe Elohim is using me as a conduit of revelation here. A weird sensation courses through my gut. She waits for me to answer.

"I trust you," I say.

Satisfied, she gets up to get more soup for me. Cautiously filling the clay bowl, she does the slow ceremonial shuffle back to me, cradling it carefully in her hands. Soon the revitalizing soup warms my entire body.

Yet I'm still hungry.

Miramee seems content to serve me, as if this is a rare opportunity for her. I sense that hers is a lonely life. Unlike the other apostles who have founded communities and are revered leaders, each one having a large following, she seems to be a congregation of one.

"There are always two, Traveler," she says, reading my thoughts. "With me, there is always another."

"But you are alone here, are you not?" I ask. There's no one else around that I can see.

She smiles and takes the bowl from my hands.

"Never," she says.

"Then, who …" I stop myself there. I need a dunce cap. She's talking about Yeshua. I get it. In some way, he's always present here with her.

"He will be back soon," she says after a moment.

"Yeshua?"

"Yes."

"He's here? Now?"

"Yes, he is here now, always. But in the flesh, he will return soon to us. He promised this before he was lifted up. He will be back with me soon. With all of us. It is one great thing, one wondrous expectation that gives us hope in the midst of so much suffering.

"If he does not come back right away?" I venture.

"He said it, and so it will come to pass," she replies. "And soon, before we all die, he will bring the New Time with him. He will restore order to the world with the light of the Father."

How can I tell her that for two thousand years, people will continue to wait for Yeshua to return? She sees that I need more.

"In my homeland, our religion helps us to keep the Laws of Moshe—peace be upon him—and thus we prayerfully live our daily lives and have our dealings with one another whilst keeping close observance of what Elohim wants from us. Yeshua upset all that. He turned us around and gave us a new urgency to see that everything will change on the inside and the outside, that there will be a new observance, a new daily life that will fulfill the Law of Moshe in a brilliant, joyful way."

This is the division between the Hebrew and early Christian approaches to life. She just described an ancient religion whose divine guidelines help people firmly rooted in the world negotiate each day, each Shabbat, as they move through their lives. The Hebraic worldview is a very material one.

However, the new covenant gives the followers of the Way a sense of impermanence about everything around them.

Mystical ... and miraculous. The material leads to the divine *immaterial*.

In some ways, these people are a lot like twenty-first-century Christians in some Evangelical and Baptist sects, who believe that the last days are right around the corner. It lifts any deep meaning from acquiring the material in this world, and it lasers the focus on the future coming of Yeshua. In Miramee's view and the views of other early Christians, it's about how we treat one another while we tread water in the *between time*, which, in this period, is thought to be only a few short years in duration.

It's all about perception, isn't it? What we sense leads us to knowing. This sparks another question in my mind.

"Miramee, may I ask you something else?"

"Of course. I will answer as best I can. But no *whys*," she replies with a smile that would light New York.

"No *whys*, I promise. After Yeshua's immersion, when the Immerser was returning with him to shore, he felt great heat from Yeshua. Yet

Andreas found him as cold as icy winter water. Whose perception was real: the Immerser's or that of Andreas? Did Yeshua truly radiate heat?"

Miramee sets down the ladle and bowl for a moment as I see her roll the question around in her mind.

"Yeshua is a man, but he is also not a man. Similarly, the immersion is both death and birth captured in a moment of time, a single breath of life. Because one has to hold one's breath under the water, it is a small death. When that breath returns, it is like the first breath taken after emerging from a mother's womb. So, it is an ending and a beginning, evening and morning. One could feel the death, the evening, which is the coldness of the body—as Andreas and some others may have sensed that day. The Immerser, who perhaps held Elohim more deeply within, could perceive the birth, the morning. He felt the warmth of Elohim moving out from Yeshua."

"So, each person perceives the man Yeshua differently?"

"Of course. As a man and not a man, he reflects each of us back to ourselves," she replies, picking up the ladle and bowl again.

"Like a mirror, then, each person perceives himself or herself when encountering Yeshua?"

"Yes, Traveler," she says as she slowly stirs the pot with the ladle. "And sadly, that is seldom comforting at first. It stirs things up rather than giving peace."

"Peace is later," I say, staring off into space, not knowing where that came from.

"In the fullness of time, everyone and everything returns to peace," she says, filling the bowl. "It is not for us to become distracted by trying to learn when and where. Yeshua's return to lead us is soon. That is enough."

Holding the bowl, Miramee comes toward me with the slow and cautious steps that are becoming a familiar sight.

"When did your falling sickness end, Miramee?" I ask, changing the subject.

She kneels and then relaxes back, resting on her calves. She pulls the brown blanket across her lap again and focuses her deep, lovely eyes upon me as I eat yet another bowl of soup, waiting for her answer.

Chapter 8

Miramee:

My father's identity was my mother's guess.

She could remember nothing about him and had forgotten my true age. Perhaps he worked on the caravans that passed through, or perhaps he was a fisher or even a Roman soldier. Considering of the color of my skin, he must have been dark, maybe a *Nabataean*. My mother was lighter-skinned and was proud to be fully Hebrew.

All that I can remember from my earliest years was that we were desperately poor. My mother and I begged near the marketplace of Magdala of the Fishes, a village by the Sea of Galilee near Herod Antipater's new city of Tiberius. Most of the catch from the west coastal towns is salted and prepared for market there.

My mother was a gifted storyteller, and to pass the time, I would implore her to tell me again the tale of Adam and Eve, loving especially to hear about the beautiful garden. She described Eden in such wonderful detail that I felt I walked around it in my imagination. There were shady trees bearing fruit, so many trees that anyone could simply stroll about and eat her fill any time of the year.

A girl would not feel hunger there.

There was a beautiful stream with warm, fresh water flowing. A girl could bathe every day without fear of catching her death from cold. There were animals too—all the animals of the world—but none would harm the other. All were at peace in this small, leafy haven of Elohim.

On many days, my empty stomach ached and rumbled, so I would walk around a grove of trees just outside of town and pretend to be

Mother Eve. As I walked around in the cool shade, I sometimes felt very dizzy, and I would pick imaginary fruit from the barren trees. I pretended to eat and then look around for my Adam. I looked desperately all over the grove, hoping he would appear and take me from this place, but he was never there, and I would begin to cry. It was on one of those walks that I first experienced falling sickness. I don't remember it, but I woke up with a boy on top of me with his hand on my mouth, trying to hold me down.

"The demons are in her!" he shouted to his other companions.

"Get off of me!" I said and easily threw off the confounded boy. I was hungry and exhausted, but I was also strong for my age, and I knew how to defend myself.

The seizures happened more regularly after that. My mother was alarmed, thinking that a demon possessed me. She took me to a charitable woman who was married to the physician in town. He examined me and pronounced that I was not possessed but that I had the falling sickness. My mother did not know what to do with me, and when seizures occurred in the marketplace, people began to shun us. She told me to wander around and find food in the rubbish heap outside of town. She would never have me around her again when she begged.

As I got older, I could not cry anymore. I did not walk in the grove and pretend. I searched the rubbish for food with all the other poor people and ate the scraps the dogs did not find first. I found enough to eat and made sure my mother did as well. When I would fall sometimes, I was alone. I would just wake up—bruised, dirty, and exhausted but unharmed.

One morning when I was twelve or thirteen, my mother was coughing violently as she shuffled toward her spot in the marketplace.

She turned to me and said, "Remember the garden, Miryam. Walk in the garden for me today."

She longed for paradise, and she knew it was there somewhere, maybe to the east as she had always told me. That afternoon, I did stroll in the grove, but it no longer took me to that magical place, and I felt no need to search for Adam. Toward evening, I brought her some fresh bread that a kindly housewife had offered me. I was so excited to share some fresh food with her, and I found her sitting in her usual spot in the marketplace. She was slumped over with her hand outstretched upon her knee. I thought she was asleep, but she had died sitting up.

Sadly, someone had placed a coin in her hand … a final gift. I still have that coin.

Some men helped me bury her in the common grave for the poor. After they left me, I went to the wall where she sat in the marketplace. It was night, and I realized how alone I was. The tears came then, buckets of them. Holding tightly to her last coin, I wept until I fell asleep, sitting in the place where my mother had died.

I was alone, an orphan and a young girl with falling sickness. Some people in the town were charitable, but that charity lasts for a short time. Life became very dangerous to me in my seaside village. I scavenged for food and tried to beg, but I knew my mother's destiny would not be mine. Fortunately, because I ate so little, I was thin and wiry like a boy. I had not yet developed the womanly endowments that good nourishment would soon bring forth.

My mother had been very beautiful in her youth. If that was to be my fate, it would only make me more vulnerable. So one morning, in my hunger and desperation not to be raped or killed, I cut my hair, found some discarded clothes so I could dress as a boy, and walked the two hours down to Tiberius. It was there that a man hired me to care for the camels in a caravan headed south and east to the Nabataean city of Philadelphia. Elohim blessed me, for I had not fallen since my mother's death.

When doing my private business, I took care to be safely out of sight, and the lifesaving deception worked well enough for the first six days of the caravan's journey.

On the seventh morning, we climbed a parched, rocky trail. When we finally topped the little crest, I gasped at the sight below me. Like a blue jewel in the harsh desert, a twinkling pond lay nested in a deep, small valley.

This was the water encampment about which I had overheard the others speaking, the place where we could rest and take provisions.

I marveled at the groves of date palms, olive trees, and many other types of trees I had never seen before. Trees and flowering bushes surrounded the lake, and a dozen tents and a stone building were clustered in a small clearing nearby.

I had never seen such a wonderful place! In my child's mind, I thought it was the garden of Eden, for my mother had told me that the garden was located in the east, and I knew we were in the east. Yet for all its beauty, the encampment was a busy, bustling place.

When we arrived, I was amazed to see the many provisions traded there. In addition to the water, of course, there were jars of wine, and there were goats, chickens, extra robes, and other food as well. One could buy anything needed for the hot, dry journey to Philadelphia.

A man and woman came out to meet us and to greet the caravan master. The proprietors were a married couple: the mysterious husband, strong and dark, and his much shorter—and wider—wife, who called him only "the Nabataean." She was from Jerusalem and had a queenly way about her. At that time, they were both thirty years old and had four boys around my age. The whole family seemed so healthy and happy that I thought I'd found a place where problems did not exist. I imagined what it would be like to live with them in this paradise.

After all the riders dismounted and their men began to assemble the tents, I began to water the camels by the lake. There I felt the urge to do my private business, so I scanned the area to see if there was anyone in sight, and seeing no one, I found a suitable spot. In the middle of it, I got very dizzy, and I do not remember anything until I woke up, exposed, with the owners' youngest boy squatting over me.

"I told the caravan master you were sick," the little brat snickered, "and that you were a girl."

"What?" I shouted. "You stupid boy!"

My eyes darted about, searching this unfamiliar place for a hiding spot, but it was already too late. I stood there helplessly, unable to run, as the caravan master and two younger men approached me contemptuously. He lifted my robes to certify the boy's claims, and when the caravan master discovered my sex, he slapped me hard across the face, knocking my head to the ground.

"If you want to deceive me, you wretch, you will pay the price," he said malevolently. "Boys, this little virgin is all yours!"

Horrified, I felt myself going into another convulsion as a couple of the young men moved toward me like jackals approaching an injured lamb. As one reached for me, grinning, his expression changed to a painful grimace as a stick struck his back. The wife had come with two of her older sons and had begun to beat back the young men ready to pounce on me. Even though she was short, she was as strong as a man twice her size. My attackers knew better than to challenge the owner of the provisions they needed, so the caravan master barked them back to camp. He turned to face the scowling little woman who stood defiantly, hands on hips, facing him and the retreating men.

"Well, looks like you got yourself a daughter, Havalah, because this lying wretch goes no further with me!" the caravan master said, shooting me a disgusted glare as he stormed off.

The woman turned to look at me with fury in her eyes.

"Are you trying to get yourself killed? Who are you? Where did you come from?" she demanded in her strong Judean accent. In spite of being angry, I could tell she was afraid for me. No one had been afraid for me in a very long time. She appeared kindly and safe. Most importantly, she had beaten back my attackers and saved my life. I had grown used to trusting no one, but I felt I could trust her. Her sons helped me up, and the younger son who had told my secret sheepishly approached, his mother pushing him forward.

"Israel, say it!" she said.

"I-I am sorry I told the caravan master you are a girl—but you are!" Israel said. I nodded, dusting myself off. His brother's hand slapped the back of the boy's head, his signal to get back to the camp. He bounded off like a rabbit in the bush.

"What is your name, child?" she asked.

"Miryam."

"Well, Miryam, let us hear it all," she demanded. She was gruff, but I sensed a motherly concern.

I recounted my story: my mother, Magdala of the Fishes, the falling sickness, her death, my disguise, all of it. She said nothing but listened carefully. She asked one question about my father, but when I stayed silent and hung my head, she quickly understood. She was away from the world out here, but she knew its ways very well.

"Hmm. It seems you are half-starved, but you are still strong enough to work. We will try you out here, doing chores. Can you sew? Or cook?" she asked.

I looked at the dirt. In my life so far, there had never been enough cloth to sew or food to cook.

"Very well then, you shall care for the animals. You seem to have some knowledge of that. But if you give me any trouble—any trouble at all—I will ship you back to Galilee on the next caravan through here! Understood?" Her words were stern, but I could see a softening in her sun-burnished face.

I nodded again. With a regal sweep of her arm, she motioned the boys to take me back to the camp. There, she washed me up, burned my old clothes, and dressed me as a girl again. For the first time in my life, I had fresh clothes and felt truly clean. She spun me around to see how well my transformation had turned out. Satisfied, she faintly grunted her approval.

"Does that feel better, Miryam?" she asked.

"Oh, yes! Thank you, kind lady!" I said.

"Call me Havalah," she said.

"Havalah," I repeated, enjoying the sound of the name of my rescuer.

"We found this in your pocket before we burned your clothes," Havalah said as she handed me my clay fish, the one on the shelf up there. The tip of its little tail fin had chipped off when the caravan master slapped me to the ground.

As I looked at it, she said, "I can fix that."

And I loved her then.

Elohim was good to me. He had led me to the garden, the garden in which my mother wished me to walk. In my young girl's mind, I thought even more could now be possible. As I stood there, I quickly scanned the lake, the groves, and the whole oasis.

"What are you looking for, child?" Havalah asked.

I could not tell her then, but I was looking for my Adam.

As the years passed, Havalah and her family brought me into theirs, and I grew in peace in that little Eden in the desert. I was free and loved working with the animals. I learned to recognize the caravans that regularly came through on the trade route. Well nourished and cared for, I grew rapidly into my womanhood, and as I grew, all of my mother's beauty came to reside in me, except that my skin was gold in color and would burnish darker if I stayed in the direct sun. Havalah and her husband became concerned for my safety. When a caravan came in and I was in the public spaces of the camp, I had to wear a veil covering my nose and mouth. It was uncomfortable because of the heat, but it was my protectors' rule, so I wore it. In my old life, no one had protected me—perhaps Elohim, but no other.

Do not misunderstand: my maidenhood needed no protecting. I am afraid that was lost long before I came into the desert on the caravan. Girls like me, who do not have the care of a family or a home, have short childhoods. I was damaged early, violated by some drunken hired hand whose fishing boat came to port one evening in Magdala. I was about nine or ten; I do not remember exactly. In fact, I do not remember much, because I had a seizure during the attack.

As I matured—and since the opportunity presented itself frequently—I had learned to enjoy the embrace of a man, or a boy, for the sake of the embrace alone. There was something of a prayer in it. It set a fire within me that could burn as bright as the sun, and it filled me with this tremendous power! I did feel powerful, like the deep fragrant earth encountering, then folding into, the paradise lying beyond the heavens.

I was content with my life there as I grew into my full womanhood, and I was happy to spend my days away from other people. Even though Havalah's medicines from herbs worked well, I still suffered occasionally from the falling sickness. Her sons and husband knew what to do when I fell. I grew past the age of marriage, for none of the Nabataean's sons would have me as wife because of the falling sickness. That was the spoken reason. The unspoken one was that, after all the embraces, I had never conceived. They felt I was barren. However, I was happy, at peace with the understanding that alone I had come into this place and alone I would leave. For the second time in my life, I no longer looked for my Adam.

As the years passed, my friendship with Havalah deepened. She was more of a mother than my own mother had been. I worked with her when the caravans came in and spent many hours in idle chatter when things were quieter. She accepted me exactly as I was, and I never had to pretend with her. My life was serene, although something I could not name nagged at me, something in the air that managed to pry itself into my spirit.

A portent came on the morning a man arrived in camp. I walked out of my tent to fill a jar with the morning water. As I filled the jar, I looked up to see a young man standing with his back to me. He was not from our camp, and there was no caravan here. He was dressed in fine clothes that were so white that they almost seemed to shine. When I approached him, he turned to me. His face was beautiful and beardless like a young boy.

"Hail the Beloved. Pay attention! It is time," he said in a low voice that left a fragrance of flowers in its wake.

He pointed to the road toward Judea, and following his finger, I walked past him and squinted to see where he pointed. When I saw nothing, I turned back to him—and saw only the date palms swaying in the morning breeze. Alarmed and suddenly dizzy, I fell.

They told me later that I had dropped the empty jar, and a shard of pottery had cut my right foot like a knife.

Israel, Havalah's youngest son, had apparently picked me up and carried me into the tent for the sick. This tent was away from the others and carried all the unguents and supplies for those men of the caravan who were injured or ill.

When I awoke, I felt searing pain in my foot. I discovered the gash and was relieved to be in the comforting presence of Havalah. Over the years, she had tended many sick and injured people, being as skilled as the best physician in any Galilean or Judean town.

Elevating my right leg, she washed the wound with cold water. She applied a towel with warm water to my forehead to draw the blood upward. Then she put olive oil on the cut and applied some herbs that slightly numbed the skin as she took a needle and silk thread to sew up the gaping wound. Tears streaked down my cheeks from the pain, but I did not cry out. Havalah sewed with great care, stitching me back together. She finished it off with a flourish of red wine over her needlework. She then gave me a healthy gulp, took one for herself, and carefully bandaged me up.

"Take her back to her tent, Israel," she said to the son who had told everyone I was a girl so many years ago. A big, strong man now, he carried me to my tent and laid me on my cot, having that look in his eye that he would like to do more than tuck me in. I sent him away and laid back on the cot, looking at the roof of the tent as my foot throbbed with pain.

I wondered what all this meant.

Who was that man in white?

What did he mean, "Pay attention"? To what?

Hail, the Beloved? Who was that? I had no one but my little group of people in this oasis, but I was not the beloved of anyone.

The morning's events shook me to the core of my being, leaving me with the disturbing feeling that something was about to change my life forever.

And I was right.

Chapter 9

AD 43, and the third year of the reign of the emperor Claudius, Ephesus

Miramee fascinates me as much as her story does. She's like no one I have ever met before. She looks and talks like no one I know. She stops speaking, resting for a moment in the memories of what is long past. When she recounts the events of the desert, it's as if she's describing what happened yesterday.

She sits cross-legged on the mat with her blanket across her lap, holding her right foot as she speaks. I notice a respectable four-inch scar across the top of her foot, and it stabs me like a knife. That scar marks the time in history when she met Yeshua!

This is almost too much to absorb, and looking at that little band of healed, white flesh makes me feel dizzy. Then, as if returning from another place, she looks at me, becoming aware of my presence again. Her brow wrinkles in concern.

"Are you all right, Traveler?" she asks gently, touching my shoulder. "Do you need another cup of soup?"

It feels nice, too nice. I raise my hand: no more! And I smile. A longer period of silence follows. She takes in a deep breath as an idea pops into her head.

"You should meet Havalah!" Miramee says. "She is my dear and sweet old friend. And do not be fooled by her bluster. She raised four boys and ran a desert water camp for decades until her death. She is tough *and* gentle. You know, she never left it. She never left the garden. Yes, it is time for Havalah. I should rest for a moment."

Her smiling countenance fades.

Chapter 10

AD 38, and the second year of the reign of the emperor Caligula, Desert Oasis Camp

Amazing!

But nauseating. Again.

The transition is barely perceptible this time, like a dark elevator shooting upward in a skyscraper. Feels like my stomach dropped off five floors below—complete with the bucket of soup in it.

Now I see the date palms. They're just as Miramee described them, the fronds swaying as if dancing to the unheard music of the desert. I smile at the thought, but my wonder remains.

An old woman comes up to meet me. From Miramee's description, it's Havalah.

Kind of sad. By the time I'm born, she'll be long, long dead—like the Immerser … and like Miramee.

I sigh aloud. There will be a time when I am long dead as well. But right now, she and I are both living human beings, and even though time bends like the palm branches here, this moment is what we share together. In the oasis, I sense a natural rightness and balance, understanding how Miramee loved it at first sight.

"Come over here. There is a place to sit by the water," Havalah commands in a full voice that can be heard across the camp.

I follow her, liking the energy emitted by this stout and sturdy little woman. Her hair is iron-gray mixed with black, her jaw strong and set. Her skin has borne the years of the sun with a handsome, wrinkled grace. I admire her before she utters a second sentence.

The lake is large and fed by a number of artesian streams, like blood vessels trickling life up from under the canyon's boulders. The water is relatively clear, although it's a bit murky in places. I take in the stark contrast of this view: the reddish, dry hues of the rocky ridges framing the greens and blues of the oasis. It's a magical place in its natural meeting of opposing forces.

God's contradiction.

Like me.

By the lake, Havalah points to a low bench made of rich-grained wood. For a seat like this, placed in the open air, it looks astonishingly unweathered—polished, in fact—and almost new, and I think how lovingly someone must care for it. It looks familiar too, as if I've seen it before. Maybe I'm thinking of my wife's small bench in her flower garden.

"The wood is from Lebanon," she says. "He made it while he was here. He made it for her. Sit!"

Yes, Ma'am!

My butt plunks down obediently as I notice the fronds of a giant date palm planted directly behind the bench, shading it perfectly. It's the only tree out here; the others stand in the groves nearer the camp. Settled into our seats on the bench, Havalah begins to speak. I suddenly realize how totally comfortable I am, considering that it's about noon and it's hot.

My clothes have changed again into the correct and insulating wardrobe of the times. The white, flowing robe is made of rough but comfortable cotton, and my *keffiyeh*, with its red decorated band, fits my soccer-ball head perfectly. Its flapping cloth protects my neck from the unrelenting sun as well as the sandy gusts of wind that like to surprise me with a painful whip from time to time.

"There are many things I must prepare before the *Shabbat* this evening," she says, "but I will do anything my Miramee asks of me. I did not call her Miramee before he came, and now she prefers that name, so that is what I call her. She was taken away from us by that name and by the man who gave it to her." Her voice softens a bit, tears moistening the corners of her eyes. She swallows hard, readying herself to continue.

"Excuse me," she says. "Old age has made me sentimental. I do not like it. I never had much time for sentiment, but Miramee is as close to a daughter as I have ever had. Even my daughters-in-law are not like

Miramee is to me. And I will tell them all that. It is no secret. I do not have time to pretend."

"How did you end up here, Havalah?" I ask, changing the subject so she won't break down and start crying on my shoulder.

Recovering quickly, she now forages around in her satchel. She grunts with satisfaction as she lifts out a small wineskin and two cups. Without asking me if I want wine, she pours the thick, red fluid into the cups and hands one to me. She lifts her cup.

"Shalom."

I nod the toast back to her.

She takes a healthy gulp and stares out at the lake.

"When you help someone—and you must always help when you can—you never know where Elohim will take you, or what he will take from you," she says wistfully. The wind gusts up across the lake, disturbing the quiet surface of the water. "It is as if each person you meet is like the wind on this water. He or she pushes you along like the wind pushes the little waves toward the shore."

"And then you break," I add. She turns her golden, gray head to me and burrows deep into my eyes.

"And then you break," she says, nodding slowly, "into Elohim!"

Chapter 11

Havalah:

"Caravan coming! Samaritan coming!" shouted my youngest son, Israel.

Of course, a number of Samaritan people came through our water camp, but there was only one *Samaritan*. He was the richest, most frequent, most reliable client I had. He made this trip from the coast of the great sea to Philadelphia at least four times each year. We had a special tent for him and went through a little ritual every time he arrived. We would offer him the tent, and then he would graciously decline and have his own personal tent pitched. He even brought his own women with him, so I did not have to worry about Miramee, although the previous time he had visited, she had gone unveiled, and I saw him taking notice of her.

That could have been trouble, and we did not want to lose his custom, but in this, the desert is our partner, as there are no other water camps within four days' journey of ours.

The Samaritan was a large, generous, and joyful man, a pleasure to have in the camp. He was a good friend of my husband's and mine. That could never be the case in Jerusalem, the town of my birth, at least not publicly. The Judeans shun the Samaritans, because the Samaritans claim they are descended from two ancient tribes that remained in our homeland during the captivity of my people in Babylon. Their blood mixed with the blood of Assyrians, while our ancestors supposedly kept their bloodlines pure. The Samaritans celebrate the Festival of Passover on Mount Ar-Garazim, while we celebrate in the great Temple in Jerusalem. There are many differences, but in my view, none are big enough when weighed against all the hatred that has passed between our peoples.

Out here, it does not matter.

I remember one year at Passover, the Samaritan brought us several flawless lambs from Jerusalem so we could celebrate the feast appropriately and deliciously. A good friend.

I treasure my friends here and my family. Life depends on them. When I was young, I did not fit in very well in the great city of my birth. It is a big city, magnificent, not like the other country dung heaps they call villages. Most of my family still live there: brothers, sisters, cousins, and my father, who disowned me.

Certainly, he is dead by now.

When I was fifteen, I fell in love with a Nabataean trader visiting the city. He was dark, handsome, and maddeningly mysterious. I was only a girl, but I knew at once that I wanted to spend my life with him. He was dashing, and with every glance, every step, he carried the romance of his desert nation. He was tall, a head taller than most of the men in Jerusalem, with broad, muscular shoulders and the powerful arms of a man who worked hard for his living. His face bore the high cheekbones and the elegant, prominent nose of his people, but his eyes had a gentleness that almost belied his physical strength. I was smitten! He told me of the vast desert, of the camp that his family had owned for hundreds of years. He said it was the most beautiful place on earth.

"Is it the garden of Eden?" I asked him.

"I don't know," he replied. "I have not heard of that garden."

His religion was not the same as mine. He worshipped many gods, but he was especially devoted to the warrior god of his people, *Al-Qaum*, a god who protects caravans. And caravans were the Nabataean's lifeblood. Such talk was blasphemous for a daughter of an observant Hebrew family. He was a Gentile, but it did not matter. All I wanted was to jump on the back of his horse, ride into the desert, and find this garden.

Yet life is seldom that easy. My father had already selected a husband for me from a great family: a boy named Yosef bar-Kayafa, whom everyone called Caiaphas. My marriage to Caiaphas would enhance my parents' standing in the city, and it was a match that my family prized. I was young, but I knew I did not want to spend the rest of my days bearing children for that arrogant, pimply-faced boy.

I married my Nabataean love one night, and we hid in the house of another man of his country. My father and brothers came looking for me. They were going to stone me for disrespecting the family, in accordance with the precepts of the Law. They searched the whole city but could not find me, and we rode out while it was still night, into the freshness of the open country under a resplendent, starlit sky.

When we arrived here, I thought it the most beautiful place I had ever seen. And I never left. The caravans are regular and the trade good. The Samaritan's caravan always brought the richest treasures.

When he arrived that day, I was happy to see him. We could predict his arrival within a day, so we were always prepared with ample provisions to send him and his caravan on to their destination. What I could not have planned for was the man the Samaritan brought with him.

Slung over an ass was a dirty, lifeless body. I was confused. Why had he not buried the dead man out there?

"Havalah, you rose of the desert!" shouted the Samaritan.

"Why do you bring in a corpse to stink up my camp, old friend?" I shouted back.

"He is not dead," the Samaritan said, glancing at his charge. "At least he was breathing the last time I checked."

"Who is he? Where is he from?"

"Well, Havalah, I asked him, but I did not get much of an answer." The Samaritan's camel knelt, and the boys helped him down. "I found him unconscious by the side of the caravan road, sprawled out in the camel dung. A couple of travelers going the other way said they saw him but did not stop. They feared it was a ruse for robbers!"

No robber could stay alive out there long enough to enjoy his spoils. It was a very small community of people who wandered this stretch of the desert, and we all knew each other: every man, woman, and child.

"So you picked him up and brought him here?" I asked.

"What else was I supposed to do with him?" he said, shrugging. "You are the best physician in the desert, my sweet rose!" Then he embraced me. Israel took the camel's reins as it wavered up to standing again and the boy led it to water.

I looked at what was left of the man who was wrapped in a beaten and ragged mantle. Underneath, he wore a filthy, light-colored tunic caked with deep-red blotches of blood that had been baked dry in the heat. Surprisingly, he did not smell.

Normally, someone in his condition would stink up a circle ten paces wide, yet when I was right beside him, there was no odor. This piteous creature then took in a deep breath and exhaled.

"Well, I suppose he is alive after all," I said. "This is not going to be cheap." I lifted the hem of his mantle, let it drop, and then regarded the Samaritan sternly. "And he will probably die."

"We all die, sweet rose," he said. "That does not excuse a man from helping another in the desert. I will pay all of his expenses." I pretended to consider this carefully, stroking my chin for a moment.

"Oh, very well, then. Boys, put him in the sick tent!"

This was going to be a challenging job. Of course, I had no idea what I had just agreed to or whom I had just allowed to enter my perfect, hidden world.

Lying on his cot in the sick tent, the broken man looked dead, and I thought he soon would be.

Pity too, because he was handsome enough.

The boys had stripped him and bound him loosely in new white linen. I dropped his tunic and mantle into a large pot of boiling water to cleanse them. The caked blood flaked to the churning surface, turning the clear water to a brownish-red. I cleaned him up, dressing his wounds and scrapes. And he had plenty. He looked as if he had been in a fight, or someone had thrown him into a patch of thorns. I picked the needles out of him for over an hour.

While I cleaned and bandaged him, he made no movement at all. I gave him sips of water mixed with wine to keep his mouth moist, and without waking, he swallowed a drop or two. The water dripped out the side of his mouth and trickled down his cheek and neck. It created two pale red streaks, like tiny rivers coursing down his sun-browned skin and disappearing into his beard. I left the tent to let him rest until morning. I took his clothing out of the pot, the brownish water now cool to the touch. I put the wet clothing into a large basket I'd woven from reeds growing in the lake. None of my sons was nearby, so I walked out with the pot and emptied it upon a small date palm that had sprung up by the lake. It was browning and struggling to survive in that spot. Since it was too fragile to move, I thought the bloody water might do it good.

I told Miramee to stay in her tent and off her sore foot for the whole day. Otherwise she would have been hopping around like a wounded gazelle. It was important that the foot had time to heal. The next morning, when I came out of the sick tent after checking on the man, I was not surprised to find her walking gingerly on her right foot, so I decided she could help me. I asked her to go into the sick tent in three hours and change the man's dressings—if he was still alive. At midday I looked up from my cooking to see her slowly limping over to the sick tent, carrying in her arms a jar of ointment to dress his wounds. A gentle breeze blew the tent flap open.

That was the first time she laid her eyes upon him.

Suddenly Havalah is gone.

The oasis disappears as well, and I'm back in the stone house with Miramee—no transition. It happens in a flash.

I gasp.

No delay. The story goes on seamlessly without missing a beat—except it is in the music of Miramee's voice.

Chapter 12

Miramee:

When I first saw him, his eyes were shut firmly, and I thought he was ordinary, no one special. As I was to discover later, his eyes were bright and astonishing. When he looked at you, you could feel something shift and change inside your heart. You had to be able to see his eyes or, if you were blind, to feel them. When I limped into the tent with my jar, all I could see was a young man sleeping in his bandages, wrapped in linen dotted with irregular islands of blood.

In these first moments, I noticed that, oddly, the pain in my foot had suddenly disappeared. As I began to change the bandages on his arm, I saw that he possessed the most beautiful hands. One does not think of a man's hands as beautiful, but his fingers were elegantly long, and although he clearly was a man from the laboring class, there was a masculine perfection about them.

His hands reminded me of the potter's hands in Magdala near whose shop my mother begged. As a child, I had watched the potter's hands forming the clay on the potter's wheel. Like this wounded man's fingers, his were long, and they moved the clay masterfully, helping the jar to emerge from the formless, red-brown lump. I loved the smells of the potter's shop: the earthy clay and the burning wood of the hot oven where he fired his creations.

There were jars of all sizes. Some large ones were for the water to drink or to fill the *mikveh*, the pool for our holy bathing. There were beautiful smaller ones used for ointments, and the medium-sized jars for wine were against the farthest wall. With their lovely curves, I always pretended they were a line of well-born ladies standing. Taking pity on me one day after my mother had died, the potter fashioned a fish out of some extra clay that had fallen on the floor of his shop. He made a little slot on top to hold my mother's last coin, and then he fired it, giving it to me as a gift.

I possess very little, but there are three things that go with me everywhere, and the clay fish is one of them.

In the sick tent, a feeling came up from my heart. I took the sleeping man's left hand into my hands and felt an incredible warmth rush through me as if I had added another heart to my body. I sensed it pumping much more than blood through my veins. My head began to pound, and my face flushed. Perspiration beaded on my forehead.

With a slight hesitation—wondering if I should, if it would be proper, I brought his hand to my breast, to my heart, and let this second heart fill me up. I thought I would faint or have a seizure, but I did not. I remained awake and present. It seemed like the sick tent disappeared around me, and I was standing in a blissful nothingness, just this man and me. It was then that Havalah came in and saw me.

"Miryam!" she said with a reprimanding tone.

I gently and unhurriedly placed the beautiful hand across his abdomen as if I was replacing the rib of Adam, returning it to him with gratitude for the second heart. Even though Havalah attempted to shame me, nothing could diminish the bliss that enfolded me like gentle, warm water of the lake.

Havalah came over to the man and began to change his bandages with me. She said nothing and did not look at me for several moments. I was sorry she thought I had acted improperly, but I'd had to follow my heart. When I began again to bind his wounds, the sensation of the second beating heart returned.

"Will he live?" I asked Havalah.

"That is up to Elohim," she said, not looking up. "We do what we can do."

The young man continued his deep slumber. As I could not walk around much, Havalah told me to remain in the sick tent with him. She said that it helps the spirit of a man to return if he has company. "Aloneness can often create loneliness and cause the spirit to join with other spirits rather than return to the body," she said.

I did not believe that about this man. His spirit was here, sleeping but present. Havalah turned and gave me a stern maternal look as she left the tent. "And leave his hands where they are."

I nodded and merely sat with him. Israel brought me my needlework, and I busied myself with sewing, for I delighted in this work at those times when I had to sit. Havalah taught me many useful skills, like sewing and cooking, and over the years, I have enjoyed these quiet labors.

The man stirred slightly once, and I thought that he might awaken, but he lay motionless again without so much as a flutter of his eyelids.

As Havalah ordered, I periodically moistened his mouth with special unguents she had made. In the late afternoon of that first day, he swallowed as I held his bearded jaw with one hand and let the cloth soaked in water and wine drip into his mouth. When he swallowed, an odd thing occurred. I felt the most intense rush of energy course through me, like a calming wavelet of peace. I knew then that he was no ordinary man. I wanted to take his hand again as I had done before, but I remained obedient to Havalah. Several times, I brushed his fingers lightly with the backs of mine—and then turned sharply to see if anyone had entered to witness my sin.

He slept for six days. Each morning, Havalah thought we might discover him dead, but I believed he was going to live. He continued to sleep, though he swallowed tiny amounts of water and wine. My foot healed rapidly, so I resumed my chores, but I took whatever sewing time I had to spend in the sick tent. I mended his mantle and tunic, which were made carefully and well. Someone at home loved and cared for him. Was he married?

As he lay there, I talked to him, simply saying aloud whatever was on my mind. We passed the hours together, and I was happy to be with him, though he had yet to open an eye or speak a word. Perhaps I was losing my mind—or my heart.

On the sixth day, at noon, Havalah came in to share the midday meal with me. Our lake had some delicate-tasting fish, and Havalah was skilled at roasting them over the wood fire, basting them with salt, spices from the east, and olive oil. She served this treat with freshly baked bread.

"What did the Samaritan tell you about him?" I asked as I chewed a piece of bread.

"The Samaritan was on the road to Philadelphia, and several other traveling groups led by important-looking men passed him on their way to Galilee. Remember? Those were the people we had in the camp two days before the Samaritan arrived."

"Oh, yes," I said. "There was an officious man, a priest from the Temple, who could not keep his hands off me as I served supper."

"Yes, precisely. I was happy to see them all leave." She continued. "So the priest warned the Samaritan that there was a robber's trap ahead and that a man was lying on the road, supposedly left for dead. It was true that no man out in that part of the wilderness would be without a companion or a group, so the priest was being reasonable, I suppose. Another group told the Samaritan the same story, but he did not believe them. He knew they were excusing themselves from helping someone in need. So, when he saw the man lying there in the camel dung, he took great pity upon him. But he believed that the man was already dead—until the breeze kicked up some sand into the man's face and his hand twitched."

At that precise moment, as Havalah recounted the Samaritan's tale, our sleeping patient's left hand jerked, giving us both a start. I let out a short shriek and jumped a bit. We both laughed.

"Just like that," Havalah continued, fully enjoying her storytelling. "The Samaritan had the man lifted onto an ass and had his servants bandage the poor creature's eyes. You were injured, so you did not see him, but he was as filthy a human being as one could imagine. It took me until the midday meal to clean him and pick out the thorns from his flesh."

"The Samaritan is a good man," I said.

"Yes, he is. And rich. Which is good, because even if this wanderer dies, the Samaritan will have to pay for all his care."

Behind the brusque, business-like tone of her language, I knew that Havalah would have cared for the man even if she had received no payment.

"It is odd how we look down upon Samaritans at home," I said.

"It is worse in Jerusalem," Havalah said. "Of course, there we look down on everybody!" She laughed again.

"Yes, but out here, we are just human beings: men, women, and children," I said. "Where you are from and how you speak to Elohim does not matter."

"In a way, it is like Eden," she replied.

"I often feel that way," I said. We both paused a moment, and I imagined this as the great garden created out of love by Elohim.

"Havalah!" We heard the Nabataean calling for his wife. Havalah wiped her fingers on her apron, hurried out of the tent, and, looking back at me, raised her hand in an "until later" wave. I wondered if I would ever have a husband to call my name. With my falling sickness, I doubted that anyone would want to marry me.

A breeze moved into the tent, pushing upon the sides and roof, making it breathe. It moved sadness into me as well. I wondered what Elohim wanted from me.

I returned to my duties and wiped the forehead of the sleeping man who had sent fire from his hands. He was as alone as I.

While I concentrated my efforts to clean his face, I barely noticed him swallowing hard.

"What is your story, young vagabond?" I asked him aloud.

During the six days he had slept, the man's wounds and bruises had vanished. I remember that on the third day, I cleaned and dressed a deep, oozing gash on his right forearm in the morning. When I returned to change it at midday, I noticed that it had stopped leaking. I feared it had begun to swell again, so I carefully removed the bandage to inspect it.

I gasped.

No swelling. Indeed, there was no wound at all—only healthy, smooth skin!

I thought I should call Havalah to share this wonder, but a small whisper guided me to hold this within my heart, for I was coming to understand that some things must remain inside the precincts of my inner Temple.

His wounds disappeared, one by one, and after witnessing this for three more days, such miracles became the norm for me. I somehow accepted wonders I could not explain as the sacred and mysterious movements of life. By the sixth day, I could see nothing other than the faint scar arcing down his right cheek. It was the only remaining mark on his body.

"Such a shame," I said. "Your wounds have healed, but you cannot awaken. Is your voice deep and rich, or is it high-pitched and nasal? Perhaps you have no ability to speak at all! Who would know?"

I rinsed out the cloth in a bowl of water and began to put the unguent on his lips again. They were now back to normal, and I noticed that he had full lips for a man, rather sensuous beneath his bearded countenance. As I put the ointment on them with my two fingers, his lips quivered ever so slightly. Startled, my fingers recoiled, folding into my palm. I stood there, looking at him expectantly. Was he about to awaken?

His eyelids remained firmly shut.

"I feel you being more alive now," I said to him, resuming my comfortable conversation with a sleeping man. "That is good. Maybe you will wake up after all."

Lifting his left arm, which rested just below his chest, I began to wash it, cleaning down to his fingers. I decided to put the special unguent made of olive oil upon the skin, because it felt dry. With my oily hands, I caressed his fingers and noticed that the webbing at the base between was scaling and chapped. So I carefully ensured that the healing balm covered each small valley.

Suddenly his long fingers closed around mine. With a start, I looked up to his face and saw his eyes open, looking blearily back at me! I shrieked and jerked backward, knocking over a jar of Havalah's oil and spilling its clear, green contents into a pool on the ground.

He closed his eyes again, and I went speechless, dropping my hands to my sides. It was like seeing a dead man live again. When I had collected myself, I asked, "Sir, are you awake?"

No response.

"Sir?"

His eyelids fluttered open again, and a groan came from his lips. He could speak after all, and his voice was deep and rich. His eyes focused and became instantly bright, fully awake, as if someone had lit a torch behind them. They were very light brown, almost golden: two small suns. He regarded me carefully for a moment and then slowly turned his head to look around the tent. Casting his eyes downward at the spilled oil on the ground, he was taking it all in, trying to make sense of his surroundings.

"I am sorry your oil was wasted," he muttered.

Each word rolled around in the air and lingered in the opening of my ears as if they were deep notes from a horn played softly.

"The oil was for you, sir," I said. "It was your oil."

"It anoints the earth now," he replied more clearly.

"Yes, so it does." I smiled. "As if the earth needed anointing." He did not answer but coughed the dryness from his throat. I quickly retrieved a cup of wine mixed with water and offered it to him.

He took the cup and drank, looking at me intently as if agreeing with me. I felt somewhat invaded by his eyes.

"My name is Miryam," I said.

He smiled. "I know."

How could he know? He had been asleep. *Adonai!* Had he heard all the nonsense I'd chatted up while he'd appeared to be unconscious?

My faced burned into an embarrassed bright red. He stretched his open palm, still glistening with oil, and held it out to me. I quickly scanned the entrance to the tent and then took his fingers into my oily hands. The warmth shot through me again, but I was not alarmed. It felt as natural a thing to do as breathing while standing in the rain.

For more than an hour, I held his hand as he dozed and woke—until finally this nameless man fell into a deeper sleep. I no longer cared if anyone entered the tent. Nor did it matter if a thousand people were watching me watching him. The world itself seemed to vanish in his sleeping presence. He was beautiful to look at as he lay there with the most peaceful expression on his face. His breathing was light but constant. I realized that I had spent more time with this man while he was asleep than I had while he was awake—and both experiences of him, waking and sleeping, were deep and wrapped in warm mystery.

His few words echoed within me: *it anoints the earth now.*

I wondered what he'd meant and how he knew my name. He was right. If we need anointing, the earth must need anointing too, because we are the earth. I feel sometimes as if all I am is a piece of the earth that is privileged—or cursed—to walk and talk.

What had he stirred up in me?

His brow furrowed suddenly into a scowl, and with eyes still firmly shut, he groaned softly. I squeezed his hand tightly to let him know I was still there, and his expression relaxed into peace again.

I wondered what dreams disturbed the sleep of this strange and beautiful man?

I was unaware how long I'd sat there, but the light began to dim as the sun journeyed beyond our western ridge. I felt content to stay beside him—for the rest of my life if he needed me to.

Was he my Adam? Had he come for me at last?

I heard Havalah calling me to help with the supper. I gently returned his hand to rest across his abdomen and remained beside him. I sat a bit longer, not wanting to break the spell, letting this settle within me before I returned to the ordinary: to the jostling of pots and bowls, to the jumping aside when yet another winking, traveling man decided to pinch my bottom.

Leaving the tent, I told him I would return later with some food. I would say nothing about his awakening yet. For this moment, I would hold all this within my heart.

For this small measure of time, his golden eyes and the deep music of his voice belonged only to me.

Chapter 13

AD 43, and the third year of the reign of the emperor Claudius, Ephesus

Falling asleep. Exhausted from my journey here and to the other places, I need to rest, but I also seem to push myself more when I feel spent. It's like an unconscious wrestling match with my body to see who's boss.

"Before we finish, what did you mean by *inner Temple*?" I ask, forcing my bleary eyes to stay open. "Temples are buildings."

"The Temple is a place on earth, built on sacred ground that the prophets and priests have anointed," Miramee says. "It is a place to remember our love for the Father."

"Yes, but what is the *inner* Temple?" I ask, my insurance-agent persistence emerging.

"Yeshua taught me that each of us has within us a holy and silent place, a Temple," she says quietly. "We all contain this inner Temple, so any place we stand on earth can become sacred ground. It can become anointed with our oil when we remember the love that is Elohim." She smiles and stands and then moves slowly to her chamber for the night.

As she leaves, I say, "The way you say 'heart'—it sounds different from the organ that pumps our blood."

"*Heart* or *lebak* means more than the organ that pumps blood. *Heart* is what pumps life through you, and then it delivers your essence from you to the world. It is the love of Elohim coming from your Temple. It can also be …"

Why does she hesitate?

"It can be something that the Tempter uses to deliver darker things into the world." She finishes with a thoughtful glance and then disappears into her chamber.

I pull myself onto a mat by the fire. In only a minute or two, I sink into the benevolent oblivion of sleep.

I wake to the sounds of chirping. Close by.

Squinting in the morning sun that streaks in the window, I see a small brown bird hopping a few feet away. I watch it peck around on the floor for any overlooked remnant. It doesn't care about mashiachs, kings, desert oases, or the garden of Eden. It's got no story to live by except that which leads to the next bite of food.

That's a very short and simple story.

It stops to check me out, its small head jerking this way and that in an apparent effort to make bird sense of me. Suddenly its legs bend, and it flutters up to the windowsill to streak out to a nearby pine branch. I turn my head toward the entry of the house, and Miramee stands there with a jar of water. She nods and proceeds to go about making the morning meal. Soon she does her customary careful walk and hands me a bowl of steaming grain cereal flavored with pine nuts and honey. She sits near me and eats as well. Suddenly she stops and looks at me.

"Does your wife make you meals?" she asks.

The fateful question.

"Sometimes I do, or our housekeeper does," I say as I chew.

"You have servants?"

"Well, not servants exactly." I clear my throat. "Well, yes, you would call them servants."

"Are you a rich man when you are home?"

"Ah, yes, I suppose, relatively, I guess."

She tilts her head in the same puzzled way as the bird visitor.

"Yes, I am a rich man when I am home."

She nods. She's right, of course. What material wealth I will amass lies twenty centuries in the future. Here, I am a pauper, like that homeless kid in the park—as dependent as a baby in a crib.

And it feels fine. Not only fine but good.

What's being revealed to me puts wealth into its *right* order of importance and gives it a mystical context. I'm learning that wealth is truly the resources flowing toward me from God—and only that. What work I do in the world may seem to generate wealth, but that's really only incidental to it. Nurturance, what sustains us, which is all that wealth is, comes entirely from God. And in time, it moves out from me to others, ultimately returning to God, like electrons moving back and forth through a wire to charge and discharge a battery.

"So, who are you, Traveler? The rich man or the beggar? Who?" She wears a wry smile.

Grinning, I eat my cereal without answering. I'm not trying to be cute or flirtatious. I really can't answer that question right now. Besides, I don't know if she really wants an answer from me. Maybe it's simply a question that's supposed to sort of float around between my ears until it's answered, or until it no longer needs to be there.

I munch more of the cereal. The grains taste different, nuttier than the grains I'm used to. I think of how simply the farmers must harvest these few fields in comparison to the mechanical and gigantic agribusiness that my insurance agency serves. Most people in my community buy their cereal in boxes, with no thought of where it came from, who tended it, or how the rivers and sky watered it. I taste more than the grain now. I taste everything that went into the grain as well.

Her face brightens. She is ready to continue. As she sets her bowl down, I imagine the floor changing from stone to earth, and as I listen, my mind's eye returns to the sick tent.

Chapter 14

Miramee:

That first day, Havalah and I returned with the man's meal, and we marveled together at his recovery. She recommended that I stay with him throughout the afternoon to ensure that he did not lapse back into unconsciousness, but I felt as if she was granting me some hours with him.

By evening, he managed to take a few steps but was unbalanced, requiring my arm and shoulder to lean upon. I was happy to help, and his closeness sent a peaceful, warm sensation throughout my body. He seemed to enjoy it so much that I wondered if he really needed my help after those first steps. Perhaps it was partially a boyish deception of his so he could walk with his arm in mine. He tripped up once as we reentered the tent, and I spoke to him after keeping him from falling. I realized that I did not yet know his name.

"Who are you, sir?" I asked him as he plopped down onto his safe cot.

He sat at its edge and wiped his mouth absently. I had the feeling that he was wrestling with that question himself, judging whether this was the proper time to render an answer. He looked up at me, holding my gaze solemnly, and I returned the stare boldly, transfixed by the suns of his eyes.

Remaining silent but smiling, he simply sat on the cot. I felt confused and hoped I had not insulted him. Then I suddenly knew to ask the question another way.

"By what name are you called?"

In that unforgettable voice, the name he uttered seemed to contain all the sounds of the world within it, as if the very air released from his mouth flew like a flock of white seabirds carrying the joy of our people. I felt my own breath escape me, leaving me empty, when I heard him say,

"Yeshua!"

Chapter 15

AD 43, and the third year of the reign of the emperor Claudius, Ephesus

The story stops. I look up from the floor and see that Miramee is staring into the fire, continually but gently kneading the blanket.

I wait. Clearly, she is off somewhere in her thoughts, nowhere close to this stone house. She snaps her head toward the door. A moment later, a simply dressed man appears in the open doorway, bows a greeting, and humbly waits there. He's holding a little girl who coughs roughly. Under his other arm, the man carries a bundle covered in cloth. Miramee rises slowly and walks over to greet him.

In their whispered exchange, I hear him tell Miramee of his daughter's illness and then ask for her blessing. I can't help but turn and stare, wanting to see a miraculous healing. I scold myself for this magic-show mentality and watch reverently as the woman lays her hand on the child's red hair. The girl's saucer-sized brown eyes show her uncertainty with all of this, but soon the blessing is complete. I hear no celestial voices singing, just the fire crackling and the birds chirping in the pine branches outside. The man uncovers a large block of white cheese punctured with holes the size of a bird's eye. He gratefully hands it to Miramee, and she accepts it with a gracious smile. As he leaves, she sets the wheel of cheese on a table.

"From the time he first spoke his name in that very rich rumble of his voice, Yeshua amazed me," she says.

"Do people come here often for healings?" I ask.

"You are distracted once more, Traveler," she says matter-of-factly, again without correction or judgment.

"I am sorry," I say. "Yes, I was, but I'm ready now."

"No need for sorrow," she says. "That is also a distraction. Your eyes are opening. You will close them from time to time, which is the distraction of your meandering thoughts. I simply remind you to open your eyes again. That is all.

"I have lived in amazement from the moment that name was first uttered. Yeshua, my Rabbuni, opened my eyes in that moment, in that tent for the sick."

Chapter 16

Miramee:

For four full days, he talked to me as if he could not stop until he had told me everything.

He began to speak about his boyhood, what it was like to be a *different one* in Nasrath. Around the town, there were rumors buzzing about his legitimacy. The respectable people always looked down upon him, and no girl would have him for a husband because of his questionable birth. Yet he could speak in synagogue, because his father had declared openly that Yeshua was the son of his blood, not a bastard born outside of marriage, and therefore of the lowest status. All declarations aside, Yeshua was a legitimate Hebrew according to the Law, but he was illegitimate by rumor and by the whispers of small-town people. He was both a rightful son and a bastard at the same time.

The more he talked, the more I realized that we had both drunk from that same difficult cup of life. Our stories varied slightly, but they were the same in many ways. The next day, Havalah told me to go keep the man company again. I asked her about my chores.

"Don't worry about those," she said. "I will have the boys take care of them. Just tend to your patient."

I wondered if Havalah was trying to match me with Yeshua. I was very happy to sit with him and listen to him talk, even though he did not want to stop. It was as if he had to unburden himself. For some reason, he took me into his trust and told me everything. I only interrupted him with a question for clarification from time to time, but mostly I sat mesmerized by his elegant, poetic speech.

One morning, Yeshua asked me to accompany him on a walk. He was improving, and I thought he was ready to go outside again. He took my arm for support as we emerged from the tent and squinted in the bright daylight. He seemed happy to be in the open air.

"It is quite lovely by the lake," I said, and we set off slowly, arm in arm.

The path to the lake was narrow and uneven, so, even with his holding on to me, he took great care to keep his balance. His legs had regained some strength but remained a bit wobbly. When he saw the lake for the first time, he sighed. It was a sparkling blue piece of heaven on earth. Startlingly framed by the dry, rocky hills surrounding us, they always reminded me how fragile was this little spot of safety in the middle of a parched and unforgiving wilderness.

Some reeds grew at the edge of the lake, and he brushed them lightly as if he was greeting the plants themselves. We both stood for a long time, looking at the mirror-perfect water. A bird dived suddenly, breaking the surface, and emerged with its catch. The ripples formed wavelet circles that intersected one another with dispassionate order and sequence. We stood like the father Adam and the mother Eve in this tiny portion of creation, clothed yet somehow naked, childlike in wonderful and awe-filled witness.

"There should be a bench here," Yeshua said finally, pointing to a spot by a single small but thriving date palm. I recalled him telling me that he had been a carpenter.

"Are you serious?" I asked him. Seeing that he was, I said, "Well, a caravan master who could not pay all that he owed us left several cedar planks from Lebanon. They are stacked behind the sick tent."

"Then I will make a bench for you," he said with a radiant smile that lit up his face.

Oh, my! I thought. It suddenly got hotter, and I clenched my teeth to return his smile. *Do not fall in love with him, Miryam!*

But this warning had come too late. Through his hands while he was sleeping that first day, my heart had felt the echoing beat of another, his own heavenly heart. If this most intimate and private part of me had changed so quickly and completely, how could anything else ever remain the same again?

"That would be lovely," I said. "Thank you." I cleared my throat, and we returned our eyes to the surface of the water.

PART II

IN THE DESERT

Chapter 17

AD 43, and the third year of the reign of the emperor Claudius, Ephesus

Miramee sits quietly, remembering. I'm anxious to hear more of her days in the desert before the Samaritan rescued Yeshua, but I don't want to intrude on the moment she's having.

I'd never before thought of Yeshua flirting with a pretty girl. Yet I suppose he was like the rest of us in that way. Why wouldn't he be? Beside all that he ultimately became to the world, Yeshua started out as a man, a man who had friends. And like anyone else, he probably had favorites.

For an instant, I muse about living at that time and perhaps even being one of his buddies. What would it be like to have Yeshua, the Son of God, as a buddy?

I glance back to the face of the woman who truly was his friend. She deals me that "you're distracted" card again, but it's not true this time. I'm learning.

Yeshua was a friend to people, a buddy, a real guy. That discovery is a Traveler-generated lesson. But I need to know how he ended up thrown like a saddlebag over the back of a donkey and hoofed into Havalah's "Eden" oasis.

How did he go walking into a dust storm at the River Jordan and land in an Arabian version of Palm Springs? Time to find out.

"Miramee, how did Yeshua become unconscious, almost dying on the caravan road?"

"Everything about Yeshua's journey through the desert was a mystery set into motion by Elohim," she says.

"May I ask when is it proper to use *Elohim* and *Adonai*?" These names throw me every time someone uses them both.

"When we talk about the name of the Father, we use Elohim," she explains. "When we talk to the Father, we address Him as Adonai. Yeshua called him a very intimate name, *Abba*. It's what a small child would call a beloved father."

"Like *Eema* for mother," I say.

She pauses when I say *Eema*. A long silence follows.

"Why, yes, like Eema for mother."

Miramee glances around the house quickly. She takes a moment. When she becomes aware of me again, she shakes her head.

"Where was I?"

"The Immerser said that after his immersion, Yeshua went into the wilderness alone," I answer.

She nods confidently. "Such a time he had," she begins.

Chapter 18

Miramee:

When Yeshua left the Immerser and his family at the river, the wind was howling about his ears.

The storm from the west pushed upon him with such wrath, pummeled him with so great a force that he felt as if seven thousand demons had picked him up and were casting him eastward into the desert.

But they were not demons. In truth, legions of *angels* were sending him forth!

Before him, the path was barely visible except for some scattered, dry remains of camel dung. Here and there lay the discards of humans, blown in from the vast expanse surrounding him: shards of broken pottery, a torn white head covering, and the rotted remnants of food, which were now unrecognizable. Soon, even these fetid signposts faded into sandy oblivion.

Yeshua kept the mantle tight over his nose and mouth, thinking of how, over the ages, these storms had buried many men's bones, without prayer or reverence. The dust still seeped through, making his breathing difficult. Behind him, the wind continued to raise the sleeping floor of the desert like a giant wave of the sea, sending thousands of sand daggers into his back.

Suddenly, within three heartbeats, the wind died down. The day's bright light returned with the same blinding blue sky arching over his head once more. Yeshua turned to look back, and seeing only desert, he remembered leaving the river without a word to Eema or Tzadik.

He walked until the sun had completed its journey to the west. He was very far now from the river or any place that was familiar to him. As he walked, the hues of the horizon shaded into deeper reds and golds, and an inner conversation began. A kind of wisdom declared itself. There were no words, just sensations throughout his body, settling into the center of his being. With each step, he graced this new wisdom with surrender, permitting it to find its home in him.

Through his heart, the new wisdom unveiled a vision of the life he was to lead. He saw the beginnings of his journey stretching out before him in pictures, like the paintings of the Ephesians. It was clear now: he would be a teacher and healer, but a wanderer as well. Like the bird diving into the lake for food, he would have no permanent home, and he doubted sadly that he would have a wife, children, or any familial hearth as his sanctuary from the hostile world. In these moments of revelation, Yeshua resolved that if this were to be his life, then he would face it with the knowledge that the Ruach Kudsha, the Spirit of Elohim, would give him the fortitude he needed.

With darkness near, Yeshua looked up and saw a small outcropping of boulders. There was a cavern large enough to make a serviceable camp. He set a fire and drank more from the water-skin given to him by Eema. Yeshua thought of it as his faithful companion, helping him feel less alone, reminding him of her loving care. Weary from the day that had begun with the Immerser, his disciples, and Eema—and now ended with solitude in the wilderness—he slept hard and long until the next morning, awakening when the sun climbed high enough to shine directly into his eyes.

He drank a sip from the water skin and rolled the water around in his mouth before swallowing it. He wanted to take a handful of water and wash his face and eyes, but he dared not. He had very little of the precious fluid remaining, and like all desert travelers, he knew to save some drops until he could see the source of the next. It would be a day in which he only moved forward and looked for water.

The sun was already bright and hot, impeding his steps, so Yeshua sought some shade under another of the endless outcroppings of rock. Squatting on his haunches beneath the protective hand of stone, he took another tiny sip. The wind whispered through the spaces in the rock, as soft as the breath of a small child. Then all became still and starkly motionless.

So quiet, he thought. *I can hear the rocks crack from the heat.*

His mind wandered as he surveyed the barren landscape. The only movements were mirages, the hopeful reflections of undulating lakes that seemed to recede with every step forward. As he rested under the rock, he began to see more than the mirages. The sunlight dimmed, no longer bleaching the scene a blinding white. The shapes of the rocks themselves took on a radiance all their own, separate from the reflected light of the sun. He heard a resonance: a low, vibrating hum.

He thought the sound could not be coming from insects, for there were none visible in that parched patch of earth. There was something else about the way he was seeing and hearing, something different and new, a way of perceiving that he had not before encountered in this lifetime of many strange experiences.

Yeshua also had a sense about things for which he had no explanation. He felt the goodness in each particle of dust, each stone. Shaking his head as if to rid himself of these bizarre thoughts, he wondered if he was truly losing his mind.

How can rocks be good?

He resumed his walk. In a loud voice, he sang psalms as his steps began to slow. He soon realized that singing made him thirsty, and from that point, he only prayed in silence. He walked and searched, but there was no water in sight. There was only one long stretch of sandy dirt framed by the mountains in the distance. Only a gulp or two remained in his water skin, and there was no food or living thing in sight. His empty stomach ached, and he felt nauseated. His mouth was as parched as the desert floor that lay beneath his stumbling feet. Determined, he kept walking, unwilling to empty his water skin of the final drops.

"If I am to die out here, then it is Elohim's will," he said to the barren earth.

He slumped to his knees, feeling them burn in the sand beneath his robes. He closed his eyes as he knelt and breathed in the fiery, hot air. When he opened his eyes, he saw beings of light all around him. They were not human, although they were shaped like humans, and their images remained motionless, like sculptures in a garden he had seen in Tzippori, the Greek-styled town near Nasrath. Each of the light figures was a different hue, and some were brighter than others.

Am I awake, or am I dead?

The pain in his knees told him he was still alive. Shaking his head again, thinking he was losing his mind, he closed his eyes. When he reopened them, the beings were no longer visible, but he still felt their presence.

With great effort, he pulled himself up and stood again. His mother, Eema, had always said, "The angel protects."

"What angel is out here with me?" he asked the sky.

As he began to walk again, he thought about how much he needed Eema's bottomless faith. Yeshua felt strange, aware of how he ached from the lack of nourishment and from being unsheltered from the sun's intense heat, aware of how he thirsted from the lack of water. But he also felt empty in a way that he had never felt before. He was drained not only of water and food but of all that had filled him up, of all that he had thought he possessed before stepping from the river's edge into the desert.

"Adonai, what will you do with this empty vessel? What do you want with me?" Yeshua asked the blue nothingness above his head.

There was no answer. None of the signs he promptly received in the past when he posed such questions came to him. There was just his walking and stumbling, his parched mouth and empty stomach.

He fondly remembered his beloved father carrying him on his broad shoulders, raising him and his brothers to be just and observant men. He remembered the day Yosef had collapsed at his woodworking in the stall outside their home. This was one of only two times Eema had asked Yeshua to *do something* miraculous.

"Save him!" she demanded as Yeshua and Tzadik carried Yosef into the house, laying him on his cot.

Yeshua had been obedient and had laid his hands on his father's chest as his brother cradled his head. But he'd sensed his father's spirit moving away from the body, unwilling to return. Yosef's soul and Yeshua both knew it was finished.

"Yosef, Husband, do not leave. Please!" Eema had cried, weeping in agony. Yeshua had felt her faith waver in that single instant. But it had only been for a moment, and within the hour, she'd joined the family in washing and anointing her husband's body for burial.

Yeshua then laid himself down in the dirt and sand, the serene and loving expression on her face in his mind's eye. He wanted to weep because of the remembered grief welling up inside his heart, but he could waste no water.

Yeshua picked himself up and dusted off. He scanned his surroundings and spied another pile of boulders, this one forming a natural low arch through which he could see the bleak sands of the landscape ahead. Because of the sun's position, it now provided much-needed shade. He sat down in the shadow, for the rock arch was so low that he could not stand underneath it. As he sat there and rested, his mind started to reckon how many leagues and how many days he had traveled from the river. In his fatigue, these weak attempts at calculation began to divert his attention, so he straightened his back as he dismissed them gently. He wanted no distractions. He knew he was not there to die. He was there to learn what Elohim wanted of him.

He was there to hear Elohim call his name.

Human conventions, such as counting the number of leagues or days, served only to keep him from hearing and to turn his eyes from seeing. He was becoming the empty cup, the human chalice made from the earth. Elohim could fill this cup now with the Ruach Kudsha.

Lowering his eyes, he reverenced his emptiness and sat under the stone arch, feeling no inclination to save the life in his body. He knew somehow that angels defended and cared for it in the most intimate way. Suddenly, he felt a thick, wet coldness rub the back of his bare arm. He sprang up, hitting his head so hard on the low rock arch that he knocked himself unconscious for a moment. When his eyes snapped open, his face felt slimy wet with the hot, moist breath and sloppy tongue of a dog licking his cheeks and forehead. Yeshua sat up, his head pounding, and placed a hand on the sizable lump swelling on top of his head.

"Aderes!" he said, managing a weak smile.

The stub of a brown tail wagged, and then a respectable canine sneeze completed the noble greeting.

"What are you doing out here, my friend? I was to come out here alone."

Yeshua reached out with the hand not covering his lump and gave the dog a tussle and pat. Aderes sat on her haunches, regarding him carefully, her still-wagging tail kicking up some dust. The response was clear: she was staying. He looked at the dog and noticed the light again.

Effortlessly, he could see the light everywhere, in all things—even the dog. The light surrounding her was a glowing white and green. He could see the love within her canine heart.

As he shared the last sips of water with her, Yeshua wondered just how hard he had hit his head.

"Well, no spring is going to bubble up here, Aderes," he said to the panting dog, "so we had better look someplace else."

Head still pounding, Yeshua began to walk. Aderes bounded out in front.

"Do you smell the water that I cannot?"

Voicing her answer, Aderes looked back at him and barked. As he followed her, Yeshua understood why she was there and why he must follow her rather than head in the direction his mind told him was correct. Elohim was leading him, like a father, to the place where he needed to be. It was an act of faith, and in an instant he understood the deep trust in Elohim that Eema possessed, for she had instilled it in him as well as his brothers and sisters. Her faith was absolute, and it had made her fearless—gentle yet fearless.

Aderes's gait remained steady. She did not stop to sniff the ground but trotted along with an assured and expectant air. She would stop when the distance was too great between them, give a canine glance back and wait, and then resume. They passed the hours of the long afternoon in this way, until slowly Yeshua's thoughts began to blur. His thirst had long ago overpowered the hunger pains cramping his stomach. When he stumbled over a stone and fell into the dirt, he could only lie there, panting, his eyes closed.

"Water, Adonai," he whispered, inhaling the clear, dry air mixed with dust.

His head was afire as he slipped in and out of consciousness. Fortunately, the flaps of his head covering had fallen over his face, shielding his eyes and skin from the searing rays of the sun. An unlikely sound finally stirred him, but when he opened his eyes, he still saw only the glaring, hot landscape. He closed his eyes once more, thinking he must have dreamt it, but then he heard it again.

Impossible. The sound …

Yeshua questioned himself. *Was that a tiny splash? Like an animal lapping up water?*

His thirst welled up in his dry throat, and he coughed and wretched into the dust. He lifted his eyes from the ground, weakly turning it in the direction of the sound, and saw Aderes, head down, only ten paces from him.

She looked as if she was drinking!

With that, Yeshua slowly wobbled to his feet, and when he stood, he beheld a beautiful sight. As he moved closer, he realized that this was no mirage but a small pond filled with clear water, apparently fed by a source he could not see. Joyfully uttering a prayer of thanks, he leaned into the pond and drank until he felt his head begin to clear. He filled his waterskin and then removed his sandals and mantle and eased himself into the water. The dog sat watching him bathe.

"Thank you, Adonai, my Father in heaven, for leading me here, and thank you, my Nasrene mother on earth," Yeshua said. "And you, my friend, Aderes—thank you. Now, let us celebrate!"

The dog leaped into the water with a resounding splash. They dove and swam, jumping about, and for a moment, Yeshua felt the exuberance he had as a young boy swimming with his brothers in the pond near Nasrath. As Yeshua moved back to dry land, Aderes bounded past him, shaking mightily and joyfully spraying him with a shower. The dog then went sniffing about the thick shrubbery bordering the pond.

Once revived, Yeshua could clearly see that this was a good place to make his encampment. He found some edible grasses near the pond and then turned to see the fronds of a lone date palm tree rising above some tall shrubs that were so thick, the trunk of the tree was not visible. Probably seeded by an overlooked date dropped by a wanderer visiting the oasis, the tree had grown undisturbed for many years. Giving rise to no children, the large palm yielded its dates year after year in the great silence of the desert.

"Thank you, tree of life," Yeshua said, and he began to eat its fallen fruit.

Later, after he had eaten, he gathered some dead fronds and other kindling to ignite a fire using the oldest method of two sticks and friction. He also used the fronds to construct a makeshift shelter. Aderes returned to the camp with a desert rat and sat apart, relishing her prey.

This would be a good place to stay for some days, Yeshua thought wearily.

He did not lie under the shelter he had constructed but let the stars form a canopy over his head. The desert had turned cold after the fiery furnace of that day. He covered his head with his mantle, enjoying the warmth of the fire. Aderes settled in next to him just as she did with the Immerser. Yeshua was grateful for her company and the additional warmth of her body. He was tired, and soon the sounds of the night led him into a welcome sleep.

In his dream that night, Yeshua waded through deep water and moved slowly, each leg straining to take the next step. All at once, he was on a mountaintop, reaching up into the thin air, trying to touch the firmament, yet with each upward thrust of his arm, his legs became mired even more in the white, skull-like stone beneath them. He grew more anxious as he sank deeper and became more a part of the stone. Finally, his fear and frustration overcame him. Yeshua awoke, bathed in a thick, sleeping sweat.

The dawn was breaking, and Yeshua sat up, tossing off the covering of his mantle. Aderes jerked to attention. The dream of the mountain came back to him along with a message.

Go to a high place and see!

The command was clear, urgent, and direct. He knew he must obey. The camp was comfortable, but he knew that Elohim had sent him into the wilderness for a purpose, and he knew he could not fulfill this purpose by resting comfortably there. His duty was to prepare. He did not know for what, but in his newly discovered emptiness, he was ready to move into his destiny.

Yeshua looked around. There were no true high places visible to the north or south, but there were mountains to the northeast. With his waterskin full and the pockets inside his mantle filled with dates and grasses, Yeshua set out, Aderes contentedly trotting by his side. On the first day, he crossed a valley of sand and rock. They found a ravine with a pool of water no bigger than a well and made camp for the night.

Yeshua slept uneasily. His body ached, and his stomach was queasy from the light sustenance he had eaten. During the day, he had not seen even a locust or fly. In the middle of the night, his eyes snapped open. The moon was full and high in the sky, a beautiful, silver light. Its beams cast Aderes in blue hues as she lay beside him.

Walk now. Do not wait until morning!

A voice spoke to him as a deep, wordless inner direction: silent, urgent, stirring. He sat up. He would obey. He rose and quickly filled his waterskin. Aderes read his urgency and began prancing with anticipation. They set off for the mountains in the moonlight. It was warm that night, but he began to shiver, feeling a sudden chill pass through him.

Was it a portent?

Moonbeams lit their path, folding imperceptibly into dawn as morning grew closer.

The sun rose like a psalm: slowly, beautifully, like a single voice singing. It emerged from the ridge of the now-closer mountain. Yeshua's pace quickened, even though his legs were sore and his body weak from lack of adequate food and sleep. Arriving at the base of the mountain by midday, he saw their passage to the summit blocked by a pile of boulders. They would have to climb over them.

Aderes took the task's measure and found a way up and around them, and then she was quickly climbing the craggy path as Yeshua followed her more slowly. Ahead, he heard the dog bark ferociously. Feeling dread tighten his stomach, Yeshua called out to Aderes. He heard her scream in pain several times.

When he finally found her, he saw Aderes lying on her side, struggling to breathe, her tongue lolling to the side. She had come upon a den of cobras. One loomed over the fallen dog in a menacing strike position. It lashed again at Aderes's left shoulder, which was already bleeding from three bite wounds. The dog's breathing slowed and stopped.

Yeshua cautiously reached for Aderes' hind legs and pulled her away from the four cobras that now defensively swayed side to side like leafless tree trunks in the wind. When he was far enough away from their dangerous reach, he lifted the large animal and carried her down the path. It was not easy. She was heavy, and Yeshua was feeling the weakness from too little food and rest.

Deep sadness overtook him, for this reminded him of the day his father had died. After Eema and his sisters had washed and dressed Yosef, he and his brothers had carried the body from the house for burial. Now, the ceremony was lacking, but the grief weighed like a sack of stones on his heart.

Descending to the foot of the hill they had been climbing, Yeshua placed Aderes's body in a small, natural pit and sat with her, a hand on her exposed flank. He knew he could call her spirit back—it was one of his gifts—but she would have to carry the desire to return, and he did not sense that, so, sadly, reviving her was impossible. Her body remained lifeless and still.

Amen.

He covered her body partially with stones.

Soon she will be food, he thought.

All dead things became life-giving food for other created things. Only fire prevented that.

He would miss Aderes's company. Yeshua stood and began his climb back up the mountain. An hour later, when he paused to rest and sip some water, he could see where he had left his friend. A lioness was dragging the carcass out from under the rocks. An imposing male lion with a large chunk of his mane missing entered the scene regally. Two smaller cubs followed him tentatively. Soon other animals would finish what they left behind. With a heart still heavy, he turned and resumed his climb. Her death would bring more life.

By midafternoon, Yeshua had reached the windy peak of the mountain. He stood and took in the full panorama, and the vastness of the varied desert landscapes spread before him. He knew the wilderness for what it was, both the womb of life and its destroyer. There he could find the greatest silence of earthly peace and the wildest sounds of its fury. He knelt with the wind whipping his mantle like a battle standard of his namesake, Yeshua, the great warrior of Father Moshe.

Elohim is here. I Am is here.

Yeshua breathed in the mountain air and felt the wind. He closed his eyes and let himself feel his exhaustion and hunger, his sadness about Aderes and his father, and his thoughts about his mother, brothers, and sisters. Mental images of food and drink assaulted him for a moment, and then he remembered the Jordan's current washing over him. He wondered where he would make his bed and whether rain would drench him tonight while he slept. All these busy forms of thought flew through his mind like bees in a field of flowers. They lit and then went on their way.

He brought his attention to rest and cleared his mind for prayer. As a youth, he had wrestled with his thoughts, trying to force them into silence so he could enter into the "inner Temple," that vastness of love, the eternal remembrance of Elohim. Now he waited and watched, and as evening fell, his prayer became prayer. He was no longer trying to pray a prayer or sing a psalm. It was wordless, thoughtless, and timeless. In the silence, focused and fully aware, it became simple joy and a peace that exceeded what a mind can know as peace.

I am peace. I AM *peace.*

Yeshua knew that he sat once again on sacred ground, and he remained in that state for half the night. His awareness was knife-edge sharp. He could be both immersed in prayer and aware of the fly landing on the boulder behind him, feeling the air move from its fluttering wings. He saw the formless rain clouds edging onto the horizon, and he sensed the eyes of thousands of small creatures watching him from their hiding places. With lightning-like intensity, he felt power—the naked power surrounding him.

He felt no cares about his future. He did not wonder about what was next or what his discomforts might be. There was no *my* head, *my* comfort, or even *my* life. There was no *me* left in him. There was only the trust in Elohim.

The prayer time seemed to end, but there was no end. The revelation came to him that there was another mountain to climb. This was not where he was to stay. He would need to move again to another place, another summit. Even though he had expended great effort to scale this peak—though Aderes had given her life for him to climb this mountain—he accepted that there was another. He simply stood and began to walk the slippery, gravel path down the mountain.

Yeshua felt the living perfection of every bush and rock. Each step was complete in itself, not dependent on the step before or the next one that followed.

As he walked down the mountainside in the dark, he stumbled on an exposed root and fell hard onto his right forearm. He felt the searing pain as the bone snapped. He gasped but moved into the pain and detached himself from it as if there was no *self* part of him at all. Yeshua felt like a witness to the incident; he sensed the pain, but it did not possess him. This amazed him. He reached down, and with one great *snap*, the bone moved back into place. The pain was now beyond searing; it was hot, like the red tongs of a metal smith. He kept his free hand in place upon the break and prayed. Instantly the wound tingled, and the palm of his hand heated up like a desert rock and then immediately cooled. When he opened his eyes, he saw that the bone was straight again, and all the flesh was healed. He felt the heat recede from the wounded area. He sang a psalm all the way down the mountain and then continued to walk onto the sandy plain that yawned wide before him.

Yeshua felt the festival of starlight, sensing everything inside being outside and everything outside being inside. No borders separated the end of one from the beginning of the other.

After walking for a while, he felt his ears prick at a nearby sound. As he passed near a small patch of green, he heard a reed bending ever so gently a hundred paces away. He stood and waited—and saw the large tousled mane of a male lion as it walked out of the shadows toward him. He realized that it was the same lion that had made a meal of poor Aderes. The lion bore the scar of missing flesh and a large chunk of the mane on the right side of his head.

The two stared at one another, the lion panting.

Neither was fearful.

Yeshua understood that in the fullness of time, our bodies all become food for other living things. This moment was either that time or it was not. When it was right to do so, Yeshua looked away and resumed his walk. Soon the lion was trotting past him and then staying about ten paces ahead, much the same as Aderes had done. Yeshua was content with his royal company, for it felt familiar, as if Aderes had returned in a mysterious way. He gave the lion his peace. And as the dog had been his food, the lion and Aderes were one now.

It came time to stop. The night was warm again, and Yeshua felt no need for a fire. He spread his outer mantle on the sand in peace. If the lion ate him in his sleep, he would awake as a lion.

He smiled at the thought and fell into a deep sleep.

He rose, as did the lion, before dawn. A large outcropping of rocks lay in the distance, so they set out. The sun was very hot, and after several hours, his thirst again became severe. The lion's tongue hung from his mouth as he trotted twenty paces in front now and turned sharply to the right before heading off in another direction.

Yeshua decided to follow the lion, which led him to a stream hidden by the cavern it had carved out of the rock for a thousand years, making it invisible from the path on which they had been walking.

The stream fed three pools with high reeds emerging from the blue-green coolness and he relished the relief the water gave his skin. The lion and he drank and lay at its edges until the sun went down. Yeshua made camp, building a small fire by the bank of the stream. He ate a handful of dates from his pocket. In the darkness, he looked around for the lion, but he saw only his lengthening shadow ghosting slowly away.

On the other side of the fire, Yeshua's eyes saw something else: a freshly killed rabbit left by the lion as a parting gift. When he had set out, he decided to eat only enough plant life to give his body the strength to keep walking, yet this was a friend's gift, which he could not refuse.

He picked up the limp and bloody body of the rabbit, immediately feeling his palms burn. The light around the rabbit had not faded; in fact, it was radiant. He began to understand this gift of sight and sensation he was being given. He knew the rabbit was not finished with its time in the body. He instantly felt that young rabbits needed the food this mother had been about to provide them when the waiting lion had snatched her as she prepared to dive into her burrow.

Yeshua raised his eyes to the brightening stars as he held out his other hand and prayed over the rabbit's limp body. Feeling his hands cool, he looked at the creature again. The blood remained on her fur, but the massive wounds to her head and neck had disappeared. Suddenly the mother rabbit squirmed and leapt from his hands, scratching his wrists and forearms with her nails, and then darted back into the brush.

Wiping the traces of blood on his mantle, Yeshua happily returned to eating his dates and then reclined by the fire, feeling a mixture of wonder and loneliness. His weary mind and body merged in quiet thanks for his life as he slipped into sleep.

He awoke again to the full morning sun shining brilliantly in his face.

Chapter 19

For what can scape the Eye
Of God All-seeing, or deceave his Heart Omniscient,
Who in all things wise and just,
Hinder'd not Satan to attempt the minde of Man,
with strength entire,
and free Will arm'd,
Complete to have discover'd and repulst
Whatever wiles of Foe …
or seeming Friend?"
—John Milton, *Paradise Lost, Book 1* (AD 1667)

AD 43, and the third year of the reign of the emperor Claudius, Ephesus

Almost imperceptibly, the darkening afternoon fades into evening, the sky now laden with clouds.

Tap.

Tap, tap-tap-tap.

Thick raindrops pat the rooftop and splash their dance upon the stone window ledge. I pick up a pine log from the large stack to the right of the hearth and place it on the fire. Miramee prepares vegetables in a broth for supper. She stopped her story an hour ago and began to busy herself with cooking. She baked bread earlier in the afternoon, and now she takes it out of the brick oven with expert ease and grace. Once again, the aroma fills that small stone space, and my stomach responds with a rumble as she tears off a piece and offers it to me. I eat it and then eat some more.

"Here's a little broth before the supper," she says as she takes her familiar cautious steps and hands it to me.

As I eat, I sense my hunger for more than the bread and white cheese brought by the visiting father and daughter. I want to learn more of Yeshua's journey through the wilderness. At the same time, understanding how deeply she loves him, I know that speaking these memories back into life must be very painful, draining her energy. Maybe the simple actions of baking and ladling broth give her a needed break so she can continue.

It's been only thirteen years since Yeshua left her, so these memories are fresh and intense. I am still curious about Eema.

Is she the friend who died here?

I'm reluctant to broach that subject head-on. I know tradition has St. John living to a very old age and dying naturally here. My mental computer clicks on, and I determine that he would be younger than Miramee, possibly in his midthirties at this time. I clear my throat.

"Where is Johanan?"

I feel a bit uncomfortable asking, but I know Miramee answers only what she chooses to reveal, and she clearly decides the timing. I'm uncertain if the question transgressed her very well defined boundaries. This is to satisfy my curiosity, after all. One interminable minute of silence passes before she speaks again.

"Perhaps after your supper you will regain your attention, for you are very distracted, Traveler," she says, again not in a reproving or stern way but in that even tone, sounding like a doctor prescribing a drug therapy for my sickness.

I feel chided anyway, and we eat in silence. The soup is salty but delicious, and the bread tastes like bread from heaven. I'm beginning to understand that most of the thoughts occupying my mind are distracting.

"Before she left us, she taught me how to bake bread the way Yeshua liked it," Miramee says. "It is unfortunate he is not here in the body to enjoy it. He loves to eat."

So … Eema *was* here.

This revelation changes nothing, and Miramee smiles, almost flirtatiously, as she delicately chews another morsel. We both taste the cheese as well, which is sharp but very good. I smile my gratitude for her kindness.

"I will tell you about Johanan when it is time," she says. "One thing must follow another in the right order. Otherwise, there is distraction and the danger of losing that which is most important."

I wait to hear what that might be, but she'll not hand that to me like another morsel of bread. It's clear I must learn it myself.

Later, we clean up, preparing for the evening's rest. She's too tired to speak again tonight.

"In the morning I will tell you about Yeshua's first encounter with Satan," she says simply and nods her good-night.

Returning the nod, I sense that her words, especially in the naming of the Devil, seem to hang like a cloud of thick black smoke in the room. It completes a disturbing equation: if I'm to meet the brightest of the holy ones through her, then on balance, the cast must also include the darkest one as well.

The rain brings a damp chill to the night air, and I try to settle into sleep nearer to the fire. I both dread and am strangely excited about the story to come. What is inside and outside of me is unbalanced, and contradictions push and pull at me. Like an old washing machine stuck in spin mode, I feel bounced around, knocking back and forth, totally out of whack.

Perhaps this is "the outside and inside opening," as Miramee said about me on the first night.

I stare at the darkened roof above me, entering finally into an uneasy sleep. Dreams come, disturbing images of that damn leopard chasing me, and I can't run, mired in the mud and the rain. I sweat in my sleep, even in the damp cold, and then wake up shivering. In the earliest hour of the morning, I rise to put more wood on the fire. Stripping off my wet bedclothes and standing in my cold, clammy nakedness, I reach for the blanket Miramee keeps folded neatly by the wall.

"Not that one," I hear Miramee say. Snapping my head around, I jump as I see her figure outlined in the dim light. My startled heart races, keeping time with the rain that drums upon the roof. Thunder rolls and lightning flashes on all sides, as if we are standing at the center of a battle between two primeval gods. The flames of the fire and lightning make her look like a ghost, which, I admit, creeps me out.

Sooo.

Here I am.

Standing buck naked, staring back at her.

My hands fold quickly and reflexively across my crotch. Naked *and* spooked by a woman who has already been dead for two thousand years by the time I first kicked my way into the world dressed in this birthday suit. Getting weirder and weirder by the minute.

She's holding another blanket, and she hands it to me.

"Since you are awake, we can talk."

I wrap myself up quickly as she takes her seat next to the wall. She doesn't give two damns that she saw me as bare as a boiled chicken. That's another "Grandpap-ism." She pulls the brown blanket over her legs and stares at me intently. I sit upon my mat, bundling the new, dry blanket about me. The warmth of the fire is now comforting, and my eyes begin to adjust to the semidarkness. I'm still feeling a little edgy, which amps up when—

Boom!

Another bolt of lightning strikes a tree right outside the window. There's a great blast of noise, shocking light, fire, and then smoke. The storm rumbles and grumbles grudgingly down into the valley below. The best way to deal with fear is to work the mind on something else. I mentally grab at any wandering idea, and a question that has bounced around all night now moves to the fore. The violent storm drifting away lends it a meaningful context.

"How *did* heaven and earth open for such a meeting between Satan and Yeshua?" I ask her. She stares at me for a moment. The question clearly does not stump her, for she knows the answer. She's deciding how much to give to me, a spiritual toddler.

"Your question assumes that there are times when heaven and earth are closed to the interaction of evil and good. I can say that the opposite is true. Everything is possible at all times if the conditions are in the right order, especially the encounter of truth with that which is untrue."

Clearly, I'm not getting the lingo here.

She sees my clueless expression but doesn't seem to care, and she begins to speak. She knows I may not be many things, but I am a quick study. I'll catch up.

Eyes down, I let the dancing shadows from the fire mesmerize me, and my imagination changes the floor into sandy earth on a cloudy and humid desert morning.

Chapter 20

Miramee:

There was not yet rain, but with every breath he drew in, Yeshua felt the weight of water.

The day before, when the sun had burned into him, Yeshua had seen the promise of heavy rain clouds on the horizon, and now they had arrived. He savored this heady irony: the scent of water in this driest of places. It had been days since he had eaten more than a handful of dates and plants, yet Yeshua noted that his senses had grown more acute. He could see color and hear sound, even in the fragrances and odors he breathed in. When he drank from his waterskin, it felt like music coursing down his throat. Even the sweat soaking the hair under his head covering felt like a cool anointing laid upon him.

He told me how sensitive his hands had become; just by touch, he could feel the stories of things. Once when he was famished, he picked up the lifeless body of a locust and seriously considered how to eat it. He stopped in wonder, for the moment he took it into his hands, he could sense its past life. Suddenly he felt the thrill of its memory, its exuberant skimming upon the updrafts of earth-warmed air.

His alertness now was constant, effortless, and all-encompassing. He sensed things in a way he could not measure with the calculating abacus of his mind. Yeshua told me he felt calm, yet his heart beat as if he were excited. The joy came into him deeply from both the outside and from the heart, the very center core of his body. He could feel the love everywhere, and it was Elohim the Father! His hands radiated great heat, nearly burning his thighs when he rested them on his legs. He felt as if he was emerging from a chrysalis—but far more powerfully and wonderfully. There was a change in the light all around, as if he himself had become the new sun, the blue-green pools, and the small cavern. All the plants seemed to reflect this freshly discovered brilliance.

Then, just as suddenly as it had come, the light receded, and Yeshua's hands were cool to the touch again.

Inhaling deeply, his nose sensed something else in the air: an intermittent fragrance as incongruent to this place as to be summarily dismissed as a trick on his sense of smell.

It was the aroma of baking bread!

His empty stomach stirred and growled like a waking lion, and his mouth began to water. He saw a plume of smoke rising above a cover of reeds rooted in the third water pool. He waded through the plants and soon came upon a small camp on the sandbar of the stream. There was a spacious tent set up beside the stream, and an ass was tethered to a narrow, thumb-like boulder protruding from the sandy dirt. He walked into the camp, emboldened and excited at the thought of company—and bread.

In front of a small campfire, a princely man was enjoying his meal near the opening of the finely made tent. He was young, clean, and well dressed for a traveler this deep in the desert. Even stranger, he appeared to be alone.

Yeshua's body tensed slightly, his human defenses alerted, for this was an old ruse: leading a man into camp and distracting him with the aroma of cooking food, while one's cohorts jumped the victim from behind.

Yeshua felt no immediate danger, but he remained vigilant.

Except for the flames of the fire, nothing and no one moved. The situation remained like this for several moments. Like a painting on a wall, it appeared to be an illusion. Just as Yeshua thought this, the man suddenly stirred, snapping his head sharply to stare at him. He smiled, but Yeshua saw no expression in his eyes. In fact, he could see no eyes at all—only two black, vacant holes in his sockets. Blinking hard, Yeshua looked at him again, and the eyes of the man appeared normal and dark, like the Nabataean desert dwellers in that country.

Yeshua wondered if he was so hungry that his own eyes were playing tricks on him. He scanned the area for the source of the aroma but saw nothing. He felt the pain in his sore, tired body. The regal man continued to stare, as would anyone surprised by a stranger appearing suddenly from the reeds. Yeshua discerned unease but no fear in him, and he also noted that the man radiated no light.

He could see the light around everything else now, even the rocks and boulders. Yet this man was only a form and nothing else. He did not give the traditional greeting of peace exchanged between men in the desert. Yeshua's heart pounded in warning, and his skin began to heat up. He felt the already humid air grow warmer and then stifling. Beads of sweat trickled down his forehead, but despite the uncertainty of this strange encounter, he yearned for the food that he smelled but could not see.

Yeshua watched the young man as he pulled out a piece of unleavened bread from a pocket and pop it into his mouth, smiling as he chewed slowly. Yeshua understood what he had sensed when he'd first laid eyes upon the man.

This was no traveler. He was not even a man. He was a *demon*.

Then the revelation came: Yeshua was in the presence of the Tempter, the Prince of Darkness himself.

"What are you doing here?" the Tempter asked.

The aroma of bread made every part of Yeshua's body cry out for food, and his stomach walls ground against one another in response. All he needed was a tiny morsel, anything to take away the pain. He tried to focus on something else, on the Tempter or the surroundings, but his mind would not let it go. His every impulse was to snatch the bread from this creature's hand. Yet he knew he could not and would not. He did take a step closer to the Tempter, feeling his very human body move toward what it needed without the mind's consent, so weakened that it acted as if it were a separate being.

Yeshua could not answer the Tempter's simple question. Even in his state, he still possessed a deeper knowing that if a question did not have a practical human purpose or bring with it the possibility of a new or richer understanding, there was no point in answering it. In asking what Yeshua was doing there, the Tempter was truly questioning him about something so profound that there were no words with which to answer. Therefore, the only possible, teachable truth was silence in the face of that query.

He stood still, looking into the shadows, his shadows. Self-doubt plagued his thoughts, and his hesitation was mirrored in the Tempter's eyes.

Still munching the bread noisily, the Tempter grabbed his bejeweled staff, rose to his feet, and walked around Yeshua, smiling broadly at his bedraggled appearance as if enjoying some private joke. He pinched Yeshua's dirty mantle, massaging it between the two fingers, and released it. Then he laughed loudly, showing a set of dull, yellow teeth and the little chewed lumps of bread on his purplish tongue.

"You travel light, I see. No supplies. And when you run out?" he asked, raising his eyebrows into a peak. "Let me guess. You pray?"

"I pray always," Yeshua replied. "Circumstances change; prayer does not."

The Tempter nodded and then used his staff to hike up the tattered hem of Yeshua's robe, regarding the remnants of his sandals.

"Hmm. Perhaps you should be a little more specific in those prayers?"

"I am here and alive."

"Yes, you are, brave Yeshua! Here *and* alive. That must mean that you get all the manna from heaven you need." He dusted the crumbs from his hands. "Mm-mm. That is good, because I just finished the last bite of my own manna. Ha!"

Yeshua looked deeply into him, beneath the endless layers of putrid hatred, anger, and evil accumulated through countless generations. He saw the created thing, the spark of life, and the divine source that unites all creation. It was small, almost imperceptible, but the life of Elohim, the Father, was in this creature too—covered up, warred against, hidden.

Yeshua's unease changed for a brief moment into compassion for this being who stood so smugly in front of him.

The Tempter picked up a stone.

"Still, a man must eat, and, my friend, you know you will not last long out here, eating weeds like a musk ox."

He tossed the stone from hand to hand.

"But you don't need my bread, do you, Yeshua? You could command bread at any moment, and you would receive. True? Of course!"

Yeshua was uncertain if he could do anything of the sort. He was not a worker of magic. He was able to heal some by touching them, and he had even delivered a few afflicted people from demons. He had known about these gifts since he was a young boy. But could he turn stones into bread? That was something different. However, he was perfectly aware that the Tempter could hurl that stone at him, so he remained on guard and alert to his movements. He returned the glare but said nothing.

"I will make a bargain with you," said the Tempter, "though it is such an easy task for you, I am a fool to make such an offer." He tossed the stone at Yeshua to catch.

Still unsure whether he was throwing the rock *to* him rather than *at* him, Yeshua caught it easily.

The Tempter pointed to a stack of rocks beside Yeshua that had not been there an instant ago.

"Make bread out of these stones and eat your fill," he said. "Then even *I* will believe! You can turn history on one little act."

Still holding the Tempter's gaze, Yeshua continued to see the deep darkness within him, a profound sadness that contained all the misery and suffering of the world. He saw that it was a mirror of his own suffering too, here and in the days and years to come. This moved him again into a deeply felt compassion for this hapless creation of Elohim.

The Tempter must have sensed Yeshua's empathy for him, because his eyes now smoldered with fire. No one should ever pity the prince of this world!

Yeshua knelt in the sandy dirt, and using the Tempter's stone, he wrote "I AM" in the earth. He looked up at the Tempter and they locked eyes. Calmness settled upon Yeshua as he looked at the name he had written and bowed his head.

"Bread is not enough, and you know that," he said evenly. "We live not by bread alone but by the grace and power, the mercy and love, of *I AM*!"

Yeshua closed his eyes, and after a few moments of great heat, he felt the earth shake slightly—a vibration, really—and then suddenly the wind changed. It remained humid, but a cool breeze bathed him, bringing welcome relief.

When Yeshua opened his eyes, he was kneeling alone in the sand. The camp, the man, the tethered animal, the fire, and the aroma of bread were gone. The cooler air carried with it only the sounds of water flowing, and its breeze played lightly among the reeds in the pond.

Soon, the softest of rains began. He let his damp clothing fall to the earth, and he stood naked, with heaven's water showering down upon him. He rejoiced in being alive in this body. He felt power course through his veins as deep love welled up in his heart. Yeshua knew now that all protection, all knowledge, and all life came into him from Elohim, his Father in heaven. As he waded into the water with the rain falling upon him, he saw where the stream emerged almost imperceptibly from the cavern's rock wall in a small, thin waterfall. He knew this was the *av'va*, the source of the stream, just as the Father was the Av'va, the source of all that is, whether seen or unseen.

Yeshua thought how *Av'va* sounded like the word *Abba*, the name that, as a small boy, he had called his father, Yosef. His Father in heaven would be Abba from now on, the name closest to his heart.

Abba, the Father and the source, would lead him to where he must go next. He was content to spend the day in prayer, as joyful in that little oasis—and as innocently naked—as Adam, who must have stood on the first morning of his creation and gazed in wonder at the garden as Abba bathed him like a newborn son in the warm, gentle rain of Eden.

Chapter 21

AD 43, and the third year of the reign of the emperor Claudius, Ephesus

Miramee smiles, gazing down at the stone floor, and shifts in her seat, wrapping her ever-present blanket more tightly around her bosom and folding her arms beneath it for warmth. The rain subsides. Now there's only the after-storm water dripping off the roof. It's still dark but I hear morning birds chirp the impending dawn. We've talked most of the night, and she gets up slowly to return to her chamber.

"Do not be afraid," she says quietly. "Just continue to breathe and know it is of Elohim, of the Father. And this is desired for you." She returns to her chamber without saying another word.

Cryptic. I'm puzzled. Again.

It's been a long night, and I lie back down on my cot for a few hours of rest. As soon as I close my eyes, the darkness turns to orange, like someone has switched on the lights. But of course, there are no switches in AD 43.

My eyelids flip open, and I hold my breath as my heart races. Seated in Miramee's spot is a young man who is radiant with light. He has no beard, and what looks like hair on his head is luminous, almost translucent. His mouth is closed tightly, and there's no movement—by either him or me. Next to him, propped up against the stone wall, is what appears to be a sword of light. Orange laser-like rays shoot from the sides of the blade, giving it the appearance of being on fire. I sit there, mouth gaping in my amazement, and I wonder if I've just kicked the bucket. Is this angel the one who crosses people over and into the tunnel of light?

My heart starts racing. Damn! Maybe Miramee—maybe all of this—was to prepare me for my own death!

I shudder.

"Peace be upon you, Traveler," the man says, only his mouth isn't moving. The sound of his voice comes through in clear, masculine, and familiar tones, with no movement of face or body. I want to reply. I want to say, "And also upon you," but no words come. My throat is dry, my tongue thick. I'm unable to speak.

"The people call me Micha'el. The name is a question: 'who is like Elohim?'" His voice continues as he sits, and light emanates from him like a shooting star that has made a soft landing on earth. *Who is like God?* The answer is "no one," but I sit like a mute, facing this incredible being.

"That is true, in part," the voice of Micha'el replies, reading my thoughts.

For a moment, nothing else happens. The fire burns, the first crimson streaks of daylight appear in the window, and the sounds of dripping water subside into the moist, predawn stillness of the forest. The birds are silent now. The man's features are familiar, but I can't place him. Besides, where would I have seen an archangel before?

For a long period, I sit in awe-filled silence, waiting for Micha'el to speak again. My thoughts begin to slow down, moving toward rest. Calmer now, my traveler's heart drums with a new, more leisurely rhythm, feeling deeply the archangel's peace.

I'm ready to hear him, now.

Chapter 22

Micha'el, the archangel:

At that time in the wilderness, Yeshua had only begun to understand the significance of what was happening around him. His eyes were newly opened, and yet he did not understand *who* he was. The time was not full, and like all things, that revelation must follow in the right order.

As I said, the day I AM allowed the Tempter, whom the people called Satan, to converse with the Holy One, I wondered whether any man was ready for such a direct encounter. The Tempter face-to-face, can be more than the human eye or heart can bear. Just as I brought my power down—almost to the dimmest light possible—so I could appear to you and not send you into an explosion of a million million bits of fire, so also did the Tempter bring his power to the lowest level so that Yeshua could see him as an ordinary man.

He is very skilled at that ruse, but Yeshua was learning to see on many planes. When he saw beyond and through his own physical hunger, the Tempter's illusion could be seen for what it was: another trap and manifestation of evil. I saw that Yeshua's human body could hold vast amounts of power now. He had received and manifested great light during the revelation before the Tempter arrived.

In fact, Yeshua's light was what called him forth.

Since the Tempter was the brightest, most radiant being before his great mistakenness, he remains attracted to the brilliance of good, if only to smother that light with his deep and fathomless appetite for darkness.

I watched the encounter, but I could *only* watch. This test did not involve me. I AM, who was in the Holy One's heart, brought it forth, *allowed* it to take place.

In order to align himself with his destiny, Yeshua had to master his own appetites and any delusion of his own human control. Perhaps he *could* turn stones into bread. That merely involves switching a few atoms around. But he was not there to do tricks for the Tempter. Yeshua was there to understand fully that all life and all nurturance come from I AM.

Now, when the Tempter heard the name of I AM, Yeshua's eyes were closed. Yeshua did not see, but I did. The name made the Tempter tremble. His skin turned red—deep, bright-red like blood—and he was furious. He grew to the size of ten men and loomed over Yeshua as if to squash him like a rat.

I made myself manifest and lifted the sword. The Tempter looked at me with his leg raised and foot poised to stomp upon Yeshua. The flames from my sword shot across the air toward him, nearly piercing his side. He brought his foot lightly down upon the ground next to Yeshua. We felt the earth shake slightly. I looked at Yeshua and could see that he was still sitting, calm, and unharmed, with his eyes closed. The Tempter glared at me, and then, like soap bubbles popping, he and all his illusions dispersed into the air.

The Master of Illusion.

Only Yeshua remained, a solitary man kneeling on a sandbar of a stream.

Chapter 23

AD 43, and the third year of the reign of the emperor Claudius, Ephesus

Micha'el, the archangel, finishes speaking. He looks at me directly. There are no pretenses and no games. Nothing has been withheld. I nod reverently to let him know that I now understand, that he's opened my eyes. Even the Tempter was necessary to help crystallize Yeshua's awareness of his calling and to slowly move him toward his destiny.

Miramee enters. She has her hair completely wrapped in an orange head covering that has faded white spots on top, as if she accidentally dripped bleach on it. Incredulous, I watch as she begins her daily routine by making breakfast.

Doesn't she see that there's an archangel *over in the corner?*

I notice a change of light in the room and snap my head back.

Corner's empty.

Of course, he's disappeared. That's the way everyone seems to move around—here one moment, teleported somewhere else the next. I'm getting used to it. Almost.

I smell the fragrance of flowers coming from the place where he sat. It's all that remains of the great archangel's visit, but a fresh, wet breeze from the open window disperses it swiftly. The sun now shines, and I feel energized. There's a promise alive in any sunlit morning after a storm.

We eat a simple breakfast of grains and yogurt, and Miramee tidies up quickly. She turns toward me and motions me to stand up.

"Prepare, Traveler. We must walk down the mountain into the city for some provisions."

Miramee gathers her shawl about her shoulders and ushers me toward the door. No wasting time with her.

I notice that her clothing looks to be of the highest quality, well-made but washed and worn for many years. The shopping trip surprises me, because I did not think that Miryam of Magdala would actually need to hoof it down to Ephesus to buy her own food. She smiles at me. Her face shines like gold from underneath the head covering.

"The man who usually brings us provisions lost his young sister," she says. "He travels to her village, a day's journey from here. So, either we eat only the eggs of the chickens, or we go into the city and buy our food."

"How do we go down there?" I ask. Because I arrived at the house by just showing up, I haven't a clue as to how people actually get to Ephesus from here.

"Why, Traveler," she says, "we walk, of course!"

"Sounds good," I say.

Outside now, she hands me a skin filled with water, and I put it into the saddlebag of her young donkey. I take its tether in hand and begin to hike down the path, with Miramee striding vigorously alongside.

"It is, of course, mostly downhill from here, so the way to the city is not difficult," she says. "Save your energy, though, for the climb back up is very steep and can be tiring."

Not for me, Miramee. I'm a hiker, after all.

She tells me of the short three-mile trek to the northeast, winding among and down the slopes of beautifully forested mountains, and then dropping finally into the scrubby lowlands that lead to Ephesus.

"Let us talk as we walk," Miramee says as she pounds ahead of me. "This little journey in the mountain air will help my memory." My competitive gene kicks in, but the donkey refuses to pick up the pace.

Olive and other fruit trees surround the house, but here the trail cuts through large stands of evergreens. Finally, the donkey shifts into second gear, so I can at least keep up with her. The forest is peaceful and a luscious green. The trees are tall, conical pines and cedars, with the shady ravines laced with leafy hazel and maple trees. I'm loving the first exercise I've had in a while, and this walk in the woods reminds me of home again.

Miramee glances back at me as I approach her, leading the less-than-enthusiastic donkey. I'm irritated because my sandals don't fit me well; Johanan has large feet—too large. Then the realization that these are

St. John's sandals sends a light-speed shiver down my spine. Throngs of people would come into a church on their knees to kiss the remnant of a strap, and I'm bitching to myself about them being too big!

Just then, the flap of the left sandal catches a stone on the path, and I stumble. I quickly remind myself that I have to focus on every step. Miramee catches me again, keeping me from falling as she did that first night.

"Pay attention to the path, Traveler," she says. "You are on it for the first time." She then walks arm in arm with me for a short distance. For her, it's a natural gesture of care, and once more I feel a sense of peace coursing through my body.

I have to admit that I like the feeling of her arm in mine.

"Yeshua was not yet certain what the Father wanted of him," she began. "He needed to be constantly aware, ever attentive, for the voice of the Father is often subtle and easy to miss. Even if one can hear it, the guidance of the Father is often completely misunderstood if one is distracted."

"As I am often distracted?" I ask.

"Yes. But you are hardly alone. Many brothers and sisters walk the journey of their earthly lives in a state of continuous distraction: worrying about their treasure, the future, their children, and their bodies. How can anyone hear or take the tiny whisper of the Father into the inner Temple with such a din of noise going on in the head? It is impossible."

"Impossible?" I ask.

"Almost impossible. But with the right awakening event, which is usually unpleasant, you can hear above the noise of your life. One can hear the Father. At last."

"And then?" I press.

"And then you can finally learn who you are and to whom you belong."

I look at her face now as we continue to walk arm in arm. She smiles serenely as if fondly remembering him.

No wonder he loved her. I would too … if I were Yeshua.

As she begins to tell her story, I pay enough attention to my loose sandals that I can keep pace with her. As I glance downward, I feel a low branch of pine needles lightly brush my scalp. Then, as she begins to describe Yeshua's next encounter in the desert, I feel as though I'm right there with him.

Chapter 24

Miramee:

The rain continued after the Tempter left Yeshua. There was a flash and a resounding clap of thunder that echoed through the little canyon. The sound returned again and again, the earth absorbing more of it each time. Finally, all became still. The rain was warm, but Yeshua sought shelter under the rocks, sitting upon his wet clothes in a shallow cave until it subsided. His stomach groaned anew. He pondered his own momentary wish for the bread of the Tempter and then breathed in very slowly and looked into the freshened sky.

"Abba,

Who is in heaven, May I hold Your Name in holiness,

Your Kingdom, Your Sovereign Presence, is always near,

Your Will be done here as it is done in heaven.

Give me what I need to eat each day, Abba!

Forgive me my many distractions and errors,

Please do not put me again to the test! Rather, lead me away from the wiles of the Evil One.

For I am only human, Even though I love you with all my heart and mind, with all my soul, and with all my strength. So, thus may it be."

Soon Yeshua realized that his stomach pains were gone. Like a phantom that haunts and departs, the emptiness left him. The raindrops still danced upon the surface of the water. There was an exquisite movement in the stream. A green-gold fish leaped into the air as if rejoicing in the freshened water and its newfound breath.

Abba's will be done!

The prayer he uttered was the true prayer, because it contained all prayers, all words, all sounds, and even all the silences that lay between the words. Relaxing back into his little cave, his breathing eased.

Yeshua told me that around him every grain of sand, every reed and raindrop that moved toward reunion with the stream—all seemed to speak to him of the Creation doing his Father's will with joy. The lives in the very stones and boulders that made up his cave—and even the space of the cave—were a sacred tabernacle themselves, a psalm to the ever-creating Creator, the nameless I AM.

Yeshua sensed the spirit of the Father lift within him. He had felt the rain, but he knew there would be no flood. This was the gift of life the Father gave to the desert, an affirmation of His gift of life to Yeshua. All this penetrated him, making him dizzy with the ecstasy of revelation. He had not forgotten the Tempter's test, but it paled when compared to the infusion of grace he experienced in the cave. All at once, he felt drowsy, and his body fell into a deep sleep.

When he awoke, the sunlight shone like diamonds on the wet sand and the stream. The relentless heat had returned, and the afternoon wore on. He did not know why yet, but it was clear to him that he had to make his way up a mountain in the distance. He liked praying on a summit, for it was like praying nowhere else on earth. Yeshua felt that he could touch heaven there. When the wind whipped the mountaintop, he would breathe purer air, with little dust, and only the lightest fragrance the shrubs stirred up when it rained. In that wind, he could hear the voice of the Father.

There was no need for plan or provision other than a skin full of water taken from the refreshed pond. Soon he was again walking out on the vast sandy plain. He carried no thought of what would become of his body. After the revelation in the cave, all he longed for was the ecstatic communion between the Father and himself again. It would take place on the mountain.

He trudged on for hours, until each step became more difficult than the last, the sun's arc slowly moving toward the horizon. In his head, he repeated a verse over and over. It was a prayer from a psalm of King David.

"Abba is my strength and my shield; my heart trusts in him and I am helped. My heart leaps for joy, and I will give thanks to him in song. Abba is my strength and my …"

Sometimes as his fatigue grew, he would confuse the order of words, and it would come forth as "strength is Abba my shield."

He plodded along the barren landscape, chanting the psalm in his mind. He sang it aloud a few times, but his mouth went dry, so he continued to sing in silence. As the hours passed, he stopped sweating, and his sight began to blur. He felt very light-headed as his legs began to give way under the weight of his body. Finally, at the foot of a small rise, protected from the final rays of the setting sun, he dropped to his knees. His mind raced. He wondered if this would be his end, the place where he would depart from his body.

He saw a shadowy thing rustle on the ground in front of him. There were squawking sounds above his head.

Vultures. Four dark silhouettes circled ominously above him.

Was his body to be their next feast? Was this flesh, which had come from the body of Miryam of Nasrath, destined to become the stuff of the vulture's young?

There was a rustle again under the dried branches of a dead bush a few paces away. He had trouble focusing his eyes, so he sipped from his waterskin.

Rustle.

Now, less pronounced.

He squinted to see the form come into focus. It was feathered and prone. Then he saw it clearly: a large, tan-colored dove. It was dying. His hand went out to touch it but then faltered. Like the dog, this one was determined to die. Its body shivered and went still. He saw a small light emanate from the center of its belly. It surprised him that his weary, weak eyes could yet *see*.

Yeshua lay still and felt relief settle in him, then a slight surge of energy. He propped himself up on an elbow and looked around weakly. He slowly rose and moved toward some dried fronds he could use for kindling. This would be camp tonight, and the dove's body would let him gather strength and live. After he'd built a fire and roasted it, he ate every part he could. The flavor shot through his mouth and body in bolts of pure pleasure. Each small part of him rejoiced.

Yeshua looked at the now-clear night sky. He did not feel alone, for he was in the company of the small lights of heaven. He thought of how Eema had loved to tell the story of a star that hovered over the birthplace of a magical baby whom many said was the Mashiach. In the darkest nights, when there was no moon and the clouds covered the stars, she would tell him, his brothers, and his sisters about the wicked king who wanted to kill the newborn baby. Even though all the children knew the story well, they would still beg her to retell it.

"One more time, Eema, please!"

Laughing as they implored her yet again, she would smile, pretending to need convincing. Then, in her captivating voice, she would weave great mystery into their favorite part, the part where it was foretold that one day the baby would be crowned the greatest king of Israel.

She told of the three astrologers from the east who had followed this star. The king told them he wanted them to find the baby and then inform him of the child's resting place so he could worship him. But an angel told the astrologers to go home another way, and the parents secreted the baby away to far Egypt where the harsh king could not find him.

The king, angered by this deception, cast a net of death, ordering the murder of all boys in the village who were less than two years old.

A terrifying story.

Eema could tell a tale so well that the child Yeshua believed he was there, witnessing it all.

For years, something had nagged at Yeshua. During this storytelling, his eldest brother Tzadik always remained silent and aloof. He did not join with the other children in pleading with Eema to tell it again. Yeshua then remembered one night in particular, when he was about seven years old. Tzadik had argued with Yosef and Eema earlier that day, and when night fell, Eema told the beloved story again. Tzadik, still angry, came into the room and blurted out to them all that this was no child's tale but a real account of Yeshua's birth.

In an instant, the playful mood vanished. Yeshua remembered a shocked expression contorting the features of Eema's face, and he remembered how harshly she had reprimanded Tzadik. Yeshua never understood his mother's reaction, or his father's. Yosef came in, took Tzadik roughly by the shoulders, and ushered him outside for a muted but hot discussion.

A growing number of questions roiled through his mind like a tempest.

Why had the very air in the room that night become thick with tension?

Why had the adults' faces grown stern instead of everyone laughing at Tzadik? He could not have been serious in making such a ridiculous statement.

Had Tzadik somehow mocked the only mother he had ever known, or in some way that was mysterious to Yeshua, disrespected her confidence?

As the years passed, this one act was inconsistent with the absolute hunger for truth that Tzadik possessed. It had never made sense to Yeshua. Tzadik had always been a strong, loyal, and above all, truthful brother.

So why had he said such a strange thing so many years ago?

Like the heads of the Hydra in Greek legends, one unanswered *why* question seemed to give rise to many more. Settling his agitated thoughts, Yeshua placed his cloak out on a soft, sandy area and lay down with his hands behind his head, looking up at the starry sky. On previous nights, he had watched two planets slowly approach each other. Tonight, they were nearly aligned, creating a bright heavenly light in the sky. He reached up and traced the short space between them with his finger. Another shooting star crossed the sky right under his pointing finger with a sudden luminous streak.

He laughed.

At once, he could see the faces of thousands of souls in the night sky, as many as the stars spread out endlessly before him like a canopy of distant suns. So many people, countless in the human mind, yearned for him, called out for him, and hoped for him.

Yeshua shook his head as if to shake away this vision, but it continued, even with his eyes tightly shut. The feeling of a heavy, terrifying, yet wonderful burden of their longing invaded his heart and was just as inescapable as the vision.

His thoughts absently returned to the memory of that tense night in Nasrath.

What had Tzadik meant?

He closed his eyes and remembered more details of the scene: Eema's concerned expression, the look of defiance crossing his brother's brow, the darkness and disbelief on Yosef's face as he pushed Tzadik out of the house.

A sudden clarity, a streak of insight made his eyes snap open.

"Abba, you do not mean …" His mind stopped him from completing the question.

But it was too late. A terrible sweetness had settled into Yeshua as subtle as a deep breath. He began to *know*. The revelation was coming into him, and he was passively listening as if he were a three-year-old harkening to his father's instructions—except that there were no words, no sentences, and no complete thoughts. It was rather a knowing that instantly transformed every blood vessel in his body.

This is my beloved Son. The words from the day of the immersion.

On that morning, Yeshua had understood that *Son* meant only his calling to be a prophet of Israel. He was willing to wear that mantle, but what was coming into him now was a burden he felt completely unworthy to bear and terrified even to consider. His mind finally gave voice to it. He summoned all his strength.

"Abba, am I—could you have chosen—*me?*" Yeshua blinked up into the vacant sky, which stared back at him with twinkling indifference.

One raindrop hit his forehead and startled him, because he could see no cloud above him. A few other drops plopped around him, but not another touched his body, and then there were no more. Yeshua finally saw the filmy traces of a small dark cloud above.

He squinted up at the sky with a questioning stare.

"You anoint me?" he asked, his voice barely a whisper. "And the earth as well?"

A breeze brushed the desert floor. Yeshua thought it was the intonation of a natural psalm, and he felt as if his body was the center of some kind of ritual, as if he were the sacred axis of all things in that moment. He could hear a low, and then high, vibration that was beautiful and exciting. The tones went into Yeshua's body, and he could feel the singing sounds move upward and downward.

The music of the angels.

The vibrations engulfed Yeshua, swamped him like a small boat battling a storm at sea. He felt them press upon him, push against his skin and pulsate through every fiber of his being. With his whole body, Yeshua heard the harmonics of an ephemeral and celestial music.

"*Baruch haba b'shem adonai!*" Blessed is he who comes in the name of Adonai!

They were startlingly clear, as if thousands of human voices were singing. It was both exquisite and deafening. Yeshua sat up and reflexively covered his ears. Then all sounds stopped as suddenly as they had begun. All that remained was the night's silence. He filled his lungs and turned his face to heaven.

"Who am I?" Yeshua shouted.

No answer came, not even a breeze to rustle the leaves of a squat shrub next to him.

Absolute stillness.

Yeshua waited.

Nothing. All of nature held its breath.

He continued to keep vigil in silence as the night wore on and the moon rose, bathing him in light. His troubled thoughts abated as the comfort of the patient moon kept him company.

Peace came to rest in him, and Yeshua's mind no longer yearned for the Father. As the moon drifted directly overhead, catching him in its silvery beam, a small bit of pure-white down descended slowly and came to rest on the back of his right hand in the small valley created by two prominent veins.

He stared at it.

"What young bird is out here in this harsh place?"

As he looked, the inescapable truth settled into him, and tears filled his eyes.

Whose am I?

He wiped his runny nose with his dirty sleeve, smudging his lips with mucus and sand.

"I am the son of David, the shepherd of Bethlehem, David the king!" he said hoarsely.

He brushed at the tears, marking his cheeks with tracks of moistened dust.

"I am the son of Miryam of Nasrath," he said.

He hung his head and coughed hard, as if he had to force the next words from his lungs.

"I am … Abba, why? I am not worthy!" he said. He could not utter the words. Then a force came into him. A powerful energy filled his body, as if all the light from the stars and moon above had entered through the crown of his head.

"I am the One like a human being, the Anointed of Adonai, the beloved of Abba," he said. With newfound certainty, Yeshua inhaled deeply, pausing before he pronounced the words that would change him—and with him, the whole world—forever.

"I am the Son, the Holy One of Elohim. I am he who is to come into the world and save his children."

He coughed phlegm into the dirt, eyes reddened and leaking precious water.

"Hear me, O Israel!" he shouted as he turned to the west. "I AM is One!"

The night air was suddenly fragrant with the subtle scent of flowers, and there was a crack of thunder from the cloudless sky.

Then the resonance of all tones pierced the moonlit silence with a strange, new harmony, as if to sing, simply and forever:

"Alleluia!"

Chapter 25

AD 43, and the third year of the reign of the emperor Claudius, Ephesus

"It is the last day of the goddess's celebration," Miramee says, her mouth turned down as we walk along with the crowds, edging toward the gates like a forceful high tide. I wonder if she can continue her story with all these people chattering, dogs barking, and animals raising dust.

The little donkey I'm leading begins to bray, apparently wanting to add its voice to the cacophony of sounds. I wish this thing I'm pulling along had an owner's manual.

Only moments ago, while we were still in the silence of the pathway, Miramee finished her story of Yeshua's revelation, and the tall pines subtly gave way to the fruit trees and grasses of the foothills.

"What goddess?" I ask, and we are back on topic.

Astonished, her eyes search my face to see if I'm really that ignorant.

"Some call her Diana, others *Artemis Ephesia*, the patron goddess of the city," she says patiently.

I nod like one of those dashboard figurines from the sixties, but I don't know who the hell she's talking about. Miramee's eyes roll up to the sky in exasperation, as if asking someone up there why he sent her such an idiot.

"She is the hunter and protector, the twin of Apollo, the sun god," Miramee explains.

I stay quiet, steeping in my ignorance.

"We may run into a procession or two while we make our way to the market," she says. "It is a very large festival, and there are many people in the city."

As we approach ancient Ephesus, it's an amazing sight to see. We enter through the great city gate and go to the Agora, the wide principal thoroughfare lined with elegant marble buildings, libraries, and temples, all so dazzling white in the sunlight that it hurts my eyes.

As we make our way down the boulevard, the crowds of people and animals everywhere jostle us about. I pick up a mixture of odors, some identifiable and some not: perspiration, animal droppings, and rotting garbage overlaid with roasting lamb and onions. The combined effect adds a dimension of experience, a coloring of the real, convincing me once again that this isn't an illusion but a true experience. And I'm acclimating to all this now, even getting comfortable.

I just wish I could call Sharon. I always call her every day when I'm on a business trip. I miss her voice.

The sound of drums and flutes announces the procession passing right in front of us, and I stop to watch the approach of fourteen dancing girls and boys, colorfully clothed in rich linens.

"Are the colors and hues significant?" I ask.

"No," says Miramee. "Those are just the colors of their class. These are highborn children." I sense her distaste for all of this as the young people sway and pirouette in front of us.

After them come the musicians, drummers, and men playing flute-like instruments. The Temple priests follow, making their way reverently toward the large amphitheater, where they coax the *epiphany,* or presence of the goddess, from the statue. Finally, we see the bizarre sight of the statue itself. The sculpture of Artemis Ephesia is larger than life, probably about twelve feet tall and borne on a sacred wheeled cart drawn by two antlered stags.

There are eight burly men surrounding the cart to ensure its safety from the increasingly hysterical crowd that hypnotically chants her praises. The men are there to control the behavior of the less enraptured stags as well. The goddess is dressed in silks and other rare cloths dyed in vibrant colors and festooned with flowered garlands.

"They dress the statue in what they call the *kosmos,*" Miramee adds with disgust. "Worshipping this carved stone is such a flagrant affront to the Father!"

"But the Father would understand, because these people do not know him yet," I say.

Miramee snaps her head at me as if I have breached a protocol of my instruction. She does not answer but turns her head back to the procession. As a reverent Hebrew and a follower of Yeshua, she doesn't agree.

When the statue arrives right in front of us, I notice something peculiar. Even stranger than the dress of the statue is the number of her bare breasts. I count at least twenty. At one point, a priest pulls a cord and a liquid leaks out of every stone nipple. Eyebrows arching up into my wrinkling forehead, I blink in amazement. I can't think of a way to politely ask Miramee what this means.

"She is both the protector of the city and their goddess of fertility," she says, reading my reaction.

"And she is the twin of the sun god?" I ask. "His mirror image but feminine?"

"Yes, I believe I said that already," she replies. Clearly, her patience with all this is exhausted.

We leave the procession behind and enter a colonnaded market area near the Agora, which is a wild, bustling, magnificent sight to see. The donkey and I follow Miramee like kids following Mom into an unfamiliar but wildly exciting place. There are stalls with every imaginable spice, gem, or piece of cloth: silk thread being spun from cocoons fished out of a pot of boiling water; chickens and young goats hanging skinned and ready for roasting; the fragrance of cinnamon mixed with saffron; and many spices lying in colorful heaps upon a vendor's counter. Sellers call out to customers as they pass by. There's a carnival atmosphere as the feast and the sweep of its celebration fill the air with a joyful spirit.

Miramee selects measures of wheat and barley. As we load them onto the donkey, I notice that the vendors simply let her take what she wants—without payment. When she goes to the stall for dried fish, she offers some coins. The woman accepts, but the husband comes out from the rear of the stall, takes the coins from his wife's hand, and returns them to Miramee. She nods gracefully to him and his wife. The man returns the nod, as does the woman, although she doesn't hesitate to grouse at him.

"That was our best fish today, you superstitious fool!" she whispers loudly. He smiles as he puts a hand over her mouth, apparently not wanting to be embarrassed in front of Miramee.

If I did something like that to Sharon, I might put a hand on her mouth, but I'd pull back a stump!

Miramee obtains other items. Some she pays for; most she doesn't. Many people in the market nod and smile at her. They are members of the nascent church in Ephesus, and they call themselves followers of the Way at this early time. They obviously know who she is, yet no one greets or speaks with her openly. I get that it's for her safety that people don't call attention to her. I wander off for a moment, looking at a table with brightly colored beads. As I notice a string of green and golden beads, the vendor, a middle-aged man with no front teeth, hands them to me. I take them and admire the intricacy of the artistry and their exceptional beauty.

"You keep it for her," he says, causing me to look up at him with a start.

"For the lady, for the Beloved," he says. "You give this to her for me. Yes?"

Another follower of the Way?

After this surprising request, I pause, assessing him carefully. Is this dude going to yell "thief" after I walk away?

Alarm bells are sounding in my head, but the man looks so damn sincere, I suspend my suspicions.

"Uh, yeah, yes. Of course, thank you," I answer.

"No, thank *you*!" he says. "Tell her the bead merchant gives this to her. Tell her that my wife is now well because of her blessing, the blessing of the Holy Beloved." His voice breaks slightly as he speaks. He looks down for a moment to compose himself. His watery eyes then return to mine.

"The Holy Beloved is our treasure," he says quietly. "Can you remember to tell her my wife is well?"

I incline my head respectfully and take the gift over to Miramee, who waits for me under a line of vibrant banners whipped by the breeze. She receives it happily and nods her gratitude to the bead merchant. He beams, and then, looking around quickly, he bows low toward the woman he calls the Holy Beloved.

We both sit in the shade of a large date palm near the snapping banners, watching people go about their business. This is a little strange for me, because I'm usually too impatient to sit and watch other people working. Typically, I'm the one in motion. In the distance, the drums and music of the festival continue their unfamiliar but intriguing rhythms. I'm a little hungry and wonder which stall might offer something my Californian stomach can tolerate. Right now, a giant beef burrito bathed in cheesy enchilada sauce would be perfect. The thought makes me miss my home for a moment.

But I'm not letting my mind go there. I can't miss a minute of this incredible experience.

The baker's son comes running up with some warm bread. A woman walks toward us and sets down a wineskin—and then walks on without looking at either of us. A toddler tentatively pads toward us, holding something wrapped in a blue cloth towel. He plops unceremoniously on the ground in front of us and then giggles as he waddles double-time back to Mom as fast as his chubby legs can carry him. From the towel, we smell the indescribably rich aroma of roasted lamb with garlic and onions.

I'm not quite sure what's in play, and I look at her quizzically.

"People are afraid for me," she explains. "Many powerful people cannot hear the triumphant message of Yeshua in Ephesus. They love their festivals, their grand shows, and their tributes to the emperor too much to allow any of us to speak publicly. We will not sacrifice to their gods or to the emperor, so they call us atheists."

She pulls off a piece of the bread and fills my cup as she continues.

"Johanan had to return for a period to Jerusalem, because the leaders of the city forbade him to preach the message or the Way here, on pain of death. Yet the people have a great thirst to drink of the living water of Yeshua. They are fearful that I will leave them too, and they are right, for I must depart soon."

"Why?" I ask.

Her response is a smile. It's the wrong question … again. I'm not picking things up too fast. We eat a little more. I absently wonder how farmers manage the crops to produce this variety of grains and vegetables. I'd like to see a harvest while I'm here.

But that's curiosity, distraction.

"Go over there and sit for a moment," she says, pointing to a marble bench behind us on the other side of the thick, scaly trunk of the palm.

"Why?"

Miramee's mouth tightens with her growing impatience.

"It has a view you need to see," she says. "Go now and sit!"

Okaaay.

She's not doing too well today so this is probably all the explanation I'm going to get, so I stand and walk over to the bench. It overlooks the large amphitheater of Ephesus as well as some lesser temples. People throng into the theater from every direction. I see slaves handing out coins to the spectators, gifts from wealthy citizens who are the patrons of the great festival. The final day of religious rituals is under way, and it's a multicolored and fantastic scene to behold. The crowd breaks into a mighty roar as the stags and men carry in the bizarre, multibreasted statue. The priests take their places, and all await the epiphany of the goddess.

As I sit upon the bench and watch all of this, I glance to my right absently. With a start, I realize that Micha'el, the archangel, stands only a few feet from me, silent in his glowing presence. He raises his hand in peace, and I hear him talk once more. He makes no facial movements.

"Hail," he says.

"Uh, hail, Micha'el." I return the greeting, unsure exactly what the proper form of address is for an archangel.

"My name is a question. It means, 'Who is like I AM?'"

He said this to me before, and now he waits for some kind of answer to the question that defines his name.

"No one and nothing," I reply.

"That is the beginning of the answer. You will answer fully in time," Micha'el says solemnly. "Traveler?"

"Yes, I am called Traveler here," I answer, but I feel something change inside me as I speak the name. I feel this tingly sensation throughout my body, like a feather drawing up my spine.

"You must know your true name, or I AM cannot call you out. If you doubt your name, then many others can call you out falsely. Thus, you will live in untruth."

"But a name is only a collection of sounds given to us before we know anything," I say, realizing that I'm arguing with an archangel. I'd better watch out.

"No! I AM calls you out with the only name that is true. You must know your name, or the Tempter will call you by another name, a false name, and you will be deceived."

"So, what is my true name?" I ask. I want to drill down on this. Apparently, archangels don't drill down. He stares at me impassively.

"Listen now," he says in the customary cryptic answer of all these holy ones. He begins a story, still without facial movement. The words slip into my ears effortlessly, like kids down a waterslide. In a way, he's the real speaking statue, not the twenty-breasted stone goddess to whom everyone is now shouting in the amphitheater below us. His words take me from a sultry Ephesian afternoon into the deep mystery of the Jordanian desert night.

Chapter 26

Micha'el, the archangel:

The Tempter and Yeshua were to come together again. What I AM ordained for Yeshua had been imagined before time. What was written for him would not be changed or altered.

That truth did not make the confrontation less repulsive to witness.

Yeshua slept well after the humble supper and awoke while it was yet night to begin his walk again—or at least he thought he was walking. Suddenly the desert floor fell precipitously away, and he found himself stepping precariously upon a narrow battlement, with a deep gorge, an ominous dark void yawning out and beneath him. He realized that he was standing on the high parapet wall of Herod's Portico. This wall is found at the perimeter of the Temple compound and the gorge was the Valley of Jehoshaphat right outside Jerusalem that he knew well from his many pilgrimages to the Holy City.

For several moments, Yeshua wondered if he was dreaming.

He knew he was not. He squatted and breathed slowly for a moment, trying to focus and bring his mind into communion with what he was experiencing. He quickly sensed something, and as he looked around him, he discovered that he was not alone. A few paces away, the Tempter manifested as the same young man from the small oasis. He stood with his arms folded across his chest in respectful silence, waiting for Yeshua to regain his composure.

We find it remarkable that human beings tend to imagine the Tempter as frightening and hideous. He does manifest like that if the situation warrants, and he is always dangerous, but that is mostly because the Tempter makes himself attractive, amiable, and enticing. It is far easier to seduce the strong but inattentive than it is to overtake them with strength, and the Tempter finds the results far more satisfying.

That night, the Tempter seemed cordial and relaxed, considering that they were both dangerously perched on this very high point of the Great Temple. Yeshua lost his balance and seemed just about to fall off the edge into a certain dark death below, when the Tempter caught his arm and helped him regain his balance.

"You choose another strange place to meet," said Yeshua as he righted himself.

The Tempter released his grip and moved closer to the edge, looking down to the valley below— a chasm that in Roman measure plunged over six hundred feet deep. He raised his eyebrows as if waiting for Yeshua's response.

"Surely you are amazed at what I can do, Rabbuni?" the Tempter stated more than asked, then turning toward the Temple buildings and the great city beyond, opening his arms to indicate the scope of the spectacle before them.

Yeshua looked too but remained silent, squatting down to the right of a loose tile.

"An astonishing amount of power, is it not?" The Tempter was not relenting.

Yeshua looked him in the eye. "From what source, what Av'va, does the power come?"

The air suddenly became hotter and humid.

"No Av'va! I need no one to accomplish this!" the Tempter lashed back with an angry hiss in his voice.

Regaining his composure, he slowly wagged his index finger at Yeshua as if to chide a young boy. "Ah … Rabbuni. This is my game— my game and my rules."

Yeshua dusted off his hands and shook his head. "You have no power, Tempter, except that which comes from Abba."

The Tempter surveyed him coolly, pausing for a moment to let the impact of his next statement pierce Yeshua's heart.

"The Mashiach would know from where my power comes. The Promised One knows. And you know. Therefore, you are … you must be the Holy One, Rabbuni," the Tempter said in a slow, icy tone, as if he was unveiling a verbal statue.

Sacred titles sounded filthy issuing from his lips. At this moment, the revelation about Yeshua's destiny was only hours old, a truth he was still absorbing himself.

"You will not address me in that way," Yeshua said. "When it comes from your mouth, it is not to honor the Father but to blaspheme."

Undeterred, the Tempter laughed. "Ah, you do not command me, Nasrene! But tell me: in truth, in your most secret room, is it not blasphemy to be a holy one, crowned with the greatest sacred calling, and yet be possessed—no, *demonized*—with such doubts as twist and torture your mind?"

Yeshua stood up and again nearly lost his balance. The Tempter moved to assist him, but Yeshua recovered himself. A part of him wanted nothing more than to get off that battlement, out of the Tempter's loathsome presence, and get back to his lonely desert, to the place where he was not the Mashiach but simply a thirsty man walking. A nagging pain pierced him, and a crawling darkness seeped into his heart.

How can I be the Mashiach of Israel when my mind is cluttered and confused? Abba, help me!

Yeshua's father had taught him how to build tables, benches, and even houses, not how to be the saving force of Elohim to His people. Yet from his father, Yeshua had also learned that the craftsman had to complete each task of a process in the right order. He or she could not be casual about the proper sequence of the work or the critical time in which to do it. The artisan had to pay attention, being exact in his measurements and cuts, and must understand how much weight the wood could bear. He must examine it and watch out for any cracks or fine splits that indicated its potential weakness under pressure.

In this moment, and in the presence of the Tempter, Yeshua understood the steps through which the Father was leading him, although he was yet uncertain about where those steps were taking him. His memory shot back to the many years when Yosef had hired out his brothers and him to farmers to help bring in the harvest. All able young men of the village did the same. There was a sequence, a combination of waiting and watching until the time was full, until the wheat had ripened and was ready, and the olives and grapes were fat. One had to understand the signs, had to learn when the time was precisely right and know how to reap in order to garner the greatest yield. When he came to the realization that this great calling would be a process that he would learn as he had learned to build, as he had learned to plant and harvest, he understood how even a man like him could be the Anointed, the beloved Son of Elohim.

Ironically, by calling Yeshua the Mashiach, this mocking creature had given him a great gift. In essence, he had driven the inevitable truth of his calling deeper into Yeshua's heart, where he felt pain like a dagger's thrust. But he also felt hope that fired into every muscle in his body. Yeshua knew now that Abba would teach him how to heal and shepherd his flock, just as Yosef had taught him how to understand the strength of the wood and how to build with it.

"Thank you, Abba."

Yeshua was stuck.

The area of the battlement where they stood was small and cut off. Only five or six men could fit on this slice of space, and it was much higher than any other parapets nearby. Yeshua could hardly stand the close presence of the Tempter, yet he knew the jump to escape this creature would certainly kill him.

"I see you are finding this revelation unsettling. I am surprised your *Abba* did not reveal your important burden sooner. And your mother …" The Tempter hesitated as Yeshua's eyes sharpened into a glare at the mention of Eema, his mother.

"You may not speak of her in my presence," he said, barely controlling the rage he felt growing in him.

The Tempter ignored him and continued, smiling. "Because you are aware, of course, that she knew about you before your birth, perhaps even from your conception. So sorry to have to be the one to inform you of this rather intimate deception. No? Difficult news for you to accept, I am sure."

Yeshua felt this creature's unworthiness to mention either the name of his Father in heaven or Eema. She had always been a wise, strong mother, as pure and good to all his brothers and sisters as she was to Yeshua. And they had not even been her natural children. For an instant, all their faces passed before his eyes. These children he had always called brothers and sisters did not share Eema's blood, for she had married Yosef after the death of her cousin, his first wife. Eema's cousin had borne Yosef five children before growing ill and dying suddenly of a feverish infection. Sad to be leaving so many little ones behind, his dying wife had begged Yosef to betroth himself to the future mother of Yeshua. After coming into the carpenter's house, Eema faithfully and lovingly reared all of them, becoming the only mother most of them remembered.

Yeshua felt warmth fill his heart and wash away the last doubt he had about his calling. In a way, the Tempter's revelation had helped him by confirming what he had sensed since childhood. It was true that his mother had withheld his sacred destiny from him, and Yeshua now understood why that was right for her to do. Whatever his mother had done had been for his safety and well-being.

Always.

Nothing could ever dislodge his complete trust in her motives. She had known, as he did now, that he had to learn his Father's calling on his own. No human or angelic one could tell him who he truly was. That revelation belonged to the Father alone.

Nevertheless, with his body weakened from the lack of food and water, and exposure to the wilderness, he sensed it was dangerous for him to be this close to the Tempter. He felt him draining what remained of his physical strength through the lethal ability to sow doubt and fear. Yeshua closed his eyes and opened them, looking down to the hard blackness below. The Tempter followed his gaze.

"Go ahead, jump," the Tempter urged him with a wide smile.

Yeshua looked into his eyes and said nothing.

"It is fine, truly. Throw yourself down. It is the only way out for you. After all, you are the Mashiach. Nothing will happen to your precious body. Your Father is not done using you up yet. However, when he *is* through with you, the Mashiach will become food for the worms, just like everyone else."

The Tempter's voice became smoother, almost purring. "One day, he will spend you completely. He will pour you out like wine from a skin until you are spilt, spread, and absorbed back into the earth." The Tempter lost his smile as he said, "He will snuff out your light … but that day is not today."

He folded his arms again and stared at Yeshua, clearly enjoying himself once more. "Remember the passage from the Torah about you—and be assured, it is about *you*: 'On their hands they will bear you up, so that you will not dash your foot against a stone.'"

The Tempter gestured to the valley below, completing his invitation.

As much as Yeshua was inclined to jump, he knew that if he did, he would fall like any full wineskin thrown from that height and explode his entrails on the pavement below. He knew that if he permitted his personal desire to overcome his faithfulness to the Father's will, his body would be like that flattened wineskin, its life-giving contents leaking back into the earth. Yeshua understood that he could not jump to escape evil, for there are no easy ways out.

Perhaps the Tempter was right, and he would land on a cushion of angels, but even then, he would have vanquished no evil. In fact, he would have enhanced it, for he would have put the Father to the test. Yeshua knew that he needed to stay there with the Tempter, holding the tension of good and evil together, resolving it within himself.

He stood and faced the Tempter defiantly, locking onto his vacant eyes, and he instantly saw the only possible conclusion to this test. By tempting the Mashiach, the Tempter was testing the Father, the great I AM himself. Such a temptation was impossible. Yeshua realized now that the Tempter was pressing *Yeshua* to the limit.

As he watched Yeshua's eyes, the first inkling of doubt crossed the Tempter's own face. Where only a moment ago, he'd seemed to have the upper hand, both of them understood in an instant that everything had changed. The Tempter had lost.

Yeshua said, "It is also written: 'You shall not put I AM to the test!'" He used once again the most sacred and seldom spoken name of the Father.

At the mention of that name, the Tempter's face blanched with fear, his eyes darting about as if he expected some immediate retribution. But in a split second, he regained his composure. In his darkest, most loathsome fury, the Tempter glared at Yeshua, his eyes burning with fire. The Temple briefly shook beneath them. Yeshua sought to keep his balance, but he knew in his heart that no stone of the sanctuary could be overturned unless it was the will of the Father. He watched, alert but unafraid, as the Tempter tried again to ignite fear in him.

It was pointless. The Tempter knew it was over. He could accomplish nothing else there. His eyes became two holes of fire, and then slowly, like lava dripping down from a volcano, his face and body melted, immolating himself like a burnt offering. Yet there was nothing sacred about this fire. It was a gruesome and stinking sight.

Yeshua closed his eyes and reopened them. He now saw only the campfire in the desert with the dove's bones strewn about. It seemed as if he had never left the campsite. In the distance, the first rays of sunlight etched the ridge of the mountains. Today, he would again walk toward them. As the new morning dawned, his body brimmed with an energy he had never before experienced.

In those first hours of light, everything was different, including how he felt about Abba. The knowledge that he was the Mashiach sat heavily upon his shoulders, like a thick wooden beam he once used to support the roof of a new house. He had carried many such beams upon his shoulders before, and he would carry this one, his arms strengthened with the fire of the Ruach Kudsha.

The Tempter had not changed anything. In truth, he could not. Everything he had done had only helped to reveal the Father's will. Yeshua understood the revelation when he surrendered his human will to the Father. All this served to make the burden of the Mashiach much lighter to bear.

He raised his face and smiled as the path to his destiny spread before him. Ignoring the pain in his feet and legs, renewed in spirit, Yeshua began to move toward the mountains with labored steps as a sense of triumph lifted his heart.

Chapter 27

AD 43, and the third year of the reign of the emperor Claudius, Ephesus

The archangel is gone, instantly, without a good-bye.

The temples reemerge in my line of sight. To the Ephesians, they are as sacred as the Great Temple was to the Hebrew people, or Westminster is to the Brits. They are merely different temples with different gods.

I think of the countless skilled and reverent hands throughout the millennia that spent lifetimes of toil on building such holy places—all to help make us feel less alone on our sojourn here as we precariously ride a wobbling, wet rock that spins faithfully through the darkness of space. I'm learning how differently we humans saw the world in this earlier time and place. We did not know that the land belonged to that spinning rock called Earth. We did not know then that Mother Earth was only another planet like Mars and Venus.

That it was perishable and simply another traveler.

Like me.

In the twenty-first century, the names of God have changed, but the longing for him remains in the human heart. It will never leave us, no matter how much we forget about what made us sacred.

Have we permitted the Tempter to plant doubts in us about our Father, our Mother?

And who, or what power, do we mean when we say Father or Mother?

A hand gently takes mine, interrupting me.

"The journey is more difficult going home," Miramee says.

I stand, viewing the great scene of Ephesus for the last time. My eyes will not see it like this again. In my time, all that will remain is pile upon pile of broken stone. The spectacular and grand sight will become a graveyard in a way: broken columns lying like dead trees in a petrified forest. Instead of the vibrant banners snapping in the breeze, the color and sounds of the procession, the aromas from the markets, and exuberance of the people celebrating, there will be tour buses stinking of diesel fuel, bare-legged tourists in shorts and sunglasses pointing cameras at things they don't or can't understand. They'll snap photos of the remnants left behind, of these haunting stone vagrants, and for these visitors, it will be just another site on another tour. At home, they might look at these photos once, as we did. Then they'll put them away in a drawer or close the digital file, sending the remains of the great temples back into darkness again. Closing my eyes on the scene, I turn toward the mountains, the stone house, and my rest.

We make our way back up the road. The uphill hike is more strenuous, which feels good, but the donkey, now laden with our food, brays loudly, annoyed that he has to move against gravity. Miramee doesn't speak until we reach the section of the trail shaded by pine branches. The wind picks up suddenly, and the boughs sway overhead. It blows harder, directly at us, and makes the trudging uphill tougher.

"The rain comes again," she says, and I look at her lovely face. That sentence stays in mind, the lilt and her voice caressing each sound. Then the sky seems to break open, and it begins to pour buckets. Although I'm pulling a reluctant donkey along, although we are facing into the driving, windy rain, there's no other place on earth I'd rather be right now. In the presence of the Holy Beloved, the beating rain is more than bearable.

Even joyful.

We find shelter from the downpour in a tall but shallow cave by the side of the trail. It's large enough to shelter the two of us—as well as a donkey that is happy to take a break. The roar of the wind and the torrents bathing the forest outside bring a strange peace to this moment.

"If you wish, I can speak more of Yeshua," she says. I give her a wet nod, drops falling from my hair and my sprouting beard.

"Often, when we finally discover who we are, it takes some time to believe it," Miramee says as she bundles her mantle tightly around her. "When we first begin to see the truth, there are many false ideas about ourselves that we need to release and let die in us. It is the only way to enter the Kingdom. And Yeshua was learning that he was the way to that Kingdom."

As if in an act of reverence, the rain slows to lighter showers now, and the tree branches no longer sway. It's as if the forest, the rain, and the rocks are waiting. The whole earth is quieting itself to hear the tale of the Holy Beloved.

Chapter 28

Miramee:

As Yeshua walked out onto the plain of sand that extended to the base of the mountains, his mind turned over the amazing revelations of the previous night, ending again and again with the affirmation by the Tempter that he, Yeshua, was the Anointed One, the Mashiach. Yet also within himself he felt another self, a close companion, unknown but sensed since he was a young boy.

Could this part of me be the Mashiach? And if indeed I am the Anointed of Elohim, what am I supposed to do differently?

When Yeshua asked himself this last question, only one answer emerged.

Nothing.

He had to remind himself of a basic fact. Whether he was the Mashiach, the King of Sheba, the beggar on a corner in Nasrath, or a shepherd, he was still walking in the desert. The rest were names with stories to believe in. Stories had power that could rule over men and women. But in this moment, his story was only that of a wandering man.

Yeshua took his thinking to this place: supposing that inside this body, he had a part that could be called the Mashiach. "All right, what if I can do the magic the Tempter says I can do? Suppose that I could cause changes in these stones to make them into bread."

As he asked himself these questions, the aroma of bread suddenly enfolded him as if he were back by the hearth in Eema's house. Before him, he saw hundreds of loaves of freshly baked bread lying on the ground. Immediately, dozens of vultures appeared and began diving for them. The moment before they reached their incredible feast, Yeshua understood that he had manifested this from his thoughts and not from the Father, so he undid it. The bread returned to rock. Confused vultures swung out of their dives and resumed circling overhead.

He did not fully understand the power residing within him, but he knew he would use it only in the moments revealed to him by the Father.

His head ached, and even though it was only midmorning, he was already exhausted. He sank to the earth and sat for a moment in the dust. Looking up, Yeshua watched the vultures move languidly in their flight patterns, catching the wind currents and gliding effortlessly. His momentary miracle with the bread no longer interested them, for they were death's custodians. He envied their freedom, but their freedom was also his.

In an instant, they gathered and drifted away.

Yeshua's spirits lifted as he made himself stand and began to trudge again toward the distant mountains. As he walked, his prayer kept his mind off the pain in his legs and feet. He had little remaining energy to spend on movement.

Even if he was the Mashiach—as unworthy and imperfect as he was—he would give all that he had to the Father. He saw now that he could accomplish the majestic and confounding task of saving his people only by doing the next small thing the Father led him to do, as small as one forward step. Yeshua, and indeed any man or woman, could do that!

By nightfall, he arrived at the base of the final mountain he would climb.

Chapter 29

AD 43, and the third year of the reign of the emperor Claudius, Ephesus

There's a lull in the storm and Miramee stops the story. The rain will ruin the provisions, so we dart out of the cave, making a run for the house, but we feel the first drops of the next torrent. Pushed by a steady southerly wind, the rain soon falls in sheets, the water pounding our faces as we labor up the final hill toward the house. Miramee covers her nose and mouth with the spotted, orange head covering, eyes squinting to see the path, which has taken on the gravelly consistency of liquid concrete as small rivulets of water rush past us.

The dryness of Yeshua's desert has a lot of appeal right now.

My buddy, the donkey, gets spooked by the rain-river and stops as abruptly as the story. He's done; there's no more stomping through the thick mud for him. I try coaxing him, but he doesn't budge. I admit I know nothing about donkeys. There are no gears to shift, batteries to charge, or hard drives to reboot. Forgetting that Miramee is within earshot, I cuss at the damn thing, spraying some water out with the f-bomb.

Miramee stifles a laugh from her linen-covered mouth.

I know. Pretty pathetic.

A grown man who can't get an idiot donkey to move his *ass*.

Literally.

"We will have to carry the provisions to the house," I announce irritably.

Wordlessly and expertly, she takes the reins of the obstinate animal. She puts a hand gently under its jaw as if she is caressing a child's face.

She smiles, and in a moment the donkey takes one tentative step and then another. I scratch my very wet and astonished head.

"Thank you, brother," she says to him, but she doesn't lead him by the tether. Rather, he simply follows her up to the house like a pet poodle. I stand there in soaked amazement, my pride injured. I remember now that she knows how to wrangle any four-legged beast. It was her job in the desert.

With a satisfied smirk on my face, male ego safely intact, I trudge up behind Miramee and her poodle.

After we get all the supplies inside and dry ourselves off, I decide to help Miramee prepare the supper. She looks very uncomfortable as she lays out some pieces of flat bread. In this era, it's an insult to a woman's competence if a man helps in the preparation of a meal. Undeterred by convention, I don't retreat to my seat by the fire, but I keep standing next to her as an idea leaks into my skull. I spy some herbs and the white cheese left by the grateful father. Too bad there won't be any tomatoes here for another eighteen hundred years.

"What is that cheese called?" I ask.

"*Tulum.* From the goatskin in which it is stored," she replies. "It is made from the fattest milk of the goat."

"Do you mind if I try something here?" I say it with no question mark in my voice and without waiting for her consent. She stands away from the small preparation table as I begin to slice the cheese and place it on the flatbread, sprinkling some herbs over the top. There's no need for salt, because the cheese is briny enough.

"Okay, I need to put this in the brick oven over the fire," I say, and she assists with a puzzled smile. We shove the flatbread pieces covered in cheese into the oven. If I can't have pizza, this will do.

"What are you making?" she asks, barely stifling a giggle.

"It's called a *quesadilla*. That is Spanish for *pizza*," I say, not caring what is translated and what is not.

"Kaysa—" she repeats.

"Yes, Kaysa-dee–ya," I say, smiling at her effort to pronounce a word that doesn't exist.

"Kay-sa-dee-ya," she mimics with a laugh. "What was the other word?"

"Pizza."

"Peesa."

"No, but close. Pee-tsa!"

"Pee-tsa! Pizza." She says it perfectly.

I just taught Mary Magdalene how to say *pizza*. Sometimes, life is very cool.

As the baking commences, I take a steaming cup of chicken broth, and we find a comfortable place to sit, enjoying the warmth of the fire. Miramee begins to speak, and I listen to the rain beating against the sturdy stone house. It provides a natural counterpoint to the dramatic, measured music of her speech.

"Like the rain, slowing and strengthening, stopping and starting, so often would Yeshua accept his calling with grace, then doubt it, then learn the patience his doubtfulness taught him. From each of these risings up and fallings back, he would reach a new level of understanding." She moves about, working as she speaks.

These lessons fall from her lips easily, and I sit forward, arms around my knees, completely captivated—like a twelve-year-old. Here's a woman whom Yeshua loved, the Jesus whom billions have worshipped through two millennia of human history. Here is this amazing, important person, eating pizza with *me* and talking lightly about things that popes, emperors, and patriarchs would gladly prostrate themselves before her to learn. And I'm sitting by the warm fire as *comfy as a bug in a rug*, as Mom would say.

Who picked me to listen to her? Here I go again, but seriously, what cosmic lottery ticket did I win?

No answers or downloads come. It's the *why* question, a dead end. I am resigned simply to wonder at the miracle unfolding, and I refocus on the fascinating woman and the beauty of her speech.

Chapter 30

Miramee:

Yeshua dug with his hands at first, then with a sharp stone, clawing away at the mud that lay underneath a patch of plants at the base of a boulder. He created a small pool of water from his digging and let it settle until the water cleared of sediment. Then he drank and filled his waterskin. The grasses fed by this tiny underground stream were edible, but Yeshua had decided to fast until the Father revealed his will and led him away from the wilderness. He drank amply but slowly, not wishing to cramp his stomach. He still felt intense hunger, but he stretched out on his cloak and fell into a deep sleep. His body was exhausted, yet his soul was at peace, for Yeshua had arrived at the mountain to which the Father had called him.

In the morning, refreshed, he climbed the steep trail leading up to the summit. It started, stopped abruptly, and then began again, for animals, not men, had blazed this path. Yeshua scrambled up boulders, and at times his lungs labored painfully to catch a breath. He demanded much from his body, but he did not care; getting to the summit was what mattered. The Father waited for him there.

At the eighth hour, he reached the summit, tired, thirsty, hungry, and grateful that, at last, he was where he was supposed to be. He drank the last drops of water, made a circle of small rocks, and sat in the middle of the circle. There he listened and waited.

He did not sleep.

The stone ring became his sacred fortress, as if it were the protective wall or *temenos* encircling the ruins of the ancient Greek temple near

147

Nasrath. After discovering it in the hills as a boy, he used to play around it with his brothers and sisters.

There in his temenos, the temple of Yeshua's body felt neither hunger nor thirst. He prayed hour after hour as unwelcome thoughts charged into his head like herds of swine. Some were prideful thoughts. In one reverie, he imagined himself as the traditional Mashiach, made to be a king like David and unite his people again into one nation. He might bring back the glory of the Hebrews, driving the Romans and their foreign slaves from the hearths of the Father's chosen ones. Many other ideas invaded his head as if they were trying purposely to reroute his attention to the vanities of the world. At times, his mind jumped on a thought for a ride of fantasy before he caught himself.

His parents, and especially Eema, had taught his brothers and sisters that they were on earth to serve Elohim alone. They were not to expect earthly treasure. Yeshua greatly respected Yosef, because the man understood his wife. Even though Eema loved his father dearly, Elohim was always first in her life. She had absolute faith, and Yeshua had learned that faith from her. She accepted everything that happened. She grieved when people close to their family died, but she never doubted for a moment that the death had occurred at the divinely appointed hour. "Death comes to every one of us in the fullness of time," she always said.

Yet in his experience, her compassion for the suffering of other people was great and all-encompassing, without parallel in their little town or anywhere else.

Yeshua's initial excitement at receiving the revelation from the Father waned as the day stepped into the silence of the night. He grew more fatigued as he sat, and two vultures landed a few paces away from his temenos.

"Sorry, sister birds," he said solemnly from inside the circle. "There is nothing here for your children to eat but skin and bones."

The vultures flew off, and Yeshua marveled at their patience. As the hours of the night passed, he continued to wait and listen, but he heard nothing.

His leg muscles were sore from the climb up the mountain, and numb from the loss of circulation—the result of being crossed on the ground for too long. Yeshua lay down flat on his back, letting all the blood flow evenly again, and he was grateful for the momentary relief. He dozed fitfully as another hour went by. The cramping muscles in his legs continued to wake him. He realized that they hurt not only from the climb but also from the lack of water. He sat up again. He sighed, and his thoughts drifted.

"Why do I have to wait to hear the Father's voice?" The complaint move across his tired mind like a gray wave on the sea.

"Forgive my impatience," he whispered. He held his throbbing head. "Open my ears so I may hear you clearly. Set my feet upon your path, and guide my hands in your service, my beloved Abba!"

Yeshua breathed slowly to calm himself, but his head was hot, and the constricted muscles of his legs ached with pain.

"How can I be a good servant when I do not know when the Father will give me guidance?" he said. "Abba, I thirst!"

From behind him, a flash of brilliant light and the deafening clap of thunder almost threw him out of the circle. Then came another. He saw that in front of him, the night sky was clear and scattered with stars, but when he turned to look behind him, he witnessed the blackness of an enormous thunderhead fomenting directly above him. Yeshua looked up as a few heavy, warm drops of rain bounced off his forehead. Then torrents of water showered him. He opened his mouth and drank the water from the Father in heaven. Soon, pebbles of hail followed and pummeled him. He sought no shelter but accepted the tiny, icy stones. It was strange and miraculous to receive the guidance from the Ruach Kudsha.

Yeshua understood that the Father would care for his body when he needed it.

The rain shower ended, leaving a watery perimeter around the stones of his temenos. He lay down again, this time in warm mud. Slowly his leg muscles relaxed. The sky was brilliant with stars again, and the night air was pungently moist. The water was not only for him but also for the shrubs, the snakes, the scorpions, and the lions.

"Elohim waters us all together," he thought.

Lying in the sandy mud, he quickly fell into a deep sleep.

When Yeshua awoke, he immediately sat up, shivering. It was still night, and he was completely wet and covered in mud. He doubted that anyone would mistake this muddy, emaciated man for a king, much less the long-awaited Mashiach. A flash of memory took him back to his boyhood and a man he had once known, a scribe named Nathaniel from the synagogue in the city of Tzippori.

Nathaniel first told him about the "one like a human." Even as a young boy, when he could sneak away from his work in the fields, Yeshua eagerly set out on the short walk to Tzippori just to speak with Nathaniel. The older man was a welcome change from the narrow-minded elders in Nasrath's synagogue. Yeshua's unspoken but accepted status as a bastard made the men at the synagogue treat him with indifference.

Much larger than Nasrath, Tzippori was an ancient city, destroyed many times and currently rebuilt in the Grecian style. Yeshua liked the bigger city, for it gave him a comfortable anonymity. Nathaniel weighed him by his mind and heart, not by the gossip about his questionable paternity.

Yeshua could walk in the gardens of Torah and be taught without being rejected. Nathaniel was an old man who often made time to speak to the younger men, helping them memorize the *targums*, the short passages of Scripture men could pass by mouth to others who could not read. Some wore the written targums on their body or head to remind themselves and others of Torah in the midst of their daily work.

Yeshua did not wear the Scriptures, because he wore them on the inside. Nathaniel understood this, and thus he gave more time to the boy. Often when Yeshua arrived, Nathaniel would dismiss the others present, ignoring their protests. The old man relished teaching Yeshua the great stories of Eden and the fall, the exodus from Egypt, and the forty years in the desert. He spoke about the great kings: David and his son, the wise Solomon. Yeshua learned about the sadness of exile in Babylon and the people's return to the land of their fathers. Most important of all, he learned the stories of the prophets, and especially Isaiah.

Yeshua remembered the balmy Galilean afternoon when Nathaniel discussed the name "one like a human" as it was used in the book of Daniel. After some bread, dates, and nuts, the scribe took his customary rest. Yeshua felt unsettled and agitated, but he did not know why. He walked all around the quiet city wrapped in its afternoon rest. He passed the great amphitheater and walked through the majestic colonnades of its temples and public buildings. When he returned to the synagogue, Nathaniel looked up at him and beckoned him over.

"I have prayed about this for some time, Yeshua," he said while sipping a small cup of warm wine and water. Yeshua sat at his knee and waited anxiously.

"You know that I have studied the prophets for many years," he said, "and I understand many of the signs and portents that herald the coming of the Holy One, the Mashiach, the one Daniel calls 'the one like a human.'"

Yeshua nodded intently.

"Yeshua, I do not say this lightly or casually, nor will I repeat it or say any more." He looked in from side to side and lowered his voice, speaking slowly and deliberately. "But I believe the name of "one like a human" is for *you*. You came *from* our people, and you came *for* the people Israel."

Nathaniel lowered his head slightly, letting this take hold, watching a quizzical expression flash across the boy's face.

"What are you saying, Rabbuni Nathaniel?" asked Yeshua. "That I am called out to be one of the holy prophets?" He was truly confounded, unable to take Nathaniel's words into his heart.

Nathaniel's expression changed to one of surprise and then resignation. Saying nothing else, he remained silent for a long time. Then he only spoke to teach another segment on temple sacrifice. He never mentioned Yeshua's calling again, silently waving off the boy's questions.

Since that afternoon, Yeshua had often asked himself why Nathaniel had told him such a thing without any further explanation. He did not believe Nathaniel meant to hurt or confuse him. He was a good and kindly man, but his cryptic revelation had caused a puzzling, unsolved riddle to smolder in Yeshua's mind.

As he sat on the mountain summit, staring at the sky and feeling the coolness of the rain but no longer shivering, Yeshua knew now what he could not have known then. The Father had shown Nathaniel the destiny of his student, and the teacher had tried to convey that revelation to the Holy One. By Yeshua's response and his inability to comprehend immediately, Nathaniel saw clearly that Yeshua's time had not yet come.

Even then, upon that mountain, tiny pustules of doubt grew in his weary head. Yeshua blinked into the comforting darkness of the night.

"Doubt has long been my companion, coming and going without notice," he said aloud. "Yet despite its many warnings and concerns, I am still here … waiting."

Exhaustion crept into his bones, and his thoughts wandered. Dark questions persisted, like thieves climbing through the open windows of his mind.

"What if I am not the Son? Perhaps I have gone mad out here."

His head continued to pound. His stomach no longer asked for food, but he felt that at any moment his brain might push right through his skull. Again he lay flat upon the earth, facing the heavens with his arms wide apart, and closed his eyes.

"Abba, what do you want of me?" he shouted out.

There was no response from the silent desert that held him.

Chapter 31

AD 43, and the third year of the reign of the emperor Claudius, Ephesus

Miramee pauses. We've finished our quesadilla/pizza supper, which I must admit was pretty damn good, and the house is now quiet, except for the occasional snap from a burning log. Staring into the flames, I feel the loneliness of Yeshua on that desert mountain. I remember my own impatience and how I've awakened many times, feeling alone and anxious to understand where I fit in. After a moment, Miramee searches my eyes and then narrows her gaze, her face a question mark.

"Miramee, you seem uncertain about something."

She shakes her head. It's amazing how I never tire of looking at her.

"This next part does not belong to my voice. I know the story intimately, but it falls not upon me to tell you of the last test," she says.

"Who then?" I ask.

She pauses for a moment, staring at the fire, and then she inclines her head forward, and closes her eyes briefly. She's got it now.

"The archangel will come again," she says, opening her eyes slowly. "But before he does, know this: Yeshua did not ever doubt the Father. He was tired; his mind had no food and little water to feed it. He was a man like you. His faith remained strong, but his flesh was human, and that is why he grew impatient. The human body faltered, but Yeshua never did, not once. At the last, he knew who he was, and he trusted in the Father."

Okaaay. What's with the disclaimer?

Without another word or even a glance, she rises and walks away, disappearing through her chamber door. I don't want her to leave. Her presence enriches any moment, even the simplest act of eating a first-century quesadilla. As I think this, the room fills with golden light.

"Peace be upon you." The voice of Micha'el fills the air, but as I spin my head around, I notice that the sound is coming from all four corners of the room.

"And also upon you," I respond automatically, marveling again at the miracle of the archangel's radiant presence. This time, I'm not afraid. I look at the fire, and out of the corner of my eye, I see him sitting in Miramee's place. When I turn to face him, he nods. His clothes and skin aren't luminous. He looks like any guy sitting by a fire, a buddy ready for a talk. All we're missing is the Guinness.

The archangel manifests with Nordic features: fair hair and ruddy face with the prominent forehead and angular facial bones of the Vikings. He looks less like the Norse god Thor and more like a soccer player from Stockholm. I smile at my thought, and he does as well. Apparently, at this level of existence—or in this dimension—spoken words are good but unnecessary.

He rises after a long, silent moment.

"I am called to tell you of the last test in the desert." His voice is warm and strong. This time his mouth moves with the words, which makes the conversation feel less like a badly dubbed foreign movie. He chuckles at my thought. Micha'el has a sense of humor.

All at once, as if the inky vapor of the Tempter begins to settle into the room, invading each darkened corner, the atmosphere becomes very solemn and heavy.

"I am ready," I say.

Not really, but jumping in anyway.

Chapter 32

Micha'el, the archangel:

On the mountain, I was near the Holy One called Yeshua as he sat in the circle. He neither saw nor sensed my presence but kept his eyes lowered.

"Abba, I am ready. Be it done unto me according to your will," he said.

Suddenly, there was the smell of smoke and incense burning, and I saw that we were both in a grand palace. From human perception, it was majestic, luxurious, and brightly lit, and gold gleamed off the walls and sconces. Candles and large, intricately ornamented lamps hung from the richly carved and painted ceilings. Yeshua found himself in a great room that led to a large marble terrace. The opening was a series of archways supported by marble pillars in the style of the Greeks, but the polished stone was of every possible earthly color.

From the arches hung long, white, silken curtains that swept elegantly into the room, dancing upon the breeze wafting in from the outside. I could not see beyond the balustrades of the terrace, for the light that poured into the room was blinding white, as if the sun had moved closer to the earth. All around us were urns and baskets filled with every type of blossom and flower imaginable.

Out from the sun-drenched terrace, a silhouetted feminine figure appeared. Yeshua noticed her and invited her to come forward. From the brightness emerged what appeared to be an angel—although, to be clear, *not* an archangel. She was clothed in radiant white robes, her uncovered head revealing a cascade of luxuriant, dark hair, black as a moonless night.

"My heavenly Lord Yeshua," she said as she entered and genuflected with her head bowed low. She looked up at him, smiling, and then rose and graciously took his hand.

"I am not a lord," he said.

"How shall I address you, then?"

"My mother and father named me Yeshua. That will do."

"May I address you as Rabbuni, as Teacher?" she asked with charmingly sweet concern.

"If you wish. By what name are you called?"

"The Angel Nura, Rabbuni." She bowed her head as she answered.

"Angel Nura. What does it mean?"

"In the language of this region, people understand *nura* as *light*," she said, smiling.

Yeshua nodded.

"This is a beautiful place," he said, scanning the room quickly. "Especially as I have been sleeping in the desert."

"We have every type of bloom from the earth, all the loveliness of creation just for you," Angel Nura said, "but your human body is in need of nourishment and drink. We have prepared a refreshment for you."

She took a handbell and rang it. It emitted a warm, pure tone.

"What do you call this place?" Yeshua asked, watching her closely as she moved about gracefully. She bowed again and smiled.

"This is a respite from your arduous journey, a way station where you can regain your strength before going on to your great calling."

There was a long silence as Yeshua looked around. I followed his gaze too, wondering what he was thinking.

"You were asleep. Now you are awake," she added, bowing slightly. "You are the king of Israel, Yeshua. The great king!"

A man wearing the short *chiton* entered, carrying a golden chalice and a diamond-encrusted decanter. He was dark-eyed, lean, and muscular, and he moved with the athletic grace of a marathon runner. He set the chalice on the small table and poured the deep-red wine into it.

"You must be thirsty," Angel Nura said, offering the golden chalice to Yeshua. "Permit me, Rabbuni."

He held up his hand and declined it.

"Many thanks, but after my time in the desert, my body still needs water." He smiled as he took a gulp from his own waterskin. Wiping his mouth, he asked, "You say this is my home?"

She laughed, "You are in your kingdom! You are the *Kristos*, the Anointed of him who sent you!"

I found it odd that she used the Greek word rather than the Aramaic, his language. What was she up to?

"But there is more, Rabbuni. Come out to the terrace, for I have something to show you!" Angel Nura opened the silk curtains that partially obscured the view.

Still invisible, I followed them onto the terrace. The brilliant light abated, and suddenly a panoramic vista came into sharp focus.

"Behold your home, Rabbuni," she said.

Circling the terrace as far as the horizon in each direction, the great cities and civilizations lay, grouped tightly together from different times and places. There were pyramids, the legendary library of Alexandria, magnificent Grecian and Hindi temples, the Great Wall weaving its way through the high country of China's north, the white frozen mountains of Antarctica, a cascading waterfall in the lush Amazon rainforest, the Temple of Diana, and the Colosseum of Rome. In the region to the farthest left, I saw an incongruent image, the shadowy outline of what appeared to be the New York skyline in silhouette. Like two fingers pointing to heaven, there were the twin towers of the World Trade Center.

In the vision, we saw millions and millions of people with every color of skin and of every age, wearing every type of clothing, riding on every kind of conveyance, speaking every language known in the world. It was an astonishing spectacle.

Yeshua stepped back slightly, for it was almost too much for human eyes to behold in one moment. He then stepped forward again and nodded approvingly.

"It is truly an unimaginable sight you lay before me, Angel Nura," he said.

She smiled and nodded. "It is all here for you to rule as the King of Kings!"

"It is true that my time has come."

"We are filled with joy that it has."

When she uttered that sentence, I sensed that this creature did not know joy, would not know anything like joy.

"People need your leadership, Rabbuni," she said. "Look at the disarray the world is in. Rome holds the entire Mediterranean hostage to their abominations, their cruel hands meting out horrible suffering. If they were not here, there would be conquerors like the Assyrians, or if not them, some others—always others. And even some others that we cannot yet name." She then gestured to the parts of the panorama that reflected the world of your time, Traveler.

Yeshua watched her as she paced back and forth.

She was right about the horrible state of the world, and there was so much grief and injustice yet to come with the Tempter's full support and helping hand.

"You can change it all forever," she said, her voice a purring entreaty. "We know who you are, and we understand your true power."

Yeshua looked at her, his hands clasped in front of him. "And in truth, I know you too, Nura. We have met before, many times."

This was the Tempter wearing another disguise, but it failed to deceive Yeshua. Nura shot an irritated look at him, but after a long moment, she bowed her head and continued as if he had said nothing.

"You can see the state of affairs, but you are the chosen one who can help straighten this world out now and for all time to come. It could be the Kingdom of which you speak!"

Yeshua remained unmoved.

"You are strong!" Nura continued. "Moreover, I know from my tests that you are not easily tempted. You think clearly and fairly. A great woman raised you to be a good and strong leader. The one you call Abba and I are in agreement on that single point: you are the best suited to heal this broken world."

Yeshua kept his silence.

A vulture slowly circled the terrace before landing on the railing near the manservant who had come out to wait upon Nura. He glowered at the vulture. With that expression, I suddenly was aware that the manservant was also a disguised fallen angel known as Ose, Lord of Hell and the Tempter's second-in-command. I knew the vulture as well; he was Azra'el, the archangel of death. He was there to remind Yeshua that all is passing in this world, and the promise of permanent earthly power by force is a devilish illusion.

Yet Yeshua did not seem to be aware of Azra'el. Hunger and fatigue had weakened his body. Nura was the Tempter, and as much as I wanted to intervene, Yeshua had to reject the Tempter unequivocally on his own. Until that time, I was commanded to wait. I could do nothing, for the test was between Yeshua and I AM. Even the Tempter had little to do with what was happening. That it should be between Father and Son may confuse you, but all had been designed and set into motion before time began.

I was present in the event that the physical person of the Holy One was in danger. Numberless angels—what humans would call an army—awaited my command.

"Rabbuni," Nura purred, encouraged by Yeshua's silence, "if you wait for all this to be accomplished without having access to the power I possess, the wait is going to take an eternity. These humans are so out of touch with who they are, they fall into violence and treachery at the first sign of conflict or affliction."

"You mistake the sheep for the wrong-headed shepherds who guide their sheep astray," Yeshua replied.

"You could help your sheep get their lives back on the right path, the chosen way, if you ruled them as king," she replied.

"I am only a shepherd," he said.

"Shepherds are not kings," Nura said.

"David, my father, was both shepherd and king," Yeshua answered.

Nura nodded. "But you are the one who was foretold. You are a king first," she said, "and these are your kingdoms! And this would be accomplished with no spillage of blood."

Yeshua bowed his head in a prayerful silence that broke the rhythm of Nura's entreaties. She began to pace restlessly. For some interminable moments, we all stood looking at Yeshua, wondering what he was thinking and what he would do next.

"All that you see can be changed by you, Rabbuni. All you need to do is quickly drop down on one knee before me and swear your allegiance. It will seal our covenant, our pact of mutual respect and cooperation, and the healing can begin."

She pointed to the ground, gesturing for Yeshua to kneel before her.

Yeshua remained silent.

One thing was clear: in the unlikely event that Yeshua paid homage to the Tempter disguised as Nura, Yeshua would be disposed of immediately, like rubbish to be burned. He would be of no further use to the Tempter or anyone else, and I could do nothing about it. Like a violent and unmoving but fully sensed wind, I felt the mighty tension between heaven and earth as his silence drew on. I would not be concerned about Yeshua paying homage, but I knew how weakened his body was. I left the terrace for another vantage point.

Yeshua then turned to face the Tempter, and slowly a smile crept across his face. He laughed. "You are clever and persistent in whatever guise you choose," he said, raising his hand and pointing heavenward. "But did you really expect the 'one like a human' to be distracted from his Father's path by a false display of earthly power and pain?"

Nura frowned.

From my vantage point, I saw the illusion as Yeshua must have seen it. With that voiced rejection, I took my flaming sword and cut through the fabric of Nura's illusion. The views of all the kingdoms of the world were divided, flopping down and smoldering as if they were part of a painted canvas. The sword was aflame, and it cut so wide a swath that Yeshua could see the desert night and the view of the valley from the mountaintop where he had sat in his sacred circle.

"Micha'el! You vile—!" The Tempter shouted as if she was going to burst into flames herself.

The Holy One smiled weakly.

"You think this is a game, Rabbuni?" she shrieked. "Do you know what you are turning away from? Have you lost the courage to do what is right? Be the man your mother raised you to be. Be the Mashiach of Israel. This is your chance. Kneel! Kneel, and the world will be given to you! Now!"

I could sense that the force beneath the Tempter's words was gone. The flaming sword had cut through the illusion, but Yeshua had already seen through it from the start. He needed no rescuing. He knew the Kingdom would not come through the Tempter's illusion of earthly power but solely from the hand of I AM. There are no shorter paths. There are no faster or easier ways than the way revealed by I AM through the Ruach Kudsha.

"The children will never be healed through a covenant with evil," Yeshua said. "The saving mission will have little to do with kingships and titles and palaces. It will come from the roads, the wells, the camps, and the village houses, from countless points as yet unseen and from generations yet unborn. I am here to show the way, to be the Way."

The Tempter's eyes shifted from false friendship to fear to rage.

"Leave me now, Satan, for it is written, 'Worship Elohim and serve him only!'" Yeshua said in a commanding voice.

She closed her eyes in furious frustration. "You just made the biggest mistake of your insignificant life!" the Tempter roared, the beautiful voice of Nura now gone. "You will live to regret this day, and I will be there to see it!"

Yeshua raised his arm and pointed straight to his left.

"Be gone!" he commanded in a thunderous voice.

Cadenced, drumming sounds caused the furniture to turn over and one of the great hanging lamps to crash to the floor.

The faces of Nura and the manservant, Ose, contorted in fear as my hosts of angels appeared, approaching the terrace. A blinding, hot rush of air swept into the entire scene, and Yeshua covered his human eyes.

When he lowered his hands, he had returned to the mountaintop. He was alone in the mud and surrounded by his *temenos* of stones.

Chapter 33

AD 43, and the third year of the reign of the emperor Claudius, Ephesus

My sleepy eyes open to the unblinking stare of a cat that sits just a forearm's distance from my face. He is large with a grey, longhaired coat. He twists his head to the left in feline curiosity, wondering what in blazes I'm doing here.

"Hello, cat," I say, reaching out to him. He jumps back and away from my hand, emitting a loud hiss.

"Petros!" Miramee exclaims as she walks out of her chamber. The cat bounds toward her, and she leans over and sweeps him up in her arms.

"Where have you been? I have not seen you for so long!" she coos.

"I didn't know you had a cat," I say, rubbing my eyes as I sit and pull up the blanket over my bare chest. I can see from the right window and the absence of sunlight on the floor that it's midday. I blink hard, trying to get my bearings.

"This is Petros," Miramee says, nuzzling the gray ball of fur. "Our friend affectionately named him after Kefah, who is known as *Petros* in Ephesus and the Hellenes. She called him that name because he is strong but a little hardheaded, like a rock! He ran into the forest the day our friend left us."

"He has been out there all this time?" I ask through a yawn, rubbing my eyes.

"Yes, but he is very strong and smart. I knew he was safe. Our friend loved him very much, and Johanan permitted him indoors, even though he had difficulty breathing with cats around. He loved our friend and could deny her nothing."

162

Instead of her usual flitting around the kitchen and fire to make a meal, Miramee sits down. She is wearing a pale-blue, loose-fitting tunic or gown that reminds me of the kaftans women wore in the seventies and eighties. She takes Petros into her lap, replacing her blanket. She gently strokes the cat's fur and seems quietly content.

"Petros's coming home makes me feel as if our friend is here with us right now," Miramee says dreamily. "I do miss her very much."

A cat cannot shift my mood so easily. The images Micha'el gave me reach down and eat away at my gut. The impressions of the Devil so sweetly manifested, of evil deceptively posing as innocence and good intentions, writhe like a devouring snake inside of me. I have seen it in the world myself. It moves about and self-righteously destroys whomever and whatever it wants in the name of the "greater good" or in the name of God or Allah. Yet the Tempter became frustrated, and Yeshua finally stretched out his arm, banishing evil. This all boils up tumultuously within me, starkly contrasting the sight of a happy woman petting her returned cat.

Still, there's something very alluring and lovely in watching Miramee sit there in her comfortable gown, her hair in tangled tresses falling down upon her shoulders, her long, elegant fingers stroking the cat. I feel my breath shorten, and I catch myself. I make a focused effort to change my thoughts and stare again at the embers in the hearth. I distract myself by putting on some logs and stoking the flames.

The cat purrs in her lap, and the first sliver of afternoon sun spills onto the stone sill of the window.

"Yeshua knew," she says evenly. "All the doubts ceased in his mind." She looks down at her hand as she continues the gentle and loving strokes.

"It must be unbearable not to see him," I say absently, feeling her emptiness at the loss of Yeshua's physical presence.

"At first, after he left, all I did was weep," she says as her eyes moisten. "Even now I think of him and the feeling of his hands as I applied the oil, and the tears come again."

Her voice thickens, and she returns her gaze to the cat. She brushes her cheeks self-consciously with the backs of her fingers. She sniffs as I hand her a small towel.

"Thank you," she says with a smile as she wipes her face and eyes. "And now you shall hear how he began all that came afterward."

Chapter 34

Miramee:

For three days after his final encounter with the Tempter, Yeshua sat in the circle and prayed. He did not sleep. He drank no water. He simply waited for Elohim to send him guidance about what he was to do next. As I said, he knew who he was now, and he was ready to commence his work as guided by the Father through the Ruach Kudsha.

On the evening of the third day, just as the sun was setting and the moon was beginning to rise on the eastern horizon, a white bird came to land on the boulder just a few steps from the sacred circle. It fluttered its wings, and Yeshua heard a voice as the wings moved the air toward him.

"Go now, Shepherd of my flock," said the voice. "Feed my sheep."

Yeshua sat in total peace. The wings fluttered again.

"Go now, Shepherd of my flock," the voice repeated. "Lead my sheep."

Yeshua lifted his eyes to the crimson-streaked sky. The wings beat once more.

"Go now, Shepherd of my flock," the voice said finally. "Feed my lambs." Yeshua inclined his head forward three times, closing his eyes briefly as an affirmation; each was a pronounced and slow bow from the neck. He could accept his calling if the lambs of the world—the very young and very old, the sick, the poor, and the powerless—were the last and, therefore, most important part of his saving mission.

The bird shot down the mountain toward the caravan trail at the base. In one direction, the road would return him to the Galilean Sea, and the other led to Philadelphia by way of the Nabataean's water camp.

Yeshua stood and began to descend the mountain in the waning light. He did not realize how weak he had become, but because the Father had sent him forth, he trusted his body's safety to him. On a steep section of the path, the gravelly dirt tripped him, and he slid on his side for the distance of a man's height. With his arm cut and bleeding, he struggled to his feet, regained an unsteady foothold, and edged downhill, determined not to rest until he returned to his native soil.

An exposed root tripped him again, and he fell facedown, skinning his knees and palms badly. Oddly enough, he felt no pain. He felt warm blood trickling off his jaw, and he realized he had sliced his right cheek on the thorny bush he'd fallen upon. He was exhausted and starved, and his mind seemed to go in and out of consciousness. He moved slowly in the darkness and managed to get near the base of the mountain before dawn. As the first rays of light illumined the starry sky, he could see that the road was very close now. Soon he would walk upon the flat land again, on the wide road to Galilee.

"I am almost there, Abba."

No sooner had he spoken those words than he passed out. His unconscious body rolled down the slope and over brambles and stones until he came to rest right beside the road.

You will now see and wait with him, Traveler.

Prepare!

Chapter 35

AD 27, and the fourteenth year of the reign of the emperor Tiberius, Jordanian Desert

No emotion or passion inflects Miramee's powerful final sentence. It's as if she was telling me that supper was ready. It was so matter-of-fact that I don't understand at all.

I will see and wait with him.

See him? See who?

Prepare? For what?

My mind doesn't let me go there yet, but deep inside, I know. Traveler understands exactly what she means and *whom* she is talking about. As this finally seeps into my awareness, a chill shoots through me as fast as the messenger bird darting down the mountain.

I'm not ready for this encounter.

Never did I wish to be at a conference in San Jose more than now. I'd be in control there, doing the talking with others listening to me, the master instead of the student. Yet here I am, so not-in-control that it boggles the mind. But I am in wonder. And with me, wonder is winning!

I draw in a breath, bulk up all my courage, and nod slowly at the pretty woman calmly holding a cat by the fire.

It's dawn, and I'm now in a desert. Cat, fire, Miramee, and house all vanish in an instant.

No downloads yet.

The moon is still full and present in the brightening sky. I sense the dampness in the air and savor the smell of the desert after a rain. The few thorn bushes and shrubs that stubbornly cling to the gravelly hillside give up a wet fragrance, an aromatic alleluia to the heavens for this gift of water. It's similar to the California desert, but there's a different quality to it. The rocks and plants tell me I'm somewhere unfamiliar, still on my voyage of discovery but on a new ocean—this one of sand.

Without fully acknowledging it, I know where Miramee has sent me and who is here. Like a child overwhelmed by excitement, I look all around, but not at what is right in front of me. It's too much to handle. But I feel his presence. Tears unexpectedly spring from my eyes, for I know whom I am going to see next, and my brain comes up with a hundred reasons to ask Miramee to take me back to the fire and the cat.

I'm not ready. But she wouldn't have sent me here until the time was right. With him, with Yeshua, it has to be perfectly right.

Questions boiling over in my brain, I stand still, unable to move. I look anywhere but right in front of me, where I know I should look. I can't face the reality of it until I hear a man's groan—a sudden, very human sound of distress. The rescuer instinct takes charge, and I immediately look down. About ten feet away lies the filthy, limp, and bleeding body of a man lying spread eagle in the dirt.

My heart is racing as I move a little closer to the man. It's perfectly still here, as quiet as a tomb. Yet my ears buzz with a silence so loud I can't hear anything. He's lying on his stomach with the left side of his face in the dirt. His head is covered by the dirty keffiyeh except for a small part of his bearded jaw and his neck.

"Wait with him." I hear Micha'el's voice.

When I look up, I see Micha'el and three other archangels surrounding us, each standing and facing outward—north, south, east, and west—like luminous guards keeping their watch. I think I'll choke, for I stop breathing at the sight. I sit in the dirt beside his body, which is covered with a bloodstained mantle. The other archangels turn and see Micha'el nod at me, so I proceed. I sit down by him and take his keffiyeh to cover the rest of his face and neck. The sun will come out with a searing vengeance in an hour or two. I see the deep scratch on his right cheek—just as Miramee described it. It will heal into the scar that he'll carry for the rest of his days. I have never thought of Yeshua as having scars. The holy pictures always show a glowing, baby-smooth complexion. There's nothing baby-like about this man, and he's in a world of hurt. As I sit, I feel my right arm lift as I gingerly place a hand on the bloody cloak covering his back. There's a tingling sensation, like a very light, very subtle electrical current flowing up my arm.

As the sun rises, the archangels don't move, and neither do I. We all wait with Yeshua for the Samaritan to come.

For two days, we stay there at the base of the mountain. During those two days, I don't sleep, nor am I hungry or thirsty. My body asks nothing of me except to stay and wait with him.

Who gives me this honor?

No answer is needed. I only know that whether this is a dream or I'm some kind of cosmic time traveler, I'm kneeling here in a desert twenty centuries before my birth with the Mashiach, the Holy One of God, and the great Redeemer of the world: Jesus.

But at this moment, he's only an injured, sleeping man with whom I must sit. A hurting man upon whose back I am able to place my imperfect but very human hand, letting him know—in a way that an archangel cannot—that he is not alone.

Chapter 36

AD 38, and the second year of the reign of the emperor Caligula, Desert oasis camp

In the dark of a moonless night, I sit all alone on a bench looking out at the oasis lake. I am panting as if I've just scaled a peak. I stare at the water reflecting the nothingness of the black sky, and I shut my eyes for an instant as my breathing slows.

I know now how it feels to touch Yeshua.

I know where I am, and for once, I don't care how I arrived here, or why. My awesome, direct experience with Yeshua lingers and wades into my cell tissue like that subtle electrical current.

How am I supposed to go back and write crop insurance policies after this? I can't even move right now.

"My son, may I sit beside you?" A woman's voice snaps me into the present. I see that it's Havalah.

I manage a weak smile and pat the place next to me on the bench. The wood feels cool, polished, and smooth, as if it has just been finished that day. Havalah plops down and takes my hand affectionately, as if she senses my bewilderment. She looks up at the fronds of the palm barely swaying in the night breeze. I get it then.

"You poured the water and his blood upon this tree. True?" I ask, already knowing the answer.

"It was green and a hand's width taller the next morning," she replies. "I knew something was strange about him, but I sensed something wonderful as well." She speaks without taking her eyes from the fronds gently brushing one another like two sisters slowly combing each other's hair. Then her eyes return to mine, and with a sad smile, she says, "She could not tell you the next part of the story."

"I have already heard about how they met at the encampment at the oasis," I say as I clear my throat.

"No. She cannot speak of when he left her," Havalah says with a slight smile as my eyes adjust to the ambient light. The stars seem brighter now.

Havalah may be older, but she remembers what longing feels like, and she is well acquainted with the passions of youth. In the warmth of the desert night with the unseen rustlings in the surrounding plants, the interlacing fronds, and the smoky fragrance of the campfires nearby, we both turn our gaze upon the perfectly still surface of the lake: a mysterious, dark mirror reflecting heaven.

Chapter 37

Havalah:

He stayed with us longer than I thought he would.

I had decided that Yeshua was a restless type, a wanderer, a "man with an itchy foot," as my grandmother would say. He stayed three weeks after I took him out of the sick tent and put him into a tent with my boy Israel. I think Miramee would have preferred that he stay with her, but I would have none of that. I run a respectable camp. He worked hard: pruning trees, harvesting dates, and even building furniture when he could find enough wood.

After he made her this bench, she sat with him, and they talked together the entire time, night and day. When anyone approached, they stopped or lowered their voices. They were falling in love, yet he was a different type to fall in love with. He had an unusual quality about him. Even though he was always respectful, friendly, and cheerful, he was … apart from us. He required large amounts of time in solitude.

"He goes off to pray," Miramee would say.

We received word from the Samaritan that he would arrive the following day on his return trip to Galilee and Samaria. My intuition told me that Yeshua was about to take off again on his own into the wilderness. It was not anything he said, exactly, but I have seen enough men to know when they are about to leave. There was a difference in his manner, and he spent more time alone. He was restless and distracted, as if something called him away. Miramee did not sense it, because she could not bring herself to do so. She was too deeply in love.

When I heard that the Samaritan was coming, I took Yeshua aside.

"Your benefactor is returning to pay for your care," I said.

"The Samaritan?" he asked.

"How many benefactors do you have?" I answered.

He smiled at me. He enjoyed that I wasted no words.

"I want to thank the man who delivered me."

"I think you should go back to Galilee with his caravan," I said. "It is safer than the way you came through the desert."

He paused and thought quite a while. Impatient by nature, I got restless standing there, but I wanted an answer, and I was not leaving without it. Obviously, his friendship with Miramee weighed heavily in his response. When he coughed, I knew his throat was tightening up with anguish. Closing his eyes for a moment, he opened them sharply and suddenly. He cleared his throat.

"Yes" was all he said, and then he turned to go.

As he walked away from me, he glanced back and thanked me, but he was unhappy about his decision. I stood there dumbfounded. No man around here does anything I suggest without arguing with me. I put my hand to the side of my head because it began to ache.

Oh my! What am I going to do with Miramee once he tells her?

The day before the Samaritan's caravan arrived, Yeshua took Miramee for a walk by the pond. I saw them sitting on the bench, talking and then not talking. They simply stared out at the surface of the pond together for a long time. She later told me that he was expecting to see her again, but he did not know when. His life belonged to Elohim. I remember giving her hand an affectionate pat. I had heard all the excuses of a man, but this one was unique. With that, I gave up on him as the man for Miramee.

The Samaritan arrived, jovial as usual. He was very happy to hear of Yeshua's recovery and paid the fee without question. He also agreed to take Yeshua as far as the Jordan.

"We still have the donkey you rode into this camp," he told Yeshua good-naturedly. The Samaritan was unfailingly likeable. Miramee was devastated. She even dared to ask Yeshua to let her go with him.

"It is not yet the hour for us to walk together, but the hour will come in the fullness of time. Trust Abba, Miramee," he said, and I saw his eyes well up.

They looked as if they would stand there together forever, so I went over and took her arm. If he shed a single tear, then she wept the summer rain down. He rode off on the humble donkey to the sound of her sobs. Miramee was inconsolable. She could not pull herself together. She stayed in her tent for a week and did not come out. I brought her food and felt terrible. I suppose I wished he had not left as well. He was … wonderful. Nevertheless, I was convinced he would have left somehow, sooner or later. At least he would arrive back in his country alive.

And she could not have gone with him. It was clear that he did not have two shekels to rub together. At least the Nabataean had a water camp, a thriving business to support a wife and children. This Yeshua was a wanderer—a beautiful, deep, and achingly mysterious wanderer—but he was clearly not made to be a husband. I thought then that she would just have to cry it out. The heart would mend. It's a very strong muscle.

When she emerged from the tent, she came out with a plan. She did not share it with me then, but Miramee could not forget the man from Galilee, and she was determined to find him again.

Two weeks after he left, another caravan arrived from the west. The leader, who knew the Samaritan, said that he and his cargo had made it safely to the Jordan. He spoke of a wonder-worker and of the Immerser, but at the time, I did not know about whom he was talking.

Miramee did, but she kept her silence.

PART III

In the Beginning

If you were faced with Him in all His glory,
What would you ask
If you had just one question?

—Eric Bazilian, *One of Us* (1995)

Chapter 38

AD 29, and the sixteenth year of the reign of the emperor Tiberius, Machaerus

"Shit!"

I gag and put my forearm over my nose and mouth.

I'm back in that hellhole of a prison cell.

Strains of tinny music mince above me, and the revelers' shouting seems to grow more brazen as the night wears on.

The wild man remains in the corner, sitting with his back against the bars, barely visible in the faint light. A few torches are stuck into the crude metal brackets wedged into the seeping walls. These serve only to make the miserable place hotter, more humid and fetid. Essentially, it's an outhouse/steam room combo. My gag reflex triggers again, but I hold back the vomit this time. I will do that only once to this pitiful man.

I still wear the Jordanian desert clothing, which is stifling in this place. I remove my mantle and squat down to maintain balance on the moist and slippery stone floor.

"I may not see him again with these eyes, but I will tell you of the last things said."

The Immerser doesn't greet me. I settle from my squat into a sitting position in the now familiar straw pile I made on my previous visit.

I've no idea how much ancient mold and unseen contagion I'm taking into my lungs, but I refocus, determined to stuff those thoughts down. The angel protects ...

He begins, and in my relieved mind's eye, I can join him at the river.

Chapter 39

The Immerser:

There are times when we sense that we are speaking to a person for the last time. I felt it at the river that day as I stood in the shallows, as was my custom. Ah, I can still feel my nose and lungs filling with the fresh air of the wilderness and the water!

As if out of nowhere, Yeshua stood on the bank. He waded out and stopped to face me.

"I gave you up for dead," I said.

"One day this body will change, but only at the time the Father ordains, and not a moment earlier or later," Yeshua replied. "Until then, I remain a breathing servant like you."

"We serve Elohim in different ways," I said, "and I know that my service in the river nears its end."

Yeshua's eyebrows rose slightly. "I need your wisdom, Immerser. How can your service be finished?"

"I am the voice crying in the wilderness: 'Prepare the way of the Mashiach,'" I said with a smile. "Are you he, kinsman? Are you the Anointed of Elohim?"

Yeshua was silent but held my gaze.

"You may be the Holy One, but Elohim has not revealed this truth to me yet. I pray for the revelation."

"All revelation comes in the fullness of time," Yeshua said.

"Yes, I understand. You cannot tell me. The words once spoken create the possibility of their opposite meaning. If you say, 'I am he,' instantly there arises the possibility of the opposite: 'I am not he.'"

178

"Words can be dangerous, for they are only sounds that point," Yeshua said. "People imbue them with a meaning within themselves. They point to the truth but are not the truth themselves, nor can words alone encircle all that is the truth."

"The silent and speaking being of the Mashiach conveys the truth," I said.

"The Mashiach *is* the truth," Yeshua replied.

We had said enough. Our time in one another's presence was complete.

"I will be listening with interest for news of you, Yeshua," I said, gripping his shoulder. "Until our paths cross again, in this body or in spirit, his blessing and peace be upon you, brother."

Yeshua gripped my arm in farewell. "And peace be upon you, Johanan. Amen."

He turned and waded back to the riverbank, and that was the last time I saw him.

I nursed the thought that I was the herald of the Mashiach, but Elohim had left me uncertain if Yeshua was the Holy One. I proclaimed my whole life, yet Elohim chose to withhold this knowledge from me. The prophet Isaiah told us that the ways of Elohim are not the ways of men.

As this complaint flowed away from my self-centered mind, I moved toward the next man, a timid pilgrim who knelt in ankle-high water. Lifting my shell full of water, I poured it over his head as Yeshua crossed the river upstream to begin his journey back to the Galilean Sea.

Each to their own way, I thought as the last drops fell from the shell's lip.

When I rested that afternoon, a pilgrim came into camp and told us that Yeshua, treading the path along the river to the Sea of Galilee, had joined a band of travelers returning to Capernaum.

I wondered what destiny awaited him on those shores.

Chapter 40

AD 29, and the sixteenth year of the reign of the emperor Tiberius, Machaerus

I come back from my imagination to the dank reality of the dungeon. Reflexively, I cover my nose and mouth.

"I am sorry you must keep returning here, my friend," the Immerser says sadly.

His words stab my conscience, and I feel small and American-spoiled about my own temporary discomfort. I'm in the presence of the actual wilderness prophet. I have to spend only a few minutes in this stench and squalor, and he has been forced to live out his final days here.

The Immerser hacks into another coughing spasm, interrupting my realization that God goes pretty tough on his friends. Adding to this sonata of suffering, the groans of the other prisoners combine with the odd congruence of joyful shouting from Herod Antipater's drunken guests above.

"The king's birthday celebration," the Immerser explains. "One of the guards assigned to me is up there right now, standing watch at the feast. That guard is a nice enough fellow. He is a seeker and good company. We have many comforting discussions."

The humility of this man overwhelms me. There is a long silence as I wait to see if something will zap me out of here. I stay put. I must not be finished here.

I look at the Immerser and try to convey my great respect.

"You know, my grandfather was named after you. His name was Juan Bautista. That's Spanish for, uh, John the Baptist." I pause for a beat, realizing that this conversation is getting dumber by the second. "You see, Spanish is a language from the time I live in. We mostly speak English now, but before it became America, many people spoke Spanish …"

My speech slows to an awkward stop as the Immerser regards me kindly, like a grandfather listening to a toddler mumbling pure gibberish.

He, of course, hasn't a clue what a *Juan Bautista* is—or what Spanish is, for that matter. He has never heard the words "John the Baptist" or any version of that name in any language.

Upstairs, the music beats faster, and the shouting grows louder.

"It is time for you to return to a more peaceful place," the Immerser says gently.

"I am very sorry for your being in this prison, Rabbi."

"Oh, Herod Antipater will free me eventually," he says as if to make me feel better. "He likes to come down and visit with me from time to time. He has the beginnings of faith, and we should never give up on one another, especially those who are easiest for us to discard or judge as hopeless. Only Elohim knows the heart. We cannot."

"Yes," I say, but I doubt that there's little faith stirring within the heart of someone who can keep people in a place like this. I can't tell him what Herod Antipater has in store for him—not that I would. According to the rules, he couldn't even hear me if I tried, yet I long to do something, to make it *not* happen somehow, but there's no changing the shape of the past. No matter how many times I walk, sit, and talk with these holy ones, I am no actor on this stage, so I must resign myself to the role of spectator, of someone who can't do any good for these people, or return anything for the abundant gifts they give me.

"Go in peace and serve Elohim. That gift remains yours to give," the Immerser says as if I'd voiced my thoughts.

"I will," I assure him, mustering a smile through my frustration.

The room begins to darken even more, which is difficult to imagine. As I transition into Ephesus again, I hear a fading voice, someone from upstairs, shouting, "And now the daughter of the queen will dance for the king. Enter now, the noble Salome!"

Oh, God.

It's her.

It's tonight.

Damn.

My heart freezes faster than a Sierra mountain pond in winter.

Chapter 41

AD 43, and the third year of the reign of the emperor Claudius, Ephesus

As if lead weights have dropped onto my shoulders, a heavy realization bears down on me, the realization that the Immerser and I have been sharing his final hours.

Yet it's now some fourteen years later.

Shaking my head to clear it, I refocus on Miramee, content to be resting again on my mat by the fire. It's nighttime, though it's not yet late.

She sits, quiet and composed, in her usual spot with Petros nestled in her lap, his feline eyes pinning me suspiciously, unsure whether this human who can pop in and out of the room suddenly is safe enough company for his mistress. Miramee remains silent for what must be three minutes by my reckoning. I've learned not to initiate the conversation; it must always come first from her—from all of them, really. Here, I'm the student, and I understand my place. She appears to be mentally deliberating something. I've seen her face through many conversations, and by now she's becoming familiar.

"It is time," she says finally. "There is no one else who can tell you the next part except him."

Except who? Now what?

"Listen carefully to me, Traveler. Listen with all your heart," Miramee says with her eyes tearing up.

What is going on here? Why are their tears? What does she have planned for me now?

"Every word from his mouth, every movement, every silence has meaning. You must pay very close attention. You cannot be distracted," she says, her voice breaking.

She's having difficulty maintaining her composure, and she wavers. I fear she is going to go into an epileptic fit, but she steadies herself and stares at me. The lovely face, the beatific features change into a focused intensity, as if she has become a laser boring right through me.

Now I know she is telling me that I'm going to *him*, and my stomach seizes and churns nervously.

"And do *not* be afraid!" she says, reading me clearly as the room darkens around me.

Chapter 42

AD 30, and the seventeenth year of the reign of the emperor Tiberius, an orchard very near to Jerusalem

The hazy sunlight of late afternoon slants through the olive tree branches, dappling an orchard's path with the play of shadow and light.

What is this place? I have seen this stand of trees before, but I receive no download. I start to walk up the path. It is about four feet wide, and it climbs steeply through the grove. Judging by the short, bright green and unbarbered grass under the trees, it must be early spring or perhaps late winter. I troop to the top of the rise, which reveals suddenly and magnificently the thick fortress walls of Jerusalem.

The pinnacle of the Temple sanctuary rises like a rocket above them. The sun's retiring rays shade in gold the ancient stone walls, yet the sky remains a deep azure. The panorama is so moving, I gasp aloud. This is not the fought-over city of late twentieth-century Israel. Spreading out before me is the great capital, the very seat of God, the last city in which Yeshua will walk, and through its gates, he will carry his cross.

Then I remember the one I think I'm here to meet, and my stomach flips an acrobatic somersault. When I waited with Yeshua in the desert, I had my hand on his back, which was covered by the bloody mantle, but I saw only his form. Other than his wounded cheek and bearded jaw, his face remains a mystery to me. My breaths shorten, and I feel as if I'm ready to burst into flames like the wood in Miramee's fire. I fear many things.

How does one meet the Holy One of God?

All I can think of in that moment is the old pop song, "One of Us."

If God had a face, what would it look like,
And would you want to see,
If seeing meant that you would have to believe?

I am only a guy from California, a nobody from two millennia in the future. Who the hell do I think I am? I'm no priest or minister. I go to websites I shouldn't go to. I wrote off some personal meals on last year's taxes. I'm imperfect, flawed.

So, why am I the man granted the insane high honor to look upon his face? Who is the one choosing me to hear his voice?

I decide to take a minute and let all of this settle in my bones. I know that I'm delaying the meeting.

Even when Yeshua was unconscious, the air around him seemed electric and living. I walk down a steeper grade for another hundred feet and come across a long stone wall about five feet in height. It ties into a tall, jagged escarpment of rock. Between the path and the stone wall are olive trees; no space is wasted. These appear less tended than the others on the Mount of Olives do, their branches almost obscuring the stone wall in places. Is this where I am to meet him?

I scan the area and see a tree that has a large root that arches up and then dives down into the earth: the perfect natural bench. I sit down and only then notice that directly in front me and across the path is a pair of partially open gates made of wooden slats at a break in the stone wall. They're wide enough to allow wagon traffic in and out of a large service yard the wall encloses.

What is this place?

Feeling lost and unsettled, I see a man on a ladder. He is pruning one of the olive trees near the gate and a little to the left of where I sit. He wears only a tunic—working in his underwear, so to speak—which observant Hebrews in this era would consider so underdressed that they would call him nude. It's nice and warm today, and he's working hard, so he should dress any way he wants.

The man expertly swings a metal-toothed sickle to separate the dead branches from the boughs and trunk of the tree. The branches fall onto the ground with a thud and a rustle.

He's in his late twenties or early thirties, in my judgment. His head covering is a modified keffiyeh that looks more like a shortened chef's hat pulled down like a cap. It sits low on his forehead to his eyebrows and covers his head down to midear on the sides, with a short flap protecting the neck. This is the first time I've seen anyone wearing this type of headgear.

He has a dark-brown beard, and I am close enough to spot a few premature flecks of gray. He turns from his surgery and quickly checks me out with a brief up-and-down glance. Every man in this country seems to size me up to determine if I'm dangerous. Well, I am taller than most of them.

By the speed of his appraisal, I guess I'm not much of a threat. He wordlessly returns to his work.

"Peace," I say in greeting.

He inclines his head forward, still looking at the tree in his acknowledgement, and keeps to his work.

"Sir, this may sound stupid, but—where am I?"

He turns again, frowning slightly, probably wondering if I'm a lost pilgrim.

"Whom do you seek?" he asks hoarsely.

"I'm not sure, exactly," is my weak reply. Under his cap, I can see his forehead lift quizzically.

"From where do you come?"

Why doesn't he just tell me where the hell I am? I know I'm near Jerusalem, but where is this place?

"From Califor-, eh, Ephesus."

Without looking, he snaps the remaining fibers with his free hand, and another sucker branch falls. He looks at me blankly. Ephesus means nothing to him. Why would it? He's a gardener, not a traveler. Many people in Jerusalem would not be familiar with the great city of the Roman province of Asia. I feel like I'm wasting time talking to him and decide to move on. The man calmly returns to his pruning, carefully trimming the remaining splintered stub of the fallen branch from the bough. I take two steps, and then it hits me like a brick: Jerusalem, olive trees. I spin around on my heel.

"Is this place, damn, *what* was the name of that place?" I ask myself aloud. He neither turns nor responds right away.

"*Gat-Shemanin*," he says at last.

"No, that is not it," I reply absently, still lost in the memory retrieval process. I stand in the afternoon sun, working my brain hard, burning through synapses by the second. And then I remember.

"Gethsemane! Yes, that's the name of it! Gethsemane!" I'm thrilled to have pulled that one out of the cobwebbed memories of religion class. I smile, self-satisfied, as if I just guessed the right answer to the bonus-round question on the TV game show *Jeopardy*.

The feeling is short-lived as the gardener shakes his head vigorously. "No. Gat-Shemanin is the name given this place!" he says. "It is called thus because of the oil press inside the cave." He indicates the yard, which must contain some kind of cave, but I can't see it from here. Noticing my uncomprehending expression, he continues. "You know, for all these olives?"

"Gat-Shemanin," I repeat, unwilling to yield up my Jeopardy victory so easily. "Are you sure?"

He frowns and turns back to his pruning. Finally, a dim light switches on in my brain. Gat-Shemanin must be the correct pronunciation of Gethsemane. I am in that holy place.

How about that? Oh, shit! I'm in Gethsemane—Yeshua's Gethsemane!

Like having a laden bookcase topple over on me, I feel like I'm going be crushed under the weight of the next realization. If I'm in Gat-Shemanin, as he says, then I am certain to meet Yeshua in the next few moments. This is really going to happen—face-to-face, one-on-one.

I'm not ready. I need to go back to the stone house and have some soup. I need to hear more *about* him. It's too soon to *see* him.

I run my hand over the surface of the root, which is as thick as a tree trunk. It burrows into the stony dirt, like a giant sea serpent or a python plowing into the earth. I examine the tree to which it belongs: an astonishingly ancient olive tree. I marvel at its mottled trunk, which must be five feet in diameter, and my eye takes a spiraling trek upward into the thick, gray-green lusciousness of its canopy. Gazing at the intersecting branches silhouetted against the sky reminds me of the tangled limbs of that old oak near the streambed in Monterey, the tree next to which I asked the question that began all this. I lean back on the serpent root, using its gnarled tree trunk as a backstop. I let this reality slowly sink into me.

Not worthy. A sinner. Never will be worthy—or ready. How do I get back to Miramee?

"Whom do you seek?" The gardener repeats his question with his back to me.

He needs to butt out of my anxiety.

The guy slices off another branch with that sickle, which looks like a lethal weapon in its own right.

Leave me alone, dude.

I've got stuff to deal with. Well, I might as well ask him as ask anyone.

"I suppose I seek Yeshua of Nasrath," I say as breezily as I can, trying to keep it as light as if I'm chatting about the weather. The man says nothing in reply, continuing to hack at another sucker branch, which is wrestling well with his killer sickle. *Whack!*

Down it comes.

"And who told you he is here?" he asks in a hoarse but louder voice. Sounds like he has a cold.

"I was sent here by a woman to see him."

"A *woman* sent you?" he asks and turns toward me. I see something in his face I have not seen before.

"Yes," I say, looking into his tired, light-brown eyes.

"And what is this woman's name?"

"She is called Miryam of Magdala. Miramee."

The gardener turns toward the tree again, but only to descend the ladder. He pauses at the bottom, just for a moment, and looks at the pile of branches thoughtfully. Then he turns and walks slowly toward me. Now I can see his features clearly in the golden rays of the sun.

"Other than me, you are the only one ever to call her Miramee," he says.

Everything inside of me—my heart, my breath, my circulation, my mind—hits a dead stop, and time freezes. A mini-death reaches from within me and moves silently to the outside as the world becomes perfectly still. In this breezeless moment, even the branches and leaves cease their sway. I feel as if the whole earth pauses, making a noiseless genuflection to honor this very simple, very natural encounter.

I am looking into the eyes of Yeshua. Jesus.

I'm going to throw up.

The moment passes, and everything begins again: my breathing, my heart, the world, even the dappling play of hazy light upon the path. I feel his presence now as I did in the desert, although my preconceptions did not include the sight of a man hacking away at tree limbs or talking with his back to me. He looks younger than me, about thirty, with a dark, sun-burnished face, which is not as long as almost all the paintings of him suggest. He has prominent cheekbones and narrow, bright eyes that glint at me, reflecting something like amber firelight. He has a strong jaw beneath his light beard, and he is certainly "handsome of face" as Miramee elegantly put it. His hair is black, more curly than wavy. He is of average height and athletic looking: fit and tough. In the afternoon light, I can see the curving scar on his right cheek, just as Miramee described, like an opening parenthesis on one side of the face with no closing parenthesis on the other.

In all, this man bears no likeness to the sentimental pansy you see on holy cards. With a kindly expression, his eyes meet mine.

"My Lord" is all I can say, and even that is with a raspy quiver in my voice.

"I am no one's lord," he says. "A lord possesses much and commands much. I have only my mantle, and I am *commanded* rather than *commanding*, Traveler."

He knows my name. He said my name!

Through my amazement, I notice that in addition to his hoarseness, he seems tired and even a bit irritable. That changes as he gets closer and his eyes rivet into mine. An alchemy happens then: things start changing, and the universe seems to spiral in the opposite direction, mirroring itself. He gives off energy, exciting billions of atoms that make up my body and the air around me.

As his eye lock onto mine, I feel the inner warmth course through me again, and I find that I'm no longer nervous. This relative comfort in the presence of the Mashiach should startle me, but somehow, incomprehensibly, it doesn't.

"How does Miramee teach you?" he asks.

"She guides me and sends me to others for more guidance."

As he weighs my response for a moment, I finally get the download that this is the year AD 30, roughly three years after I waited with him when he was unconscious in the desert. But his ministry only lasted three years. Jerusalem was his last stop, and here we are staring at its imposing walls.

A chill runs down my arms, and my fingers tingle. This must be close to the time of the Passion. A profound sadness wells up inside me as I look at him. I know already that I'm powerless to ease his suffering or prevent the spillage of a drop of blood by even one of those excitable atoms. Never have I felt so frustrated, so useless. A sandbag of grief hits my chest. He coughs, then sneezes, and clears his throat for a moment.

"Bless you," I say reflexively.

Now it's his turn to be startled, and he eyes me curiously as if to ask, *"Are you blessing me?"* As he looks at me carefully, a radiant expression crosses his face. Perhaps he senses the sadness and frustration I feel. His expression moves me even more deeply, and my throat begins to close again. Now it's my turn to cough.

"Blessings upon you as well, Traveler," he says to me with a wry smile.

At the sound of him speaking the name Traveler, joy surges through me again. Yeshua knows me. Most of my neighbors at home have no idea who I am, but the Rabbi Yeshua of Nasrath, the Mashiach himself, knows me. I break out into a broad grin as he squats to sit under the olive tree next to me. Out of respect, I begin to get up, but he motions me to sit again. He clears his throat.

"What happened to your voice? Are you sick?" I ask.

Yeshua smiles the same smile that they all seem to have mastered, the one that tells me I am being distracted again. If it's important for me to know what contributed to his rasping voice, then I will know it. Otherwise, I should focus on what they are telling me. I feel stupid, as if I'm the Disciple Lite from twenty-first-century California. Obviously, anyone who speaks in public without the benefit of a microphone would have to shout at the ears of his listeners and thus would lose his voice from time to time.

He puts a kindly hand upon my shoulder, and I feel energy pulse through me once again. It almost feels—please forgive me—*orgasmic.* Now, it's not the same thing at all, but the intensity is like the all-encompassing passion at the height of sexual intercourse. I suspect it's similar to the form of ecstasy that mystics, spiritual masters, and adepts experience in the moments when they encounter union with the divine.

Yeshua mesmerizes me, but I have to shake it off. I must concentrate on the here and now rather than lapse into a kind of waking dream state.

"Traveler, you are protected," he says. As I hear his words, they move around my ears, and I feel Micha'el's presence. It's a cool and clean sensation, completely new. I feel happy, but that is short-lived. A warm gust of wind rushes through the grove, rustling the branches, causing them to swing and sway violently. The aroma of evening meals cooking in nearby homes perfumes the air, and I feel my stomach gurgle with the thought of food. Soon I forget my appetite, and my gut cinches when the wind knocks the ladder over. Yeshua frowns.

Out of the corner of my eye, I see someone standing between the trees and the wall, his dark robe snapping in the sudden rush of wind. I turn sharply to see who is sneaking up on us, and I discover a young man fiercely glaring at us like a specter. At the sight, the blood chills in my veins. I look at Yeshua, who is still frowning, and turn again to see nothing but trees. The man is gone. Satan was that close to me.

"He wants me to be aware that he is always nearby, always present, merely a blink away," Yeshua says and coughs. I feel some vague pains in my chest.

I need to dial it down now.

"But you are protected as well," I say, hand over my heart, "by the archangel."

"Now you see me because I am here in the name of the Father. In the fullness of time, this body will no longer be easy for you to see."

This discussion with Yeshua seems to ride on two different tracks. He answers questions I cannot ask and ignores the ones I can ask. At the same time, he has access to every thought that passes through my mind. It's as if two entirely different voices in my head are carrying on a conversation, one of which is in total silence.

"Perhaps you ask the right questions, but they issue from another *av'va*, another source, within you—from the heart, not your mind," Yeshua says. The pains cease when he says "heart." I close my eyes and exhale my acceptance of his answer, whether or not I understand the mechanics of this process.

"Let us begin," he says.

With amazement, I find new courage, a willingness to act on, not just witness, all that is about to happen to me. Sinking into the spaciousness of his presence, letting my imagination run wild, I settle into my seat upon the serpent root, my back still resting against the bark of the olive tree, ready to listen with as complete attention as the man, Traveler, can muster.

Chapter 43

Yeshua:

When I opened my eyes that morning, I found I had slept with only my mantle spread upon the soft sand of the beach near Capernaum. I had chosen not to sleep in the house of Shimon, whom I now call Kefah, the brother of Andreas. His house was adequate, full of bodily comforts, but I knew that the time to find shelter there had not yet come. Everything has its moment, its ripeness—even something as small as where one lays his head for the night.

Andreas had found me four days earlier at an encampment by the Jordan. I had joined a family of pilgrims who were returning from Jerusalem and was resting in my tent when he sought me out. He was greatly distressed, wet with sweat from running, and told me that Herod Antipater had taken the Immerser to his fortress at Machaerus. He thought if I knew about it that I could undo it, that I could free him from prison. Andreas's faith is great and strong.

When I told him that he needed to return to Capernaum to his brother, to his daughter whose mother had died in giving her birth, he was unhappy. He loved his rabbuni, the Immerser, and he was impatient because he yearned to be called to more than his present life. The Father calls you only to your life. Then that life shapes itself into the right order in the fullness of time.

Thus, we journeyed back together. When we reached the town, I left him to his family and found the pleasant spot on the shore to rest.

As I slept there, all that was living upon the beach came to sleep within me.

When I sat up, I felt refreshed. Unlike many of the pebbly and muddy shorelines of the sea, this one was thick with fine, soft sand. Shaking off my night's rest and quieting the morning growl of my stomach, I began to walk in the direction of the town's piers and the beached boats. As I approached, two men were eating smoked sardines and bread. As one of them looked up at me, I noticed the light around both men: a peaceful, green light. As if these were second bodies, the lighted forms made what looked like a bow toward me. One of the men stretched out his hand immediately and offered me a smoked fish. I accepted it, thanked them, and wished them good morning as I continued to walk. I knew I had business in this area, but the Father had yet to reveal it to me. Often, revelations come at the last possible moment, precisely to prevent the mind from distracting thoughts that accompany advance knowledge. The Father calls me into his *Ever Presence*, the Kingdom. If I am here and awake, I can teach the Kingdom. If my thoughts about what may happen tomorrow distract me, then I am asleep, and the gateway to his Ever Presence closes.

I had walked a good distance by the shore when I saw Andreas with another man in a fishing boat. The boat was old but well cared for, with a crossbeam intersecting the sturdy mast toward the top. Across the beam, the sail was furled, and the mast reclined into the hull like a fallen cross. The boat was an average size for two or more men to use—about fifteen *amot* long, and five at its widest, or in Roman measure, about twenty-six feet by eight feet. This boat could hold many fish.

The men were offshore a short distance, but they were well within the range of my voice. They were casting their nets. Like a brilliant spider's web flung across the early morning sky with flecks of clear-jewel drops showering back onto the surface of the waves, the men expertly positioned the nets next to the boat. Andreas noticed me standing on the shore and said something to the other man, who looked up from the net briefly before returning his gaze to the task. Andreas's light was as radiant as the sun; I had not noticed that quality of light in him before that moment.

The other man sat on the side, leaning over into the center of the boat, and when his upper body was completely visible, I could see that he also emitted this radiant light. The man was older than me by at least ten years, his hair and beard twined with gray. He was thickset and muscular, rock hard, like a human boulder. I could see his large calloused hands, hands that did work six days a week and then opened for prayer on Shabbat. They were like my father Yosef's hands.

No one spoke. Andreas acknowledged me with a nod. The older man looked up again and glared at me. His eyes were dark and set close together. With his beak of a nose, he looked like a falcon studying the approach of another predator. As I watched, they returned to the casting of the net.

"How is the fishing today?" I shouted out to them.

"Nothing—a few sardines. Bait fish," Andreas said and then barely inclined his head to the man with him. "My older brother, Shimon."

I nodded at Shimon, who acknowledged me with a brief, impatient glance.

He saw in me just another roaming rabbi whose very presence threatened to take Andreas away from his work again, thus leaving Shimon with the burden of caring for both their families. Regardless of the glance and the feelings behind it, Shimon's brilliant light did not abate; it only softened, bending toward me. The body often lags behind the spirit, because the mind's fears and desires rule it.

At that moment, the Father sent a revelation shooting through me like a lightning bolt. I could see these men serving him with as much dedication and love as they now labored to support their families, as Andreas had served the Immerser. I lifted my eyes to the heavens and gave thanks. A moment later, I heard the men begin to yell in disbelief.

"Ad-o-nai!" Shimon shouted.

I opened my eyes and saw them struggling as they pulled in their net, grappling with the ties that gathered the net together. After a moment they stopped, breathing hard, gasping in wonder at what they saw in the water. The sea was churning white, a small tempest centered in their net as they discovered a whole school of *musht*, a local fish considered a delicacy. Musht can weigh more than three pounds, always fetching a good price in the market, but even I knew they were a rarity this late in the spring.

With their nets full, the boat took on water and appeared about to capsize, so they called out to the other fishers nearby for help in bringing the catch to shore. There was plenty for all. With the kind of laughter and happy shouting that seems to belong only to brothers of the sea, the men merrily beached the boats.

Once ashore, Shimon and Andreas began the age-old practice of separating the musht and other good fish from those considered unclean by the Law of Father Moshe. However, one by one, as they opened the nets and spread the catch across the beach, they noticed something different. They all exchanged astonished looks.

"There is nothing but musht!" one fisher said.

It was true. The nets gave up only the finest of fish. Overjoyed, the men settled in, cleaning their surprising catch and taking it to market. By the time of the afternoon rest, the job was finished. The men busied themselves cleaning and refolding their nets.

I could see Andreas and Shimon speaking in muted tones as they worked. Shimon glanced in my direction occasionally but said nothing. He was wrestling with what he had seen, trying to find some *reasonable explanation* for this miraculous gift. Finally, he had had enough. He laid down his net and walked over to where I sat on a boulder that was chiseled wide and flat to make a bench. He regarded me carefully for several moments, evaluating me by sight as if he were a caravan master purchasing a camel. The brilliant light around him shone directly into my eyes, making me squint.

"Rabbuni, my brother believes you are the Mashiach, and maybe you are," he said finally, nodding as if considering the idea for the first time. "But maybe you are not."

"Brother!" Andreas shot at Shimon, fearful of giving offense.

Shimon raised his hand to silence him.

"Since I was a small boy on my father's boat, I have fished this part of the sea," Shimon said.

"You are the son of Jonah," I said.

"Yes, I am the son of Jonah," he replied. "But I swallow the fish; the fish do not swallow me!" His rocklike features cracked into the briefest smile. It was a remark that sounded humorous but was really a deflection. Shimon was sensing something he did not yet want to acknowledge.

"What happened today has never happened before in my life," he said. "Musht, out of season, in such great numbers our nets could barely hold them. And there were no other fish, not as much as a shell or minnow in our nets. It was all bounty. Our purses are full, and what's more, our nets are in the same condition they were before, though they should be in shreds. Perhaps it *is* a miracle."

Yet something else troubled him. His questions about me aside, he clearly did not want to be ungrateful for what had happened. This strong man had endured great hardships and believed he had earned what life had given him by the sweat of his brow. And he was no one's fool, either.

"Or perhaps it was the work of a spell-caster."

He watched me carefully as I arched an eyebrow in response. He moved closer and sat beside me, staring into my eyes.

"But it is good to be a fisher on days like today," he added, "and I give thanks for what was given."

He fell silent, hesitating to continue for a reason.

"Ask your question, Shimon."

Shimon kept his gaze fully on me and then blinked. "*Whom* do I thank for all this?"

"You ask what you already know," I said, laying a hand on his shoulder. "All good comes to us from the Father, from Elohim. Give your thanks to him alone."

"Then tell me now, Rabbuni, what does it mean for simple fishers like us to see such wonders?"

Under the cover of his tough exterior, I felt a deep hunger for the Father. The radiance behind him grew more dazzling in its brilliance. Then I saw clearly a wondrous sight. Through him, the Father would change thousands of thousands of lives. Countless generations would come into the Kingdom. As if drawn into the light of this vision, Andreas moved closer and stood next to his brother. Into the bright gold-whiteness, I held out my hand and beckoned to them.

"Come, Andreas. Come, Shimon," I said. "I will show you. Follow me, and I will make you fishers of men."

For a long moment, Andreas and Shimon looked at each other— and then intently at me. They did not turn to cast a glance at their boat or mended nets. They gave no care to the abundant catch. As the brilliance intensified, growing larger and more magnificent, the two men simply stood there. I could almost hear and taste the light. Without a word or movement, they had given the Father their answer.

Their *Yes, Adonai*!

Chapter 44

AD 60, and the seventh year in the reign of the emperor Nero, Patras, Achaia (Greece)

The story ends. I can't see Yeshua.

I blink hard and open my eyes to the sight of a pebbly beach among a cluster of rocks jutting out into the sea. This time, there is no darkness, no flashing light streaking past me. My transport took place in the space of a blink, like one beat of a gypsy moth's wings. Yet I feel rested, as if I've slept for eight hours.

It's morning now.

Moving out from behind a cluster of beach boulders, I see against the gray sky a mostly flat shoreline, interrupted here and there with outcroppings of rock.

Is this the Sea of Galilee?

No.

There is a huge mountain across the water that looks vaguely like a purple clothes iron perched on the horizon. It must be five thousand feet high or more. Nothing that high borders the large lake known as the Sea of Galilee. Besides, from the salty, marine smell, I can tell it's low tide.

Lakes do not have tides.

The murky surf laps onto the pebbles, causing them to lazily rattle and repack. The air is cool now but much more thick and humid than the olive orchard outside Jerusalem. About a mile from where I stand, I see what I now know is the city of Patras, which is really a cluster of squat, white buildings. This part of the beach is isolated, but about a hundred feet away, six men, mostly clean-shaven with curly, short-cropped hair, stand facing the surf. The brain feed tells me that they're Greeks. The men intently watch an old fisherman as he readies his boat to put out to sea.

I also get another download that we are later in time. The number comes first as the seventh year of the notorious emperor Nero's reign and then backs into AD 60. My math-loving mind clicks the calculation efficiently. It's thirty years after the time in the garden with Yeshua—just a blink away. The physics strains my gray matter, but I never understood physics anyway, so I let go of it all.

Walking toward the men, I approach a youth who's trying to help the fisherman, but the seemingly irritated old-timer waves him off with a convincing Oscar-the-Grouch expression.

"He no longer catches any fish," says the young man as he takes a quick glance at me.

I know suddenly that his language is Greek, with the Achaean accent of the northern Peloponnese. Before my dive into the forest, I couldn't have told you where to find the part of Greece called the northern Peloponnese, *nor would I've given a shit.* Now I know exactly where it is, and that's good, because at this moment, I very much give a shit.

"Why does he go to sea?" I ask the young spectator as the old man steadies the boat with his oars.

"He is the apostle, of course!" he says astonished at my ignorance. "He goes out every day to pray. He goes to catch *Theós.*"

"What's a *Theós*?" I ask.

He appraises me now, eyeing me up and down with great suspicion. "*Theós* is the Father, of course. The one the apostle's people from Galilee call Elohim," he offers cautiously. Another name for God that doesn't translate. "Who are you?"

"I am called Traveler," I reply. "Is that Andreas?"

"Who sent you?"

This dude seems to be more helpful than threatening, so I decide to bring him in, but I wonder whose name I should give—not Yeshua, that's for sure. Perhaps I could say Miramee. I wonder by what name they know her here.

"Miryam of Magdala," I venture.

He continues to survey me carefully but doesn't speak. We both turn to the old man again. I notice he is large with huge hands, a fisherman's hands.

"Yes. As you said, he is the great Andreas the Apostle. He knew the *Kristos*!"

So, this elderly man is one we will later call Saint Andrew. The instant I think this, Andreas jerks his head sharply to scan the shore of men and then locks eyes with me. Like the Immerser, he has a penetrating glare, as if the weight of the years has compressed his eyes into a pair of burning coals.

"How does he catch Theós?" I ask the young man without taking my eyes away from Andreas. There's no answer, and the old man motions to me. The hand he uses holds a knotted tassel.

"He counts the prayers with that," the young man tells me. "It is a tradition from his country."

"You, there! Come with me. Now!" Andreas shouts to me above the crack and splash of the wavelets on shore. Seven pairs of eyes are on me, but I hesitate, so the young man pushes my forearm toward the boat.

"You had better go," he says. "He never asks anyone to go with him!"

I roughly shake off the man's hand on my arm. No one pressures me. I get that this is the experience awaiting me, but no one needs to push me. Wading out to the wooden tub, I extend my hand, and the big man pulls me up and into the boat with a single movement of that arm and meat hook of his. Andreas may no longer be young, but he is very strong, his face weathered with deep and craggy lines etched by the years on the sea. His nose is flattened, broken many times. He has led a tough life, buffeted by more storms than I'll ever see.

Without a wasted movement, he pushes off skillfully with his oars. It's as if we are gliding on an early morning pond rather than setting out to sea. The smell of the open water reminds me of sailing at home with my family. Like him, I've been on the sea my whole life. Like him, I find my *Theós* there too.

We row out in silence. Andreas studies me carefully, making me feel a bit uneasy. After all, he is the brother of Shimon, or Kefah.

Alone with Saint Peter's bro!

The cumulative experiences of being in the personal presence of these holy ones—of Yeshua, Miramee, the Immerser, and now Andreas— weigh in, and I shudder. Thankfully, he's looking out to sea and doesn't notice my moment of awe. When the boat is some distance from shore, he lays aside the oars and pulls up a bag looking like it's made of hemp. It holds a smoked fish, a skin of wine, and a skin of water. As we rock back and forth with the shoreline still in sight, he mixes the water with the white wine, offering me both fish and drink. I eat part of the fish, and I find the wine/water refreshingly light.

I can see that the men on the beach aren't leaving. They stand patiently, almost reverently, and because it's early morning, I wonder if they have jobs. I check myself because I've no idea how a preindustrialized world functions. This is as foreign a time and place as if I were visiting another planet. There are no time cards or time clocks here. Hell, there are no clocks, period.

Now that I think about it, it's been some time now since I've looked at a screen or seen a single electronic device—no phone, PC, laptop, TV, electronic billboard, car dashboard, or even a microwave oven display. That's almost as amazing as anything else that's happened so far. There's no gadget with juice running through its circuit boards, yet there's plenty of juice here, and it's running through the people I'm meeting.

He hasn't spoken since I climbed aboard. After he takes a bite or two, washed down by a gulp of watered wine, Andreas wipes his mouth with a clean, white cloth folded neatly beside him. He pulls in his oars, letting us drift. Among the distant mountains to the north, I notice the lone clothes-iron peak.

"*Paliovouna,*" he says.

An amazing sight, its slopes crashing down from the mile-high crest directly into the sea, like a giant, unmoving wave beckoning us. Scanning the span of the huge bay, I get the download that this is one of the many islands making up the jigsaw puzzle of islands and inlets we now call ancient Greece. As we bob on the gray waters, the sun emerges, burning off the morning cloud cover, repigmenting the grays into startling shades of turquoise. A gull lands on the stern's gunwale, greedily eyeing Andreas's burlap bag of wine and bread.

"Ah, my first pilgrim!" he says and reaches into the hull for another sack.

"They put this sack of bread in the boat for me," Andreas says. "It's the blessed bread left over from the Rabbuni's Supper—in case I hunger for more than what I bring with me." He pulls out two large rounds of pita bread. I register that the roundness of the modern Catholic wafer and the shape of the pita are the same.

"By the Rabbuni's Supper, do you mean the meal when you say the words Yeshua said over the bread at the Last Supper?"

"Yes," Andreas says nonchalantly, breaking the pitas into small pieces.

"So that's …"

"The bread, yes, from last night's Rabbuni's Supper—*as I already said*." He squints at my denseness.

Obviously, I'm having some trouble swinging at the slow pitches.

I'm shocked. I may not be practicing, but I know the reverence with which Catholics and Orthodox Christians treat the consecrated bread. I feel that deep respect. It's contained in the fifteen hundred years or so of my European DNA. Yet this Holy Communion did not come out of an ornate tabernacle for a priest to give sacramentally to the faithful. Andreas simply and unceremoniously pulls it out of a rough-sewn bag to be given to—to whom, or what?

Andreas tosses the first piece into the water. Suddenly the gull kamikazes in, snatching it up. It's clear that we're going to have a lot of company soon. In seconds, the flock is bearing down on us like bombers in an old war movie. Andreas smiles and throws baseball handfuls of bread to them. I am amazed that he keeps reaching into the bag and pulling out more. Huge numbers of gulls and seabirds circle over, diving and flapping as they sing their calls to the others. For about five minutes, he keeps up this steady pace as I stare with my mouth agape. His eyes crinkle as he sets the bag down and finally looks at me.

"Your mouth is open, Traveler," he says, enjoying my astonishment. "Do you want me to throw a piece in there as well?"

I shut my mouth and manage a grin. The bag lies flat on the deck for a moment, and then he opens it and reaches in again. He pulls out one pita after another, continuing with the feeding for another half hour, until slowly the animals begin to fly away.

"And now it's time for us to eat," he says as he pulls out another round of pita with his man paws and offers it to me. I accept it.

"Amen," I say almost as a reflex, and I chew it down, enjoying the fact that the apostle, the great Andreas, is feeding me like the birds.

After we eat, we drink some now warmer wine/water, and he neatly arranges the wine, water, bread, and bottomless bag behind him in the bow. He is ready to speak. As I watch him, I marvel that a man who spent his life taking from the sea and eating its gifts now spends his days nurturing the sea by feeding its hungry inhabitants. I had to see it to understand this communion, the slow and rhythmic pace, the repeated giving and receiving. Without doubt, I know that on most days, this unhurried ritual is private, witnessed only by Andreas and the animals he feeds. I begin to understand what sacrament truly means: the ordinary and the miraculous combining to bring us together, connecting us in a way that wasn't possible a few moments before. And there is great love in it. There is Yeshua in it all. I savor this elegant simplicity as we bob on the sea in silence.

Now he's ready to speak.

Chapter 45

Andreas:

That morning, Kefah and I sailed out to another spot, because we had no luck in the usual place we fished. We remained unlucky that day and headed into shore with nothing to show for our labor but a few sardines. The morning sun was hot, and there was no wind, only a light breeze luffing the sail. Kefah rowed and I looked over at him. My oldest brother is a good and practical man. Quick-tempered, he is no pushover. If someone wants trouble with him, he can find it.

My father taught us how to fish when we were very young, and it seems we have lived more upon the sea than upon the land. In truth, I am more at home on the water. Perhaps that is why I find my own kind difficult to understand. To me, fishes make sense; people do not. Fishes swim, eat, and make other little fishes. They live life fully, right up to the moment they enter my net. Then, thrashing and fighting, they yield up their bodies for our food. It's simple.

Life makes sense on the water. The weather is what the weather is. When the sea dances with the sky in a storm, she can take your life in a careless moment, but if you respect her, take time to learn her ways, she will give you amazing sun-filled days on blue-green waters, royal days to harvest her abundant gifts.

When I came back to Capernaum, I told Kefah about the arrest of the Immerser and about this new rabbi, Yeshua of Nasrath.

He smirked and shook his head. I knew the scolding was coming.

"Brother, you look for the Mashiach in everyone. I am not that easily swayed. Lately, many holy people tell us that the Mashiach is coming soon, and it cannot be soon enough for me. No one hates the Roman occupiers more than I do. But as I see things, you have a daughter and responsibilities that you chose to leave to me so you could be free to spend your days listening and helping this Immerser fellow. Now he is gone, but you managed to find his replacement within a few hours?"

I could understand why he was angry with me. He could not yet see why I had to leave.

"I know it sounds crazy, but you need to meet him," I said. "And I never said he was the Mashiach."

"And he did not come to the house ... because?"

"He likes sleeping under the stars since he was in the desert for forty days," I replied a little weakly. I could see in his eyes that he doubted me. He nodded slowly again and sighed, resigned to my blindness.

"All right, bring him to the house for Shabbat tonight," he said wearily as he plied the oars through the murky water. Even though he was agreeing reluctantly to meet *this prophet of mine*, Kefah discovered quickly how fast things can move when you give your consent to Elohim, even unwittingly. My brother did not have to wait until Shabbat to fulfill his promise grudgingly given. When we approached the port of Capernaum, we saw Yeshua standing on the shore, and I pointed to him.

"That is him, right there!"

"Where?"

"There. What are you, blind? On the shore," I said as I waved my pointing finger at Yeshua.

"Hm," Kefah huffed, glancing at him and resuming his preparation of the net. The two of us work in a familiar rhythm, and without saying a word, we decided to cast one more time, even though we knew it was too close to shore to catch much at this time of year besides maybe a broken jar or a chewed-up sandal.

The Rabbuni shouted out a question about our luck. I told him that we had no luck today as we placed the net where we wanted it. Suddenly our nets sank as if filled with heavy rocks—so fast that we both lost our footing and fell against the low gunwale. Near to capsizing, we threw our weight to the high side immediately, no thinking necessary. Had we snared a submerged boulder?

As we regained our balance, we looked down into a foaming storm of fins flapping madly in the water. Our nets tugged at the boat sides, and we instantly began to pull them in. We gasped in disbelief. This time of year, we are happy to net one or two fish, but our nets were bulging full, and the fish were *musht,* the finest fish we could catch in the Galilean sea. We called some of the other men from boats near us, including Kefah's oldest son, and we all hauled in a catch so heavy that we were certain our nets were shredded.

"Good fortune, eh, Brother?" Kefah slapped me on the back with a loud chuckle.

I said nothing in reply but kept working, and Kefah noticed my solemnity. I knew what had happened, and I felt the heaviness of it bear down upon me even more than the catch. I grunted something and looked toward shore where Yeshua still stood. A chill ran up and down my back, and the hairs on my neck stood on end.

"This wasn't luck, Brother," I said. He followed my eyes.

He laughed loudly and derisively.

"Are you saying that *he* had something to do with this, Little Brother?" Kefah asked, peering at me, but his laughter was hollow. He knew this was no ordinary play of luck. I kept silent and worked. The other fishers helped us, and we brought the massive catch into shore. We all emptied the nets and sorted the fish, but there was no sorting to be done.

All musht.

Soon Kefah's son and the other fishers took the catch to market, and we stayed on the beach, mending our nets. Yeshua remained standing in the same place. Kefah glanced at him more thoughtfully, still considering what I had said earlier. Yeshua looked at us and then out to sea.

"How could it be?" Kefah said. "He was standing there on the shore the whole time!" I'd had enough. I glared at him.

"When did you last see musht in these waters at this time of the year, Older Brother? And there is nothing in the net *but* musht! No half-chewed sandals, no wood scraps, no rocks. Enough for us and enough for every other fisher who helped us."

I held up our nets close to his face.

"And how is it that our old nets, which we have to repair each afternoon, show only a tear or two? You know our nets could not look like this unless we had caught a handful of sardines. You tell me how that can be."

"Fine, fine," Kefah said, recoiling. He looked over at Yeshua again. "Elohim was generous to us today," he said finally.

"You do not understand, do you?" I said, irritated. "He is the Mashiach!"

Speaking these words surprised me. It was always present in my thoughts, but I had never before pronounced it aloud. I'd seen the wonders he worked, but more than that, there was Yeshua's presence, which shook me to my core, grabbing me by the heart and pulling me into his heart. At that moment, I felt like one of the musht caught in our net, writhing and squirming to set myself free, hoping to find a tear I could open with my teeth and escape back into the unpleasant familiarity of my life. What Yeshua's presence stirred up in me drew me toward him, but it brought me fear at the same time.

Kefah looked at me and the color drained from his face. Calling someone the Mashiach was close to blasphemy. He made no more casual remarks about Yeshua, not because he believed he was the Mashiach, but because he sensed the mighty weight in all that was happening, forces he could not understand. He looked concerned, considering my serious face, the catch, and the undamaged nets. I think that both of us—together, at that same moment—began to learn that we were all participants in this power rather than merely its witnesses. I felt this deep revelation flow through me. It seemed that something similar was happening to Kefah. He had suddenly ceased talking and joking altogether.

Kefah is nothing if not direct; he decided to deal with all this head-on. He rose to his feet and plodded over to Yeshua. The Rabbuni looked at me as Kefah approached him. The strangest sensation ran through my whole body again. It was as if he saw into my soul itself and talked with it rather than with me. All at once, this warm, brilliant light overwhelmed me. I knew that what I had blurted out to Kefah was the truth. Yeshua *was* the Mashiach. From that moment on, I was convinced he was the Holy One about whom the prophets spoke.

When the Rabbuni asked us to follow him, we did not answer with words. We were both looking into a hole in this world's screen, permitted to gaze into a country no man in the flesh had seen. Kefah and I stared in amazement as an unfamiliar conversation between our souls and Yeshua took place, where all was being decided. Somehow, we understood what we were supposed to do. A deeper wisdom settled into us, and I felt a foreign feeling in my heart. What was it?

Joy. For the first time in years, I was truly happy. There was no answer but the answer of movement. In wonder, as if having one mind, we brothers followed him. There was no surprise in it, either. It was as natural as eating or sleeping.

Yes, we followed Yeshua, walking away from the nets and the boat. There were no horns from heaven blowing, but I knew everything had changed in those few moments. Some fishers, our longtime companions of the sea, called after us, but we did not turn back. When Kefah saw his son, he called out to him.

"After Shabbat, upon the first day of the week, take the boat out and see that the catch reaches market before midday!"

Bewildered, the young man nodded in reply as he watched us step away from the only life we had ever known.

Chapter 46

AD 60, and the seventh year in the reign of the emperor Nero, Patras

Andreas turns the boat toward the Achaean shore. The communion with the animals is complete, as is his memory of Yeshua for now.

"So you three just walked together along the beach?" I ask, back on track with the important part of the story.

"What follows is not for me to say," Andreas replies cryptically, and he pulls the oars with greater urgency. It seems the retelling of the story depletes him in a way. I'm learning that telling is nothing like listening. Telling *costs* a person somehow, even if it gives peace.

One black-headed gull zooms across the bow as if dive-bombing into the green-gray sea. The gull does not dive but fires toward the shore, which lies dead ahead. Then two more gulls and a few sandpipers skitter low above the swells, creating an impromptu parade, an escort leading us home. Overhead, a magnificent flock of seven pelicans flies in a *V* formation, like an arrow in the heavens pointing the way, and then they angle slightly to the right. I laugh lightly at the coincidental beauty of all of this taking place, but in a few seconds, my laughter ceases as I gape in wonder at a pod of porpoises steadily arching their way along our starboard side. On the port side, three flying fish skim the waves toward shore, and like the others, they veer across our bow to the right. I blink as my stomach does a flip-flop.

What kind of power is this?

As astonishing as it is, I wonder at the hulking man to whom the earth and sea bow in reverence. Andreas strokes along without taking notice, as if this parade is nothing out of the ordinary. We see the faithful followers patiently stand again on the beach.

Suddenly, about twelve uniformed Roman soldiers come onto the shore and begin to disperse the men. These men are doing nothing, harming nobody. Some of the men are outraged and shout at the soldiers. Andreas stops rowing, and we watch as one soldier unsheathes his sword.

"No, no, no," Andreas mutters. "Go away. Simply walk away." As if they hear him, the men go in three different directions.

Close call. We simultaneously exhale with relief. Yet the soldiers stand there, looking out at us.

"We will land at another place. A place where you will feel safe," Andreas says.

"Where I will feel safe? What about you?"

"The lambs know they are never far from the Shepherd. The sheep are also close, but they have much yet to learn." He breaks into a rare smile, telling me I am definitely in the *Sheep* category. The man of the sea turns the boat to starboard, and I remember the animals pointing us that way. I absorb all of this as the sun slants the golden rays of late afternoon upon the face of the water. The gold turns to burnished orange, then red, then darkness. Only it's not darkness. Millions of stars emerge, and we row for shore into a rocky cove that is about as secret a place as one can find around here.

The beach is no more than twenty or thirty feet wide, and the surf is higher here, so Andreas maneuvers the boat in to shore in precisely the right position and angle. Otherwise, it would have broken up on the jutting rocks that cup the cove narrowly like a nearly closed hand. As we beach the boat, I look at the moon, a slim, yellow crescent as it rises on the horizon. The same men the soldiers dispersed, the wordless faithful of Andreas's flock, come out of their hiding places behind the black boulders. In the dim moonlight, they look like phantoms who are stalking us. Two of the younger men wade into the surf and help steady the boat as we climb out.

"*Abouna*, Andreas. We will take the boat back to the other beach so it will be there by morning if you should want to take it out," one man says with deep respect.

Andreas nods his consent, places his hand upon the young man's head and then gives his blessing to the others. The two men climb in, and Andreas and I join in helping them shove off. He turns and raises his hand as a blessing to each of them as they row away. We climb over a few rocks in the dark. I am concerned about him slipping, but Andreas is the one who leads me over the boulders and onto the flat sand.

"We need to go to the house of Demetrius tonight," Andreas says.

"Is it not safe at your house?" I ask.

I can see those eyes pinning me again, this time in disbelief.

"I have no house, Traveler," he says with an astonished smile. "The Rabbuni had no home, and neither do I."

I consider this, but I cannot help thinking that, beyond its humility, this nightly moving from home to home is a shrewd strategy as well. It's a way to stay ahead of the Roman soldiers. They seem to be chasing him but not aggressively, because they could certainly find him any day they wanted. Apparently, they pursue him with only minimum effort to comply with their orders. Before spending time with him, I knew little about Andreas's traditional story, except that he was the brother of St. Peter and that the Scots use his cross as their national symbol. His cross: the thought of a torturous death awaiting this large, gentle man saddens me as I walk now beside him—a very much alive and breathing human being.

Clearly, the Romans will catch him eventually, crucifying him in a strange way that the Scots will incorporate into the X-shaped cross of the Union Jack. This pang of sorrow shoots through me, because in trying to tell him of his grisly fate, nothing but noise would come out of my mouth. Even if I could tell him, I am ignorant of any details about his execution, so again I feel useless. Sadly, I resign myself to the humility of just being here with him. For a guy like myself, who is used to being the animator in any situation, the mover and shaker, this passive role of being a mute—here only to witness everything—tests the limits of my patience.

Andreas interrupts my thoughts.

"Traveler, you think like a man and not like God," he says. "Remain with what is important, and forget the curiosities that amount to distractions and nothing more."

Curiosities?

I nod my agreement, but being human, I will continue to care about these people, and I will feel bad when I know something terrible is going to happen to any of them. That's not going to change, even if Andreas,

Miramee, or anyone else in this time considers my powers of attention too meandering.

"Traveler, you cannot find the Kingdom there," he says, his eyes like coals burning into mine.

Once we reach the dark streets of Patras, we make our way across the huge town square, past the reproving statue of Caesar Augustus, who put this place on the map by making it a Roman colony, and we move into a warren of narrow alleyways toward a freestanding house at the end of a dirt road. As we approach, I see it has a walled courtyard and is larger than most of the surrounding huts. A sizable black rat scurries across our path, traveling with prey-animal urgency from one hole at the base of a building to the next. The air is completely still; there's no hint of any salty breeze to sweep away the merciless stink of raw sewage.

Andreas knocks a code on the gate, and a middle-aged man with a coronary-inviting midsection opens it instantly, as if he has been waiting for us. He smiles with strangely colored teeth bordered by a gold bridge, which punctuates his grin. His mouth reminds me of Captain Jack Sparrow's teeth in *Pirates of the Caribbean*. He inclines his head with a small bow in wordless welcome. We cross the few steps of the courtyard, and Andreas places his hand on the lintel, giving the house his peace. I do the same. Then my nose and I happily enter the home, which is bright and warm with the aroma of onion soup. A curtain sections off the foyer.

When our host opens the curtain to allow us in, I'm startled to see thirty people, adults and children, standing in a large room with a fireplace. It's a dining room and a kitchen together. The tables are low with cushions, placed in the shape of a *U*. I recognize some of the men as those who helped on the shore.

Andreas walks down the line and greets each person with a kiss on either the cheek or the mouth, his big hands blessing each child's head. A young mother, no more than sixteen, grabs his hand and kisses it. While Andreas allows her to do so, he frowns slightly. He is not royalty and wants no one to treat him as such.

Several people eye me carefully. I look foreign and weird to them, with my mother's Irish upturned nose, my straight, brown hair, and my light skin, which is surely getting red from the day at sea. I wouldn't know, though, because there are no mirrors around these parts. Although it remains unspoken, the question hangs in the air. Who's this sunburned stranger with the apostle?

Our ample host shows us to a table that connects both of the other tables, all running parallel to the walls of the room. The little congregation waits for Andreas to recline on his cushion, and then they all do the same.

A toothless woman merrily begins to chirp a hymn, and everyone joins in. "My soul magnifies *Kýrion*, and my spirit rejoices in *Theós*, my saving One." I remember those words as the ones Eema sang in one of the gospels when she greeted her cousin before the birth of Yeshua. They sing softly in deep, hushed tones, so no one outside these walls can hear them.

Hey, I get it. This is a Mass! Or what will eventually become the Mass.

At this point, it's what the early followers of the Way do to celebrate the memory of Yeshua. The wonder of it passes through me as if my heart is opening up like a present on Christmas morning. This is how it all began: a group of people, a reverenced leader, a table, and singing. Andreas says some prayers, takes the bread, and breaks it. All are silent.

"*Touto mou estin to soma*," Andreas pronounces slowly.

For some reason, I hear this in Greek because I need no translation. I know the words. *This is my body for you.*

He does the same with a large cup of wine and then passes the bread and wine around to each person, beginning with me sitting to his right. I tear off a small piece of bread and pass it along. I take a small sip of the wine and then hand the cup to the woman on my right. Men and women sit together here, or at least they do at this celebration. There doesn't seem to be the usual division of sexes I've seen at other social gatherings. More prayers and a psalm, again sung in the softest tones, follow the eating of the sacred bread and sipping the blessed wine.

The secrecy and stealth reminds me of how dangerously illegal all of this is. I remember the Roman soldiers on the beach staring out at Andreas earlier. History was stalking him. Yet at this moment, none of the faces in the room betrays worry or concern. They all seem ... well, very happy.

Seamlessly and with no real division between the sacred meal and supper, some of the women get up and begin to serve the soup. When it's served, I'm astonished to see that the guests use the remaining sacred bread to sop up their soup! I check out Andreas to see if this is permissible and find that he is blissfully sponging up his soup as well, so I join in.

As I stuff some delicious onion-soaked bread into my mouth, I'm thinking that this is real communion: the sharing of Yeshua together. I smile, savoring the simplicity and the love among these people, which feels as satisfying as the soup. When the supper concludes, all the guests stand, and Andreas rises and closes his eyes. All are silent until a toddler burps, which causes a ripple of muffled laughter among the children. Smiling through that amazing, craggy face, Andreas raises his hand in a blessing.

"May the Rabbuni, the Holy One, guide you and all of the called-out brothers and sisters of the Way in Patras. May the ears of our enemies be opened to hear the triumphant message. May we know his peace until the day he returns to us, and may that day be tomorrow!"

"Amen!" say the guests. They break out in another hushed hymn as they leave in pairs or threes, with a generous spacing of time in between. When the room is finally empty, our host, still affable but tired, shows us to a sleeping chamber, the luxury of a larger house. We make ready for the night's rest and lie down on our mats. Andreas is only a few feet away, and in what light there is, I see that he is lying on his back. So am I. Both of us stare at the low plaster ceiling.

"Even though we wait for the day he will come upon the clouds, each time we meet, he is truly here with us again," Andreas says as if speaking to himself.

"I know."

"Did you feel him?" he asks.

"All day."

"But *him*. Did you feel *him*?"

I felt the communion all day, the giving and receiving, with Yeshua's memory present and all done in his name. But I'm not sure what he means by "feeling *him*."

"I do not know," I reply.

When I was with Yeshua by the side of the road in the desert and later in the orchard, his presence felt much more electric, like pure energy running through me. This supper was warm and gave me a connection that's very real and comforting, but it's not the same.

"When you find him in the bread, then you will find him everywhere," Andreas says and then rolls over on his mat.

Soon, as Andreas is peacefully snoring, I continue to stare at the plaster ceiling and watch the dance of the fire shadows. I remember how he gave the blessed bread to the birds—the rhythmic, gentle gestures with those big hands. At the time, the bottomless bag grabbed my attention, so I was missing the real miracle. He was giving Yeshua back to them. Yeshua came out of creation and returns into it, over and over again. When Yeshua died, he belonged to us, but he belonged to the rest of creation as well.

I turn on my side and wonder if I'll ever have that experience of Yeshua everywhere and in any time. The mat is thick and comfortable, and I leave this weighty question for now, replacing it with another.

Where will I wake up tomorrow?

Chapter 47

AD 30, and the seventeenth year of the reign of the emperor Tiberius, Gat-Shemanin

Tomorrow is a vague, elastic concept in this experience. Tomorrow might be yesterday or some day three decades past.

Outside the olive press cave and yard enclosed by a tall stone wall—the place called Gat-Shemanin—in the same waning afternoon light that I left, the first thing I see is Yeshua's bright eyes staring back at me. Startled, I jump a bit, even though I'm sitting. He still sits under the shade of the old olive tree about two feet away from me.

Okay, I'm sitting now. What the heck happened to sleeping?

The scene is precisely the same as before. No time has passed, as if there's been only the space of a blink since we spoke our last words here.

"Have you returned now, Traveler?" Yeshua asks.

I wipe my eyes, yawn, and blink—and give up on assessing the situation. I feel the electricity of Yeshua's presence again. It's comforting, and I remember Andreas's words before we slept: "When you find him here, in the bread, then you will find him everywhere."

Well, Yeshua is right before my eyes, looking at me and into me, so the mystery of the bread will have to wait for now. On the other hand, maybe that was the purpose of the experience: the mystery of the bread is playing out in a kaleidoscope of encounters. I don't know yet, but I'm learning to trust—and limit the interior commentary as much as possible. That's a tough one.

"Let us walk," Yeshua says, standing and dusting his hands off.

The idea of a little physical movement is appealing. It's energy in and energy out, and Yeshua is generating a lot of juice right now. I need to walk—or better yet, run. I jump to my feet. What I'd give to have my running shoes right now. I'd like to fire off down the path for thirty minutes. Maybe this feeling of being a human nuclear power plant would ease up a little. Maybe I'd understand more than I do.

As we begin to walk down the narrow trail through the olive trees, I wonder if the others who meet Yeshua experience this energy surge in the same way. Does it course through their systems like jolts of power, as if they're hooked up to two cosmic jumper cables?

I begin to get nauseated. It's not "throw up" nauseated but "jittery" nauseated, just like in college after pulling an all-nighter, studying, and drinking too much caffeine—after too much alcohol.

"Traveler, give it to something else, just as it was given to you," he says quietly, his voice still hoarse.

"Give what?"

Yeshua inclines his head to the thick, twisted trunk of an old olive tree a few feet to my right.

"Put your hand on the tree trunk and give away what you cannot yet use. The tree will know how to receive it and use it."

I'm thinking that this is a strange request, but a part of my mind agrees. It makes sense. Give away what you cannot or do not know how to use.

Energy we can't use correctly can be destructive. Anyone who has seen a documentary on Hiroshima can understand that. I step over to the tree and look at Yeshua. He inclines his head, closing his eyes briefly, a sign of his approval, and I place my hand on the tree trunk. I feel the energy, which is needling me like a million pinpricks, move down my arm and then burn into the palm of my hand that rests on the coarse bark. The tree seems to absorb it like a sponge. Nothing happens to it; there is no visible or dramatic transformation. The trunk remains gnarled and old. All the brown leaves spotting its branches here and there are still brown. But I feel different. There are no more needles pricking me. There's no more vague feeling of nausea.

Calm. My mind can focus again.

Content, I return to Yeshua's side, and we continue our stroll. We climb a small grade, and then we see the resplendent sight of Jerusalem once more. The Temple is like a lighthouse, the beacon of the Father rising above the city. It stands illumed in golden hues by the slanted and weakening rays of sunlight. Above the olive trees, we can see the fronds of large date palms bordering part of the grove. The fronds rustle and dance in the evening breeze. Both of us pause to hear their music.

"It is like the water camp," Yeshua says. "It reminds me of the palms framing the far shore of the desert lake."

"With Miramee?" I ask.

He looks at me with a trace of a smile.

"Where did the name Miramee come from?" I know I'm prying, being distracted, and all the other wrong things, so sue me. I'm curious. I see that he decides to humor me this time. But it's more than that: I sense that he wants to talk about her as one friend to another.

"There are many names given in a lifetime: those given by parents, others by friends, and others still by enemies," he says solemnly. "Then there is the name by which one is called out. Sometimes it takes a whole lifetime to learn that name. Other times it comes earlier, but seldom does it comes very early."

"But aren't all names just sounds we learn to respond to?" I ask.

"What do the sounds of her name bring up in you, Traveler?"

"At first, it sounds like an affectionate name, a nickname, you know, with 'Miryam' as its root," I say. Suddenly another insight pops into my brain. "Then I hear something else, something in my own language, in English."

"Tell me what you hear."

"Ha! Well, it sounds something like "mirror of me," I say slowly, smiling sheepishly. But then my eyes grow wide. As the truth seeps into me like seawater through sand. I'm startled by what I just said: *mirror of me!*

He feels that she is the mirror, the reflection of him.

Is she a mirror showing all others the Yeshua within them?

It's like a million microscopic neurons are firing like riflemen in the shooting gallery of my brain. How can this be? It's a nickname in Aramaic. How could its sound have any meaning in English?

Yeshua remains silent for a moment, letting this percolate. After some time passes, he clears his throat. "When I opened my eyes and saw her for the first time in that tent, I felt her powerful presence surround me completely. She covered me with her light, yet as she oiled my fingers, the form of her body was apart from me. From where she sat, she was unknowingly able to touch every part of my being as no one else ever had—except the Father. While her presence was not as powerful as his, it was pervasive, gentle, and subtle, and as encircling as the humid air before the rain."

I listen with rapt attention to the way he speaks and the resonance of his voice, which is no longer hoarse. It reminds me of the lyrical way Miramee speaks. Of course, his is masculine and powerful, while hers is feminine and melodious, but they are both like different tonalities of the same musical instrument.

"Did she know who you were?" I ask.

He inclines his head, closing his eyes briefly once more

"Before I woke, every part of her knew me. Her waking mind was slower to receive the revelation."

"What did this cause in you?" I ask as if in a trance, losing my self-consciousness before the one I dare to ask such personal questions. But I am asking him as a man like me, a buddy.

"I had been alone with the Father for many days in the wilderness, praying and fasting, thirsting and coming into understanding. Out there, I became a new creation, a new Adam, and I learned that there is no separation between Abba and me. Yet a part was missing. As my form of body lived, it contained mostly masculine energy. For the Mashiach, there has to be the opposite energy to complete the movement of the Ruach Kudsha. I required the feminine vibrancy of another, and that, perhaps, was the reason the Father delivered me to Miramee's camp and to her care."

I decide to go for it. "Do you love her as I love my wife, as a man loves a woman?" I ask without embarrassment or tentativeness.

He smiles and looks at the ground as we walk and then turns to me. "At this moment, you cannot hold the depth and breadth of my answer to that question," he says, "but the part of your mind that asks it has begun to understand the answer already."

They're together, no question. Maybe it's not at all times. Maybe it's seldom in physical proximity, and perhaps it's not in a sexual or intimate sense, but they are united. And there is love—great, passionate, subtle, wondrous, and eternal love. It's not like some romantic fantasy served up as "love" in my time. This is the true one-in-one-in-all love. My heart feels this first, and then it makes its way up to my brain.

"When I first saw Miramee," Yeshua says, "I felt the spaciousness that pointed me to her person, pointed me to the one who could help me bring forth the triumphant message in the fullness of time." He studies me carefully, his eyes crinkling. He places a hand upon my head, covering my scalp with his long artisan's fingers.

As he does, I realize that he likes to speak about her, but he is always teaching, always informing. With the Mashiach, there are no wasted words or useless movements.

"Traveler," he says, "I will tell you more now."

Chapter 48

Yeshua:

From where we stood, we could see two boats on shore with eight or nine men mending the nets inside while others were working on the catch. Kefah, Andreas, and I had walked up from the beach in Capernaum to the neighboring town of Bethsaida. I noticed the gulls swooping and hungrily feeding on the bits and pieces thrown into the waters from the boats. That morning, like every morning, the gulls awakened without knowing what, where, or from whom they would feed. They have no cares; they simply ride the currents of air, remaining watchful. The food will be there.

Kefah waved at two of the younger men, and they shouted back a cheerful greeting. An older man—I presumed the father of some of these others—smiled warmly at us. I could see that he was a good man for there was a welcoming light around him. The two younger men who had shouted the greeting stood by his side as we approached. I could see that their lights were dazzlingly bright, so full of radiance that I was truly astonished, although I knew such surprises were part of the Father's revelation.

Kefah and Andreas greeted them as longtime friends, and then all eyes fell on me. Kefah was awkwardly silent, but Andreas spoke up.

"This is Yeshua, a rabbi from Nasrath."

The two younger men inclined their heads respectfully. They were either brothers or cousins. I could see their resemblance to the older man.

"He is a kinsman of the Immerser," Andreas said. The younger man raised his thick eyebrows with that remark. Many in Galilee were disciples of my cousin.

"I am called Yakov," the thicker, older brother said in a deep voice as he extended his hand. He was large and powerfully built, and the grasp of his calloused hand was firm and strong.

"This is my father, Zavdai, and my younger brother, Johanan," Yakov said.

The father, Zavdai, looked up from his net mending and scrutinized me carefully. I could see that the old man's mind was whirling with all kinds of questions about me. He clearly felt something strange and vaguely threatening about me. Dignified, almost regal, and not fat as most rich men, Zavdai was muscular and fit. Most of all, I could see that he possessed great wisdom and love for the Father.

The younger man, Johanan, then stepped forward to extend his hand in greeting. He had the slighter build of a man with few years, but he bore a handsome face. Under those caterpillar eyebrows, his eyes squinted warmly as he smiled, but I could see enough of them, see enough *into* them, to sense that his soul was indeed as ancient as the stars. The light emanating from Johanan suddenly grew wildly bright, causing me to shield my eyes with my left hand.

As I grasped his hand with my right, I felt his innocence. He was perhaps only sixteen or seventeen years old. The fuzz on his cheeks and chin was wispy, and he still carried some blemishes on his forehead, even with the sun and sea salt tempering their advance. Yet he was a wise man disguised as this boy, and he had a profound river of compassion flowing from his heart. At once I knew what I was meant to do.

With Andreas and Kefah standing near Zavdai's two sons, they regarded me, mouths agape, like children staring at a good storyteller. My skin pricked with the radiant light and dazzling heat emanating from the four of them.

After a moment of silence and these combined lights, Zavdai got anxious and began to fidget with the net, pulling and plying the lines around his hand.

"So, you are from Nasrath?" Zavdai asked nervously. "Do you know the butcher there? Ah, what is his name—Cleopas? Good man." He sensed correctly that something was *transacting* between the men and me—and the Father.

Turning to him, I said, "Cleopas is my uncle, my father's brother."

"Oh, yes, your father was the carpenter who died a few years ago." Zavdai sighed. "I am sorry for your loss."

"There is nothing lost," I said.

Zavdai's eyes widened, and his considerably bushy eyebrows lifted in shock, for he imagined that I had just disrespected my dead father.

"What issues forth from the Father, from Elohim, returns to him and then comes again," I said. "Nothing is lost."

I could see and feel Zavdai's dilemma. He was now confused instead of shocked. I could see that he still had light within him, but his ears were not yet open. I turned to his sons.

"Come. Follow me."

I said it as easily as if I was telling them to look at the seabirds feasting, and I could feel the wave of calm certainty roll over them. To the bystander, this surely sounded like an outrageous suggestion, but the true listeners, the four men in front of me, heard an invitation directly from the mouth of the Father. The sons of Zavdai found it as powerful and irresistible as Andreas and Kefah had earlier that afternoon.

When Yakov and Johanan immediately stood up in their boat and began to climb out, Zavdai looked at them with incredulous anger, veins blistering from his forehead and neck.

"What? Wait a minute! What are you two doing?" he yelled at the top of his lungs.

As they bowed respectfully to their father, we all turned from the boats and began to walk away.

"What am I supposed to do about this business? These boats? Come back here now! I am your father!" he thundered after them.

But they did not look back.

"He thunders like a storm upon the sea," I said. "So you will be called the 'Sons of Thunder!'"

The brothers nodded, and Johanan emitted a youthful, nervous laugh at what he thought was a joke. But I meant much more than a lighthearted reference to his father. These two men had a very long way to travel with me, and much of it would be as violent and disturbing as the most ferocious tempest they ever encountered upon the waters of the Galilean Sea.

By the time they were finished in these bodies, they would feel the name "sons of thunder" as the very thunder of the Father!

Yet, at that moment, there was only light. When I looked upon my four disciples, I wondered at the brilliant sun shining between them.

It was a warm evening, so we camped on the beach. Some of the men bathed in the water to prepare for the Shabbat as Kefah began to roast some fish over the fire. We would keep the holy evening observance in our camp, and in the morning, we would go to the synagogue at Capernaum. Soon we gathered at the makeshift table lit only by the firelight. Before we ate, I asked for the Father's blessing on these men.

"May Adonai bless and keep you. May Elohim make his countenance to shine upon you and give you peace." The men stood respectfully around the table where Kefah had placed the fish and some bread. There was also wine, and I filled the cup to the brim with the red vintage, holding it before me as I began the blessing of the wine.

> You anoint my head with oil.
> My cup is full.
> Only goodness and mercy shall follow me
> All the days of my life,
> And I shall dwell
> In the house of Adonai forever.
> Prepare the meal of perfect faith,
> Prepare the meal of the King.
> This is the meal
> Of the holy ancient one.

"Amen," the men muttered, the only word spoken or even permitted.

Taking the first drink, almost half of the full cup, I then passed it to each of the men, who shared it in silence. Three of us reclined and ate the roasted fishes. As a sign of preparedness since the days of Father Moshe, Johanan and Yakov stood according to the custom of their house. In some observant households, the families stand to leave at the call of the Father as the Israelite fathers and mothers did when it came time to leave Egypt as free men and women. We ate slowly and spoke little. It was a good meal and a good silence.

Satisfied and tired from the long day, each man found a place to rest upon the soft, sandy grasses. I slept deeply but only for a few hours.

In the night, I awoke suddenly and stood up. I quickly set out, walking along the shore, and when I was a distance from the camp, I found a boulder to sit on. There I watched the moonlit waves tumble easily over the pebbles of the shore, one wave following another in an unhurried rhythm.

The Father sent me a revelation. I understood now that regardless of who lived or died, of what skimmed upon the water's surface or swam beneath, the waves still beat and broke upon the stones. Like the crack of tiny thunders during a storm, it was the eternal percussion of creation. The Father abides in the waves and the pauses between the waves, and I knew then, in the presence of this moonlit music, that I did as well.

That night of the first Shabbat with the disciples, I prayed for many hours. Most of the prayer was silent, waiting for the Father and sometimes listening for Him. A solitary cedar tree stood near the boulder. I was amazed at the presence of this huge mountain tree thriving in the low, warm chalice that makes up the Galilean Sea. As I gazed up at it, I felt like the only human being who was awake, the only one who could breathe in the pungent scent of the cedar and release it back into the world. I knew the tree was old and had come as a sapling from another land to be planted by a loving hand three hundred years ago. During her sojourn near that beach, the mother cedar gave life to many other trees, her deep roots withstanding many storms. The children of the mother cedar had died at the hands of men to become houses, tables, and boats to bring in the sea's harvest.

Over time, the fishermen had spared this particular tree, this night's companion of mine, to remain alive, only because it provided shade on hot days for their rest. The cedar tree accepted all, withstood all, and gave shade and shelter to all creatures without hesitation or resentment. She sheltered even those men and the sons of the men who had cut her children down.

When it comes time for the tree to die, she will simply die limb by limb, and those living things that survive her will then use her body, partly as a home for insects, partly as firewood or another table or another boat—or a *cross*, a cross for the Romans.

She will have no memory of me, but perhaps she will have in her fibers some joy at having been there with me during that sacred night. In the wood itself, there will no longer be the memory of her aloneness. And the joy will continue in the fire from her wood or the children of the insects who feed upon her in death or in the table made from her thick branches. For most of the night, I breathed with the cedar, and I felt her gratitude.

At first light, I blessed the tree, and she blessed me. After making my way back to camp where the men still slept, I put more wood on the fire, and once it caught, I began to cook more fish for breakfast. I needed to make ready for the short walk to the synagogue in Capernaum. There, I knew we would find much curiosity, as well as a measure of anger from the disciples' families and the townspeople. Yet I knew there would also be light. Even with the men asleep, there was so much light that its gathering brightness joined the dawn. This wonder moved deep within my heart along with the memory of the night and the brave tree's fragrance.

I closed my eyes and felt Abba's peace wash over me once more, as if the company of these men and their light brought with it a pervasive and all-encompassing tranquility.

As I took another breath, I thought I could smell the distant cedar once more.

Chapter 49

AD 36, and the twenty-third year of the reign of the emperor Tiberius, in a house by the sea in Tyre

In another blink of an eye, the orchard and Yeshua vanish. Instantly, everything changes.

The gnarled spirals of olive tree trunks give way to the ordered grace of a colonnade framing the deep-blue hues of the Mediterranean and a cloudless sky. Trying to get my bearings in this totally new place, I find myself sitting on some cushions next to a low table of rose-colored marble. I'm on a terrace with Corinthian pillars supporting an elaborately patterned ceiling. It's midday, but the sun is low, far to the south, and the air is crisp and cool.

It's winter.

Like a cupped hand, a Roman-style villa surrounds the semicircular porch. I sit there in my desert tunic, which provides some warmth against the afternoon's offshore breeze. An attractive young woman enters the porch from one of the wide doors in the house. It isn't the opulence of Nura's palace described by Micha'el, but it's pleasant, situated in the best neighborhood I've seen yet. With luxuriant potted palms as well as flowers and other trimmed shrubbery, I feel like I'm kicking back in a Roman version of Hawaii. I shake my head, trying to reconcile this scene with the evening near Gat-Shemanin and Yeshua's story of the mystical night and morning by the Galilean Sea. In this fragrant, peaceful setting I think about how much Sharon would like it here and wonder what she's doing, how my kids are. Is any time passing back there? I miss the sound of Gabriella and Sophie laughing, the nightly music that wafts out of our family room when they watch their stupid TV comedy shows. The woman's voice shakes me from my home-thoughts.

"The mistress will be here shortly."

She places a cup of red wine by me on the table and a cup of white wine across from me.

"Who is your mistress?"

The woman smiles as if to question whether I'm teasing her or I'm the biggest idiot who's ever wandered through these doors. When she sees that I'm truly lost, she takes pity on me.

"Why, the mistress is Salome, from Galilee originally," the woman says as if surprised she has to tell me this.

The blood freezes in my veins. I think she speaks of the lethal daughter of Herodias, the fierce wife of Herod Antipater. A shiver runs through me now. Soon I'll be meeting the villainous princess who ordered the Immerser's head on a platter.

"Oh, here she is," the serving woman says as I brace myself. Because I received the download that only seven years have passed since the execution of Yeshua, I expect to see the lithe figure of a dancing beauty only a few years older than she was on the night she asked her stepfather/ uncle for that fearsome favor. Instead, a more mature woman, probably in her late forties or early fifties, moves purposefully toward me, her head bent slightly forward like a charging ram. She is lean and walks like an athlete.

She's not how I pictured the seductive Salome.

The download tells me that Herodias's daughter later became a queen in her own right and that she married Philip—another tetrarch, another brother of Herod Antipater, and therefore another uncle of hers. I stand as she approaches with her hand extended.

"Your majesty," I say uncomfortably and take her hand.

I don't know if I should kiss it. I'm from California, and we aren't trained in royal etiquette—or, really, much etiquette at all. Actually, I would like to yank her arm out of its socket, but I smile politely instead.

She glares at me as if I'd just called her a *bitch*.

"Why do you address me so strangely?" the woman asks me with regal indignation.

"The servant told me you were Salome."

"I am Salome," she replies.

"The daughter of Herodias?"

A look of horror crosses her face, and she scowls like the school principal, whose office I regularly visited in elementary school. I brace for the scolding about to come.

"I am not that harlot's daughter!" she shouts.

I'm puzzled, but I quickly gather my wits and put together that the dancing princess may not be the only woman in Galilee named Salome. I realize my mistake, but I am amazed that this woman would shout such a treasonous and critical name about a powerful person in a day when there's no freedom of speech. I glance around quickly, and she notices my concerned expression.

"That living horror, Herodias, and that louse of a traitor husband of hers are gone to Gaul, banished by the emperor Caligula," she huffs. "And good riddance, as far as I am concerned. When I think of their unspeakable deeds, I pray the Father deals with them mercifully when the Mashiach returns!"

She takes a deep breath and regains her composure, and then she gestures for me to sit down opposite her. She sips her wine, inviting me with a nod to do the same. I take a sip, thinking I will need all of it and more to deal with her explosive intensity.

Who is she?

Miramee must have sent me here for a reason other than to discuss the well-known failings of Mr. and Mrs. Herod.

"My name *is* Salome, but the followers of the Way call me Mother Salome," she says after another sip. "And I do not dance!" she adds with disdain.

I wait for her to continue, but she looks out to the sea that the breezes have now ruffled into a vast blue field dotted with whitecapped swells. A full minute—or two—goes by. No one hurries through anything in this time period. A memory, a meal, a walk: all are cadenced and follow a natural rhythm that is different from twenty-first-century America, and often irritatingly so. Finding a way to come into that spacing of words, customs, and actions must be part of what I'm here to learn. I check my patience once more as I wait for this regal but non-dancing Salome to speak again.

"I am a mother but the Rabbi Yeshua called me this name because of my lebak," she says, gazing at me as if I should know the deep honor associated with that word.

"*Lebak?*"

Clearly disappointed, she sees that I have no idea what the word means. She frowns slightly and sighs.

"In our language, there is a word for *heart* that not only indicates the organ but also means the center from which life radiates outward into the world. The word is *lebak*, or heart. He called me Mother Salome as an affectionate name but one that carries a deep meaning. He saw something else in me that I did not see." Salome turns her face again to the sea.

"So you were a disciple?" I ask.

She scowls again, marveling at my ignorance. It'd be helpful to receive some kind of flippin' download about her, but nothing comes. I'm drawing a total blank. Scanning what I'm beginning to trust as my sense of where and when I am at any given moment, I know that I'm in AD 36 in the coastal city of Tyre north of Galilee: modern-day Lebanon.

That's it. That's all I know. So here I sit until the mystery works itself into some kind of understanding.

Mother Salome sees that I'm waiting for her to enlighten me, exhales another exasperated sigh, and decides just to plow ahead.

"I am the mother of Johanan and Yakov," she says as if that much is obvious. But it's not. I do remember that it was Johanan and Yakov whom Yeshua called forth in the previous story, so I know that much.

Okay. Lost again.

This scowling woman is sitting in an oceanfront villa in Tyre, and when last I heard, her two boys and husband were fishermen in Bethsaida on the Sea of Galilee.

What's happened?

Where does all the money for this lifestyle come from? Do they have lottery winners in the first century? Where are the others: the husband, Zavdai, and the rest of her family? Why is she so far from home in an era when most people die less than ten miles from where they were born?

As I soak in my bewildered stew, Mother Salome sits staring at me, smirking. I don't mean to second-guess Miramee's wisdom, but what am I doing here talking with this perturbed woman?

Scanning the exits, I say, "Maybe I should come back at another time."

As I stand, she puts a hand over my wrist and yanks me down. Like the Greek guy pushing my arm to get on Andreas's boat, it pisses me off when people touch me like that.

"Stay here," she demands as if speaking to a tyke. "We have work to do."

"But it seems I caught you at a bad time," I say between my teeth, and then I stop as she puts a finger to her lips.

"Listen now and stop talking," she says. "With what I have seen, with whom I have walked and all that I am commanded to share, you need to sit and silently listen."

Elementary-school-principal Mother Salome brooks no argument, so I settle back on the cushions and take the cup of wine, swilling it down. The attentive servant girl appears out of nowhere, refilling it. The breeze now fills my lungs with its salty freshness, and I sip more of the wine, forcing myself to calm down, relax, and focus on what matters most, what brought me here in the first place.

The fulfillment of my longing.

Chapter 50

Mother Salome:

As you must know, I am not from here. My father purchased this house when I was a girl and the times at home were uncertain. He felt we needed a safe place to go if things in Galilee went badly. We came here every year, and since my father's death, Zavdai and I have continued that tradition. We enjoyed traveling here and living by the Great Sea instead of the Galilean Sea, but now I stay here only for safety when Galilee or Jerusalem are too dangerous—as they are these days.

Bethsaida will always be home. We were so proud of the synagogue in nearby Capernaum. It's a solid stone building, simple and spacious. We all sat together, *men and women*, in *that* synagogue. Moreover, we could have ten *persons* as opposed to ten men to make the quorum. Being a Gentile, you must understand that we required at least ten in order to have the blessings and say the *Sh'ma Israel*: "*Sh'ma Israel, MarYah Alahan, MarYah Khad Hu.* Hear, O Israel: Adonai is our Elohim, Adonai is One!"

Men, women, and children all said the holy prayer in our synagogue. We could have prayed alone, of course, but if we wanted to pray together, there had to be ten of us.

On that morning, I had another reason to go to the Shabbat service. I wanted to see this young man who had taken our sons away, for I was very angry and shocked at the change in them. Yakov and Johanan sat with Yeshua, when I thought they should have sat with their families. They were on the stone benches directly across the sanctuary from us, and I did not turn my gaze away from them. I wanted to see them squirm!

Poor Kefah's wife and her mother were also there. The mother, Rina, did not look well at all. Those two women had taken such good care of Andreas's daughter after the death of his young wife—bless their kind hearts—as if she was theirs. And there was Kefah, sitting with the young rabbi rather than with his family. I could not believe my eyes, nor could anyone else. The story about those four had traveled fast: how they had dropped everything to follow this strange Nasrene rabbi. *We* had heard that he himself had just returned from wandering like a madman alone in the desert for nearly two months!

These were my thoughts at the time. I wanted to be there to glare some sense back into those men. I had heard from my friend that the elders would let Yeshua speak that day. I hoped so. My heart was so full of rage. I wanted to hear how he'd sent my boys into a trance and gotten them to follow him around like well-trained dogs! As we sat on the stone benches, I wished for the sitting blanket that I had left at home, for my backside was aching. I was furious about that too, because if the boys had not angered me so, I would have remembered the blanket.

All of us, and especially Zavdai, had suffered a sleepless night. I saw how betrayed he was by his own sons. I felt the betrayal too. How sinful it was for them to leave their father and his boats. My husband has many boats of his own and all of my father's, so this was no slight matter. Most people consider my sons very fortunate, as they were set to inherit a large and profitable business just as I had. All their father asked of them was their hands and their loyalty. What was even more painful was that they seemed at peace with themselves. They did not even look my way. I was impatient for my chance to grab their ears and tell them what I thought of their behavior.

Kefah's wife got up to help her poor mother out of the synagogue. Kefah stayed seated, letting his wife struggle. I prayed to Elohim to give me patience with these men. Oh, how I wanted to take a sturdy stick to them!

I rose to help them, taking Rina's elbow to steady her. "Dear, what is wrong with your mother?" I asked.

"Oh, she has not felt well these past two days," she whispered.

Once outside, we set Rina on a bench.

"She was very upset when Kefah did not come home last night, as everyone seems to know—as you know yourself, poor Salome! Your two boys as well!"

"I don't like the look of the young rabbi!" Rina croaked angrily.

"Mother, it's all right. He is just passing through. Everything will be back to normal by next week."

I nodded my agreement, but Rina turned and gave me a frightening glare.

"Mark my words, Salome, mark my words! He is passing through, but he will take our men with him!" With that, she coughed so violently, I thought she would vomit right there in the street. As the two women turned and limped down the street, arm in arm, I felt a streak of fear climb up my backbone. I returned to the synagogue with a tight knot in my stomach.

The readings from the Holy Scrolls were already completed, and the elder introduced the young rabbi from Nasrath. He was very thin. *What does a mother feed her son that he should look like that? Either one of my boys would make two of him!*

He stood in the center of the synagogue for several moments in complete silence, simply looking around at us, a pleasant look on his face. I remember thinking that he was rather handsome, like Zavdai so many years before. Then he started to speak, and I felt my heart begin to warm. I don't know how to describe the beauty of his voice. He began to speak of his Father's Kingdom. As he was obviously no prince, I knew he was referring—almost blasphemously—to Elohim.

Yet there was that voice. It was like a warm breeze over a field of spring flowers. It wrapped me up like a lovely blanket of lamb's wool. His words were wise, but the sound, the vibration I felt when he spoke, moved through me like waves of cool water. It made me feel connected, as if we all knew that Elohim was with us right here in Capernaum in that very moment. I do not know how long he spoke. I only knew I wanted to hear more.

My life was never the same after that first Shabbat encounter.

When he finished and sat down, I began to weep. I could not control it. That surprised me. I always keep a dignified presence, but I found myself sobbing. My daughter put her arm around me. In my mind, the ancient words of Job echoed again and again: "Yet in my flesh shall I see Elohim!"

I raised my head to find Rabbi Yeshua looking directly at me in the kindliest way. My tears ceased, and I felt the greatest contentment I had ever known. From deep within me, I could feel something moving out to him. At first, I thought he was pulling my heart from my chest, but then I realized it was the other way around; my heart sought to give itself to him.

All irritations, aches, and pains left my body at once. This was remarkable, because at that time in my life, I was usually irritated or aching about something. My heart responded and went out to him, and I instantly understood why the boys had followed him. We were of one mind, and I vowed never to say anything to dissuade them.

Chapter 51

AD 30, and the seventeenth year of the reign of the emperor Tiberius, Gat-Shemanin

The brilliant afternoon by the sea in Tyre changes back into the olive orchard at dusk. My heart seems to sink with the dwindling light. These transitions are wearing me out. I'm unsure whether I'm the best candidate to be witnessing all this. Never will be saint material, I guess I'm only a family man who's beginning to feel the absence of my ladies. I sigh deeply as the shadows lengthen with the evening's approach; the thick tree trunks stand like dark figures keeping vigil, silent witnesses of the night's approach.

I'm feeling very alone in this orchard. Creeped out a little. I scan the area, looking for Yeshua but I can't see him.

Smoke curls into my nostrils, but I am not near enough to the encampment to smell the fires. My imagination begins to run wild. Is the Tempter close?

I feel something like a presence, an evil presence. Is he here for me? Blood freezes in my veins, and my chest begins to hurt.

"Hey, listen to me, universe, or God, or Elohim," I shout. "Why me? I've got news for you. I'm nobody! So what am I doing on the great stage of Yeshua's life? Why should somebody like me interest any of these magnificent and terrible beings? I'm so not a player in this league."

I understand that it's an unimaginable honor to have spoken with Miramee, Andreas, and the Immerser. It rockets far beyond words to encounter Yeshua in the flesh. But the Tempter's knowing about me is as incredibly frightening as those others are amazing. It's like knowing I'm on a Mafia hit list.

There could be danger waiting for me around any bend in the path, danger that could erase me from the lives of my wife and daughters. I breathe slowly, trying to calm down and bring myself to center again. I know fear accomplishes nothing, but that information by itself doesn't lessen my terror.

Rustle. Damn!

Branches move about twenty feet behind me. I turn suddenly to see nothing but a swaying lower limb of a tree, some of its dead leaves somersaulting to the ground.

"Who's there?" I ask.

Silence.

I begin to stride as fast as I can, short of breaking into a full-on sprint. I'm back on the path I remember walking with Yeshua. I hear the rustling behind me, closing in, and I feel as if I'm in a slasher movie. But I'm not. This is happening.

Holy shit, what am I going to do?

I can't hurt a fly or permanently crush a dried leaf here, but somebody, anybody—even a second grader—could kill me. I've never felt so vulnerable. I keep walking, but to where? It all looks the same, and it's getting darker.

What am I doing out here in the middle of the goddamn night anyway? What am I doing out here, period? Right now, I should be at a podium in San Jose, sipping burnt coffee and fielding questions from insurance agents.

I walk faster, looking furtively around for Yeshua, or an exit, or something that will get me out of here. I don't want to meet the Tempter.

"Deliver me. Deliver me from him. Deliver me."

This is the shortest version of the Lord's Prayer, ever. I stand, scanning the endless, darkening limbs of the trees. Now the horror-movie scene is complete, as a ghostly mist fingers and spreads into the orchard, covers the low bushes, and filters onto the path like a waiting phantom.

Then I feel the hand on my shoulder. I jump and think my heart will stop, but it doesn't. I don't want to turn. I don't know if I can face him. If it's the Tempter, he's too close. Every cell in my body seems to constrict in fear, but, instead of panic, I feel an odd comfort and warmth, like a remembered Tahitian rain falling inside me. I turn my head to the side, mustering what is left of my waning courage, looking but afraid to look. I feel my lungs fill with smokeless air. The hand tightens its grip upon my shoulder. Then, I know without knowing.

The hand belongs to Yeshua.

I exhale a relieved breath into the evening trees.

"Peace, Traveler. Peace!" he says. With that voice, that intonation that defies description, tranquility edges slowly, lightly into my mind. "You cannot see if your eyes are filled with fear. You cannot hear if your mind is always speaking."

"I could not see you," I reply.

We begin to walk. He repeats what he said, because my rattled nerves left me half deaf the first time. I am trying hard to focus, and I note that Yeshua shakes his head.

"You stagger under the weight of your effort. Release mercifully the mind's grip upon you. Do you see how you witness everything and everyone through your own ideas? You even see me through the veil of your thoughts. Your beliefs color all that lies in front of your eyes. When you encounter those who do not meet the ideas you call beliefs, you judge them harshly. When your own actions do not meet your ideas, you judge yourself even more fiercely. You are not mindful of how often these ruthless judgments occur. You condemn yourself and others seventy times seven every day."

Yeshua is correcting me—personally. As the recognition of that singular honor recedes, I immediately think about how I judge others continuously. It seems to be nonstop and automatic. The seventy times seven (my brain reflexively clicks out the product, 490) occurrences every day may be a conservative number.

He's right. Once you stuff a human being into the pigeonhole you create, you can only see them through the opening in that pigeonhole.

My daughter came home from science class one day and told me about Dunbar's Number. It apparently refers to the physical limits of our human brain—and the primate brain as well—in that we can only truly know about one hundred fifty people as *people*. Beyond that number, we have to stereotype, categorize, and infer group characteristics, because we cannot *know* them individually. I'm not sure that's the only explanation, but it makes sense to me when I consider how I clump people together in order to make sense of my world—or the one I'm in at present.

This inability to see a person as she or he truly is causes immense suffering. It's a dangerous form of human blindness.

There's another rustle in the mist-covered shrubs by the side of the path. I smell the fireless smoke once more. My heart jackhammers inside my chest.

Yeshua beckons me closer. "He comes at me in many ways. He never lets me forget that he is lord of this world. Capernaum was one of the first times he challenged me in public. And it will not be the last."

Chapter 52

Yeshua:

I stood before the gathering. It was my first time in synagogue since the wilderness, since the Father's great revelation. Expectant faces regarded me curiously, but the words did not come out immediately. I waited for the Father to inform me, and many people found the silence awkward and unsettling. The Father waited for their minds to slow down enough so they could hear his words. Therefore, I waited with him. The minds of this congregation settled quickly, because I could begin after a very short time.

"The Father wants you to know that the Kingdom is already here. You must gain the eyes to see it, for now darkness enshrouds them. I am here to bring the light back into your eyes so that you can see what the Father has prepared for you. Do not turn and face the other way. You show your backs to him without knowing you are doing so. Turn yourselves around, and see! The Kingdom is here. It is not somewhere else. It cannot be. If the Father is here, so is the Kingdom."

After some discourse on the readings from Torah, I ended the talk with a parable.

> The Kingdom is like the man who lives in a stone house, who orders a delicious supper for his family and then discovers that there is a hungry, blind beggar outside the house. The poor man smells the delectable meal being prepared and begins to search around the walls of the house for the food he smells. As the meal

is served, the master of the house sends a servant out to invite him in to eat.

The servant says to him, "The master invites you in to eat the meal with his family!"

"I cannot trust you," the beggar replies. "I know the meal is nearby. I can smell it!" He picks up some grass, eats it, and spits it out.

The master of the house takes greater pity on the man and sends the cook out to him. The cook implores, "The master assures you that the meal I prepared is inside where it is warm and safe."

"Ah, now I know you are trying to trick me!" the poor blind beggar says as he touches the stone walls of the house. "There is no house. This is the rocky part of a hill exposed by the cut of the road."

The master's love for the man has not diminished, so finally he sends his eldest son out to the beggar. The cook has thrown some fat out the window for the dogs, and the beggar finds it and begins chewing on it.

"My father insists that you come in and share the banquet with us," the son says as he tries to help the man up by taking his arm. "You need the nourishment and the warmth of our fire."

"Leave me alone! Liar!" cries the man, shaking off the hand of the son. "I have found what was making the delicious smell, and I am not letting go of it for anything or anyone! You lie about this banquet. If it is true, then bring it to me here! I will not go a step with you! Now, be gone!"

There was some laughter at the stiff-necked beggar's stubbornness.

At that, the master sends a plate out to the man, who eats voraciously and then drops the plate on the ground, breaking it. The beggar walks off into the cold wilderness without looking back or offering his thanks.

Nonetheless, the master sends his son to follow the man at a distance. He gives him these instructions:

"Stay with him for seventy-seven days, but do not let him be aware of your presence. If he turns around to find his way to our house, lead him back. If he falls sick, bring him here for care. If he dies, bring back his body to bury in our tomb.

If, after seventy-seven days, he continues on without turning around, you must leave him, for there are others to serve."

The son goes out after the blind man and does his father's bidding.

I stopped speaking, and all the people looked at one another quizzically.

"What happened to the beggar?" a young man shouted out. "Did he return or die?"

"He did not turn around, but he did fall ill," I said, musing briefly how the human mind takes a created story and weaves it into something real. "And when the beggar was so desperate that he thought he would die, he let the son take him back to the stone house to be cared for by the master and his household. Just as the master never gave up on the ungrateful beggar, so too does the Father wait patiently for each one to come into the Kingdom."

Story is a powerful teacher. Heads nodded throughout the synagogue, approving its wisdom.

"Let those who have ears, hear this!" I finished and sat down.

Chapter 53

My words fly up, my thoughts remain below:
Words without thoughts never to heaven go.
-William Shakespeare, *Hamlet, Act 3, Scene 3* (ca. AD 1600)

AD 30, and the seventeenth year of the reign of the emperor Tiberius, Gat-Shemanin

Among the trees, the night falls quickly. Their sinewy boughs capture and hold the fading light, as if somehow bringing it greedily into themselves and thus casting into mysterious darkness the path that lies before us. Thankfully, the moon arose before dusk, and I step cautiously within its silvery, muted beams.

Yeshua still wears the chef's cap, his mantle slung around his neck like a stole. As we walk in the late-winter evening, I feel peaceful, even though my mind transitions rapidly between multiple times and places. Yet all of it somehow melds together in this single moment. Yeshua is a lone encounter with a dizzying variety of nuanced colors, moods, and sounds. Words fall short when describing my happiness in his presence, but it's like the absolute wonder and joy a kid feels on Christmas morning. He's like Christmas morning every moment. If he says nothing, if he is only breathing and walking, it's enough.

All at once, he stops on the shadowy path. I'm on his right, and I watch as he turns to look right past me at something in the trees. He has almost an animal attentiveness in the way he moves and peers into the bush. I suddenly think of Aderes, the dog who protected Yeshua from the cobras.

I hear a growl, and my circulation ices up again. Slowly I turn my head to the right, following the direction of Yeshua's gaze. I see a leopard, its fierce eyes trained on me, poised on its front paws with its hind legs arched, ready to attack.

My memory sparks the image of the leopard in my dreams before all this happened. Identical. The download tells me this is Ose, Lord of Hell. My heart slithers up into my throat. Without moving, my eyes furtively scan the orchard for the best direction in which to bolt. My awareness of Yeshua disappears, and my attention zaps back to Ose, who continues his low growl. Only then do I see the dark-robed figure standing directly behind the leopard like a column of black smoke. All that I can see of him is his pale, silver-lit face. In a reflexive and noticeable alchemy, my peace of a moment ago transforms into horror, for I see that, like the leopard, he looks not at Yeshua but at me—at me?

The Tempter glides forward a few feet closer to me. There's no clear end to his robe or the background of the trees; it's blurred and smoky, as if he emits darkness and confusion rather than the clear light Micha'el exudes.

Where is Yeshua?

I hope he's still beside me, but I don't know for sure, for I cannot feel him. I want to turn and see, but I can't risk taking my eyes off the leopard or the Tempter. All I feel at this moment is a heart-stopping fear.

"You are right to be afraid, Traveler," the Tempter whispers slowly.

I stare evil in the face, and staring back at me, as if contained in one solitary figure, is all of the cruelty in Hitler's holocaust or the undiscriminating devastation of Hiroshima.

"Or is it *John?*" he taunts. "That pretty nurse far away calls you John or Jack. Yes, Jack. Ah, yes, maybe even … Jacky. Ha! Cute. The other two call you Daddy, don't they?"

If a sewer could speak, it would sound like this thing. He's talking about my family.

Why?

I smell the smoke again, its thick coils constricting my throat as my bronchial tubes start to shut down. I start coughing as the worm of fear burrows deep into the lining of my stomach.

The Tempter approaches me, his eyes looking like two burning holes. As my panic grows, I still don't feel Yeshua's presence. Maybe he's left me alone to face this horror by myself.

*Is this another one of God's stinking tests? Damn it! Where **is** Yeshua? Why did he desert me? What am I going to do?*

How am I going to stay alive? Why is God doing this to me? Fuck!

I know I can wrestle and pin down most of life's challenges but the Tempter is way above my lightweight class. Or anybody else's. I cock my head slightly to the left, attempting a glance behind me, but I quickly stop myself. If I look away from the Tempter toward the place where Yeshua stood, I'll see that I'm truly alone, and then, surely, the Tempter will devour me alive. He knows my name. Satan knows about my wife and daughters. I cough and shudder as the sweat of deep fear claims me. Heart pounding, I try to get my breath, and find I cannot fill my lungs. The fear is fluid, flowing like a cold, constricting solution injected into my arteries.

The Tempter raises his smoking finger at me, and it comes within inches of my left eye. The fingernail is a dull-yellow spike, and I think he is about to put out my eye with it. I can't move defensively. I'm frozen with terror, but I'm also entranced by this most sinister of creatures. I feel like a cobra in a basket, swaying to the charmer's music, imprisoned by the sound, unable to lash out and protect myself.

Then I remember sitting by the sleeping Yeshua in the desert, my hand on his back. I remember that there exists no time when we are alone.

The angel protects. Yeshua protects.

This is like any other illusion of evil. False.

Whoosh! Suddenly, in the space of a few inches between the nail and my eye, a black metal sickle swings down with the precision of a surgeon's scalpel. I fall back, and so does the Tempter, as Ose rasps a high-pitched snarl. At once, a sphere of light about the size of a volleyball comes out from the trees behind Yeshua, who remains motionless, his sickle dangling from his right hand. He never left me.

The ball of white light dodges about and then hovers between the Tempter and us. Is this some kind of fantasy or science fiction? Is Spielberg or Christopher Nolan standing somewhere around here with a megaphone and a baseball cap?

As a boy, I used humor to deflect my fear. Right now, I'm scared, but I know I'm not alone. A bit of courage seeps into my heart.

"Micha'el," the Tempter says. There's the orange flash, and then a small fire bursts out next to Ose, igniting some grass. He snarls and jumps backward.

"Fire. Interesting tactic," the Tempter says, and then his eyes pin me again as he grins disgustingly. "I know your name, Traveler," he says darkly.

The words from the Sequence part of my favorite classical piece, *Mozart's Requiem*, come into my mind.

> *Confutatis maledictis,*
> *lammis acribus addictis:*
> *oca me cum benedictis."*

> While the wicked are confounded,
> Doomed to flames of woe unbounded
> Call me with thy saints surrounded.

In an instant, everyone else vanishes, and I'm on the orchard path alone with Yeshua once more. I sit down in the dirt, burying my face in my hands. I can hear him squatting next to me. He takes my hands away from my face. When I open my eyes, he's sitting opposite me, holding my hands.

"Peace, Traveler," he says. "He is always near. You have to be ever watchful. Yet as close as he is, I am ever closer."

He looks deep into my eyes, and I can feel some kind of understanding pass into me. The fluid in my veins feels warm now. The devil's ice has melted.

"Yes, Lord."

"I told you once before: I am not a lord," he says with a wry wink. "We will continue now. The Father uses all and everyone for good, but first you must pay attention so that you are able to see."

With his words, my mind dispels the darkness surrounding us, and I can imagine the brightness of a Capernaum morning again—although it is the first time since I came here that I would rather it be a Monterey morning instead.

The Rabbuni speaks, and my homesick focus returns to him.

Chapter 54

Yeshua:

The room was as silent as stone as I returned to my bench seat in the synagogue. Then, as if they had suddenly come alive, the heads of the townspeople twisted and turned in hushed conversation. They were unsure what to make of me. As they exchanged ideas, I began to notice the many-colored lights illuming them, as distinct and bright as a rainbow's shaft of radiance against the blackness of a thunderhead. It was an exquisite sight to see.

Breathing in their light as if it was air, and their colors as if fragrances, my heart was full with love for them as they noised about in wonder. Each person's radiance was a unique way for the Father to come to me, a reminder that no matter how these sheep spent their days, the essential memory of the Father resided in them all, even those who felt threatened and wanted me ejected from their town at once. Whether or not any one person might be hostile toward me, the light of the congregation in all its colors welcomed me. In truth, mindful or not, they had waited for me in hope for many generations. Their spirits felt this.

Before the service, I went with Kefah and Yakov as they approached an elder of the synagogue, a dignified merchant respected by his neighbors. They were seeking permission for me to speak. I stood a distance from them as they took the elder aside for a word, but I could still hear the exchange.

"I will have to consult with the other elders," he responded with some hesitation.

"Everyone knows you make those decisions on your own," Kefah replied.

Eyeing me, the elder was clearly uncomfortable, and he absently stroked his long, graying beard. He finally nodded. "You and your families are my friends and the pillars of this synagogue," he said. "I will let the rabbi from Nasrath speak this time as a sign of respect to you."

As I sat there, remembering that moment and enjoying the lights and noises from the congregation, the elder rose and walked slowly to the center of the room to speak.

"My friends," he began, and then he froze in midsentence, staring openmouthed at the entrance. We all turned to see, framed in the doorway, the figure of a bent-over man, who then stumbled into the midst of the gathering. Distorted and spastic, the man's body was as crooked as the limb of an olive tree, his age a mystery because of the filth covering him. His hair was matted, and his skin was a sorrow of sores and cuts. The stench from vomit and the stink of excrement caused many of the congregation to cover their noses and faces. In his rags, he was like a man who was dead but still living.

I could feel my heart fill with compassion for him. Several of the elders and other men jumped to their feet, preparing to throw him out, but I stood and raised my hand to halt them. The man staggered over to me, dropped to the floor, and then began convulsing on his back.

"Get that man out of here!" demanded a woman as she gathered her children close to her. Others sounded their agreement, and some moved toward him, but no one touched the man. They were afraid to be close to him. I paused for a moment, waiting for the people to calm down and pay attention. Then I peered deep into the man's bloodshot eyes.

The Evil One has many slaves in this man, I thought.

"We. Have. Nothing. For you, Yeshua of Nasrath!" the man snarled at me, each word tearing into my eardrums. The voice was a mixture of voices, like an odd Greek chorus speaking in a strange strangulation of sound. I looked deeper into his wild eyes. I had seen those eyes many times before. The bodies were different, but the eyes were always the same.

"Are. You. Going. To destroy. Us?" the demon shouted at me. After that question, the people began to argue hotly, all of them alarmed by this present evil, some fearful that this unholy lamb defiled their synagogue. The knowledge that these demons were familiar with me seemed to disturb the congregation the most.

I raised my hand to silence them.

With the noise muted, I prayed for the Father to release this lamb. The possessed man rolled over on all fours and then propped himself up on his haunches. He glared at me defiantly, laughing, but in a joyless, menacing way.

Suddenly, with a thick, scornful voice, he growled at me. "I know who you are," he said, pausing after each word so that all could hear him clearly. "You. Are. The *Mashiach*! The Holy. One. Of *Elohim*!"

I became aware of the seed of anger growing in me, rising like a mustard tree. It was huge, rooting deep in my heart. I cautioned myself to take great care, for even the holiest of angers is like running on a path filled with treacherous pits. Anger extinguishes the light, making true sight impossible, so the angry person is in great danger of falling into one of those deep pits—and worse, of taking others with him. This applied even more to me, as I was then fully aware of the power of the Father residing in my body. Yet I knew that my calling by the Father was still private and intimate. Its revelation to others could not come from the casual—but deliberate—banter of a pack of the Tempter's slaves.

When the creature announced that I was the Mashiach, it was not as a sign of reverence. It was a clever, calculated tactic to raise doubt and fear in the minds of the people who had just received my words. Who would believe any good news coming from one named by a demon?

And if they heard that I thought I was the Mashiach of Elohim at this point, at the very beginning of the ministry, every move I made and every word I spoke would be judged in the shadows of suspicion and doubt. They would dismiss me out of hand.

The revelation of the Mashiach must come to each human being in his or her heart in the fullness of time. Demons wished to play with this knowledge darkly, just as their father, the Tempter, had amused himself with me in the desert.

I quelled my holy fury, drew in a deep breath, and commanded him: "Silence! And leave this man, demon!"

Because of the truth, the embattled man convulsed violently, screaming loud and pitiably. The mother of Yakov and Johanan shrieked, and her daughter caught her in a faint. Noses and mouths were covered again as the air thickened with a stench so putrid that many gagged. The large lamps suspended from the ceiling swayed on their chains like reeds in the wind, their lights extinguished. Several people cried out in horror. Although it was a warm day outside, the room grew very cold, dank, and heavy with fear. The congregation rose to stand, yet they remained as hushed and still as Grecian statues. The man lay motionless on his side, like a dead dog.

"He's gone! You killed him," one man shouted.

Suddenly the possessed man's right foot twitched, and then his legs drew up to his chest as if he were an infant awakening from a night's sleep.

"Look! He lives!" a woman cried.

The man blinked hard and then squinted as if he had just stepped from a cave into the brilliant sunlight. As his eyelids fluttered, tears began to course down his dirty cheeks. All eyes were upon me as I reached out to help him up. The man's hand was rough and dry but cool, and I could feel the energy flow from me into him. He looked up and smiled widely at me—with only a few teeth present. His red eyes crinkled and danced with happiness. This lamb understood now that deliverance from evil brings relief, certainly, but that to receive the life of the Father again, deep into the tissues and sinews of the heart, is a gift that brings everlasting joy.

Once he received this gift of the Ruach Kudsha, he could see the joy of the Father in everything surrounding him, even the very stones of the synagogue floor.

Kefah, Andreas, Yakov, and Johanan came over and stood ready to assist the man. They paused, looking at one another to see who would be the first to touch him. Then, with a shrug, Johanan put a hand on the man, and the others followed along. The disciples lifted the man to a standing position. He was unsteady, working to find his balance, yet he still smiled as he coughed a loud and phlegm-filled hack, swallowing it rather than spitting on the floor of the synagogue. I nodded at Kefah, and they took him out to bathe him in the *mikveh*, the step-down pool used for ritual bathing and cleansing.

"Bathe him in the sea instead of the mikveh," I said. "The baths are for purification, but this man has held a demon within him. Only the sea can purify him, because it is the womb of life."

Nodding, the four men carefully led the dirty but almost dancing man out of the synagogue.

A young man came forth defiantly from the congregation.

"They violate the Shabbat!"

I could tell that he was a Pharisee from his dress and from the *targums*, bits of the Torah he wore rolled up in *tefillen*, the small boxes usually suspended from a hat during prayer by the very devout. The Word of the Father might have roped his mind with rigid thoughts, and the lust for certainty may have prevented any wisdom from moving deeper inside him, yet the fire of love for the Father also burned brightly in his heart. Therefore, this love joined him to us. He was my brother as well.

"Not true," the elder replied to the Pharisee. "We are here to help another if he or she needs it—even on Shabbat! You know this!"

"Shabbat is for man not man for the Shabbat," I added.

The young Pharisee did not care for these responses. His eyebrows first went high in amazement and then furrowed in anger, but he said no more.

After a moment, the mother of Yakov and Johanan stepped forward as well. I saw a beautiful and compassionate heart lying beneath her commanding airs. I looked in wonder at her, for I could see an amazing light emergent in her. She was haughty by habit and nature, but she possessed a radiant heart.

"Mother Salome," I said to myself, looking clearly at her. She had not taken her eyes from mine. She could not hear me, but she nodded. She stood and spoke loudly so that those outside could hear as well.

"I have a tunic I made for Johanan, but he has not yet worn it," she said. "I will give this to the poor man so that he can throw away his filthy rags." She walked out of the synagogue after my disciples. That caused much chatter, but soon others spoke up.

"I have a mantle," said another man as he turned to leave.

"I have a new belt," said another.

"My grandson's feet grew too fast, and the sandals made for him no longer fit. I will give them to the poor wretch," said the elder, bowing slightly, and departing. He could not sense his felt superiority in those words, but he and his fellow townspeople were opening up their hearts. They were learning that one could give a gift freely at any time on any day of the week—even on Shabbat.

Once the elder signaled his approval by making an offering, the entire congregation began to move to the door. There were other offers of food and shelter. A group of men began to sing a psalm as they left the synagogue.

Soon, I was alone in the empty synagogue—just the extinguished lamps, now still once more, and me. Everyone was working together to help this man on the day when some of my people thought such actions should be forbidden. The elder knew it, and thus did the others learn. When a lamb needs help, you find it and save it—even on Shabbat.

In the empty hall, I looked around and felt the warmth of all who were still here, but not in the body. I sat down and rested with them in the wonder that the Father gave so generously to me and through me to all my sheep. I heard the strains, the gentle vibrations of music that the ears cannot hear.

No one came to thank me, nor did I wish for some display of gratitude. This had come from the Father, but he would have to wait for gratitude as well, because his children tend to withhold their thanks. In truth, genuine gratitude, like humility, comes only in the fullness of time. I sat there alone on a bench with the colorful lights from my companions in another realm. The silence of love began filling me again. For a few precious moments, I needed nothing, and no one needed me.

The townspeople were off to see the man bathed in the sea and dressed in his new clothes, breaking the Shabbat to help him. The Pharisee man and his friends would look on with shock and anger at such offensive behavior by a whole community, talking to others about this strange day and this even stranger man from Nasrath. My enemies' ideas of what was an affront to Elohim were misguided, and such misguided, wrongly shepherded men often act on these mistaken beliefs. Sadly, these actions result in evil, and many times they end in the spilling of innocent blood.

Yet in that moment, all I had to do was sit with the Father and the companions of the light. I could have sat there for days, but soon it was over. A young man who looked like Kefah came in holding a little girl. He cleared his throat to gain my attention.

"Rabbi, I am the son of Shimon," he pronounced, his voice breaking.

"This is the daughter of your disciple, Andreas," he continued. I smiled at the little girl. When she saw my smile, she turned and buried her head into the furry neck of her cousin. He cleared his throat again.

"My father invites you to our home for the Shabbat meal at midday," he said.

There was a moment of silence. His face twitched nervously. "Will you come, Rabbi?"

I smiled and nodded. He inclined his head and walked briskly out of the building.

As she disappeared out the doorway, the little girl waved her chubby hand, little fingers moving up and down, and then she beamed a wide smile at me. It was radiant and joyful. Like her father, she possessed the same light, bright as a noonday sun. I lingered on the stone bench for a few more moments, knowing soon that I must walk back out into the world and be the Mashiach again.

A small mouse edged warily across the floor, stopped, regarded me carefully, and then continued on her search for food. I felt inside one of the pockets Eema had sewed into my mantle. There were two dried-up dates from the small oasis in the desert, which I had kept as a reminder of the Father's care. I set one upon the floor under the bench and then stood. I walked out of the synagogue, the Father's meeting house of prayer in Capernaum, leaving the mouse to dine upon a grand and unexpected Shabbat midday meal.

As I walked out into the warm sunshine of the Galilean afternoon, I noticed that the streets were empty except for the lone figure of a woman approaching me. Her head was covered, but from the fabric of her garments and the dignity of her carriage, I could see that she was the mother of Yakov and Johanan.

Chapter 55

AD 36, and the twenty-third year of the reign of the emperor Tiberius, in a house by the sea in Tyre

The sea still has whitecaps in the late Mediterranean afternoon. Mother Salome is where I left her: on the marble terrace, sitting right across the little table from me, chalice of wine in hand.

I am no longer in the presence of Yeshua. The breath leaks out of me like air out of a blown bicycle tire. Being ripped from Yeshua's presence is physically painful. My skin feels raw, and my head pounds, aching as though starved for air. My gut grinds with a wrenching sense of loss, which remains indefinable but perceptible, like that mirage on a desert highway.

Instantly, I feel small and insubstantial. My eyes fill with tears that stream down my cheeks. This sensed weakness embarrasses me in front of Mother Salome, who studiously watches my every gesture and expression. Very kindly, she hands me a white cloth made of something that looks like an intricately woven damask. Even in my time, I've never seen materials as beautiful as those belonging to the upper classes of the first century. I dab my eyes then blow a nose full into it before handing it back to her.

"Please keep it," she says, smiling. Yeah, I guess so. "You are not sad. He always has that effect when we leave his presence. Even if you sense your holiness more clearly, you cannot help but miss him when he leaves. You feel that you are diminished somehow. It is not the truth, but it is a very human feeling."

"But it was more than a sense of only being with him," I reply. "We became friends. I know that sounds pretentious. I mean, I am truly aware that he is the teacher too."

She nods. Her lack of surprise indicates that she has also experienced Yeshua that way.

"When we are invited to be a disciple, he remains the Rabbuni, the master, yet there is something different. He is not only the Rabbuni. He is also the companion, the friend of each of us individually, and all of us together. As a friend, he draws us into his heart, and we can feel what is like friendship at first."

"But it is more," I say.

"It is much more," she agrees. "Keep this in your heart."

Mother Salome is different now. She is wise yet present at the same time. She is not one of those spiritual types who look at you with a rather vacant, dreamy expression. She can walk with Yeshua in the Kingdom while having both feet planted firmly in her everyday existence.

"He told me about seeing you at the synagogue in Capernaum— and about how, when he spoke, you wept."

Her eyelids flutter shut for a moment to collect the memory and then to choose the right words. She is immaculate in everything, so she wishes to be precise in what she tells this foreigner.

"Yes, I wept because I felt something profound move within me, like a child in the womb, but truly the change inside me had not taken place yet. The words he spoke only prepared me for the marvel of witnessing the Rabbuni casting out the demon from that poor man. It was an enormous act of courage to perform such a miracle in the middle of our crowded synagogue, and on the Shabbat as well. Yeshua is always courageous."

She speaks about Yeshua as if he was in the house. I remind myself that this time in Tyre was six years after his death in AD 30.

"You refer to him like a living person?" I ask.

"Why, Traveler, of course, he is alive! We do not follow the way of a dead man. You do know that much, do you not?" Mother Salome asks this with her school principal's voice again.

I feel chided. I nod that I do. "How did he come to call you Mother Salome?" I ask.

"Ah." She waves a finger. "You must have left Yeshua before he told you of our encounter outside the synagogue."

I nod and take a gulp of wine, which is a light-red, mature vintage. With a pang, it occurs to me that it was probably vinted about the time of Yeshua's execution. That word *execution* is a strange one for my mind to pull out of the cosmos, yet he was an innocent victim who suffered the cruelest and most torturous death the Roman occupiers could administer. It was the form of capital punishment reserved for seditionists and murderers, Rome's special enemies who dared to rise from their low classes to challenge imperial authority. Mother Salome waits for me to finish my distracted thought-dance and return my attention to her story.

"After they cleansed the exorcised man, Andreas took the tunic I brought and dressed him in it," she says. "Then I left the shore to find Yeshua. I had to hear more from him. My heart ached to hear more."

I know exactly how she felt.

"I found Yeshua as he was leaving the synagogue. He turned to face me as if he knew I was coming. When I removed my head covering and showed my bare head in the sun, he was not startled. I began to tell him who I was, but he already knew. 'I know you, Salome,' he replied, interrupting me. This startled me, for we had never met."

I move my head toward her as she tells the story. It's as if I can see this happening through Yeshua's eyes, because I remember him telling me of her approach.

"I stood there, saying nothing, unable to say anything. He placed a hand on my shoulder, and I did not care that it was inappropriate for a man to touch another man's wife. I merely stood there in the street with his hand upon my shoulder." Mother Salome clears her throat, and some tears appear in the corners of her eyes.

"Did you feel him then?" I ask. "Did you feel him move into you like electricity?" She frowns quizzically as if to ask, "*What the hell is electricity?*"

I revise my question for her first-century ear. "Was it like lightning or great energy coursing through your body?"

Mother Salome nods her head emphatically. "Yes! Yes, that was the first time I felt it. Then he named me. After he touched my shoulder and stood in stillness with me for a moment, he said, 'I will call you *Mother Salome*, for your mother heart is spacious and a great giver of life and light.' He then left and walked away without saying another word. I was speechless, and that is rare for me. The spot where he touched me left my shoulder tingling. No one beside my parents had ever named me. It was like being reborn into someone new. From that day forward, I insisted that all the followers call me Mother Salome. And from that moment of my naming, I knew I would follow him."

Mother Salome does not weep. The servant girl appears again with another towel. Salome takes it and dabs her teary eyes delicately.

Yeshua has also called me by name: Traveler. It's a good moniker. I have traveled much and seen much. I've now seen through his eyes, experienced the vastness of his mind, his being.

But, it feels like enough. For now.

I've often said that life is a buffet: you take what you want, try a little of everything, and don't miss out. Now I can say that I haven't missed out, that I've even experienced the presence of Jesus and the friendship of his beloved ones.

What else is there?

I'm feeling compelled to go home and live out my life, colored and textured by the wonders I've seen. Yes, maybe I'll leave now as I sip red wine on an ocean terrace.

But wait. I must say good-bye to Miramee.

Mother Salome smiles at me as her features seem to change. Her face becomes more youthful, and the marble terrace becomes darker and then lighter again. It's the soft light of early morning. The terrace dissolves into the stone walls of the Ephesian house, and the moist eyes of Mother Salome now are transformed into the doe-like eyes of Miramee.

Chapter 56

AD 43, and the third year of the reign of the emperor Claudius, Ephesus

"You are back, Traveler," Miramee says melodiously, creating the now familiar music. My heart skips a beat, then another.

These changing faces and settings feel too much like a dream. I glance out the window and see a dense fog rolling through the trees as if a floating army is taking its battle positions silently, stealthfully. *Muskets at the ready!* It reminds me of the mist flowing through the olive orchard just as I saw the Tempter.

I'm happy to see Miramee, but I must admit I'm tired. I'm wearing the hell out. These amazing experiences have left me physically and mentally exhausted.

I've been away from home too long, and I can't see the purpose of witnessing any more. There's a time when you just go home and unpack your bags. And I have a lot to unpack. There's also the unsettling fact that what's taken place before my wondering but weary eyes could be illusion. After all, through the trick of calendar time, what I see and have seen was reduced to dust centuries before my mother popped me out.

That's the truth, no matter how keenly I feel the reality of it all now.

In the end, Miramee shows me places into which I cannot journey fully. All the people about whom I have come to care deeply are really ghosts. Those I now love are smoky phantoms.

Visions.

All of them. *Even Yeshua?*

What is real and what is not?

257

Miramee lasers in on me intently. "What appears to us happens on the inside of our eyes," she says. "Without eyes, there is nothing to behold."

Okay. That's stating the obvious. What's she driving at?

"The lion and the rabbit," she begins.

"The ones in the story of Yeshua's time in the desert?" I ask.

"No, the ones near your house in that land far away," she says to my widening eyes. She's talking about the mountain lion killing the rabbit on the forested road by my house. How can she know about that?

"In awakening, there must be a disruption to move one away from the familiar and invite him or her into that which is very unfamiliar."

"Are you saying that the lion and rabbit were not real?" I ask.

"You saw what you needed to see," she says. "You needed to come here. It was the beginning of awakening for you. Whether there was a physical lion eating a physical rabbit does not matter much."

"Whether or not I am hallucinating matters a hell of a lot to me!"

She recoils a bit at my volume.

Need to dial it down.

She nods but scowls at me. "I don't know that word, but I do know that you have seen many, many things to help you awaken. You must trust and exercise great care. You must have patience with the Father."

All this is causing rifts of uncertainty and fear breaking along a newly formed fault line down the center of my body. Part of me is sliding away, as Yeshua slid down that thorny hillside. I want this to stop. My throat goes dry.

"I am thirsty," I say. She fills a cup with water and ladles some stew into a bowl.

"Eat and drink," Miramee says as she edges toward me, cautiously carrying the steaming bowl in one hand and the cup in the other. After all these years, she still fears a recurrent seizure, and rightly so. As she approaches, she falters and drops the bowl, spilling the stew all over the floor. The clay cup of water goes flying and bounces off the crown of my head, spilling the water down my face and hair as I jump up to catch her, twisting my body to retrieve her.

She shakes in my arms, trembling as the water from my beard drips onto her abdomen. It's not a seizure as I remember my uncle's attacks of epilepsy. Miramee seems more afraid than convulsive, and I see that fear cross her eyes as she stares into mine. She unwinds herself from my grip and stands, straightening her clothing.

"So, you anointed me?" I say with a smile, my hand wiping my face. I feel a fine trickle of blood ooze slowly down my right temple. Apparently, the cup cut me when it banged my head.

Anointed by water *and* blood.

With her right thumb, she dabs the blood and marks two opposing arcs on my wet forehead. From her touch, I sense that there's one above and one below, intersecting at the bottom. It's the ancient sign of the fish used in the earliest Christian times. In AD 43, the followers would not be using the sign of the cross, an instrument of torture, for it would bring back fresh memories of horror and grief.

"You are now truly Traveler, a follower of the Way, and a friend of Yeshua, like we all are," she says quite seriously, still trembling slightly.

Did she just baptize me?

I inhale deeply, stuffing down a mixture of conflicting emotions. There's her closeness, her words, the water, the pain from the cup, the signing in blood, and a growing pain in my chest along the new fault line in my body, all of which mirror the ache that settles now into a single desire.

I want to go home.

As Father Joe prophesied, the wineskin is about to burst.

"First you were named for him, then you met him, and now you are aware that Yeshua knows you. He anoints you. The immersion, the death of the old you—the very small you—is painful, dark, uncertain, and often greatly sorrowful. The very small *you* doesn't wish to die. You emerge from this death and are reborn into the Rabbuni's flock, the Kingdom. These passages planned for you kindle your faith and make it as hard as forged steel so that when the Father calls, you will be able to hear and move with strength in his service. In finality, you come into the Kingdom, the sovereign presence of Elohim, as a newly formed lamb. That is the change he brings to you, Traveler."

"I felt it," I say, "when I saw the people at the supper with Andreas in Patras. I saw the levels, the depths of their loving beauty. I looked at them as Yeshua looks at us all. He sees the beauty through the disease and disfigurement of our pride and anger." I bow my head.

Complete stillness.

"What are you thinking, Traveler?" she asks.

"I am thinking of Sharon, my wife. And my daughters. It has been a very long time since I have seen my family," I reply.

"You will see them again," she says.

That's little comfort. She rises now and hands me a towel to dry off, but I am careful not to wipe the blood-sign off my forehead.

Miramee begins to mop up the combination of spills on the floor. As I stand, I look down. We both do. Apparently, when I twisted hard to catch her, my sandal caught on her brown blanket and tore its corner clear off.

"Oh, I am very sorry!" I say, picking up the piece of the blanket. It's strange, because the cloth doesn't feel like anything familiar. A brown fleck of something falls into my hand.

Miramee freezes and becomes very serious. "Please, very gently," she whispers, "give me what is in your hand." She opens her palm in a reverent but businesslike manner.

"You mean this? What is it?" I ask as I turn my hand over onto hers, checking to see if the transfer was successful. She doesn't answer but moves over to a blue glass jar on the shelf in the kitchen area, removes the leather lid, and places her open palm over the jar to shake the flake into it. She replaces the cover and returns to me.

"Now, the torn fragment," she instructs. "Again, very slowly and very carefully." Puzzled by this, I think she has some strange obsession for this blanket that I do not understand. The sensation of something remaining in my hand gnaws at me, and I check the empty palm repeatedly, as if the material had reappeared or never left.

"Miramee, we are friends, are we not?"

"Yes, of course," she says, examining the torn piece tenderly.

"Where I come from, friends keep no secrets from one another."

Her large eyes look up from the small brown patch of material in her hand and pin me.

"What is this blanket to you?" I ask.

Instead of sitting on the floor, she sits on the bench and pulls the blanket onto her lap as she has done so often. She frowns, deliberating over how she's going to say what follows. She looks up to me again and then away into the ever-burning fire. In its amber light, I see that the bench is no ordinary bench. Although it is worn from weather, it looks like the one upon which I sat with Havalah at the oasis. *It's Yeshua's bench!*

Clearing her throat, she begins to speak. "Yes, it is his. After Havalah's death, the Samaritan brought it to me. Yeshua's hands made it for me, so she instructed her sons to have it sent to me. Even without the bench, which is a treasure for me, you know that Yeshua is always with me. You must have learned that by now. He never leaves. However, his body did leave."

I marvel that the little bench made by Yeshua has been there in the corner the whole time. I've set my cup and bowl upon it many times.

"I have another treasure as well," she says, lifting the blanket off her lap with both hands and extending it toward me. "A follower bought this from a soldier and gave it to Johanan, who gave it to me. It is all that I have left of him, of his body."

"So that was his ...?"

"His mantle, yes. He wore it and slept upon it." Miramee's eyes redden and brim with tears. "Before he died, he bled into it." Her voice thickens at the end of the sentence, and her throat seems to close in pain still very fresh, even though over a full decade has passed.

I recognize it now. It was a more vibrant color when Yeshua wore it, but it's clearly the same garment. So the blanket isn't a blanket but the mantle of the Holy One.

I'm looking at the holiest relic on earth, and it's been lying folded in a corner by the fire since that first night.

I understand the brown flecks now. Before I can speak of them, a lump fills my own throat and squeezes off my windpipe. A pain shoots through my chest and up my back.

"That is what is left of his blood," she says, recovering now.

"One of the flakes of his dried blood was in my hand, Miramee?" I ask, astonished.

How do I weigh this? How can my simple mind construct any rational model of thought to frame this? This is beyond the human capacity to understand, at least the human capacity of the twenty-first century.

"Take this," she says, handing me the strip of brown cloth.

I cannot accept it. It'd be too much to hold in my hand. Then I understand that a gift from Miramee is a gift from the "mirror of me."

Yeshua wants me to have it as well. I take it from her and hold it gingerly in my hand.

"Put it someplace safe," she says. "There is a pocket in that tunic of Johanan's, next to the seam I sewed after it was ripped apart." I find the pocket right on my chest, which has an overlapping cover for additional safety. It's like one of those western shirt pockets with the flap that snaps closed, although this has no snap. I tap it to show her that it's safely stowed away. She smiles now.

"Thank you, Miramee," I say, but the feeling of loneliness, of needing to be home, returns. There is another anguished tug at my heart.

"You must not go back yet," she says, reading my mind.

"I need to let them know that I am all right. It has been a long time."

"It *is* a long time to be away from someone you love deeply," she says.

"Yes," I say. "I am grateful for what you have shown me, but I belong to another time. My life is part of the lives of many others who depend on me there."

"You are free to return at any time, but your body …" She halts in midsentence.

"What about my body?"

"Your body has been through much and must rest before more traveling. It can be dangerous, otherwise."

I smile and embrace her. "I will travel fine," I whisper into her ear. "There is nothing wrong with this body."

She holds me tightly, but I remove her arms ever so gently. She looks quizzically at me.

"I will come back," I say, but she looks doubtful. "Until we meet again, my friend."

She gives me a full mouth kiss. "The holy kiss," she says, blushing.

With a last glance at the hearth I have come to know so well, I turn and walk out of the little stone house. I've no idea where I'm going or how I will get home, but I know that I can, that it's up to me.

"Wait, Traveler," I hear Miramee say. "Do not leave. You need to rest! Leave in a few days. It is truly too soon!"

Rest? Too soon for what? She's making no sense.

A fierce heat fires up in my belly, and I quell the impulse to turn and take her in my arms one more time. I know I can't look back.

"Then do not be afraid!" she shouts after me as I approach the immersion fountain.

I keep walking. I'm almost there. Good timing. I'm feeling short of breath.

Miramee calls out something else, but I can barely hear her—and then I can't hear her anymore. She didn't follow me.

In the dead quiet, I lean forward to look into the surface of the fountain and see a familiar face contorted with fear. Then I feel it, that lightning strike of pain, as if an earthquake jars the center of my being.

I remember the first night when Miramee told me that here I was as real as that bench—but only for a short time. This is as real as it gets. I clutch at my chest, but the knife-like sensation sears my ribs.

I see the image reflected on the surface of the fountain. It's Sharon's face staring back at me, her double fist to my upper left torso.

"Our."

Pain.

"Father."

Pain.

"Who art."

Pain. Short breaths.

Sharon's reflection dims, and I desperately want to see her again. Then it's dark, and from the darkness emerges another vision of the seabirds and the bread. I remember Andreas rhythmically breaking the pita circles and giving them to the gulls. I remember the night in Patras in that warm room with the followers of the Way when I used the bread to sop up the onion soup.

When you find him here, in the bread, then you will find him everywhere.

As I writhe in a pit of pain, the knowledge cascades into me that he is everywhere. Yeshua is everywhere and in everything. Therefore, forgiveness and the light must be everywhere and in everything as well. My friend will not leave me alone. As the agony increases, I feel the water on my forehead and face as I fall into the immersion pool.

Chapter 57

AD 2003, and the second year of the presidency of George W. Bush, Monterey, California

"Jack! Jack!" Sharon's face is cupping mine in both hands. She's wearing her nurse's uniform.

"Oh, thank God! He opened his eyes. He's awake! Jack. Stay with me, honey."

I'm on a cart, and all I see are fluorescent lights kaleidescoping above me like a movie filmstrip whose frames have slowed to a sputtering blurb of sequential images.

Where am I? Where is Miramee and the house at Ephesus?

A pain like the pain I felt at the immersion fountain shoots through my chest and then grinds between my shoulder blades with agonizing pressure. All other thoughts sink away.

"Doctor Kohen, this is John Castro, forty-three years old, and here's the latest and greatest EKG. Sharon's his wife." It's a man's voice speaking in an EMT's clipped phrases.

Just the facts.

"Yes, I know Jack. Sharon, I'm sorry."

Dimly, I make out Mike Kohen's voice. He's a noted cardiologist in our town. Also one of my wife's bosses. The last time I saw him was at the hospital's holiday party last year.

I fade out for a moment and then feel a light slap on my cheek.

"Stay with me, Jack!" Sharon says, choking on my name.

I'm in a darker room, the operating room that I saw reflected on the surface of the immersion fountain, the one with a scan of a beating heart. I see a few canned lights and a huge, one-eyed-monster of a machine looming over my chest. My heart beats on the screen to my left. The pain is paralyzing.

"Okay, let's have it. What happened?" Dr. Kohen asks.

The EMT's voice again: "Some homeless kid found him facedown in the creek in a roadside park near his house. He called 9-1-1 on Mr. Castro's phone. Good thing it's later in the year, or he would have drowned for sure. At first sight, we thought he was gone. Mr. Castro was bleeding from a crescent shaped cut on top of his head, so the EMTs didn't know he was having a heart attack until they rolled him over."

"What the heck was he doing down there?"

Sharon jumps in.

"I don't know. He was on his way to a conference in San Jose. I thought he was up there all morning. When I checked my phone I saw that his assistant had called, but I was working."

She pounds the gurney in frustration, crying. "Damn it!"

Groggy and in agony, I can hear her fear and confusion.

So sorry, honey.

Darkness again.

Fading back in but, but I have no sight.

"Sharon, you need to leave now." It's Dr. Kohen's voice. "I'll come out and talk to you in a minute."

"No, I've heard that speech before," Sharon says. "I know what's happening: myocardial infarction, LAD 100 percent occluded—a widow-maker. I'm not leaving." She's gulping air.

That's my warrior wife.

"We can help him more without you in here," he says one more time.

"No. If he dies …"

The words hang in the darkness. *Widow-maker. If he dies …*

"Okay," Kohen says.

Am I headed out?

There's no panic. I'm not even very concerned. I know I will turn up somewhere.

"Doctor, he's coding," a flat female voice says as evenly as if she's announcing that a takeout order is ready at the Chinese restaurant.

Shouldn't I be unconscious instead of watching this like reality TV? I can even see myself—and I don't look so good.

"No! Jacky, don't leave me. I love you." Sharon says my nickname softly, sweetly, and very sadly.

I slip further down the rabbit hole. It's dark and mysterious. The drugs they have in me are making it pretty damn peaceful too.

I'm dying—right here, right now—not twenty years from now or even tomorrow.

Today.

Now.

I feel the cold steel of the defibrillator on my shaved chest.

I hear one last sound.

"Clear!"

Boom!

Darkness again.

With no sound, no movement of my lips, I somehow whisper to the firmament above.

Yeshua.

Sequentia

Sings now the Archangel of Death:
My wings are thousands,
My faces many.
Call me Azra'el.
The name's sound is light and good,
For what I bring is light and good.
Some men fear it, the death I gift to them.
Others are tired, despairing,
Hopeful to escape with me.
Yet they cannot leave much.
What is here follows there.
Only the prepared and open heart can receive great mercy.
Many small deaths should come before I do.
If not, then unprepared in the dark,
All the anger, all the hatred and fears
Engulf like a boat
The voyaging soul.
I help, and ultimately there is peace,
But souls enter the cave without knowing
That all is completed for them.
Sometimes they open their eyes, finally,
In the holy darkness of the cavern.
They can see and then hear the deep music,
Bringing their heart at last
Into His heart
In brightest glory.
Listen now to the
Everlasting resonance of redemption!

Epilogue

Boom!

I feel my back arch up and slam down again onto the operating table. I see nothing.

A moment passes.

"Clear!"

It's dark, still, dark like black—not brown, not dim. I don't feel as cold as I thought I would, nor am I frightened, exactly. I'm hyperattentive, razor-sharp aware, knowing that I may not come back, preparing for what's next.

But what if there's no "next"? What if I remain here, lost in this warm blackness?

"Come. Come with me." A child's soft voice emerges from the inky nothingness. I see him. At least I think it's a him. It's a small boy with silver hair, like the boy described in the Immerser's disconcerting and prophetic dream.

Yet this child's face is luminous, inviting. I follow him. I've followed many people in the past few weeks with few questions voiced, though many questions have rattled through my mind. I'm not sure how or upon what I am walking, but I follow him deeper into the darkness, having only his bright face as a guide. No matter where his head is turned, he is facing me, watching me with somber brown eyes.

"Am I dead?"

He doesn't acknowledge my question, and we continue down and deeper. It seems deeper, even though I can't see.

What's going to happen to me?

A sad resignation flows through my thoughts, but I keep walking. The lines of the poem written by the poet/soldier, Alan Seeger, before he died in World War I, roll through what remains of my rapidly diminishing memory:

It may be he shall take my hand,
And lead me into his dark land.
And close my eyes and quench my breath—
It may be I shall pass him still.
I have a rendezvous with Death.

"Azra'el! *Azra'el!*" a man's voice thunders, shattering the silence and echoing off the cavern walls. From the cast of his light, I can see now that this place looks like a cave. I remember when Micha'el, the archangel, told me that Azra'el was the archangel of death, that he had appeared as a vulture during Yeshua's third temptation at Nura's palace. Onto the opulent terrace, the bird Azra'el had flown, landing on the balustrade and thus reminding Yeshua of the mortality and eternal transience of all things, especially worldly power. This began the unwinding of the illusion, which ended with the frustrated Tempter Nura eventually departing in defeat.

Azra'el? Azra'el.

So, I am moving into death.

I hear no response, only the continuing echoes of the unseen man's words, and I pause for a moment. Azra'el motions to me, and then I continue to follow the boy.

"Azra'el! Stop!"

The voice reverberates through me, and I shudder as I see the boy stand still. His eyes are no longer tranquil but fierce. I wrestle again with the realization that this kid is Death's archangel. I don't want to follow him. My face, or at least what I think is my face, freezes in an expression of horror. Miramee told me that the angels would protect me. Well, this kid's an angel.

Why must I follow him down? Where is he leading me? How am I supposed to get back?

Yeshua, what's happening to me?

"Where am I?" I ask Azra'el. "Where are you taking me?"

He glowers at me as if I've just messed up some plan of his.

There is a flash, and a shaft of pure white light ahead of us illumines the entire tunnel. I can see now that it's ordinary; there isn't much to it except that it's dark. Does something like this actually lead to the afterlife? The light calms me down, and I feel more relaxed, although I'm not aware of breathing easier, because I'm not breathing anymore.

So now I'm, like, dead?

The words shoot sorrow through me like that shaft of light. The sorrow is not for me, for the loss of my life, but for my wife and two daughters. Gabriella, the older, will not be graduating high school for another two years, and I won't be there for it. Next year, Sophia will have to learn to drive without me. Like leaden water, a profound grief cascades down through me, settling into the crater of what used to be my gut. I had no business taking these risks. No matter how adventurous it seemed or how compelling the longing, I'm a husband and father first.

All the while, this harbinger of death stands staring at me. He's no longer an innocent-looking child in my eyes, even though he manifests as one.

"Jack Castro, whom the Holy One calls Traveler," Azra'el addresses me with all my names. "Who is like Elohim? Who is like God?"

What kind of question is that?

I'm already forgetting that I've heard that question before, and I can't remember the answer. He stands there without moving, staring at me in the tunnel. A long period passes, although there's no sense of time here. One moment glides seamlessly into the next with no feeling of past or future. Slowly it comes into me. I remember now.

Who is like Elohim, like God? Who is like I AM? That question makes up the name of Micha'el, the archangel.

"No one, no thing," I say to Azra'el. It's the same answer I gave Micha'el when he first asked me. I think of how my guide and friend Miramee brought him to me. My answer is the same, but a download comes into my mind.

"And everyone, and all things," I add.

Azra'el bows low at the waist.

"Right mind brings silence in the face of that question, but you have spoken well, if speak you must, Traveler," he says. In the shaft of

271

light, the radiant Micha'el now appears. Again, the features he chooses are Nordic with a shock of blond hair, and I'm glad to see him in this creepy place. His eyes have something strangely familiar about them, but I can't place it.

Yes! It's the boy, the homeless man in the park that first day, the one I gave the pizza to. That was Micha'el! He's been here the whole time—since before Ephesus!

But I notice that he isn't carrying his sword. He always has his sword nearby. Even at Miramee's house as we spoke, the sword stood propped next to him against the bouldered walls. Then I notice small orange flares sparking and dancing on either side of the column of white light, and I remember the orange flashes on the road when the mountain lion appeared and later on the forest trail. I realize that the luminous shaft itself *is* the archangel's sword. That's why Azra'el can't move me further into the tunnel. The mighty sword of light blocks us both from proceeding deeper down.

"Too soon, Azra'el," Micha'el says, looking first to the boy and then turning his eyes to me. "Too soon. In this body, Traveler, you must move further on the Way."

"What way?" I ask, seeing both the homeless man and the archangel now at the same time. Then I understand. No words are necessary with these beings, and I doubt if I'm actually hearing either of them speak. Maybe the words are resonances deep within me, entering without sound but thrumming up with a majestic vibration. My way, the Way, was for me to understand with my heart all that these sacred beings had to tell me—and then to go that way with that change of heart. Like Yeshua discovering who he was in the desert and then venturing back into the world to begin to call others out, so I must move back into the world with this pilgrim's heart.

Boom!

I sense canister lights on the ceiling, dim lights, smells of iodine, and then a beating heart on the screen—before I sink slowly back into darkness again.

"I think he's back," I hear Doctor Kohen announce, and then his voice dissolves back into garbled sounds as he calmly gives urgent instructions to his nurse. I also hear my wife's voice, muted with sobs.

Her insurance-guy husband might be back. No life insurance policies will be paid today. Clutching onto humor in the face of this now encroaching fear, I find I can't smile or even control any facial expression.

"Okay, let's move it, people! Let's get the stent in," Kohen says. "Just one. LAD only. Can't risk him coding again. Yeah, coloring's good. Jack, I think you're back!"

Then I slip again into the warm and comforting darkness. The fear subsides in these shadows. I feel heaviness and pain in my chest, a sharp, needling pain right in the center, as if someone is touching my heart. I inhale deeply and realize with relief that I'm actually breathing again. I rest, letting the breathing and darkness envelope me peacefully.

The doctor's right. Jack is back.

With this resurrection epiphany, I feel my lips twitch slightly into the weakest of smiles. Softly, but with great gratitude, I exhale the name with the certainty of knowing that it *can* make all things new, even for a Traveler, even for me.

I whisper now the name of my hope, especially when all seems hopeless. It is the name of the Holy One of God—but it's also the name of my friend.

"Jesus!"

End of the First Book

Appendix A: Dramatis Personae

Name, Character Description, and Other Names

Yeshua. The Mashiach, the Messiah, or Anointed One. Other names: Yeshua of Nasrath, the "one like a human," Yeshua bar-Yosef, *Iesous Khristos* (Greek), Jesus Christ.

Aderes. (Aramaic for "one who protects.") Pet dog of the Immerser.

Andreas. Apostle, brother of Shimon (called "Kefah"). Other names: Andreas bar Jonah, St. Andrew (English).

Azra'el. Archangel of Death.

(C.) Bronson Pratt. College buddy and close friend of Jack Castro.

Caiaphas. High priest of the Temple in Jerusalem at the time of Yeshua, son-in-law to Annas. Also called *Yosef Bar-Kayafa*.

Chuza. Chief steward of Herod Antipater, and husband of Yohannah.

Cleopas. Brother of Yosef, brother-in-law of Eema, butcher in Nasrath, and friend of Zavdai.

Demetrius. Host of a supper in Patras in which a small gathering of Andreas and the followers had the sacred meal.

Duck. Labrador retriever, the Castro family dog.

Eema. Miryam, wife of Yosef and mother of Yeshua, stepmother of Tzadik. Other names: Mother Miryam, Blessed Virgin Mary, *Theotokos,* and Mother of God.

Gabriella. Elder of Jack Castro's two daughters.

Hanina. Wife of Kelaya, the Ephesian bead merchant.

Havalah. Ex-Jerusalemite, owner of desert oasis camp with Nabataean husband.

Herod the Great. Roman client king of Judea, father of Herod Antipater, Philip, and Archelaus. Died 4 BC.

Herod Antipater. (Also Herod Antipas.) Tetrarch of Galilee, son of Herod the Great, husband of Herodias.

Herodias. Niece and wife of Herod Antipater after divorcing his brother, who was also named Herod.

Iesous Khristos. See **Yeshua.**

Immerser, the. Imprisoned prophet of the river, who baptized Yeshua. Other names: Johanan the Immerser, John the Baptist (English), San Juan Bautista (Spanish).

Isaac. Only son of Abraham, the patriarch. Almost sacrificed by his father at the command of God. Saved by an angel.

Israel. Youngest son of Havalah, grew up with Miramee at desert oasis.

Jack Castro. Insurance man from Monterey, California, and narrator of the series. Also called "Traveler."

Josh. Castro family's community gate guard.

Joshua. Second in command to Moses (Moshe), and a great warrior for Israel. Yeshua was named for him.

Joe Santroia (Father Joe). Priest and pastor of Carmel Mission.

Johanan. Evangelist, apostle, beloved disciple of Yeshua, son of Zavdai, brother of Yakov. Other names: Johanan Bar-Zavdai, John the Apostle, and sometimes St. John the Divine.

Johanan the Immerser. See **Immerser, the.**

Kohen, Michael, MD. Cardiologist and employer of Sharon Castro in Monterey.

Kefah. Shimon bar Traveler, apostle, first pope, brother of Andreas, husband of Yasmin, son-in-law of Rina, father of Hosea. Other names: Rock, St. Peter (English), *Petros* (Greek).

Kelaya. Bead merchant at the market in Ephesus and husband of Hanina.

Mother Salome. Nickname for Salome, disciple of Yeshua and wife of Zavdai. Mother of Yakov and Johanan the apostle.

Mary Elizabeth Mulholland Castro. Mother of Jack Castro and his sister, Becky.

Micha'el. Archangel, protector of Yeshua and Traveler. Also called Michael, the archangel (English).

Miramee. Mysterious guide to Traveler.

Miryam of Magdala. Follower of Yeshua and close companion.

Moshe. Moses, patriarch of the Israelites, instituted the Ten Commandments and Mosaic Law.

Nabataean, the. Husband of Havalah and proprietor of the desert oasis in which Yeshua finds himself.

Nathaniel. Mentor of boy Yeshua at synagogue in Tzippori.

Nura. Name used by a character involved in Yeshua's third temptation in the desert.

Philip (Herod Philip). Son of Herod the Great, and half-brother of Herod Antipater. Tetrarch of the far northern and eastern provinces of his father's kingdom. Future husband of the dancing Salome.

Rina. Mother of Yasmin, mother-in-law of Kefah.

Samaritan, the. Caravan master and customer of Havalah.

Salome, Princess. Infamous dancing daughter of Herodias by her first husband, Herod II. Stepdaughter and niece of Herod Antipater, tetrarch of Galilee. Future wife of her uncle, the tetrarch Philip.

Salome. Wife of Zavdai. See *Mother Salome*.

Shania. Young daughter of Andreas. Her name means "beautiful one."

Sharon Castro. Wife of Jack Castro and mother of Gabriella and Sophia.

Shimon-Kefah. See *Kefah*.

Sophia. The younger of Jack Castro's two daughters.

Tempter, the. The Evil One, Tempter, Satan.

Traveler. Nickname given to Jack Castro, the narrator of the series.

Tyler. Assistant to Jack Castro.

Tzadik. (Pronounced "Zadic.") Nickname meaning "just" given to Yakov Bar-Yosef, older half-brother of Yeshua, and his chief disciple. Other names: Santiago (Spanish), St. James the Just.

Yakov. Apostle, fisherman, son of Zavdai, brother of Johanan. Other names: Yakov Bar-Zavdai, St. James the Greater (English), Santiago (Spanish).

Yakov bar Yosef. See *Tzadik*.

Yosef. Late husband of Eema (Mary), Father of Tzadik, earthly father of Yeshua. Other names: Yosef Bar-Yakov, Joseph the Just Man, St. Joseph (English), San Jose (Spanish).

Zavdai. Father of Yakov and Johanan, husband of Mother Salome (Salome), wealthy fisherman. Traditionally called Zebedee.

Appendix B: Glossary

AD. *Anno Domini,* "in the year of the Rabbuni." The current nonreligious designation is CE for Common Era.

AUC: Ab Urbe Condita. "From the founding of the city (of Rome)." A calendar used at the time of Yeshua. AD 1 or CE 1 would correspond to AUC 754.

Abba, av'va. See **God**.

Abouna. Form of address meaning "father," used to honor Christian religious leaders.

Adonai. See **God**.

Al-Quam. Nabataean god of war and protector of caravans.

Amen. "So be it. In truth."

Apostle. Greek form of the word meaning "envoy" or "messenger."

Amot. Plural of *amah*, a unit of measurement of about twenty inches.

Bar-Name. "Son of" in Aramaic. Jesus was Yeshua Bar-Yosef (Jesus son of Joseph).

Chiton. Short Grecian tunic worn typically by men.

Crux Decussata. Reputedly one type of cross used by the Romans for execution. Shaped like an *X*.

Denarius. (pl. denarii) Silver Roman coin worth between three and four days' wages for a laborer.

Elohim. See **God**.

Eros. Greek word for the romantic and carnal type of love.

Fearers of Elohim. Uncircumcised, Gentile followers of the Way or of the Hebrew religion.

Gat-Shemanin. Gethsemane, meaning "oil press," because olives were stored and pressed in this large cave and area on the Mount of Olives, which was later termed Gethsemane in a Greek interpretation of the name. (Source: Joan E. Taylor, *Where Was Gethsemane?*, from "Jesus: The Last Day," Biblical Archeological Society, 2003.)

God, Names of.

Y-H (YHWH). Yahweh (the acronym "I AM," the unspeakable name of God).

Abba, av'va. The familiar of "Father" but also "origin" or "source" in Aramaic, used by Jesus in the gospels.

Adonai. "Rabbuni," used for God in Hebrew. Also Marey (Aramaic) and Lord (English).

Elohim. God, the unity of one, the divine. Elaha' in Aramaic, similar to *Allah*. The Almighty.

I AM or (I AM who I AM). The name given by God as his own name as told to Moses on Mount Sinai. It is unspeakable.

Kyrios, Kyrion. "Rabbuni" or "Lord" in Greek.

Theós, Theó. The Greek name for Elohim, God.

Iudea. Judaea, name of the Roman province in the first century that contained historic Israel.

Keffiyeh. What Traveler knows as the traditional name for the Bedouin headdress worn by men throughout the Middle East. A square scarf banded around the crown. The word *keffiyeh* was not used by people in the first century.

Lebak (heart). Aramaic word for "heart," but it means more than the physical organ. It is more like the life that radiates from the center of one's being.

Mashiach. The Aramaic word corresponding to the Hebrew word *Mashiach* and the Greek *Kristos*, (English *Christ*), meaning the "Anointed One."

Mikveh. Step-down pool used for ritual bathing as prescribed in Mosaic Law.

Nabataea. Desert kingdom comprising parts of present-day Jordan. The people were the dark-skinned forebears of the Bedouins.

Nasrath. Nazareth, hometown of Yeshua.

Nasrenes. The early name for the Jewish sect claiming Yeshua of Nasrath the Mashiach or Messiah.

Pharisee. Derived from *Perushkim* is the plural form of *perush* or "separate, apart." A pious faction of the religion that was strictly observant of Mosaic Law. Later, they became the sect that led to contemporary Rabbinic Judaism.

Philadelphia. Nabataean capital that later became Amman, Jordan.

Rabbuni. (pl. Rabbunim) Aramaic for master, lord, accomplished teacher.

Ruach Kudsha. The breath or Spirit of Elohim. Corresponds to the later "Holy Spirit" used by followers of the Way and Christians ever since. Used in this trilogy as both the name of the Hebrew concept of the Spirit of God, the animating force of life emerging with Elohim, as well as the name of the third person of the divine Trinity in Christianity.

Shlama. Aramaic greeting of "peace" or "peace be with you."

Tefillen. The Jewish phylactery consisting of small boxes that contain portions of the Torah. Worn most commonly during prayer by Jewish men and some Jewish women.

Tiberias. New and opulent capital city on the shore of the Sea of Galilee built by Herod Antipater in honor of the Roman emperor, Tiberius Caesar.

Tzippori. The larger, Greek-styled city near Nazareth, later called Sepphoris.

Way. The early name for Christ followers. Also called Nasrenes.

CPSIA information can be obtained
at www.ICGtesting.com
Printed in the USA
FSOW02n0250010915
10562FS